LIGHT AND SHADE

Nora Donovan

Prologue

Lord of the Manor.

King of the Castle.

He didn't look particularly regal or lordly. But that's how the fellow probably thought of himself as he promenaded around the battlements. Maybe that ghastly jacket he wore was the latest fashion back in L.A. or Seattle or wherever he came from. A really ugly colour. But as it glowed in the sunset, she had to admit that it provided a striking contrast to the castle's newly-plastered and whitewashed walls.

This was what had finally spurred the group into action. Letters to the editor were no longer enough, Aidan had said. You can't let these rich foreigners get away with despoiling the Irish countryside like this. We have to save our heritage.

Hiding in the bushes to the north of the building, the girl had an excellent view of her handiwork - or rather, that of the boys she had got to do the actual work, boys with proper expertise in spray-painting. The slogans looked effective enough, with their sharp red and green letters. There would probably be a photo of their work on the front page of next week's *Limerick Leader*. It might even make the national press!

But was that enough? The neon sign over the entrance was just the last straw.

The fellow really needed to be given a good fright, Aidan had said, and he was right. The King of the Castle wouldn't even know who was threatening him, any more than he had on the phone. So why hadn't Aidan stayed on to help her with the job, instead of making some excuse? Never mind, she would show him what a real protester could do.

As the offending figure disappeared from sight for a moment, the girl took her chance, and dashed close to the wall. There, she wouldn't be seen by the man on the roof. Or by whoever was playing fiddle music somewhere inside the building. She thought she knew who that was. One of the people she had seen going in and out earlier in the day. So, unlike the outer gate, the door wasn't usually locked.

And it wasn't this time either. Having hidden behind a potted shrub near the entrance, she finally plucked up the courage to test the handle. It worked satisfyingly, and she began to ease the heavy door ajar.

What was that?!

An almost simultaneous crash and thud, as something brushed by her shoulders, nearly knocking her sideways.

The crash was from the once gaudy neon sign, now darkened. She could feel bits of glass from it in her hair.

The thud was from whatever had landed beside the potted shrubs. It was hard to make out, now that the only remaining lamp was the one at the corner of the car park. She took a closer look, and stifled a scream. A choked whisper came out instead.

"No, Aidan! Not like this!"

Chapter 1

"No good will ever come of it."

Mrs. Margaret O'Keeffe, known locally as Maggie Mike, addressed this remark to her companion as they walked their dogs on a quiet country road about a mile north of the village of Kilbrue. She was referring to the unaccustomed signs of activity in and around the forbidding grey stone edifice that loomed ahead of them. It had previously held no significance for them beyond marking the point where they turned left to return to the village via the main Limerick road. They both knew it as Castle Green, though neither knew why it was so called.

Apart from the solid limestone walls being the usual dull grey of so many other ruins dotting the Irish countryside, neither was there all that much green around it, by the standards of the locality. A thick hawthorn hedge, now in full bloom, cut off most of the view from the narrow public road, but behind it was an empty expanse of wasteland. What had been a small gap in the hedge had been widened to create a rough access road for building machinery, and through that widened gap they could see that most of the brambles, dock, and other weeds had been cleared away, reducing further what little green there had been. Perched on a bare hillock, Castle Green looked more gaunt than ever.

The starlings whose home it once had been had taken refuge on the new electricity wires now connecting Castle Green with the main power lines, the two new support poles barely concealed behind the hawthorn hedge. With every movement of the ESB workers, the starlings hopped, exchanged perches and chattered, generating almost enough of a racket to drown out the sounds of hammering, sawing, and sanding emanating from inside the building.

"What do you mean, no good will come of it?"

"It never did anyone any good to meddle with that place."

"Didn't the land it's on once belong to your mother's family?"

"That's right - my uncle Jack farmed it for a while, before he gave up because of ill health. None of my cousins wanted to take it over, so he sold it to ... Oh, I forget, it changed hands many times before the Moynihans took it on."

"They say some returned Yank has bought it now, at least the few acres at this end. Including the old farmhouse." Maggie's companion, Celia Ryan, was usually well-informed, since she was joint owner of a pub and guesthouse at the edge of the village. Though she had recently handed over the running of the business to her niece, Celia was still in residence in an apartment over the pub, and occasionally helped out at the bar.

Maggie's eyes followed the slope of the hillock to the smaller ruined structure at its base, now also subject to building activity. It had been stripped of its dilapidated doors and windows, and a new roof was being put on. "Is that right? He must have a fortune to take on a place like that."

"Sure that old pile of stones can hardly be worth much."

"No, but the work that's being put into it! He's got to be loaded. And crazy. At least Dinny Moynihan had the sense to build himself a nice new bungalow near the main road, a fair distance from this accursed place." Maggie's dog, a reddish-brown setter, was now pulling on its leash and whimpering. "Look, even Trudy wants to get away from here!"

"You're not serious, are you?"

"I'm dead serious!" Maggie proceeded to tell a rambling story she had heard from her aunt, the gist being that Jack had once cut back the branches of an apple tree that had been overshadowing the other trees in the orchard near the castle ruin, in spite of warnings that it was unlucky to cut that particular tree; next morning, three of his cows were dead.

"Surely you don't believe ...? Maybe it was pollution from the pharmaceutical factory near Limerick. Remember, someone up in Ballyneety went to court about it ..."

"That wasn't there then, that came much later. No, nobody could explain it any other way."

"Or Mad Cow Disease, or the Foot and Mouth ..."

Maggie chose not to dignify that with an answer. They stood silently for a while, then Celia asked, "Could that be the tree over there?" She pointed at a single scrawny tree on the western slope between the two buildings. Most of its branches were bare, but one branch was thick with what might be apple blossoms. "Let's take a closer look." Her fit of bravado may have had to do with the absence of the electricians, who now seemed to have disappeared inside the building.

"No ..." But Celia was already halfway up the slope. Since Trudy insisted on following Max, Celia's scottie, Maggie was also inadvertently propelled through the gap. A lucky move, actually, since at that moment a car passed (unusual enough for that stretch of road), splashing through a rather massive puddle left by that morning's downpour. She would have been drenched in her previous position, she reflected with some confusion. As the car disappeared into the distance, she though she recognized it from the sound of its souped-up engine as one that often made a nuisance of itself flitting through the village. That Aidan Flynn fellow, always showing off ...

"It's an apple tree all right," Celia shouted, as she stumbled back down the slope.

"Hmm. Maybe they know something. Maybe they're being careful in their own way."

"Better be sure than sorry."

"Oh, that won't help them much. The whole place is unlucky. There's even some story about the fellow who built that castle. Can't remember what it is, exactly, but he came to a sticky end. They say the thing is built over a fairy ring."

"Then you wouldn't want to be one of them workers digging into the hill, over there, on the other side."

"I certainly wouldn't, and I don't think they're local boys either, or they'd know better. ... I wonder what they're up to. Putting in a septic tank, maybe?"

"Or a cellar."

"The place already has a cellar. I twisted my ankle once on the broken steps going down to it, when my aunt and uncle had the place. A dungeon, they said it was, so I had to see for myself - I was only about ten, and didn't know any better. Couldn't see a thing, though, after tumbling down the steps, it was just a damp, black hole. There were spiders, though, I well remember that. Got out quick, I can tell you, in spite of my twisted ankle!"

"So maybe they're clearing it out - the cellar, or dungeon, or whatever it is. Anyway, as you see, it's creating a couple of jobs ..."

"Jobs! I wouldn't work there if ..." Maggie broke off there, thinking of the many cleaning jobs she herself had taken on in the course of her working life, often in spite of equally emphatically expressed objections of a moral or other nature to the prospective employers or place of employment. She mentally rejected the phrase 'beggars can't be choosers', since she didn't consider herself a beggar, and graciously allowed for a similar degree of pride and dignity on the part of the workers digging the hole in the hillside. But the basic truth had to be acknowledged, that when you have a family to feed, or appearances to keep up, or even need to finance a cigarette habit or (as in her own case) the occasional bottle of Tullamore Dew, then you can't afford to be too choosy.

"What did you say the Yanks were going to use the place for?

"I didn't say because I don't really know."

7

"I mean if they're doing up the old farmhouse to live in, is the castle going to be a hotel, or a museum, or what? Or maybe something like what they have at Lough Gur?" With that she meant the new 'interpretive centre' for the Neolithic remains surrounding the lake just another half-mile north of the castle.

"I didn't get what the people at the bar were saying about it. There was talk of a studio ..."

"Studio?" The only kind of studio Maggie could think of was the photographer's studio they once had in the village before it closed down. Now you had to go in to Limerick for a proper studio portrait.

"Some kind of business, anyway."

Maggie considered this information. "No good will ever come of it," she pronounced finally.

By now, some heavy clouds were gathering in the western sky behind Castle Green. Silhouetted against one of the remaining golden streaks they could see one of the electricians perched on the pole nearest the main line connection. From that vantage point he might have observed Celia's little trespassing escapade, but after some deliberation, they concluded that he hadn't been there at the time.

Pulled by Trudy and Max, the two women headed back towards the main road.

***

Not only were the workers digging to the east of the castle not local boys, they weren't all boys either.

The men from the building company that had been sub-contracted by McCarthy & Co. Archaeological Services to cut two parallel trenches into the hillock had gone home for their tea. There remained an exact gender parity of one female supervisor and three UCD archaeology students on holiday jobs.

The upper meter or so of the earth on either side of the more western of the two trenches - the one nearer the castle and the old farmhouse - had clearly been used as a rubbish dump in the 1950s. The two senior students had amused themselves from time to time with speculations on the level of civilization reached by this long-lost culture.

"This label is in a surprisingly good state of preservation. Take notes: yellow, lozenge-shaped, with some barely decipherable hieroglyphics: 'something ... LEMONADE'. Are you aware of anything in the literature to identify this style of decor?"

"Give me that, Declan, It'll look good on my bookshelves, and they're not likely to want it in the National Museum." Una O'Riordan was from a village about five miles beyond Kilbrue, and commuted from her parents' place every day while the other two were booked into Ryan's Guesthouse at a special weekly rate. She had recognized the label as that of a local company that went out of business in the late sixties or seventies.

But Declan was still in full flight. "The yellow residue provides evidence of the import of food colouring into southern Ireland in the 1950s and 60s - unless you wish to postulate an indigenous chemical additives industry ...?"

"Write a paper on it, Declan. In the meantime, what it signifies for us is that at least we needn't sift that pile of earth."

"But I suppose we'd better get going on the pile from the next level or we'll have Sheila down on our necks like a ton of ... Neolithic axe-heads."

There was nothing of interest in the earth removed from the next level, as they had expected from the bareness of the walls of both trenches. It didn't mean there was nothing on that level. But nobody was going to strip the hillside on the off-chance of finding some medieval farm implement. So both trenches could soon be filled in and work would proceed on the foundations for the planned car park. They would then move on to next area that was already marked out for surveying.

Every so often Una or Tom (the junior student) would complain about the unfair pressure which was being conveyed through Sheila from the building contractor - or was it the developer himself? - to get the survey finished so that she could have a (hopefully negative?) report written up and made available to the various university departments and academic bodies with an interest in such matters.

"Whose side is she on, for heaven's sake? Wouldn't it be just marvellous if we were to hit on some evidence of a Neolithic or Bronze Age habitation? I wouldn't exactly expect to find anything like the Lough Gur shield, but considering the location, the earth here could be just peppered with shards and spear-heads. We just need to be thorough enough, and they're not giving us enough time!"

Before they could write off these two particular trenches, there was the lowest level to check. Any findings there would be a reason to get the local contractors to go lower still. It was still quite bright for nearly 8 p.m. (midsummer was nigh!) but clouds were gathering on the horizon. Besides, they had already done nearly three hours overtime, so they weren't surprised when Sheila decided to call it a day. She would sift the remaining pile, and then secure the site herself.

With relief, the students downed tools and piled into Una's car. She regularly dropped them off at Ryan's before continuing on home. Today she would probably stop off at the pub for a glass of Guinness with them first. It was only five miles, after all, and it had been dusty work.

The students having departed, their boss mechanically and methodically ran the earth through the sieve. Just stones so far, which she dumped to the side. Then something different caught her eye. Clearly a piece of pottery, not that that in itself meant much. It was often quite astonishing how deep the odd piece of Granny's willow pattern tea service could be found - possibly due to farming activity, earth movements, or animal burrowing. And purity of stratification could hardly be counted on under a modern rubbish dump. But this was familiar in a different way. Gently curved, as if it had come from a bell-shaped vessel of some kind - a fairly large drinking vessel or medium-sized container, and with a faint darker zigzag pattern on the brownish outer surface. To Sheila McCarthy's trained eye it looked like something from the so-called Beaker culture. She caught her breath. The Beaker Folk were pre-Celtic, therefore Neolithic or Late Stone Age, and thought to be associated with megalithic tombs. They were known to have farming, though no metal-working. It would not be out of the question to find evidence of such a settlement here. It would need careful examination.

But how bloody awkward to have made such a find on this particular spot, thought Sheila the businesswoman. She slipped the problematic shard in a transparent plastic bag, marked it with sticker, and stuffed it into the glove compartment of the McCarthy van.

***

The little hawthorn-hedged road made a curve to the north before bending back west towards the main thoroughfare. As Maggie and her companion reached the second bend, she saw a car parked on the verge a bit further on. It must have been the same one that had very nearly splashed her new skirt back at the building site.

Yes, it was the brownish metallic car that had managed to annoy her so often before. Its owner was packing something into the boot, helped by a much smaller, apparently female figure. Something about the turn of the head made Maggie start for a moment. But no, it couldn't be ... She was only a schoolgirl, she wouldn't be hanging around with that disreputable ...

Maggie was distracted from her confused thoughts by another car passing, a pale blue one this time. It was one of the two she'd seen parked on the site, near where that hole was being dug. This one hit a small puddle and succeeded in splashing her shoes. Luck was extremely capricious today.

Disturbed by the unaccustomed traffic - or had he seen a rabbit? - Celia's scottie yanked the leash out of his mistress's hand and scampered down the road and under an iron gate. The car that had been parked there was now gone, though the unpleasant sound of its engine could still be heard in the distance.

"Max, come back here!" yelled Celia ineffectually. She started to trot after him, but had to slow down to pick her way through a mucky patch in the gateway.

Maggie had walked on, but a sharp yelp caused her to turn around. The yelp had come not from the errant Max, as she had first assumed, but from his mistress. Celia was standing stiffly in a puddle with her mouth open. Then she fell back, hit the gatepost and crumpled on the ground. It was then that Maggie saw the cable dangling over the hawthorn bush and ending in the puddle in which one of Celia's brown brogues was still immersed. The pole just inside the gate might have been the one where they had noticed the lone electrician (or whoever it was).

Max had returned, and was whimpering uneasily. For a few horrified seconds. Maggie was sure Celia was dead. But then she thought she could discern a low groan. She bent to feel her friend's pulse, then restrained herself: The heel of Celia's left shoe rested in the puddle.

Maggie knew about electricity and water. She had the presence of mind to hold Trudy firmly by his collar, and to shoo Max away. But what to do now?

Tying both dogs' leashes tightly to the other gatepost, she looked around for some useful instrument, and found a fallen branch and a torn plastic bag. She wrapped the bag round the branch for extra safety, and with this tool gingerly manoeuvred Celia's foot out of the water.

Having got Celia into a more comfortable position on the relatively dry grass verge, she slapped her friend's cheeks in an attempt to revive her, but to no avail. At least she was breathing. But where were cars when you needed them?

She thought she could hear some shouts back at the building site, so at least somebody was still there. But somehow, she would prefer to be anywhere rather than Castle Green. Leaving the howling dogs to watch over Celia's prostrate form, Maggie set off in the opposite direction, towards the main road.

On reaching it, breathless, she haplessly flapped her arms at an approaching car. The driver passed by, ignoring her plight. Two trucks heading in the Limerick direction also failed to stop. Finally, a small black Fiesta heading towards the village pulled up onto the verge a few yards ahead of her.

The door on the passenger side opened and a tousled male head stuck out. It was someone she recognized: young Tim, son of the local Superintendent. Local gossip was that he had finally joined the force after resisting his father's pressure for years.

Gasping with relief, she approached the open passenger door and blurted out her story. She wasn't making much sense, she realized. But somehow the young man had filtered out the essential facts from her confused account.

"Get in."

Within seconds the car had backed up to the junction from which she had emerged, and was speeding recklessly down the winding, hawthorn-lined boreen.

Chapter 2

Garda Tim O'Driscoll put down the paper and poured himself a cup of tea to keep awake. Night duty didn't usually bother him. But seven nights in a row were beginning to take their toll, even on a night owl like himself. The mini-heat wave they were going through was making it increasingly difficult to sleep during the day. And today - a Saturday - he had given into temptation and joined Cathy and the others at Ownahincha beach. A great day, but not much sleep. And the hour or so he had dozed off on the beach mat had also earned him a serious sunburn on his back and neck, where the stiff uniform collar now chafed.

It had been quiet so far. There had been a car theft to deal with (how stupid can tourists be to leave an expensive camera in full view on the back seat?), but the report was now filed away. A few local lads had been drunk and disorderly on Main Street. Now the pubs were closed, at least officially, and he didn't feel like earning more Brownie points for raiding Walsh's, where he knew for a fact that a few harmless after-hours drinkers were still ensconced. Besides, Barbara - his fellow sufferer - was taking an illicit snooze. She would have to be woken up before taking any action, so why bother?

He picked up the paper to finish the article he was reading. It was on the front page of the Weekend section of the *Irish Times*, and was apparently based on an interview with the person referred in the headline to as 'Richard Murrough: producer, song-writer, entrepreneur'.

His attention had been first drawn to the article by the large colour photo taking up about a quarter of the page. It showed a man lounging in one of the comfortable leather-upholstered seats of the Shelbourne Hotel's Horseshoe Bar. Pink-tinted glasses, hair greying at the temples, a glass of what was probably gin and tonic in his hand.

This Richard Murrough seemed to be an interesting character, to say the least. He had certainly pulled himself up by his bootstraps, from rather humble origins as son of an Irish emigrant ('one of New York's finest'), overcoming a huge handicap on the way. Losing one's sight as a teenager ... hard to imagine what that was like. And the man had been involved in some pretty powerful music, a lot of which was preserved in Tim's extensive collection of vinyl, now taking up a disproportionate amount of storage space in his cramped Bandon flat. To say nothing of that hit song ...

But what really intrigued Tim was the mention of Castle Green.

Ever since that little incident a few weeks back when he had helped Maggie O'Keeffe rush her friend Celia to hospital, he had been coming across references to it, mainly in the local press. The first had been, of course the report on the incident itself. He rummaged for it in the pile of *Limerick Leaders* that his mother insisted on collecting for him, and which he was dutifully though sporadically ploughing through, especially on quiet night shifts like this. He eventually found it on an inside page in the third of the discarded papers he checked:

Near-fatal accident at Kilbrue

A resident of the village of Kilbrue narrowly escaped death by electrocution last Monday. Miss Celia Ryan (64), proprietor of the popular Ryan's Guest House, was knocked unconscious when she came in contact with a dangling live wire just outside the site where renovations are proceeding on the medieval structure known as Castle Green, while walking with her companion, Mrs. Margaret O'Keeffe. The Electricity Supply Board, whose workers were connecting the building at the time, deny any negligence.

What had mildly puzzled him at the time was the lack of any reference to a Garda investigation, which - if Maggie's garbled account meant anything - should have been called for. It was certainly on the old man's turf - the old man being Superintendent Paddy O'Driscoll of Kilbrue District in County Limerick, soon to be promoted (he had been confidentially informed) to Chief Superintendent, Limerick Division. This reminded Tim that he really ought to be collecting Brownie points, if only to make some gesture towards fulfilling the old man's expectations - the bane of his life, he thought with a sigh.

The renovation - or rather reconstruction - of the medieval structure was also an on-going topic on the *Letters* page, with opinions sharply divided between those who welcomed any signs of development and those who were screaming desecration. It was also the topic of a flier he'd picked up in Ryan's pub on that same weekend, just before the incident involving Celia and Maggie. A group calling itself 'Local Heritage' was holding a public protest meeting the following Wednesday. There were two signatories. Judging by the string of appended letters, 'Mary O'Brien' might well be the local schoolteacher of that (admittedly common) name. He had no idea who 'Aidan Flynn' was.

Nowhere was there any reference to what was planned with the ancient structure, or the name of the American developer. Maybe the public meeting might have revealed more, but with his duty in Bandon, attending had never been an option.

Anyway, now he knew.

It seemed a rather odd thing for Richard Murrough to get involved in. It would be interesting to find out what was behind it, and in particular, if everything was really as above board as the man claimed with regard to planning permission. A high-tech recording studio? Everybody knew how strict the restrictions had become on modifying historic buildings. Another thing to check out on his next visit home.

Murrough would probably get up a lot of people's noses with his name-dropping and his know-it-all attitude. Judging by the interview, he seemed to have researched the whole history and archaeology of the area, spouting reams of stuff on the distinction between the original *caiseal* or prehistoric fort and the medieval tower house built on top. Even managed to show off his knowledge of Irish: *Caiseal Gréine* - Fort of the Sun - Sun Studio, indeed. Ha, ha.

Tim folded away the Weekend section and went back to the cryptic crossword he'd started that afternoon on the beach. He didn't make much progress. Somehow he was finding it hard to concentrate.

***

"Jesus! He has it down to a T - just the right degree of self-deprecating humour, and the clever way he ..."

"Now don't get mad again, P.J. You've managed to ignore the man's existence for the last ten years or so - no, it's more like fifteen years now - and it's done you a world of good."

"Sure honey, you've kept me sane. But just look at that photo. It makes me want to throttle the arrogant, self-satisfied bastard. And look at this -" He got up, rummaged in the bowl of oddments (pencils, paper-clips, bits of string) perched on the old pine dresser, found the marker he was looking for, and highlighted one of the more offending passages in brilliant yellow.

"I saw it. I've read the interview." Helen Murphy took a deep breath. "Look, we both know the score. But that was in another country ..."

"And besides ..."

15

"Besides, it's all water under the bridge. I got you out of that rat-race, and since then we've been doing fine. You promised me you weren't going to look back and moan about what might have been."

"Yeah, honey, but now it's well ... different. Think of what it could be like for you now if money were no object."

"You mean, I could be miserable in comfort?"

He laughed. "Something like that. But you might also have been able to afford one of those private clinics in Switzerland or California, where you can be sure of getting the best treatment possible."

She took a puff from her joint and inhaled deeply. "Look, I'm going to be OK. I've only got six more weeks of the chemo, and with this," - she waved the reefer - "it's really not so bad. It really cuts out the nausea, and that was the worst. The hair will grow back."

"Don't wave that thing around so much, or the neighbours might start getting interested!" Since the nearest neighbours were a good quarter mile down the boreen (as they called a little country road in this part of the country) this didn't seem an acute danger. Any casual visitors to their cottage would announce their arrival by virtue of the squeaky gate, and be clearly visible from the front window, allowing plenty time for evasive action if necessary.

"I don't think you're convinced that things *are* going to be OK. But they are. Even money-wise. Our health insurance is covering everything necessary, and I think I should be able to get back to full-time work in September."

"Look, you don't have to. "

"I'd like to."

But before the conversation could deteriorate any further the phone rang. Helen went to the hall to pick it up. "It's for you, P.J. Someone called Jeannie Staunton, if I got the name right."

As he was taking the call, she realized the name was vaguely familiar.

"Jeannie Staunton. Isn't that the one who plays drums and bongos and rattles and things with Eascra?" she asked when he came back into the living room.

"Yeah, but mainly bodhran. And spoons. You met her last Christmas, remember, at that session in Dingle."

"Sure, I remember. She's got a terrific low voice, though you don't get to hear it often in the group. Especially when Niamh is in full flight!"

"Yeah. Well, she wants to know if I'd do a couple of gigs with her over the summer."

16

"So it's true that Eascra is breaking up?"

"She didn't exactly say that. But she did say they wouldn't be touring this summer. They're taking a long break after the Skibbereen concert next week."

"So are you going to do the gigs?"

"Probably. I said I'd meet her after the Skibbereen concert in the West Cork Hotel, and we'd see if we could work out a schedule."

"I hope you're not doing this because you feel you have to. You know how you hate to travel."

"It'll only be a few gigs in Cork City and down the coast. She's got a couple of dates lined up in O'Donovan's in Clonakilty, as well as Vince Coughlan's in Ballydehob and the Courtyard in Schull. Should be fun."

"Yeah, maybe. But I hope your decision will have nothing to do with this." She waved the Weekend supplement of the *Irish Times*.

" 'Course not!

***

Niamh Ní Ghráda finally reacted to the insistent ringing of the phone.

"Look at this here - What negotiations is the man talking about?"

She held the receiver back from her ear and brushed her long red hair out of her face with the other hand. She'd just washed her hair and had been towelling it dry when her brother rang. Of course she knew it was her brother Dónal. Apart from the familiar voice, he was the only person she knew who never bothered to introduce himself on the phone. Typical also that he should leave it to her to figure out what the hell he was so upset about.

"Cool it, Dónal. Would you please start at the beginning? What man are *you* talking about?"

"This Richard Murrough person. Haven't you read today's *Times*? At the end of this interview he seems to imply that he's been negotiating something with us. Well, has he? You're the one Eamonn would probably contact first. Though he knows he's supposed to keep all four of us equally informed."

Niamh took a deep breath. Eamonn O'Halloran was their agent. He probably had already contacted Jeannie and Sean on the subject, but may have thought one member of the O'Grady family would be enough to speak to. In which case Dónal may be feeling justifiably peeved at being treated as the kid brother. Or Eamonn just couldn't face another of Dónal's outbursts. In which case Dónal should learn to be a bit more amenable, then he wouldn't be left out of things so much.

" I was going to talk to you about it at Ciara's First Communion tomorrow. You *are* coming, I presume? After all you're her godfather - for whatever that's worth."

"Yeah, OK, I'll be there. I can imagine the fuss Ma would create if I didn't turn up! Anyway, as I understand it, I was to be informed in passing - maybe at the back of the church - about some negotiations that have been going on behind my back concerning the future of the band?"

"Negotiations my ass! Can't you recognize PR guff when you hear it? There was a single letter and a telephone call to Eamonn, and when he passed on the message I said we'd consider Murrough's terms, and possibly inspect his facilities when this new studio is set up. Nothing to get het up about."

"I'll decide what I get het up about!"

"And as regards the future of the band, a new album is due anyway, you know that. It's only a question of where and when, and which producer we want to work with. Remember, you yourself said you didn't want to use Jim McGreevy again."

"That doesn't mean I'd get on any better with this Murrough guy."

"Very true."

"I mean, just take a look at that photo! The fellow seems to think he's the bee's knees, as our sainted mother would put it!"

"He's done some seriously good work. I don't think we should reject the idea out of hand. He might be just the person to help us find the new direction we ought to be taking."

"What new direction? We're doing fine as we are!"

"We've been through all of this, Dónal. You know we can't just keep chewing over the same old material."

"I don't see why not. It's good stuff, and our fans still seem to think so. They're the people we can't afford to alienate, whatever the critics say. And we're in danger of doing just that by turning our backs on them like we're doing at the moment."

"You mean by taking a break from touring? Dónal, you know I just can't keep it up, and neither can Sean, with his five kids."

"Hah! That's a good one! You know even better than I do that Sean welcomes every opportunity to get away from his wife and kids!"

Niamh decided not to rise to that particular bait. "Look, we've been on the road constantly for a whole year. Even Jeannie agrees that it's time for a creative break."

"Break up, you mean. It could mean the end of Eascra. Look what happened to Moving Hearts. And to Planxty and the Bothy Band before them."

"That wasn't for lack of touring ..."

"No, it was because they just couldn't agree among themselves. Like us, now."

"Just what is your problem, Dónal? You'll have your say just like the rest of us in where the new album is to be recorded. Though up to now you've never cared much."

"Up to now we've recorded here, there and anywhere in between live concerts. Now you want us to do *nothing but* ...! Go into retreat in this medieval castle in the middle of nowhere ..."

"Middle of nowhere would suit us just fine. It should certainly suit *you* that it's just outside Limerick. And none of the rest of us would have more than an hour's drive. Jeannie could easily come up from Cork, Sean from ..."

But Dónal wasn't listening. "... and lose touch with our fans."

"We don't have to lose touch. We can start doing the odd concert again next year. By then we'll hopefully have a new album to promote."

"Well, If you guys keep deciding things behind my back ..."

"We haven't decided anything yet, you eedjit!"

"... the new album may have to do without guitar and bouzuki. Maybe Jeannie can come up with some innovative ideas just for fiddle and Indian tabla. Or get Sean to simulate a guitar riff on his pipes!"

The latter idea set him off in such convulsive laughter that Niamh had to hold the receiver away again.

"Cool it, Dónal. Can't we talk about it tomorrow? Remember: Scarriff church, 11 o'clock."

She slammed down the receiver without waiting for his answer.

Chapter 3

"Ask who?"

"Ask nobody, you ass. I'm talking about Eascra ."

Fluency in Irish was required of all members of the Gárdaí Síochána (in the second official language: 'guardians of the peace'). It was, of course, possible that Sergeant Mike Mulligan did not recognize the relatively obscure Gaelic word for a beaker or old-fashioned drinking vessel. But in the context of having got concert tickets, he must have realized that his colleague Tim O'Driscoll was referring to the popular band of the same name. Mike was just getting more and more bloody-minded as the day wore on.

"There's talk of the band being on the point of breaking up," Tim continued on a more conciliatory note. After all. the fresh-faced Mike was his immediate superior, and was probably getting a bit riled at the absence of any signs of deference on Tim's part. "The Skibbereen concert may well be their last one. But if you haven't even heard of them, you won't be interested in these two tickets I'm having to give away."

Tim had just seen the duty roster for the coming month, and realized that his purchase had been a bit rash. He could, of course give them both to Cathy. He realized he was being a bit of a heel in not offering them to his girl friend first. He just wasn't that keen on her going to the concert on her own, or with - God knows who? Now he would probably end up making a show of being magnanimous and trusting, and feeling more of a heel as a result of his little deception.

"Oh, the band, you mean." Mike managed to imply that Tim had been being unnecessarily cryptic - as one would expect from someone he'd occasionally caught doing the *Irish Times* cryptic crossword when things were quiet at Bandon Garda Station. "No, I'm not a fan." No, he wouldn't be, Tim thought. Mike's tastes were more likely to run to the rousing choruses of the Wolfe Tones than to Eascra's subtle fusion of Irish traditional music with rock and jazz elements. Uh-oh! Was he already turning into the intellectual snob he knew Mike saw in him?

For a rookie cop, Tim O'Driscoll was of relatively mature years. He had deferred entering the police force as long as he could, in spite of - or because of - the pressure being brought to bear on him by his father,

Superintendent (soon to be Chief Superintendent?) Paddy O'Driscoll. As a result, he was one of the most over-educated cops on the Bandon beat.

It astonished him how important it had become to him to get into the force before passing the cut-off age limit of 26. But he had made it - just. Even in spite of his slightly substandard eyesight (a highly ironic defect for someone nicknamed 'Eagle'!) Tim had a strong suspicion that someone may have pulled a couple of strings on his behalf. The suspicion was strengthened when he landed the Bandon posting, which enabled him to occasionally indulge his gardening hobby on a reserved patch of old Dan's farm. But Tim chose to ask no questions. Life was good. If it weren't for the Sergeant Mike Mulligans of this world.

"When did you say that concert was, the one you want to go to?" This was Barbara Brennan, the more pleasant of the two colleagues with whom he now shared office space. He told her.

"Well, I wouldn't mind doing that Friday night, or the whole weekend if you want, if you'll take over the following weekend for me. There's a wedding I want to go to."

"You're a pal, Barbara." He was about to give her a hug when he remembered the latest dire warnings on sexual harassment and though better of it.

Now he only needed to check that Cathy really would be able to go to the concert with him. That was something he should have checked earlier, but it might have meant missing out on the few remaining tickets. His desperation to get in had been whetted considerably by the connection hinted at in that article to the mysterious Richard Murrough and his Castle Green project ...

As it turned out, Cathy was delighted with the idea, except that she didn't feel like travelling back to Cork - or even to Bandon - the same night. She suggested spending the whole weekend out west. They could stay at a Bed & Breakfast, or even the West Cork Hotel, drive out to Mizen and Crookhaven on the Saturday, enjoy Barleycove beach if the weather stayed fine, and mooch back along the coast on Sunday. With her new high-powered job with a company producing banking software (cutting-edge, state-of-the-art stuff, as she put it), she liked to throw her money around, Tim thought. A bit rash, too, considering the new job was a temporary one, with no guarantee of extension beyond two years. But he basically liked the idea, and kicked himself mentally the second time that day for his ungracious thoughts.

Eascra's concert was the main event of the three-week 'Midsummer Madness' festival with which the town of Skibbereen - a rather ordinary market town situated in an area of remarkable natural beauty - regularly attempted to attract its fair share of tourists. It was assigned to the larger of the two marquees set up on the outskirts of the town. Totally sold out, it was besieged by fans who had only recently copped on to the rumour that it might be the group's last. As they shuffled along in the queue of legitimate ticket-holders, Tim and Cathy witnessed at least two attempts to breach the marquee's flimsy defences. Being off duty, Tim resisted any temptation to enforce law and order. The security men seemed to be just about managing to keep on top of things.

Before getting into the relatively orderly queue, and while still in the disorderly mass of those with and without tickets, he had also resisted the temptation to flash a badge at a tout demanding an exorbitant sum for a standing-room ticket. Looking back from the safe haven of the queue, Cathy observed that the tout was finding plenty of willing customers. "Could this be a sign of an improving economy?" she speculated. "No one on the dole could afford such prices!"

The concert itself went well, even if it didn't quite reach the standard of the one Tim had been at in Killarney about two years before. Dónal the guitarist's clownery had been a bit more manic than usual, something that went down well with a certain section of the audience, but which Tim felt distracted him from any attempt at refinement in his playing. His riffs were rather basic stuff, as he pranced around the stage using his instrument to make the stereotyped gestures of the rock musician in an exaggerated, self-ironic fashion. The piper, Sean Mills, didn't seem particularly amused when the neck of Dónal's guitar came in direct conflict with one of his chanters, but neither did he miss a beat as he laid down a rock-solid traditional foundation. To be fair, Dónal did provide a number of good songs, usually in duet with his sister, Niamh Ní Ghráda, and calmed down a bit when playing the bouzouki.

Niamh was in particularly good voice, and as she promenaded up and down the stage for the instrumental passages, her famous left-handed fiddling created intricate counter-rhythms to Jeannie's percussion. It would really be a shame if the band broke up, Tim thought, just when they were showing the potential to take up where the legendary Bothy Band had left off.

Cathy, however, was more impressed by Niamh's appearance that by her musicianship. "I wish I could get my hair to shine like that!?"

"It's the lighting. Yours looks good enough to me." He caressed her long fair hair - nearly as long as Niamh's, though not as luxuriantly wavy, or (admittedly) as shiny. " And it smells great."

She shook him off. "And that complexion - she's practically glowing! If I didn't know better, I'd guess she was pregnant!"

"What do you mean, if you didn't know better?"

"Oh, I know it's just gossip, but I've heard her marriage is on the rocks. They're supposed to be on the verge of separation."

"Well, if she were pregnant, that would be as good a reason as any to stop touring. Note that there has been no announcement yet one way or another."

Nor was there any in the remaining moments of the concert. Unless the final encore - a spoof-traditional take on the old Vera Lynn song "We'll meet again, Don't know where, don't know when ..." could be taken as a coded message. But that, as Cathy pointed out, would be seriously ambiguous.

"Don't you remember, it was used at the end of the film *Dr. Strangelove* ..."

"Yeah - *How I Learned to Stop Worrying and Love the Bomb* ..."

"... to signal the end of civilization as we know it."

Tim ruminated over that sobering thought. "It'll be the end of civilization as we know it if we don't make it to back to the pub before closing time."

"No, it won't. We're *bona fide* residents of the West Cork Hotel, remember." He remembered. He had first tentatively suggested staying at Dan's farmhouse nearby, as they had once before, but she refused to believe that the new bathroom could make all that much difference in the level of comfort offered there. Neither did she believe that Dan's glowering disapproval of their sharing a room would have eased off. He then had tried to insist on a simple B&B, but the argument that they were all booked out because of the festival had been decisive. "So we don't have to join the rush."

She was right. It made a huge difference not to have to push through the crowd, to be able to amble back in a relaxed way and still be sure of getting a nice fresh pint to end the day. Tim took the opportunity to give Cathy what amounted to a guided tour of the town he had grown up in.

Like many Irish country towns, Skibbereen consisted mainly of two straggling streets meeting at an off-centre crossroads. Since the festival marquee was at the opposite end of town from the hotel, Tim had ample opportunity - aided by the full moon and the recently improved street lighting - to point out some of the more notable landmarks.

Some - like the plaque marking the birthplace of the Fenian leader Jeremiah O'Donovan Rossa - were of a general, touristy nature. Others had only a personal significance: for example, the Garda station where Tim's father had served most of the early part of his professional career, moving up in the ranks through Sergeant to Inspector, before the next promotion called for the highly-resented uprooting of the family.

The semi-detached house they'd lived in involved a slight detour: what had been a neatly-kept front garden was now overrun by fuchsia and montbretia, the same plants that had so taken to the West Cork climate that they now ran wild all over the countryside. Back on the main street, what had once been a sweetshop, particularly memorable for its liquorice allsorts, was now sadly metamorphosed into a trendy fashion boutique.

Tim thought they might be able to walk past the offices of the local newspaper without further comment, but Cathy was not going to let the opportunity pass. "Ah, the *other* Skibbereen Eagle!" she exclaimed gleefully.

The West Cork regional newspaper was now called *The Southern Star*, but as it proudly announced on its masthead, it incorporated the now defunct *Skibbereen Eagle*. And that was the paper notorious for a certain editorial solemnly announcing that it was keeping its eye on the Czar of Russia.

A few weeks into his first year at his new (and detested) Limerick school, Tim had already been awarded the nickname 'Eagle' for his striking appearance (nose plus wing-span). When some smart alec among his new schoolmates latched onto the fact that he actually came from Skibbereen, the hilarity had been great. And neither was the opportunity missed whenever Tim could be seen as sticking his nose in other people's affairs. "The Eagle's keeping his eye on you!" became a catch-phrase in his final year of school.

In the years since then, Tim had learned to live with both the simple and the elaborated version of the unfortunate nickname. He had hoped he might escape it when he went to college - but no, there was always someone who remembered. He was stuck with it.

On their odyssey through town, Tim and Cathy had been able to relish at a safe distance the sounds of various degrees of 'crack' emanating from the dozen or so pubs they passed. Normally, Tim would have been attracted by the complex of relaxed companionship, good drink, conversation, laughter, music, and fun implied by the term, especially since he was most likely to run into some old friends. But the danger of being caught drinking after hours didn't bear thinking about. Admittedly, the Skibbereen Gardai did not seem to be making their presence felt in that respect. But as a Garda in his probationary year, he felt he just couldn't risk it. Besides, they were nearly back at their hotel.

Cathy needed to retrieve her overnight bag from the boot of her bright new Golf GTI (a good deal more respectable than Tim's beat-up Ford Fiesta), so they first went round the side of the building to the hotel car park. Parked right beside the Golf was a white mini-bus decorated with what in the moonlight appeared to be a grey pattern of spirals and zigzags, but which they immediately recognized as part of the pale-green and white Eascra logo. Yes, there was the name on the side.

Tim was sceptical, however, on the prospect of being treated to an after-hours session. "Nah, not after a major concert! They'll probably just roll into bed!"

At first it seemed as if Tim was right. There was no sign of any action in the bar. Just a scattering of hotel guests enjoying a late-night drink. They took possession of the one remaining corner table and ordered their drinks at the bar. When the barman signalled that their carefully-pulled pints of stout were ready, Tim carried them to their table. Cathy was discreetly pointing to the other corner table to their left.

"See that man over there, looks like an ageing hippie ... the girl with him, isn't she a bit like ..."

"It's her, all right - Jeannie Staunton, the percussionist. Though if you hadn't pointed her out, I probably wouldn't have noticed."

"Some eagle you are!"

"Well, she's not exactly a striking appearance - no way as flamboyant as Niamh! And in jeans ..."

"OK, Eagle, but keep your eyes open in future if you want to live up to your image!" She took a first tentative sip of her Murphy's. "But who's the old guy with her?"

"No idea who he is. Their manager, maybe? Or their roadie?"

"He's a bit too old for that."

"Oh, come on, he's not that old. Not much more than forty, I'd say. Lots of people have turned grey by then. But OK, I'll put my bet on manager."

But their speculations were put an end to when the old guy in question unpacked a guitar from the case that had been concealed behind his seat. He tuned it, and began strumming gently. The song he began singing was one familiar from many spontaneous pub sessions, though seldom heard on recordings or performed on stage, possibly because of its extreme sentimentality. The singer had obviously chosen it as a tribute to their location. Starting with a boy asking his father why he had left Ireland, it went on:

"Oh, son, I loved my native land with energy and pride
Till a blight came over all my crops, my sheep, my cattle died.
My rent and taxes were too high, I could not them redeem,
And that's the cruel reason why I left old Skibbereen."

After the first two verses, the grey-haired singer paused to consult with his companion. Jeannie was now demonstrating something to do with the rhythm on her bodhran, also conjured up in the meantime from under the table. Actually, Tim thought, the unknown singer had been producing quite a creditable version of the old song. He had a nice finger-picking guitar style with a touch of bluegrass in it, and his vocal phrasing - with its suggestion of suppressed bitterness - took some of the excess sentimentality from the lyrics. He did seem to have a bit of an American accent, which clashed somewhat with the traditional tune - or rather, with one's expectations. On second thoughts, it was actually quite appropriate for an emigrant song.

"You know, Tim, I've never visited that famine graveyard outside the town. Maybe we could take a look on our way out west tomorrow. It's supposed to be interesting." Cathy had obviously been musing on content rather than form.

"Sure. Now that we're playing tourist."

The singer repeated the first two verses at a slightly faster pace, but with extra bars inserted between each line. This time, Jeannie accompanied him lightly on her bodhran, using her fingers instead of the usual stick. When Tim noticed Sean Mills standing in the doorway, he wondered if he shared many pipers' contempt for percussion instruments. It was hard to tell: Sean's expression was as impassive as usual. Not for the first time, Tim wondered what kept him in the band. He had certainly no taste for the non-traditional innovations the women kept introducing.

When they reached the verse about the mother's death (Tim noted that the singer had skipped the one about the eviction, with its explicit anti-English sentiments), Jeannie's insistent beat was giving it the character of a funeral march:

Then the singer hesitated, as if he wasn't sure how the song went on. Tim decided to help out, and intoned in his husky voice, "And you were only two years old ..." The grey-haired singer turned around, grinned, gave him a thumbs-up sign, and continued without missing a beat:

"... ... and feeble was your frame.

I could not leave you with my friends, you bore your father's name.

I wrapped you in my *cóta mór* in the dead of night unseen,

I heaved a sigh, and bade goodbye to dear old Skibbereen."

Jeannie had been gesturing to Sean, who was still standing in the doorway. Anyway, after first giving the impression that he was ignoring her, he disappeared for a few minutes, only to return with his pipes - just in time to add a wailing accompaniment to the last verse:

"Oh, Father dear, the day may come when in answer to the call,

All Irishmen with feeling stern will rally one and all,

I'll be the man to lead the van beneath the flag of green,

When loud and high, we'll raise the cry: Remember Skibbereen!"

From the corridor outside, they heard a man's voice joining in with the more militant version: "Revenge for Skibbereen!". It was Dónal Ó Gráda, who had obviously spent the last hour or so in one of the more raucous hostelries on Main Street. He wasn't exactly staggering, but didn't seem all too steady on his feet either as he ambled to the bar, waving a rudimentary greeting to Sean, Jeannie, and the stranger. The barman hesitated at his demand for a double Jameson, but since none of his friends looked as if they were going to take him in hand (maybe his sister might have if she'd been there?), he sighed and poured him the drink. He was, after all, a hotel guest.

In the meantime Sean had launched into a solo instrumental to close out the song. "Good man, Seanie! Keep it going!" Dónal muttered. With the closing notes of the pipes, he repeated his "Revenge for Skibbereen!" contribution, using it as a link to a new song, the tune of which bore a family resemblance to 'Skibbereen', though in a major, not a minor key.

The skill with which he managed this segue put him on a level somewhat above your average pub drunk nosing in on someone else's session, Tim thought. Even when inebriated, Dónal Ó Gráda remained a professional musician. So was Sean, who soon settled into a melodic counterpoint to the new tune, and even the stranger was quick off the mark in changing over to the chords of the related major key. The words of the song were not familiar to Tim:

"It hung above the kitchen fire, its barrel long and brown,

And one way with a boy's desire, I climbed and took it down.

My father's eyes with anger flashed, he cried, 'What have you done?

I wish you'd left it where it was, that's my old Fenian gun.'"

It went on to relate how the father. his anger dissolving, began reminiscing about the part he had played in the failed Rising of 1867:

"... 'I was down then in Kilmallock - 'twas the hottest fight of all -
And here you see' - he bared his arm - 'there's the mark still of a ball.
I hope the young lads growing now will hold the ground we won,
And not disgrace the cause in which I held that Fenian gun.' "

Here Tim noticed that Jeannie was no longer present. In itself, not particularly remarkable, considering it was nearly (he consulted his watch) ten to one. She had not been contributing to the accompaniment. But her departure seemed to have been sudden and unannounced, as the grey-haired stranger was looking around inquiringly. Eventually he stopped strumming, laid down his guitar on a bench and went out into the corridor, presumably looking for Jeannie. Tim wondered if her departure could have had something to do with Dónal's choice of song. Certainly the group never performed or recorded anything so overtly political - certainly nothing extolling violence, as this one undoubtedly did.

Dónal picked up the orphaned guitar, and after mumbling something derogatory about twelve strings, began accompanying himself for the remaining verses. Here, the son takes up the family tradition, so that his last year is spent in 'a gloomy English jail':

"... I've done my part; I'll do it still, until the fight is won.
When Ireland's free, we'll bless the men who carried a Fenian gun."

An instrumental verse from Sean closed the song, as Dónal turned to the bar to pick up his glass, still holding the guitar by the neck. Tim and Cathy - now the only non-participants remaining in the bar - applauded the performance, though their applause was equally meant for the two initiators of the impromptu session, both now absent. Sean smiled weakly in acknowledgement, then turned back to Dónal, who was downing the rest of his whiskey. Sean helped himself to some of the soda left in the bottle.

"Looks like you've sent Jeannie off to bed!"

"Little girls shouldn't be up so late," Dónal replied, and guffawed at the brilliance of his repartee. Sean did not join in his merriment. In fact, it looked for a moment as if he was about to tackle Dónal for his less than gracious behaviour.

But just then the grey-haired stranger returned (without Jeannie) and looked as if he was introducing himself to Dónal. So the two hadn't met before. They didn't catch the stranger's name, but Cathy thought it was 'Murphy'. Then it looked as if he was asking for his guitar back. Since he had his back to Tim and Cathy, they didn't hear his exact words. But in the light of what happened next, they were later to compare notes and agree that his gestures had seemed friendly enough.

Dónal, however, must have picked up some note of hostility or reproof, because all of a sudden he was yelling at the top of his voice.

"What d'ya mean, you want it back? Of course you can have the thing back! Are you implying I was going to walk off with it? Wouldn't want it in the house! Only play one of them nasty, twangy things when I've nothing else!" He strummed the guitar so violently that one of its twelve steel strings snapped. Then he swivelled around, whacking Murphy in the side with his own guitar, and knocking him back against the wall.

To Cathy's mortification, Tim jumped up, and grabbed the guitar before any further damage could be done. Holding it steady with one hand (Dónal had still not released his double-fisted hold of the top end of the neck), he pulled out his Garda badge with the other. He cautioned Dónal that he could be charged with (at least) disturbing the peace, or being drunk and disorderly, even assault. He asked Murphy if he wished to press charges, but the man shook his head, nursing his bruised shoulder.

"Just get him off my back, would you? I've got to get home."

So the man was not a hotel guest. Strictly speaking, having identified himself as a Garda, Tim should now be charging Murphy with illicit after-hours drinking, and the barman and the hotel proprietor with the equivalent offence of serving alcoholic beverages outside of the official licensing hours. But that was one place he didn't want to go. He stuffed his Garda identification back into his jacket. With Sean's help, he managed to wrest the guitar from Dónal's grip, and as Dónal made a few more threatening gestures, they held him back.

But the threatening gestures were mere bravado by this stage. "All right, copper, I'll go quietly!" he said with a sneer. Sean signalled that he would make sure he got to his room, and led him down the corridor towards the stairs, Dónal still making half-hearted gestures of independence.

"Sorry about that scene. My name's P.J., by the way. P.J. Murphy."

"Pleased to meet you, P.J. You play a mean guitar!" P.J. smiled weakly at the compliment. "As you may have seen from my identification, I'm a cop, Tim O'Driscoll. And this is my friend Cathy Cronin."

He acknowledged the introductions, expressing the hope that they might meet in more pleasant circumstances, like one of their planned summer gigs. "Ask for me at the door, and I'll be able to get you in for free." They thanked him. "But now I've got to get going. I've got nearly an hour's drive back towards Cork."

"Don't you think it would be better to stay here overnight?" Tim glanced at the glasses on the table - empty except for the one abandoned by Jeannie.

"Can't afford it. Besides, Helen's expecting me back tonight, however late." He struggled into his faded orange anorak, pulled a black peaked cap out of one of the pockets, shook it out and plonked it on top of his grey locks. It wasn't raining, but he was obviously one of those people with fixed habits of dress. "And honestly, I've only had the one pint, Garda O'Driscoll!"

Tim grinned ruefully, as he decided not to push the point. He still wasn't used to playing this particular role, and wasn't quite sure if it suited him. Cathy knew it didn't. She tackled him on the subject on the way up to their room.

"I wish you hadn't got involved in all that."

"But I *am* a Garda Siochana, after all, supposed to be guarding the peace for all decent citizens."

"I wish you weren't. You should have held out for a decent programming job where you can really use your qualifications. Getting involved in barroom brawls is not *you* !"

"It was me all right. I couldn't let things get out of hand."

"But you're off duty!"

Their petty squabble was cut off by the sound of raised voices from behind one of the doors they passed on the way to their own. The man's voice sounded like Sean's, familiar from the bar. The woman's was unidentifiable. She seemed to be urging him to keep his voice down.

"Now that really isn't any of your business!" Grabbing Tim's hand, Cathy practically pulled him along the corridor to room number 37.

Chapter 4

"Isn't it gorgeous?"

The object of Maggie Mike's admiration could be seen clearly on the horizon as the taxi in which she sat (actually her cousin Dick Casey's hackney) wound its way through the Limerick countryside. As they approached from the west, it practically glowed in the late-summer sunlight. If it were on the coast it might have been taken for a lighthouse, or at least a beacon.

"Isn't what gorgeous?"

"Castle Green. Just look at it in the sunshine!" But it had now disappeared from view behind a thick hawthorn hedge. "Oh, it's gone now."

"I've seen it - driven a number of people out there over the last couple of weeks. The last lot were a pair of English journalists who were worried they wouldn't find the place on their own. Not that you could miss it, the way it is now!"

"Don't you like it?"

"It's all a matter of taste, I suppose. But I didn't think *you* of all people would be so keen on going back there. I mean, weren't you with Celia Ryan the day she nearly got killed?"

This was a topic Maggie would have preferred to avoid, since she had trouble explaining her motivation, even to herself. A streak of stubbornness, certainly, mingled with frustration at having to keep quiet about that car she'd seen drive away. "It was an accident. The ESB men left some wires dangling ... Besides, Celia's OK now ..."

"There's talk it may have been more than an accident. There's some people hopping mad at what's been done to old Castle Green."

"Sure it was only an old pile of rocks. Nobody cared about it before now."

"Well, all of a sudden, they care now!" Maggie knew that, but she let him go on. "Didn't you see that article in the *Limerick Leader* objecting to your man's colour scheme? Said it should never have been plastered over at all, never mind painted creamy-white! And there's that group demanding that the plaster be knocked off, and the natural stone exposed again - just as you'd expect from a proper Norman castle. My daughter Róisín has just joined them."

Maggie had in the meantime heard all the local gossip about the number of young girls running after that disreputable hippie, Aidan Flynn. How he'd even managed to charm prim, middle-aged Miss O'Brien, who in turn helped recruit the more respectable members ... Yes, she'd heard all about that lot from Celia.

She decided not to comment on that aspect, and get back to the safer ground of the main topic. "Anyway, the castle is nice and cheerful now! It used to give me the creeps, the way it used to be." This reminded her that her objections to Castle Green had once gone much deeper than mere appearances, and she wondered if she were making a big mistake in taking up Mr. Murrough's offer. But by now they had reached the driveway.

"I'm supposed to drop you off at the house." The driver drew up in front of the two-story farmhouse to the left of the main driveway at the base of the tower, now thoroughly renovated and painted cream like the tower. Maggie's sensible shoes crunched in the newly laid gravel as she approached the smart new front door in what she took to be varnished pine, matching the wood of the window-frames. The windows were double-glazed, she noted approvingly, though if it had been her house she certainly would not have gone for such old-style sash windows, since they collect such a lot of dust. Details like this she noted immediately, since it might well be her job to do some cleaning in the house as well as in the tower. No door-bell, so she used the old-fashioned knocker.

She was somewhat taken aback when the door was opened by a woman. Tall and athletic-looking, but a woman nonetheless, with a bright, friendly smile and tight black curls. Maggie had been led to believe that her prospective employer was living alone. She even pictured herself fulfilling the role of priest's housekeeper, as it were, though she would not be living in, and what she had read about Mr. Murrough in the tabloids did not lend itself to comparison with a priest. Maggie tried to suppress her disappointment (maybe she was his sister?), and tried to regain enough composure to stammer out her business. But the woman of the house (for such she turned out to be) took charge of the situation.

"Mrs. O'Keeffe, I presume?"

"Yes, ma'am."

"My husband will be with you in a moment to take you up to the tower and show you around."

But Richard Murrough had already appeared behind her back, and placed a hand on her shoulder. The tall woman smiled, extricated herself from the embrace and retreated to the living-room.

Apart from the white stick, you would hardly know Mr. Murrough was blind, Maggie marvelled once again. On their first meeting at Ryan's in the village, she had already noticed the way he seemed to look you in the eye, though you couldn't know for certain with those tinted glasses. That he was probably just good at orienting voices, she realized when he made his one mistake that day and continued speaking to the waitress in one direction after she had moved soundlessly on the carpet to the other side of the table.

"Well, Mrs. O'Keeffe, if you would just come along with me." He proceeded out the door and along the gravel path to rejoin the main driveway. Maggie only now noticed the continuous stone curb installed on the left side of both path and driveway which he used for his skilled navigation.

"Oh, please call me Maggie. Or Maggie Mike if you wish. It's what everyone calls me around here."

"Maggie Mike - is that because your father's name was ..."

"Mike, that's right." So she didn't need to explain the old naming custom. Mr. Murrough had, after all, grown up in Ireland in the 1950s, before moving to the states with his parents at the age of ten. All this she knew from the tabloids. But she explained anyway. "You see, there were two Maggie Caseys in my class at school, and the other one got called Maggie Joe to distinguish her from me." She was babbling to cover her nervousness, she realized.

"Well, Maggie, you have just met my wife Georgina."

"Yes, a very nice lady. But Mr. Murrough, I ... I didn't realize you, uh ..."

"That I was married ...or rather re-married? Well, Maggie, you're the first to know. We've just flown into Shannon from Las Vegas. Got married there as soon as my divorce was finalized."

Maggie opened her mouth, but no words came out. It was partly because she hadn't wanted to be confronted so directly with her new boss's marital history - she who had only recently voted a staunch 'NO' in the referendum to remove the Republic's constitutional ban on divorce, and thus been instrumental in holding back the tide of modernity for another few years at least. But also shock at being privy to such a juicy piece of gossip.

"But don't get it into your head that you can make a packet selling the story to the tabloids. I've already sent a brief notification to the main newspapers. Just in case anyone's interested."

"Oh, Mr. Murrough, I wouldn't think of doing such a thing!"

"I'm glad of that, Maggie. And by the way, do call me Richard."

"Oh, I couldn't, Mr. Murrough!"

"Well, if I'm to call you Maggie, you can't go on saying Mr. Murrough."

"Ah ... uh, well, maybe I can call you Mr. Richard, then."

"Fine, Ms. Maggie!"

Maggie practically glowed. Ms. Maggie! It sounded like Ms. Ellie in *Dallas* ! She trotted along beside her new boss on the other side from his tapping, scraping stick, still in the shade of a row of newly planted trees - though the one at the end of the row, far from being newly planted, Maggie recognized as the old scrawny apple tree that had caused such trouble for her Uncle Jack. But it didn't seem like the right time to ask about it.

As they reached the main driveway, the tower came into full view, making its dominating presence felt. Now Maggie began to notice some details. Though most of the stonework had been plastered and painted cream, the base of the tower and the edgings of all the windows remained exposed. A lot of those carved limestone edgings had to be new, she realized. Most of the western wall had been missing, she well remembered. Once again, she marvelled at the work that had been put into the restoration of the old ruin that Castle Green had been. And it was still going on, she could see now, even though from a distance it had looked finished.

The diggers - those she had once wondered about on that fateful early-summer walk with Celia - were no longer in evidence, though she knew they must be there somewhere, since the students were still in residence at Ryan's. (Of course she knew all about their business by now.) The area she'd seen them excavate was now a smooth, paved parking area, with two vehicles parked on it: Una O'Riordan's little blue Fiat and the McCarthy & Co. van. Maybe they'd moved off to dig behind the castle.

But some hammering could be heard from the roof. As she craned her neck, she could see the profile of a worker through a gap in the bare grey stonework of the battlements. All that must be new too: there never had been a top to the castle, as she remembered it from her early days - it had always looked a bit like a broken tooth. Well, the dentistry was highly successful. To break the silence which had now seemed a bit awkward, Maggie asked when the work was expected to be completed.

"By November, at the latest. It's taking a bit longer because of some problems with the roof garden. Don't ask me the details, my wife is taking care of that."

"A roof garden!"

"An unnecessary luxury, you think? Well, maybe so. But we thought it could make all the difference for the people who'll be working here." His stick stopped tapping and was now being used to make a grand gesture towards the tower. "I suppose like most people around here, you're also a bit upset about the new look we've given the place."

Maggie shook her head vigorously, forgetting that this gesture would have conveyed nothing to her employer. But before she could say anything, he had launched into a well-rehearsed justification. "Whatever people say, it's actually quite authentic. Castles used to be plastered in the Middle Ages, the colour probably depending on the mineral content of the local sand. Whether the plaster was ever painted over is uncertain, but in any case, our tower is now a lot closer to its original appearance than all those other grey stone structures you see dotting the countryside."

"Sure it's a sight for sore eyes - Oh, I'm sorry, Mr. Murrough, Mr. Richard, I didn't mean ..."

"That's all right, Ms. Maggie, you've hit the nail on the head. It *is* a sight for my sore eyes! You may have assumed that I'm completely in the dark, but that's not quite the case. What I have is an extreme kind of tunnel vision, which makes it rather hard to get around." He whipped the curb violently to make a point. "But when I concentrate on a particular point, I can usually make out its colour. Especially a bright colour. And yes, I know what colour is!"

"Oh, you weren't blind from birth, Mr. Richard?" As she spoke, she vaguely remembered reading something about him gradually losing his sight as a teenager.

"No, it's a progressive degenerative disease. It runs in my family on both sides – though only a few of us actually get it. A recessive gene is supposed to be to blame."

Most of this was a bit over her head, but she got the main point. "So it's fate ..."

"That's right. Just like it's fate that brought me here."

For some reason, this remark made Maggie feel somewhat uneasy again. Possibly it was the suggestion of powers beyond human control that she'd always associated with the ominous ruin that Castle Green once was. But it was different now, she told herself.

By now they had negotiated the curve of the driveway sufficiently to view the main entrance to the tower on the east side. Here Maggie audibly caught her breath at the sight she beheld. Over the corbelled arch of the main door was a neon sign, glowing even in the daytime by virtue of being on the shady side of the building. There was a bright yellow flaming sun on the left, out of which extended two lines of writing - the large letters in white, the smaller ones in green:

CAISEAL GRÉINNE
recording studio

The word 'garish' sprang to mind, though Maggie wouldn't think of saying it out loud.

But Richard Murrough laughed out loud. "Impressed by our new sign? Designed it myself. And in case you're wondering: I can see it in my mind's eye."

"It's ... very nice."

"Had it put up only yesterday. Not sure if we'll get away with it, though. It wasn't mentioned in our application for planning permission, so they may well demand that it be taken down."

"Oh, that would be a shame."

"They can't get us on the plastering job - we've got the historians and the heritage people behind us on that - so they may try to get us on this. What the hell - we'll take it as it comes." He was already fumbling with the large iron key which opened the heavy double doors.

Apart from what was obviously a small glassed-in office to the left of the entrance, the whole ground floor seemed to be given over to a spacious sitting-room - or would waiting room be the appropriate term? The flagstone floor would at least be easy to keep clean, Maggie noted, even if it made the room seem a bit cold. The couple of rugs would just need the occasional shaking out, and the leather-upholstered sofas and armchairs would be easy to keep dust-free. Now she saw that behind the office was a door leading to a small kitchen, with a fridge and tea and coffee-making equipment.

Murrough must have heard the creak of the door she'd pushed open to investigate. "As well as basic cleaning, we would ask you to keep an eye on the supplies - tea, coffee, sugar and things - and make a note when anything is running low. And you may be asked to prepare a light breakfast for some of our clients."

"Certainly, Mr. Murr..., I mean Mr. Richard. No problem!"

"But now you'll want to inspect the tools of your trade. All that is kept in the basement - the cleaning equipment, I mean. So would you just check what's in the broom-cupboard at the bottom of the stairs, and let us know if anything you need is missing. I'll wait here if you don't mind, but do take a look around below." He negotiated his way to the stairwell to the right of the entrance, and switched on the basement light for her.

As she descended, she could well understand that her employer would want to cut down on unnecessary stair-climbing. The spiral stone staircase was difficult enough for a sighted person to negotiate! With a shiver, she realized that it was the same spiral staircase that she'd tumbled down as a ten-year-old. At least no spider's webs this time, but spooky nonetheless.

The broom-cupboard proved to be well supplied with all necessary gadgets, including a high-tech vacuum cleaner. Missing was her favourite brand of bathroom cleaner, but that could easily be remedied.

Apart from the broom-cupboard, the basement held the toilets, marked *Fir* and *Mná* respectively, plus the usual stick figures as a gesture to the non-natives. The white tiles sparkled, and she determined to keep them that way. But the rest of the basement had obviously been turned into some kind of a gym. The purpose of some of the gadgets was beyond her, but one was clearly an exercise bike, and there were weights for lifting.

As she re-emerged on the ground floor, her employer apologized for not mentioning the main feature of the basement. "My wife and I as fitness fanatics, you might say. We find a work-out in the morning clears the mind as well as toning the body. By the way, you're welcome to make use of the facility any time before or after your work."

She looked at him sceptically. Did he really think she was the kind to go lifting weights? As if she didn't have to lug around in the course of her normal work! On the other hand, she had been putting on some weight over the last few months, it had to be admitted, and if she was being chauffeured to and from the village (instead of cycling out, as she might otherwise have done) maybe she should have a go at that exercise bike. "Maybe I will, Mr. Richard. Though the stair-climbing may well be enough exercise for anyone."

"That's only for the moment. We're having a lift put in, you'll be glad to hear." Having secured his orientation in the room, he gestured with his stick to the corner beyond the stairwell. There she saw the metal sliding doors of a lift. "But the damn thing has to be made to measure to fit into that corner, so they're taking their time about it. In the meantime, keep away from those doors. They're not supposed to open, but we found you can't depend on that. We don't want you falling into an empty lift shaft, do we?" Maggie laughed nervously. "Gonna have to put up warning signs."

Murrough was already tapping at the first step of the next flight of stairs. "So if you'd continue up the stairs to the first floor, I'll show you the tools of *our* trade."

They ascended the winding stair to a vestibule on the first floor. That, Maggie noted, was as far as the stone staircase went. Beyond that level, a spiral stairs continued upward, but that was a modern steel and polished wood construction. Of course, she thought, there had been no more than thirty-nine steps left in the old ruin. She had counted them as a child: sixteen down to the 'dungeon', and twenty-three up to the point where the wall of the stairwell had crumbled away, exposing those daring enough to climb it to the danger of a really nasty fall.

But where there had been a gaping nothingness, there now was a new stone wall with a new wooden door set into it. Murrough went through the door, asking her to wait outside. Suddenly, a red light lit up over the door. Murrough re-emerged.

"I don't expect you'll be here much during our working hours, but just in case: When that light's on, it means recording is in progress, so do *not* enter."

"I'll remember that, Mr. Richard."

"I'll show you round the studio in a few minutes, since that's where you'll have to be most careful. But maybe you could first take a look on the upper floors." He gestured towards the continuation of the spiral stairs. "I don't think I need to come with you - just check out the four bedrooms and two bathrooms up there. They won't be always occupied, but when they are, you'll need to make the beds, etc. You should be able to find where the bed-linen is stored, I think."

It took Maggie about twice as long to reach the next floor as it had to reach the first. She hadn't been counting steps, but it seemed to go on forever. How on earth was she going to get a vacuum cleaner up there if the lift wasn't in yet? Maybe it wouldn't be necessary, if there were no carpets, for example.

There weren't. It was bare floorboards all over the second floor, of the old-fashioned kind, though she knew they couldn't really be old. The accommodation actually looked quite spartan, though each room had a bedside phone and a small TV, and the beds themselves were comfortable (she tried one). It wasn't quite such a long climb to the floor above that, but it turned out to be an exact copy of the one below.

The spiral stairs continued upward, though Mr. Murrough hadn't said anything about more than four bedrooms. She had to investigate. When she opened the door at the top, the sun streamed in. She was on the roof, she realized. Not having a good head for heights, she held onto the doorknob at first for security. Then she plucked up the courage to clamber over a pile of stones and a coil of rope to take a peek around the corner to the right. There she could hear the sound of hammering. She grabbed onto an unused cement-mixer to keep her balance.

"You're not supposed to be up here, ma'am. It's not exactly safe yet." It was the worker she'd noticed from down below. Since she was now uncomfortably close to the unfinished battlements, Maggie beat a quick retreat, not bothering to ask how far work had progressed on the roof garden. Her brief look around hadn't revealed anything garden-like, in any case. They were probably just laying the foundations.

Going down the stairs was less tiring than climbing it, but she found herself getting dizzy. She hoped she wouldn't have to wait too long for the installation of the lift.

When she reached the first floor again, the red light was not on, so she cautiously pushed open the door. The sight she beheld explained immediately why the climb to the second floor had seemed so endless. The room was easily twice the height of the other stories, and took up all of the available floor space. Part of one side was glassed in, and there she saw her boss twiddling some knobs or switches on what looked like the controls of a Boeing 727.

Hearing the door open, he gestured for her to come into this control room, or whatever it was. But first she looked around the main area. A polished wooden parquet floor - of a much better quality than the ones on the upper floors - with a broad strip of grey carpet in front of the control room. This was the only floor where she would definitely need the vacuum cleaner.

In the control room, Murrough pointed out what would probably need regular cleaning, and which controls she should on no account touch. Then they re-emerged into the main area, where he pointed out that the glass would need occasional cleaning, both on the control room partition and that of what he called an 'isolation booth' - a smaller glassed-in area in one of the other corners that she had not noticed at first.

"And what might that be for, Mr. Richard?" To Maggie, it sounded ominously like some kind of obscure punishment.

"Sometimes an instrument or voice requires a different kind of acoustics from the others, so they need to be recorded separately." He took her question as betraying an interest in recording technology, so he began elaborating on certain other features of his studio. The adjustable vertical wooden panels along the walls did take her interest because of the obvious difficulty of cleaning them. She was relieved to be assured that she would not need to climb up there.

He showed her the electronic keyboard available to the musicians recording here, and demonstrated some of the sounds it could generate. Though Maggie recognized the sonorous organ piece used in 'A Whiter Shade of Pale', and a banjo phrase as being 'Oh, Susanna', most of the others she found a bit weird. But Mr. Murrough was obviously enjoying himself, and she found it rather touching that he should take such trouble to entertain her, when he was used to dealing with important musicians.

Having stopped his little demonstration, he was now groping to his left, obviously looking for something. He located it, and caressed its cold grey metal lovingly.

"Do you know what this is?"

"A microphone, isn't it?"

"Well, yes, though we don't use this kind any more." He gestured towards the array of more flimsy, wiry things suspended from a rail below the ceiling. "This was used to record some great country music back in Nashville, Tennessee. Patsy Cline, for example, and some early Willie Nelson." Though these were names Maggie had heard, she couldn't remember any songs they sang.

"And the man I bought it from claims it was the one used in Sun Studios in Memphis to make Elvis Presley's first recording."

Now that name she knew! He was the one who started off as a rough kind of singer, but had mellowed beautifully. 'Love Me Tender' had been a favourite of hers at the time Jimmy had been courting her. People don't use that phrase any more, she thought irrelevantly, as if she wanted to banish any uninvited thoughts of poor Jimmy, dead of a tumour only two years after their wedding. She sighed. To cover up any signs of getting dreamy or emotional, she commented brightly, "So you can call it the Elvis mike!"

"I wouldn't dare. The people at Sun in Memphis claim to have the genuine article, and they run the place as a museum. But I know what we'll do. We can call it the Maggie mike!"

"The Maggie mike!" No other words came to her.

She was saved on the need to comment on the unexpected honour by a beep-beep sound from Richard Murrough's pocket. He pulled out the source of the disturbance (a rectangular plastic gadget), pressed one of its buttons, held it to his ear, and after a pause, replied "Sure, honey." It was the first mobile phone Maggie had ever seen. Little did she know that she would only a few years later become the proud owner of such a gadget. On its first appearance it seemed a wondrous thing indeed.

"Georgie wants to drop you off in the village on her way to Limerick. But I think we've dealt with everything, anyway. Is everything clear, now, Maggie?" He summed up their agreement that she work on a week-to-week basis, depending on bookings; to at least get the studio done in the mornings before ten, when recordings start; the rest to be done later - bedrooms, for example, between 10 and 12 noon.

Maggie nodded her assent. "And your first booking is in the first week in September, Monday to Wednesday, is that right?"

He informed her that that would be for Máire Ní Catháin, the *sean nós* singer from Galway, with her husband on the flute; staying just two nights. And that the next booking would be later in September, for the group Eascra. "I'll give you the exact dates later, and let you know how many of them are staying overnight."

He began tapping his way to the door. Maggie followed him in a daze.

Chapter 5

He felt like the Traveller in that poem by ... Walter someone.

The door wasn't moonlit, since (P.J. looked at his watch) it was exactly 10.10 a.m. He had thought he was a little late for his appointment, but so far, 'no head from the leaf-fringed sill' had rebuked him for his unpunctuality. Besides, the sill was not leaf-fringed - the grey stonework was far too sparklingly modernized for that. But otherwise he was smack in the middle of one of the few poems learned at school that had stuck in his mind. As he stood 'perplexed and still', he wondered if he'd got the time wrong.

His horse - in the form of Helen's grey metallic Honda - had already departed. In the silence he could still hear it chugging its way back to the main road on its way to Limerick, where Helen had an appointment with her consultant oncologist at Limerick Regional Hospital. It didn't exactly suit Helen that she now had to travel so far for her check-ups. She could, of course, have changed to a different specialist after Dr. Kelly had moved to Limerick, but had decided to stay with the person she knew and trusted. The devil you know ...

So what was inconvenient for her had proved convenient for him, in that she was able to give him a lift to this strangely-located recording studio. He felt a bit bad about not driving his wife all the way in to Limerick, where she faced a gruelling series of tests to check that the cursed breast cancer was still in remission. But Helen had shaken off his concerns. Apart from wasting time, she said that being chauffeured around would even make things awkward for her. She would much prefer to have the car with her, since she expected to be staying in the Regional only two nights, and would be driving home long before the recording sessions would be completed. P.J. would return to the cottage near Innishannon by train and bus, or maybe Helen would pick him up from Cork railway station. They would keep in touch and play it by ear.

He would be playing a lot more than that by ear in the coming days, he thought. Though Jeannie Staunton, who had been responsible for recruiting him as a session musician for Eascra's next album, had assured him that he would fit in very well, P.J. wasn't so sure.

With Jeannie herself he felt quite comfortable. On their couple of shared gigs along the south coast over the summer, they had developed something of a musical and personal rapport. After that somewhat nasty altercation in the West Cork Hotel last June he was glad that Dónal Ó Gráda wouldn't be there: he was the one he was replacing, after all. But there was Sean Mills, the piper, to contend with. Though Sean seemed to respect him as a musician, P.J. could never be sure what he was thinking. On their only practice run as a foursome, two weeks back at Jeannie's place in Cork, he had got the impression that Sean regarded him as just another smart alec playing fast and loose with the traditional forms he himself so stolidly defended. He had never said as much, of course. But neither had Sean expressed any enthusiasm for P.J.'s contribution - neither his finger-picking nor his occasional use of bottleneck technique. Jeannie had positively encouraged the latter, saying the blend had worked marvellously, but whether Sean agreed, he would never know.

He was even less sure of his position with the glamorous Niamh. On the one hand, she had demonstratively turned on the charm in Cork, and had enthusiastically jammed with him on several jigs and reels. Jeannie told him afterwards that Niamh was extremely annoyed with her brother's bloody-minded decision to boycott the recording sessions. Apparently Dónal was so taken up with his new investment - a cafe and night club in Dublin's up-and-coming Temple Bar area - that he could not find the time to devote even a week to such an important band project. But Niamh was notoriously temperamental, and P.J. felt she could easily turn the other way any time. Blood is thicker than water, he thought.

And then there was Murrough, the producer. He still wasn't sure how he felt about meeting up after all these years with the man who had in effect ruined his chances of musical stardom way back when in California. It certainly wasn't, as Helen feared, that he was out for some kind of retribution or payback for real or (in her eyes) imagined wrongs. But neither had he been deterred for as much as a nanosecond from taking on this session job by the fact that it would involve meeting up with his old nemesis. A fascinated loathing might sum up his attitude to the man.

Murrough probably wouldn't even remember him, even if he were in a position to recognize the greyed version of a West Coast hippie that P.J. had become. He was probably only one of many hundreds of people that Murrough had used or walked over on his way to commercial success and celebrity status. Maybe he just wanted to see how the man would react if and when he was confronted with one of his many victims? He would have to play it by ear.

In the meantime, where were they all? Ten o'clock was the time he was supposed to arrive and present himself at the main entrance to Caiseal

Gréine Studio. And this certainly was the main entrance - that is, if one discounted the wrought-iron gates that had clicked satisfyingly open as soon as he'd keyed in the code he'd been given over the phone in the pad mounted in a side pillar. Helen had waited long enough to ensure that he'd at least got through the gates. Anyway, the neon sign that would have been more at home in Las Vegas than in the middle of the Irish countryside left no doubt about the status of this doorway as main entrance..

To make matters worse, it was beginning to drizzle again, and the doorway didn't afford that much shelter. Not that he cared much if he got a bit damp. Realizing that he didn't have his cap on - part of his regular armour - he pulled it out of one of the pockets of his faded rust-coloured jacket and placed it on his head. Not that there was much hair to protect; Helen had insisted on him having a haircut before starting on this job. But he was a bit concerned about his two guitars, neither of whose cases had any pretensions to being waterproof.

He placed them on top of each other in the doorway, put his holdall on top of that as a kind of rudimentary protection, and looked around. Two cars were parked in the paved area to the right of the entrance - a small battered Fiat and a van with a company's name on the side. Neither of their owners seemed to be in the building, since the knocker he had banged on would easily have been heard in the battlements. 'McCarthy & Co. Archaeological Services'? Maybe someone was working somewhere on the grounds?

Sure enough, a tarpaulin had been erected over an expanse of ground at the north-west corner of the castle, and he could discern some scraping sounds coming from underneath it, and some muffled voices.

"Anyone there?"

A fair-haired woman emerged, dressed appropriately for the weather. She was probably a bit over fifty, he judged. P.J. apologized for disturbing her at her work, explained his business, and asked if she knew why nobody seemed to be in the studio yet.

She didn't. "But I have known them to start work there a bit later in the day, more like eleven."

"I was told 10 o'clock."

She shrugged her shoulders.

"You don't happen to have a key to the castle, I suppose? I'm supposed to be staying in a room on the top floor, and I'd like to get my guitars in out of the rain."

"Sorry, I can't help you there. Why don't you go to the house, down that path over there. That's where Richard Murrough lives, and if he's not in the studio he's bound to be there."

"Ah ... I think I'd rather not. I'll just wait at the door then. Somebody's bound to turn up sooner or later."

She took pity on him. "Well, if it's just a matter of keeping dry, you could sit in my van until someone comes."

"Oh, thanks, that'd be great."

"OK, let me get my keys." She disappeared again under the tarpaulin and emerged again with a shoulder bag in which she was rummaging for her car keys.

"You're doing an archaeological dig, is that right?"

"An archaeological survey, to be more precise. We have to do spot checks all over the grounds before anything gets built on or landscaped."

"Found anything yet?"

"Naah. Except for a rusty medieval plough that'll go in the village museum. Nothing yet to justify any major excavations."

"Disappointed?"

"Well, in a way. I would have expected to hit on *something*, considering the nearness to Lough Gur - I suppose you know that's a famous Neolithic to Bronze Age site. We're working in an anti-clockwise circle round the castle mound, and we're now about three-quarters of the way round. But you never know. We may yet find something significant."

"I suppose the owner would prefer you didn't!"

"Oh, I don't know. Even if we do, he won't be asked to tear the castle down - that's earned its right to be where it is by now! At most, a full-scale excavation would only affect the grounds, and delay the landscaping. Mr. Murrough has even said he would regard an archaeological find as adding to the attractions of the place."

She was now opening the back of the van, and he went to pick up his bags from the doorway. A good thing, since what had been a mild drizzle was now turning into serious rain. He first ran with his precious guitar cases and piled them into the van before going back for his holdall. Then Sheila McCarthy - as she belatedly introduced herself - let him into the passenger side of the van.

"Thanks, Sheila. My name's P.J. Murphy, by the way. I'm standing in for the band's guitarist."

"That's Dónal Ó Gráda, isn't it? One of the students working for me was talking about him. She's a great fan of his, and was hoping to catch sight of him, and maybe get an autograph."

"Well, she's going to be disappointed. He's backed out of the recordings. I admit I'm not much of a substitute looks-wise." Sheila laughed, but did not contradict him. "But I hope I can do a fair job on the music side."

"I'm sure you will, P.J. Glad to save your instruments from a watery fate." She went back to her work.

He hadn't thought to get a book out of his holdall to pass the time, so he was glad to find there was a pile of recent copies of *Newsweek* in the glove compartment, which had as a result failed to close properly. As he pulled them out, a transparent plastic bag fell out onto the floor.

He picked it up to put it back, then saw it contained a muddy brown piece of pottery. A shard, he remembered they called this sort of thing. The sticker on the plastic had some incomprehensible scribbled letters and figures on it, abbreviations for something, he supposed. Maybe the "21/5" was a date from earlier in the summer. So was this from a different site? Sheila McCarthy had said they'd found nothing of interest here. Or was the shard just as unimportant as the medieval farm implement she'd mentioned? If so, why put it so carefully in a bag? He decided to ask her about it when he got the chance.

Just then he saw a figure coming up the path. A familiar figure, though, like himself, a lot greyer than when they'd last met. At the same time the familiar white and green Eascra van turned into the drive, with Jeannie at the wheel. She was obviously using it to transport her various bulky percussion instruments. Her arrival gave him the courage to get out and at least pretend to be civil to Richard Murrough.

He stuffed what he'd been holding into his pocket, put the magazines back where he'd found them, and clambered out of the van. Then he heard another car approaching - must be Sean or Niamh, he thought. It was just after 10.30. He'd obviously got the time wrong.

Chapter 6

"Jesus, they must think we're bloody social workers!"

Sergeant Mike Mulligan was pulling on his uniform jacket as Tim re-entered their shared office after a trip to the bathroom. They had both just shared a pot of strong tea on their ten-minute mid-morning break, having been on duty since 6 a.m.

"What's it this time?" Mike had uttered a similar remark only a few days ago, in connection with having to chauffeur some exhausted and dehydrated teenagers home from the local disco. Effects of Ecstasy, obviously, though the teenagers had sworn black and blue that they hadn't taken anything, and the suspicion couldn't be proved without going to more trouble than it was worth. A word to the parents, and keep an eye on that disco, was the policy.

"Informing next-of-kin. Some local guy has got himself killed in an accident. DOA at Limerick Regional last night. The fax with the details just came in."

"Anyone we know?"

"Don't think so. Someone called P.J. Murphy."

"Common enough name."

"Yeah. But it's Philip James, not Patrick Joseph as you might expect. Lives somewhere beyond Innishannon. I mean, *lived* somewhere beyond Innishannon. His wife lives there - or rather, his widow. I'm told she's a nurse. There's also a step-daughter. But she's a student in Dublin."

"And what's he? I mean what was he?"

"A musician, is what I have here." Tim's antennae were beginning to tingle.

"A road accident, I suppose?"

"No, this one was more original. A fall from a high building."

"High building?"

"A castle, in fact. Called Castle Green, or ..." - he picked up the fax - "Caiseal Gréine."

The tingling rose a couple of megahertz. But Tim had decided to keep his powder dry for the moment. "And what was P.J. Murphy, musician, doing in a castle?"

"Performing for a medieval banquet perhaps?" This contribution was from Barbara Brennan, who had just reappeared in the office, also wearing her uniform jacket and cap. "I'd better know the details. too, since I'm being used as the obligatory female shoulder to cry on!"

Ignoring Barbara's quip and the obvious sarcasm of her second remark, Mike perused the fax from the Limerick Gardai. "The castle was being used as a recording studio. And Murphy was working as a session musician for ... Hey, isn't that the group you had tickets for a few months back, the ones you were trying to get rid of?" He pointed to the name on the barely legible fax.

"Eascra, that's right." The tingling of Tim's antenna had by now reached an even higher frequency.

"Mike, I know how you hate this kind of thing, but I don't mind it. If you want, I'll take over your part of the job as the male shoulder to cry on."

"But the Super always wants a Sergeant on this kind of mission." Mike protested. "Imparts more dignity to the situation, he says. Shows the people we take their little tragedies seriously."

"Maybe so. But I'm sure a Sergeant's time can be better used on more important matters."

Mike couldn't be sure that this wasn't more sarcasm on Tim's part, but obviously decided to take the remark at face value. "You bet it can. I've got three important reports to write between now and tomorrow noon, so by all means take care of this." He placed the two-page fax on the desk for Tim and Barbara to study. Also an Ordinance Survey map of the locality.

"Have you already spoken on the phone with Helen Murphy?" Barbara wanted to know. The name, she had picked out of the fax.

"Only to check that she really is the wife of the victim, this P.J. Murphy. And of course to check the exact address. I've marked the approximate location of their house on that map. A cottage, she calls it."

"Surely you gave some indication as to why you were calling?"

"I said her husband had been involved in an accident."

"So she's prepared for the worst. OK, we'll take it from there."

Mike's directions took them south after Innishannon, on a popular scenic route overlooking the estuary of the Bandon River, before branching east towards Ballymartle, then south again towards Kinsale. They found the turn-off into the boreen next to an abandoned schoolhouse, and parked outside the gate of the second house on the left.

It was no romantic thatched cottage, but rather your standard 'two up two down' farmhouse with a slate roof and white-painted sash windows. Both of the latter were probably original features of the old farmhouse, Tim guessed. Very few of such houses were still occupied by the original farmers, most of whom now preferred the comfort of a modern bungalow, but they were in great favour among city folks seeking peace and quiet, or drop-outs from just about anywhere. Though the house sat in a hollow with no spectacular views, and seemed to be in the middle of nowhere, its location should make it quite a desirable residence (in estate agents-speak), being within easy reach of both trendy Kinsale Harbour and Cork City. The sound of a plane overhead reminded him that Cork Airport was only about ten miles north. The plane had obviously taken off against the strong west wind, and was now curving out to sea, probably en route for London.

The rusty gate squeaked infernally both on opening and carefully closing it behind them. Dahlias and other autumn flowers lined the gravel path that led to the front door. Not just the usual montbretias, hydrangeas, and the various other plants that take care of themselves in the local climate and soil (though they were represented too, further back from the path) but evidence of the work of a careful gardener, Tim noted. The gravel crunched under their feet in the silence as they approached. There was no doorbell, but a polished brass knocker. Nobody answered their first knock.

"There must be someone home." Barbara pointed at the downstairs front windows, both of which were open." Nobody would leave the windows wide open on a day like this and go away." This was true. The gusts of wind coming in from the not-too-distant Atlantic were occasionally so strong that they had to hold on to their peaked caps. The summer, which had on the whole been a good one, was well and truly over.

"Besides, we're expected. Mike phoned, remember." Tim knocked again, but here was still no reaction from inside. "I'll take a look around the back."

A path to the left continued around the house to the back. The back entrance and most of that side of the house had been afforded the additional protection of a lean-to conservatory. This was probably the south-facing side, though the overcast sky made it hard to tell for sure. Taking a closer look through the glass, Tim could see that the structure was being used more as a working green-house than as a leisure area. There were two wicker chairs, but otherwise the space was filled with plants: ripening tomatoes in at least three different varieties, some green and red peppers, and two troughs of somewhat more exotic plants. Now that the sun had broken through the clouds, Tim had to adjust his glasses and shade them to cut out the glare, but he had no trouble in identifying the plants. He was, after all, a keen gardener himself.

In spring, the conservatory had probably been used to grow from seed the cabbages and beans that grew in neat rows in an area surrounded on two sides by a high beech hedge. Behind the hedge could be seen the crowns of at least three apple trees. From that direction Tim now discerned the sound of footsteps on gravel. Rather than be caught snooping, he beat a quick retreat, nipping round the side of the house back to where Barbara was waiting.

"There's someone coming up the garden. Let's wait half a minute and try again." Having heard the sound of a door banging inside the house, Barbara knocked again. This time it was answered, by a woman in her late thirties (or possibly early forties), medium height, very slim, her pallor accentuated by very dark straight short hair with a fringe. She was wearing faded blue jeans and a long-sleeved patterned muslin shirt of indefinable ethnic origin, the kind that used to be fashionable in the early seventies.

"Mrs. Helen Murphy, we presume? Wife of Philip James Murphy?" Helen Murphy nodded unsmilingly.

"I'm Garda Barbara Brennan and this is Garda Tim O'Driscoll of Bandon Station. Our colleague Sergeant Mike Mulligan phoned ahead."

"Yes, you were quick. I wasn't expecting you so soon. Had you been waiting long? I was out in the garden."

"Not really. May we come in?" Wordlessly she led them into the comfortable front sitting room. They sat down in the two well-worn armchairs that she indicated, and Helen Murphy took what was probably her usual place at one end of the matching sofa. Then she realized that the window was still wide open, and got up to close it.

"I'm sorry it's so chilly in here. Let me put a match to the fire." The grate of the Victorian-style fireplace was already set with kindling and turf briquettes. Tim looked quizzically at Barbara. Was all this activity a ploy to stave off the inevitable conversation to follow? Didn't the woman want to know? As the flames took hold, she added a split log from the pile to the side of the fireplace. Barbara finally broke the silence.

"Mrs. Murphy, we have some bad news about your husband."

"You can cut out the usual rigmarole," she said with sudden bitterness. "I already know. He's dead, isn't he"

"You know? ... But how?"

"I rang the studio where he was working, and they told me about the fall from the roof garden, and that he'd been taken to the Regional Hospital. Then I rang the Regional."

"But they're not supposed to divulge such information until the next-of-kin have been located," Tim put in, somewhat petulantly. "And we've only done that now."

"I have my contacts. I was in Limerick Regional as a patient myself only a week ago. For a check-up, and as it turned out, a further blast of radiation treatment." She paused, probably wondering how best to phrase it. "I'm recovering from breast cancer."

"I'm sorry to hear that - I mean, I'm sorry that you're having to fight cancer." Tim mentally kicked himself for his awkward phrasing.

"The treatment is pretty tough, I believe," said Barbara. Tim was grateful for being let off the hook.

"Yes. But effective. The odds are still in my favour, even after this little relapse. I'm a nurse, I know the score." She paused only briefly, obviously not wishing to pursue that line of thought any further. "Anyway, that was in a different department, of course, but they are well able to worm information out of Casualty if they really want to."

"So you know your husband was pronounced dead on arrival at the hospital last night?"

She nodded.

"And that's basically all we can tell you right now. I'm sure you have a host of other questions ..."

"Like, did he initially survive the fall? And what the hell was he doing up on the roof, in the weather we're having right now!"

"As I said, we don't have any more information to divulge at the moment. All that will, no doubt, come out in the course of the investigation."

"There will be an investigation?"

"Of course," said Barbara. "It may look like an obvious accident. But in a case like this, we will need to rule out all other possibilities. Such as suicide ..." Tim noticed how she tensed up. "Or foul play."

"Hah! Did he fall, did he jump, or was he pushed? Oh God, I didn't want him to go to that place. But he wouldn't listen to me!" This was the first sign of any emotion from Helen Murphy, who had obviously had herself well under control so far. Tears welled in her eyes.

"Did you have some special reason to worry about his safety?" Tim put in, though Barbara's frown told him she thought such questions were not appropriate at the moment.

Helen Murphy turned to stare at him with a blank expression. "No. We just disagreed as to whether we needed the money that much."

"Would you like a drink? Or maybe I could make you a cup of tea?" said Barbara. "Or you can smoke a cigarette, if you wish, don't mind us!"

"No thanks. And I don't smoke." She realized that Barbara had taken her cue from the ashtray on the table beside the sofa. "P.J. is the smoker ... Oh, God ...*was* the smoker!" She grabbed a handkerchief and blew her nose violently. "But maybe I *will* help myself to a brandy." She busied herself at the drinks cupboard to the right of the fireplace. "I don't suppose you're allowed to ..." She still held the open bottle of Hennessy in one hand. "No, thanks," said Tim. " Never while on duty."

"Anyway," he continued, "Garda Brennan is right: all possibilities will have to be investigated. It will be mainly a matter for the Limerick Gardai, I imagine. But you will be expected to make a statement of all the circumstances known to you. And the best place for that would be Bandon Garda Station. Unless you'd prefer to make it here, since you're convalescent."

"You mean right away?"

"Good heavens, no. Maybe tomorrow, if it suits you. In either case, we - or whatever colleague is given responsibility - would either come here, or pick you up from here. But there is something we need you to do as soon as possible. You will have to identify the body."

"Oh, Jesus!"

"Unless there's some relative living nearer?"

"No. My daughter is in Dublin. She finished school this year and is studying medicine at UCD. Term hasn't started yet, but she was just getting settled into her new apartment."

"Have you told her the bad news?"

"Not yet. You were far too quick coming out here. But when she *is* told, she'll probably want to come down. Should she come here? She could drive me to Limerick - I don't feel quite up to driving that far myself at the moment. Or should she go directly to the hospital?"

"To the hospital, I'd suggest. We can drive you to Limerick, since it's official business."

"When would that be?"

"Would this afternoon suit you? That would give you time to contact your daughter. Say, 3 o'clock?"

"Very well. I'll be expecting you, or whoever."

"What do you make of her?" asked Barbara, as she steered the car down the winding boreen away from the cottage. She turned on the wipers to deal with some drops of rain, but only succeeded in smearing the windscreen, which in turn necessitated the use of the washing mechanism to get a clear view of the road ahead.

The manoeuvre gave Tim time to consider the question. "I'd say she's one tough cookie."

"Yeah, she had herself well under control. Didn't show much emotion. So at least our shoulders weren't in much demand!"

"But the bit of emotion she did show seemed genuine enough. I think she's just got good at dealing with whatever life throws at her."

"Maybe. And good at keeping her own little secrets. She wasn't being completely honest, was she?"

"How do you mean?" This was Tim's feeling, too, but he thought it wise to get a second opinion.

"Doesn't smoke - my foot! Didn't you get that smell?" He had, so he nodded and grinned, letting Barbara elaborate. "Well, maybe she doesn't smoke *tobacco*. But she must have been smoking pot shortly before we arrived! That would explain the open windows."

"Yeah, and my guess is she was dumping the evidence on the compost heap just as we came to the door."

"So what should we do about it? It's our duty to report her, isn't it?"

"Oh, come on, the woman's got cancer. She's probably on chemotherapy - the dark hair was probably a wig."

"Yeah, I guessed that. But that's probably because of the radiation treatment she mentioned. She didn't say anything about chemotherapy."

"Either way. By all accounts, cannabis is known to relieve the nausea and make the therapy more bearable. You wouldn't deprive her of what relief she can get, would you?"

"The law doesn't make any such exceptions."

"The law is an ass."

"Don't let Mike hear you say that - to say nothing of the Super!"

"I won't. But I suggest you turn a blind eye - or rather an insensitive nose to this little matter. We don't have to stick our noses into everything."

"I never thought I'd hear *you* say that! But in this case maybe it *is* our duty to uphold law and order. The law may be an ass in some respects, but it's all we've got to ward off anarchy!"

"Think about the consequences first."

"I am thinking about them. I'm thinking about the Cork drug dealers she's probably helping to keep in business, possibly the same ones that nearly got my kid brother hooked on heroin. We were able to stop him in time, but ..."

"You didn't report him, did you?"

"No, but ..."

"Anyway, I don't think our Mrs. Murphy will have much to do with drug dealers in Cork or anywhere else. When I went round the back I took a peek into their lean-to greenhouse. They've got several cannabis plants in among the tomatoes."

"What?" Barbara's mouth hung open. She stepped on the brakes and pulled in to the side of the road.

"My guess is that they're fully self-sufficient in hashish as well as in vegetables. The Skunk variety of Cannabis Sativa - and that's what I think they've got - is quite high-yielding, so ..."

"So they may well be supplying the Cork market!"

"Oh God, it's not *that* high-yielding! Don't get the wrong end of the stick!"

Barbara was silent for a while. "I'll have to think about this. If I *do* decide to report the drug-taking, I won't drag you into it. You needn't worry."

Tim decided to say no more on that matter, since he was obviously coming down with a bad case of Foot-In-Mouth disease. Instead, he said something else that was nagging on his mind.

"Listen, Babs ..."

"Don't call me Babs!"

" ... Barbara, whatever you do or don't do about the pot-smoking, I'd like you to play down the significance of the accident - or whatever it was - for the moment. I have a hunch it may have been more than an accident ..."

"I thought I noticed your nose twitching when she seemed to be suggesting her husband may have been in some danger!"

"So don't even mention the idea. You see, I'd like to do the interview and take her statement. And at present all they'd let me loose on would be a common-or-garden accident, something that seems to be an open-and-shut case. If there's even a hint of suicide or foul play, Mike will be in on the act, or even Detective Inspector Feeney."

Barbara looked at him quizzically. "What makes you so keen to get involved in this case?"

"I'll explain if you get back on the road." She raised her eyebrows and shrugged her shoulders, but obligingly turned the key in the ignition and set off back towards the N71, the main Cork-Bandon road. As they drove through an increasing downpour, the windscreen wipers now swishing a rhythmic background to his account, Tim described his brief encounter in

54

Skibbereen earlier that summer with the man he believed was Helen Murphy's husband. "So at the very least, I got the impression that something nasty was brewing among that bunch of musicians. There are a lot of questions I'd like to ask her."

They had now reached the outskirts of Bandon town, and Barbara slowed down in conformity with the speed limit. "OK, I'll play along, Eagle. But assuming you get to do the interview, don't forget to check Mrs. Murphy's alibi. If it was murder, the wife often has a lot to gain!"

"Of course. As I said, Garda Brennan is right: all possibilities will have to be investigated."

Chapter 7

Funny that Tim had been inquiring about the place, thought Superintendent Paddy O'Driscoll, as he perused the initial report on his desk. Not that he wasn't used to his son's hunches, most of which led nowhere. One or two had in the past, however, led in surprisingly fruitful directions. Which meant that it was best not to ignore them completely.

But his discreet inquiries into the background of the surprising ease with which planning permission had been granted for the radical renovation of Castle Green had come up against a brick wall. Or rather, against a Norman stone fortress. He smiled at his little conceit, and stuffed some more plug tobacco into his Dunhill briar pipe. Smoking was increasingly frowned on at Kilbrue District Garda Station, but he felt that as boss, he could afford to indulge his little habit in his roomy private office. He was, after all, willing to put it out and open a window when consulting with the more sensitive-nosed of his subordinates.

As regards Castle Green, there had been no suggestion of any sidestepping of official procedures and regulations. Richard Murrough had apparently jumped through all the required hoops, and emerged looking good. Which didn't mean that everything was completely above board. It may have helped to speed things up that the solicitor acting for Murrough was Maureen Callinan Doyle, whose brother-in-law Jim Doyle sat on the Planning Committee of Limerick County Council. But it would be hard to find evidence of any money changing hands, beyond the legitimate fees of Ms. Callinan Doyle.

Experience told Superintendent O'Driscoll that there were few Brownie points to be won by delving into vague charges of small-scale corruption in the planning process. Now, a major re-zoning scandal ... That might be different, though that sort of thing always carried the danger of stepping on the wrong toes. Besides, he wasn't really in need of Brownie points (a phrase he'd picked up from Tim). With the vacancy coming up in Limerick, promotion to Chief Superintendent was practically in the bag, as long as he managed not to blot his copybook in the coming weeks. He smiled again at the high mixed-metaphor count of his ruminations.

Neither was the promotion all that important to him personally. It was more a concern of his wife Brigid, who seemed to regard a failure on his part to reach the top rank before retirement as an affront to herself. But he *would* appreciate the honour as putting the finishing touches on an overall satisfying career. It wouldn't even involve moving house - he could easily commute into Limerick city from their comfortable home outside Kilbrue for the remaining years on the job.

It was ironic that nobody would now care if they did move house, considering the major upset caused by their last move, from Skibbereen to Kilbrue, back in 1975, that was. Eileen was the only one who hadn't minded then, having just got married and settled down helping to run a pub in Ennis. In fact, it had suited her, making visiting all that easier in the years when she was bringing up her three kids. But Brid and Tim - both had protested loudly.

When their second daughter Brid seemed to go completely off the tracks in her student years in Dublin, he wondered if the loss of the family home in West Cork had been a contributing factor. He shuddered as he remembered those years, mainly for the effect of Brid's life-style on her mother. The commune, the political protests, the weird friends, the hippie clothes ... all that may have been calculated to shock. And then the extramarital pregnancy, ending in the ultimate horror of an abortion in England - referred to in his wife's presence as a miscarriage at the time, and a taboo subject ever since. But Brid had finally pulled herself together, got her medical degree, and was now also married and settled down, with a kid of her own (his fourth and favourite grandchild), and working as a doctor in private practice. Where? In West Cork, of course.

Even Tim had finally seen the error of his ways. Not that his good science degree and experience with computers could be fairly deemed an error. But he had always been destined to join the force. There had always been an O'Driscoll in the Gardai, for God's sake! And if it had taken a period of unemployment to nudge him in the right direction ... well, God moves in mysterious ways.

And now that he was out of Garda College and on the job in Bandon (Paddy O'Driscoll acknowledged with a smile that he had pulled a few strings to land him that posting!), Tim was in a position to follow up his own hunches instead of always bothering him. Except, of course, for one directly relating to Kilbrue District.

Now, this suspicious death at Castle Green, this could hardly have any relation to Tim's hunch. Or could it? An accident, or suicide, or whatever, involving an obscure session musician? It seemed unlikely, but it might be wise to keep the possibility in mind.

The report in front of him gave the bare facts. At approximately 9.15 p.m. on the evening of Wednesday, September 30th the victim was found lying unconscious on the pavement to the right of the main entrance by a member of the band currently making recordings in Murrough's studio. Part of the neon sign from over the door (which may have broken the man's fall) lying in bits around him. Ambulance called by same band member at 9.22 p.m. (at least the hospital can give you precise times!), arrived 9.44. Gardai already on scene (alerted by Murrough himself, 9.26), Sergeant Casey detects faint signs of life 9.38, attempts resuscitation until ambulance crew take over. Victim declared dead on arrival at Limerick Regional 10.12 p.m.

The other 'facts' were less solid and would need checking: Who was or wasn't in the building at the time, when the victim was last seen alive and unhurt, when the fall took place. No witnesses to the latter had yet come forward. Superintendent O'Driscoll began to make a list of the statements that would need taking. Just then the phone rang. It was Tim.

"Dad, I suppose you're in charge of investigating that Castle Green incident."

"How the hell did you hear about that?"

"Quite legitimate. Through the correct channels. The victim is a Bandon local, actually someone I think I may have met. I had to inform the next-of-kin."

Now why hadn't it occurred to Detective Inspector Smith to pass on that little piece of information? The perils of delegation ... "Hmm. Anyway, I don't think your hunch that there was something fishy about the planning permission can have anything to do with it. I did ask around. Nothing."

"Keep on it. You never know. But what I wanted to say was something different. I suppose you'll be doing it anyway, but check the movements of all the members of the band on that evening. Especially the guitarist."

"The guitarist? But he's the victim!"

"No, I mean the regular guitarist, Dónal Ó Gráda."

"Oh, come on, according to my information he's the only one who *wasn't* there."

"Are you sure? Check him out anyway."

"Are you not going to explain what hunch this is based on?"

"It's a bit more than a hunch, Dad. I may be a material witness. I'll explain later, it's a bit convoluted. But in the meantime could you send me copies of any statements you take from the people who were present on the scene?"

"You'll have to apply for those through the proper channels, son."

"Oh, come on, you can do it if you want to. It's done all the time."

"No favouritism. You don't want to run foul of your superiors in Bandon, do you? And you in your probationary year!"

"OK, OK, I'll go through the motions. But please don't waste any time. Got to go now."

Superintendent O'Driscoll was still holding the receiver when Detective Inspector Kathleen Smith knocked and entered.

"It's another phone-call from Richard Murrough, sir. He says he's discovered some vandalism done to the castle. A chunk of plaster knocked off and some slogan sprayed in red over the north wall."

Now what the hell could that mean? The Celia Ryan incident came back to his mind. The ESB had been adamant that there must have been outside interference - but they would say that, wouldn't they? The Kilbrue Gardai had found no clear-cut evidence of sabotage, and the only witnesses, the two women in question, had seen nothing amiss. That was another thing Tim had been inquiring about.

"I'll have to see this for myself, Inspector Smith. Let's go."

Chapter 8

"How did you get on with the widow?"

Tim thought for a moment. "Hard to say. I got the impression she was constantly defending herself - herself and her husband, actually - though against what, I don't know."

"She done it, I told you!"

"I took your advice: She seems to have a cast-iron alibi for Wednesday evening."

"Then maybe it was a contract killing. That humble cottage of theirs could well be worth a packet by now, considering its location. It'd be real handy to be outright owner, rather than joint owner, or whatever she was."

"Maybe so. That point's covered." Tim had paused from his task of formulating Helen Murphy's statement from his notes, to be presented to her later for approval, possible correction and (hopefully) signature. Since Barbara was now peering over his shoulder at the computer screen displaying the draft statement, he obligingly scrolled to the relevant passage concerning house ownership. She read on to the bottom of the screen.

"Hmm, Mr. Murphy doesn't seem to have been such a wonderful provider for his family either. Guitar lessons and occasional gigs don't bring home much bacon!"

"Actually, she seemed to take some pride in the fact that *she* was the main provider. That was one of the points where you might say she was protesting too much - saying how well they'd been managing, and so on."

"My point exactly."

"But you can't be serious, Babs! ... I mean Barbara. After all, you've been saying it probably was no more that the common-or-garden accident we've been presenting it as, anyway!"

"I hope I've neatly demonstrated the dangers of developing an *idée fixe* on such matters."

Tim grinned. "Point taken."

Helen Murphy had elected to come in (under her own steam) to Bandon Garda Station - "to help the police with their inquiries", as she somewhat flippantly put it. She made this remark as she marched defiantly into Tim's office, just as he was finishing his call to his father in Kilbrue. She also took the initiative on being seated in the small interview room on the ground floor.

"Garda O'Driscoll, before you start quizzing me, could you first answer a simple question of mine."

"Certainly, if I can."

"When are they going to release the body? I've got to make arrangements, you know. And they couldn't or wouldn't tell me at the Regional yesterday."

"According to my information, the post mortem examination should be being conducted as we speak."

"Isn't that a bit late for a post mortem? Don't they usually do it within 24 hours?"

"They may have given this one low priority, since the time of death had already been established by the hospital as 20-60 minutes prior to arrival. But I can assure you ..."

"Does that mean P.J. *did* survive the fall from the top of the castle?"

This was obviously something that had been preying on her mind, so Tim decided to stretch the bounds of correct procedure and add some speculations of his own, even if it delayed answering her original question. "An ambulance was called, therefore somebody - presumably also the ambulance crew - must have seen some chance, however slight, of saving your husband's life. Which doesn't mean he wasn't already brain-dead as a result of the fall." He noticed she winced slightly at this somewhat brutal term. But she was a nurse, and besides, she'd asked.

"But all this is speculative. You really will have to wait until we are in possession of all the relevant reports."

"And when might that be?"

"You will have to be patient. But we *can* now provisionally answer your original question, namely, when the body will be released for burial." She smiled ruefully, obviously acknowledging her responsibility for the digressions. "Even if further tests are called for in the course of the post mortem, they should be completed by tomorrow morning. Which would mean the coroner will be able to sign a form allowing the body to be removed tomorrow evening, say 6 p.m. You can pass on this information to the undertaker, but have them check before setting off."

"Thanks. Now I suppose you'll want to start questioning me."

He did. The initial part of the interview covered family relationships and personal history. They had met in San Francisco in 1973. She was already an unmarried mother with a four-year old daughter, working part-time at a local hospital. Due to the shortage of nursing staff she had had no trouble in acquiring a green card. She had been born in Midleton, Co. Cork in 1949.

P.J. - or Phil, as he called himself back then - was an American citizen: born Louisiana, played with various rock bands in L.A. before moving to San Francisco in '67. Moderately successful locally, and highly praised in the San Francisco music press, but never quite 'made it'. Narrowly missed out on an important record contract due to illness, since then, career in decline. Helen then persuaded him to apply for Irish citizenship (no problem, with three Irish grandparents!) and return with her to Ireland in 1977.

"To get out of the rat-race?" asked Tim.

"Quite. It wasn't doing either of us any good."

"What was the nature of the illness that you say got in the way of your husband's success?"

"That was before my time, so I only got to hear of it at second hand. But he referred to it as 'nerves', which could be interpreted as a bout of mild depression. Possibly induced by alcohol abuse, or drugs, or simply by stress."

Now that suggested several lines of inquiry that might be worth following up, but Tim decided to save them for later, if and when they became relevant. The ensuing silence may have induced Helen Murphy to add a positive note. "But there was one good thing about ill health in those days - it saved him from Vietnam!"

"You mean, no need for any fancy draft-dodging?"

"Quite."

More silence. "Mrs. Murphy, how good a musician was your husband?"

She seemed to be giving the question serious consideration. "He was a brilliant musician. But the problem was, there were a lot of brilliant musicians around at the time. Brilliance didn't help. Only the toughest prevailed."

"How would you describe the kind of music he was involved in back then?"

"Country rock comes nearest. P.J. was always trying to blend the various country, blues, and folk styles he'd picked up in his Louisiana youth back into mainstream rock. With some success, up to a point."

"So he had a near miss with a record contract. After that, did he stop trying to hit the big time?"

She raised her eyebrows at Tim's somewhat sarcastic phrasing, and he wished he'd been a bit more tactful. "No, he kept on knocking on the doors of managers and record companies, but with diminishing success. After all, he was approaching thirty, and already looking like a has-been." His own present age, thought Tim, and then banished the thought. Police work was different. Hopefully.

"Anyway, I thought our daughter Tara deserved better. We'd got married in '76 ..."

"But P.J. wasn't her father, was he?"

"No, not her biological father. But he adopted her at the time of our marriage. He's been a good father."

"And you've been living here since your return to Ireland?"

"Practically. We found this place within six months of our return. It suited us fine - P.J. wanted a rural retreat, and it was within easy reach of my job in St. Finbarr's Hospital in Cork. The house was just about habitable, so we could move in while carrying out renovations."

"You've made a pretty good job of it."

"Thanks."

"Especially the garden - I was admiring it on our visit yesterday. Is that your work?"

"I do the flowers, P.J. does the veggies."

Tim didn't ask who did the cannabis. "In whose name is the title to the house?"

"We're joint owners. Sorry - *were* joint owners."

"Is there a mortgage?"

"No longer. Last instalment paid back earlier this year."

"Was your husband in regular employment?"

She stiffened visibly. "My husband was a free-lance musician. His earnings fluctuated wildly. But his basic income came from the guitar lessons he gave in the neighbourhood."

"Probably not enough to pay back a mortgage ..."

"Of course not. But my salary was perfectly sufficient for that. I was working full-time as a maternity nurse at St. Finbarr's until last April."

"You're on sick leave at the moment?"

"Yes. Breast cancer, as I told you when you called. My job is being held open for me. I was hoping to be able to get back to work this month, but now it looks more like November."

"You mentioned a relapse ..."

"Yes. It wasn't unexpected. I had been in remission, but you can never be 100% sure the cancer is gone. Anyway, the tests I had done at Limerick Regional revealed some remaining malignant cells, which necessitated some further treatment."

"Treatment of what kind?"

"Look, I don't know what all this has to do with your investigation!"

"Probably nothing, and you don't have to answer any questions you may object to, as I told you at the beginning. But it's hard to say at this stage what will or won't prove relevant."

"OK. Radiation treatment applied over the course of two days on the spot in the hospital. Followed by on-going low-level chemotherapy which I can take care of myself."

"Why did you need to travel to Limerick Regional for your tests? Surely Cork would have been more convenient?"

"Sure. But my consultant oncologist had moved from there to Limerick. I preferred to stay with someone I knew and could more or less trust." Though Tim hadn't asked for it, she dug out a visiting card of Dr. John Kelly, Consultant Oncologist, from her handbag and placed it on the desk.

"Was your husband at home when you were told of the need for extra treatment?"

"No, he was already on that recording job in Limerick." Her facial expression stiffened again. "I drove him there on my way to the hospital."

"Date?"

"Monday, September 21st."

"And the results of your tests were known when?"

"Tuesday afternoon."

"Did you inform your husband immediately?"

"I phoned him that night."

"And how did he take the news?"

She paused, considering the question. "I couldn't possibly tell. He made the usual encouraging noises, of course. But he did always tend to be more pessimistic than me about this damned illness. Look, you're not suggesting ... I mean, the accident didn't happen until a good week later!"

"I'm not suggesting anything. Accident is certainly the most likely explanation, but we have to keep our minds open." She calmed down.

"Were there any further communications between you and your husband after that phone call?"

"There were three more. He phoned on Thursday to ask how I was feeling after the radiation treatment. Then I called him at the studio to let him know I was being discharged, and Tara would drive me home."

"When was that?"

"The Saturday." She glanced at the calendar on the wall, whose page had still not been turned over to October. "September 26th."

"And the third call?"

"It must have been Tuesday this week. Or was it Monday? I can't remember."

"What was spoken about?"

"Oh, it was mainly to let me know the recordings would be wound up by the end of the week as scheduled, and that he'd probably be home on Friday evening." Another pause. "Which is now."

"How was he planning to travel back?"

"Lift or taxi to Charleville, to catch the train to Cork. Then I'd probably have picked him up there. If I wasn't up to it, he'd have taken the bus."

"And what was your impression of the mood he was in?"

"He seemed cheerful enough. The recordings had gone well, he said, and there was a hint of some permanent role for him with the band. I said he shouldn't get his hopes up."

"Why not?"

"Well, if he was seen as a has-been on leaving San Francisco, he was now ten years older. No good developing more illusions. Besides, he'd been doing fine with his guitar lessons and occasional gigs. No more manic depression, anyway."

"The band in question is Eascra isn't it?"

"Yes."

"What was his relation with the various members of the band? I mean, how well did he know them before he took on this job?"

"I think it was only the percussionist that he knew well. That's a woman called Jeannie Staunton. They had done some gigs together over the summer. It was she who recruited him for this job."

"And the others?"

"I don't really know. I know he met them for some rehearsals in Cork before the recordings started."

"And when was that?"

"It must have been early September. I really can't remember."

"Did you meet any of them?"

"I had met Jeannie once before all this started. And I went along to a few of their summer gigs. The others I had only seen on the stage, at a concert two years back."

"Did P.J. express his opinions about them to you in any way?"

"Mainly about Jeannie. He thought she was a wonderful musician, and they seemed to get on well on a personal level."

"Did that bother you?"

She gaped, and then burst out laughing. "Good heavens, no, why should it?"

"What about Niamh Ní Ghráda? She has a reputation for being extremely charming!"

Was there a slight flush on Helen's cheeks, spreading down her neck? But she laughed again, in a more subdued way, and said, "That's exactly what he said about her. But I don't think he was particularly susceptible."

"And the men?"

"I don't really know. He did say something about the piper's technique, but beyond that ..."

"What about Dónal Ó Gráda?"

"Isn't that the guitarist he was standing in for? I don't know. I suppose he wasn't relevant since they wouldn't be working together."

"Had he met him before?"

"I don't know. If he did, he didn't mention it."

"And the studio owner, Richard Murrough?"

There was a barely noticeable pause. "He knew his reputation. As a successful and innovative producer, but also known to be hard-driving and ruthless."

"No more than that?"

As far as I know."

Tim decided not to pursue that line of questioning any further for the moment. "Now to finish up, Mrs. Murphy, could you account for your movements on Wednesday, September 30th - say from the late afternoon on."

Helen Murphy's mouth opened, then she laughed out loud.

"I'm sorry, Mrs. Murphy, but we have to ask this of all ..."

"... the suspects."

"No, all the people involved. We're not thinking in terms of suspects - yet."

Her mirth subsided. "That's OK. I was at home all that afternoon, like I am most days now. A neighbour called around three to pick up some vegetables."

"And in the evening?"

"At around ten past seven I drove to Douglas, Cork for a meeting of my Cancer Self-Help Group. I was there until about nine."

"Could you write down some of the names of the other participants?"

She could. And that of the neighbour who had called around three.

Chapter 9

"Niamh, would you please go outside with that cigarette!"

In view of the circumstances, Jeannie had up to that point been unusually tolerant of her colleague's chain-smoking. But in spite of the window she'd opened, the air in the ground-floor sitting room of Caiseal Gréine Recording Studio was becoming increasingly polluted, and she felt a headache coming on.

"I can't. It's raining."

"It's just stopped."

Reluctantly, and with an air of martyrdom, Niamh tipped the surplus ash into the heavy ceramic ashtray that already held five or six butts, some of which got scattered onto the floor in the process. Then walked with the remainder to the entrance, tapping noisily with her heels on the flagstone floor, somewhat losing her dignity as she nearly tripped on the edge of a rug, and banging the heavy oak door behind her.

"You shouldn't have done that." Sean looked at Jeannie reproachfully from the depths of the other black leather armchair where he was sprawled.

"Why not?"

"You heard the way she reacted to that awful scene on Wednesday night. Fainted - flat out cold - at the sight of poor P.J. lying on the pavement, with that Sergeant Casey fellow making a half-hearted effort to revive him. I had to carry her upstairs. Now she's going to be reminded of all that."

"Maggie's already cleared up the mess, I mean the broken glass and all that. And we can't avoid the main entrance. It's the only way in and out of the castle apart from the cellar door and the fire-escape."

Sean continued to glare reproachfully. Jeannie was undaunted. "Besides, she had recovered enough to talk to those reporters yesterday." Sean picked up a magazine. "But OK, maybe it's not fair to rub her nose in it."

Jeannie got up and went out after Niamh. She found her sitting on the edge of the pallet of potted conifers that were still waiting for transport by pulley to the roof. Work on the roof garden, like everything else, had been put on hold, so that the neat row of terracotta pots that Jeannie had been admiring on the roof only a few days ago still remained empty of content. Now that sunny evening - Tuesday, it must have been - seemed an eternity ago.

Niamh had quenched her cigarette in the soil of one of the plastic containers, and was holding her head in her hand, so that she apparently didn't hear Jeannie approach. She started when Jeannie placed a hand on her shoulder.

"I'm sorry, Niamh. I'd forgotten you saw ... it all ... Wednesday night. It must have been awful."

"It was. And you know what I can't get out of my mind?"

"What?"

"His cap. P.J.'s silly black peaked cap - perched on top of that stupid pine tree!" She took a swipe at the innocent conifer and began to laugh hysterically.

"Calm down, Niamh, we're all a bit rattled. Me too ... P.J. had become a real friend of mine."

"But you didn't see him. You were still down at the pub when it happened. And he'd been taken away by the time you got back."

"I know it's not the same. Look, since you're not smoking, there's no reason for you to be sitting out here. Come back in, and I'll make us some fresh tea - or coffee, or whatever." Niamh obediently allowed herself to be ushered back in.

Jeannie busied herself in the little kitchen behind the office, and made a fresh pot of each. She then poured a mug of tea for herself and coffee for the others. Having taken a first appreciative sip, Sean got up and went to the fridge. He came back with a small bottle of Tullamore Dew, two-thirds full.

"Now where did that come from?" Jeannie asked. "It's not part of our basic supplies!"

"Found it in the broom cupboard the other day. Put it in the fridge in case it got mistaken for cleaning fluid. Would have been a shame!"

Jeannie laughed. "Maggie's secret hoard! But we shouldn't be helping ourselves to it, should we?"

"I doubt if she'll acknowledge it as hers. But OK, I'll replace it before we leave." He waved the bottle around inquiringly, and Niamh accepted a small addition to her coffee. Jeannie got herself a glass from the kitchen for a small dram with water.

"Now that is the question," she said. "When do we leave? Now that we've all given our statements to the Gardai, we're free to leave any time."

"Not quite." Sean corrected her. "They've asked us to wait here until they've got Richard and Georgie's version of events, in case they have any follow-up questions. That's why we're still hanging around here getting on each other's nerves, for God's sake!"

"Sure, but they're not likely to want any more from us. And we'll be breaking up for the weekend anyway. But ..." Jeannie paused to think how best to phrase the problem.

"But what?" Niamh put in impatiently.

"I mean, we've come to the end of the two weeks we'd booked, but we haven't finished our recordings."

"Due to circumstances beyond our control," Sean pointed out.

"Sure. And I'm not sure if any of us feel up to continuing. But we were doing very well up to ... when all this happened." She waited for reactions, but none came.

"I'm not sure if we'll ever be able to pick up where we left off, if we break off now, and try to get back to it later."

"But are you sure the studio is available next week?" put in Niamh, who seemed to have recovered from her fit of the jitters, probably due to the effect of the coffee or the whiskey, or both. At least she was now thinking straight on practical matters.

"Yes, I checked with Richard. He isn't taking on that many jobs yet."

"Still emphasizing how exclusive he is!" said Niamh with a little laugh.

She was definitely feeling better, Jeannie noted. "Yeah, I guess so. But it suits us fine, doesn't it? It means we could finish the job next week if we want to."

"But Jeannie, haven't you noticed we're now missing a guitarist?"

Niamh gasped. "Oh, don't be so bloody sarcastic, Sean!"

"Well, it's the unfortunate truth. There isn't much we can do without from now on. We've done all the solos and slow airs that we'd planned for the new album ..."

"Yeah, if we'd known, we could have done it the other way round!" snapped Niamh. She took another slug of her whiskey-laced coffee.

"Now who's being sarcastic?"

Niamh was about to retort, but Jeannie cut her off. "What about Dónal? The remaining numbers are familiar stuff from performances ..."

"Except for your new arrangement of 'Skibbereen', and I can't imagine him being willing to cooperate on that!" said Sean.

Jeannie laughed, remembering the incident at the West Cork Hotel. Niamh looked puzzled - she'd missed the fun that night - but nobody enlightened her. Jeannie went on, "No, but we can't have everything. I think if we ask him tactfully, he could be persuaded to come back."

"Hardly. You know his attitude to recordings." said Niamh.

"I don't see why not. After all, he does still regard himself as a member of the band."

"How do you know?"

"Apparently Richard spoke to him on the phone last week. You know, after we'd been speculating on the possibility of a follow-up album next year, possibly using P.J. again."

"And how did he react?" asked Sean.

"Apoplectic, was Richard's word for it."

"Yeah, I can imagine," said Niamh. "He'd much prefer us to get back on the road, but if we're turning into a pure studio band, he won't want to be left out of things completely."

"So let's ask him. Niamh, you must have the number of his Dublin flat."

Niamh rummaged in her Gucci handbag, found her address book, and walked over to the glassed-in office. The other two watched as she dialled a number, frowned, spoke a few words, and then repeated the charade. Finally she stuck her head round the glass door, shaking her flaming red locks as she spoke. "No go. He's not at the flat, got his answering machine. And his mobile seems to be switched off."

"Can't you leave a message?"

"Of course I left a message! On both phones! I asked him to contact us as soon as possible." She paused and frowned. "But there's another number I can try. That business partner of his in Dublin, the one who runs that Temple Bar night-club he's got involved in." She retreated into the office. This phone call seemed to have been more successful, since she was obviously engaging in a conversation with a real human. A somewhat heated conversation, judging by her expression. She slammed down the receiver and re-emerged.

"That idiot thought he must be down here with us! Apparently Dónal left in a hurry some time on Wednesday saying he had some business to deal with in Limerick, and hasn't returned. He sounded a bit annoyed at being left to deal with some awkward financial situation on his own. Something about an extension of a bank loan - I didn't understand the details."

"Never mind his financial affairs, that's nothing to do with us," Sean cut in. "Did the fellow say where Dónal would be staying?"

"No, but if Dónal really is in Limerick, I imagine he'd be staying with Christine." Christine was Dónal's latest girlfriend, a lecturer in French at Limerick NIHE, the 'institute of higher education' that was striving for (but had not yet achieved) university status. Jeannie rather liked Christine, regarding her as an improvement on the sequence of models and starlets

70

Dónal had previously taken up with. She doubted, however, whether the relationship would last.

"So give Christine a ring."

Niamh leafed through her address book, found the number, and dialled. The charade this time was rather similar to the last one, except that Niamh became even more visibly flustered, her cheeks flaming up to a shade approaching that of her hair. Too late, Jeannie thought it would have been better if she had made this call: Niamh just didn't get along with Christine.

"I am not your prozzerce keepairre!" quoted Niamh as she emerged from the office, aping Christine's unfortunately strong French accent. "The cheek! I had asked her a civil question." Jeannie wondered how civil it had been to provoke such an answer.

"Anyway, does she know where he is?"

"No, and she says he hasn't been at her place this week."

"How about phoning your mother?

Niamh looked at her sceptically. Jeannie realized it wasn't very likely, but it was their last chance. "Try it anyway." Niamh heels clip-clopped back to the office. She emerged shaking her head.

"She hasn't heard from him for over three weeks. And she talks as if I'm in some way responsible for his lack of filial piety!" She shrugged her shoulders and collapsed into the soft leather sofa, using its full length, and draping her shapely legs over the other arm-rest.

"Well, where does that leave us?" asked Jeannie.

Nobody said anything for a while. Then Sean broke the oppressive silence.

"To lose one guitarist, Ms. Staunton, may be regarded as a misfortune."

"To lose two ..." contributed Jeannie.

"... looks like carelessness."

***

The tragic incident at Castle Green had already made several regional newspapers. That it was featured quite prominently in the *Limerick Leader* Tim wasn't to know until he turned up for his sporadically scheduled Sunday lunch at the old folks' place that weekend. This time, Cathy was due to come along, which would keep any tendency to talk shop in check. That didn't mean, however, that Tim wouldn't try to weasel as much information about the incident from the old man as he could decently manage. The *Southern Star,* which he was desultorily leafing through as he watched the RTE 9 o'clock news in Cathy's Cork flat, wasn't much help. A brief item about the death of a local man was all they had, and that far back in the sub-section devoted to the Bandon area.

So he was taken somewhat by surprise to hear the RTE newsreader suddenly referring to it, as the last item before going over to sports and weather. It must have been decisive that they'd got Niamh Ní Ghráda to speak to their reporter, however briefly. Niamh was always newsworthy. What she had to say, however, didn't go beyond the usual banalities about how shocked they all were, and how they would probably have to break off the recording work that had been going so well.

"God, doesn't she look awful!" said Cathy.

"Quite a change from when we last saw her." Tim had to agree. He had almost got up to adjust the colour on the TV set. "By the way, there's no sign of any pregnancy. You must have been wrong about that, it would surely show by now."

"Yeah, OK, I got it wrong. Unless, of course, she's had an abortion."

Tim considered the possibility. The hiatus in the band's performance schedule would have easily allowed for a discreet trip to England. But if so, could it have any relevance? His mind boggled at the effort to link it with P.J.'s death.

"Come on, it's Friday night, let's go out for a pint!"

Chapter 10

The funeral was due to take place at Innishannon on Monday afternoon. Having decided it would be appropriate for him to pay his respects, Tim had made some discreet inquiries. These revealed that though the Murphys were not known to be particularly religious, Helen Murphy had opted for the usual trappings of an Irish Catholic funeral, though (his contact suggested) the parish priest may have been asked to go easy on the sermonizing. Anyway, the coffin had been taken to the church on Sunday evening, and the actual funeral procession would start from there at three o'clock on Monday. Since Tim went off duty at two, this gave him plenty of time to join the funeral party and accompany P.J. on his last mile.

But then another - less worthy - thought occurred to him, which led him to take a detour to Kinsale for a leisurely lunch at the Blue Haven (crab meat on brown soda bread, washed down by a pint of stout), before making his way not to the church, but the cottage. He timed his arrival there for three o'clock sharp. He was glad that Barbara had not opted to accompany him to the funeral, as he would otherwise have had some explaining to do. As it was, he was having some trouble justifying his actions to himself.

The cottage was deserted, as expected. He walked around to the back, and took another look into the lean-to conservatory. The same range of plants filled it, as far as he could make out. A lot of the tomatoes had already been harvested, which made the more incriminating plants behind even more visible. Barbara was still having qualms of conscience over that little matter, though she had been so far persuaded not to take any action. He couldn't guarantee for the future, though.

Tim tested the back door, but as expected, it was securely locked. He then walked down the sloping path to inspect the rest of the garden, the part he had not been able to see on his first visit. As he'd guessed, the lower part of the garden consisted mainly of an orchard, with apple and pear trees near the hedge, and some soft fruit - blackcurrant and raspberry bushes - further down. At least there were no further cannabis plantations - nothing camouflaged behind rows of tall-growing beans or maize, as had been known to be attempted in the West Cork area. Maybe that would persuade Barbara to keep quiet. Or maybe not.

Between the harvested strawberry bed and the remains of that year's rhubarb was a good-sized compost heap. Tim inspected it approvingly. It was every bit as sweet-smelling as his own one further back west on Dan's farm, and seemed to consist of a well-balanced mix of garden and household waste, lightly covered by grass cuttings from the lawn. One discordant element took his eye, however - a piece of newsprint jutting out from the grass just beneath an upper layer of household waste: tea-leaves, coffee grounds, and (yes!) the remains of a cannabis joint.

Not that Tim disapproved of putting newspaper on a compost heap. On the contrary, it decomposed nicely, and in the right proportions, was a positive element. When crumpled, it also enclosed pockets of air that aided the ripening of the mix. But that only applied to black-and-white newsprint; Tim was suspicious of the chemicals used in colour printing, and assiduously avoided wrapping any of his waste in anything with garish advertisements. And the offending piece of newsprint in question consisted largely of a bright colour photograph.

On looking closer, he saw it was part of the Weekend supplement of the *Irish Times*, with a June date. Now that was odd: who would keep a piece of newspaper that long and then dump it? On looking closer still, and yanking at it from the side (taking care not to collapse the top level of compost), he realized that it was one familiar to him - one he remembered reading while on night duty at Bandon Garda Station. The one about the record producer, Richard Murrough. And his castle.

It now appeared that somebody else had been intrigued enough to hoard the same article, or rather, interview. And that somebody was either Helen Murphy, her daughter, or her husband - the man who ended up dead from a fall from the castle in question.

Now what could that mean? It didn't exactly go with any of the half-baked theories, or rather, wild guesses he had developed so far. He would have trouble linking it with the suicide hypothesis, or with murder or manslaughter by a disgruntled rival musician. But there had to be some connection. It couldn't be just coincidence. Or could it?

Giving up on the effort to keep his hands clean, Tim scooped off some of the household waste covering the newsprint and managed to extract about half of the page, the rest having got too soggy to be salvaged. He recognized some of the topics covered in the interview, and noted with increasing interest that some passages had been marked with a bright yellow marker. One was a reference to The Hawks (a successful West Coast country-rock group of the early seventies, one that in Tim's opinion had been a bit over-hyped, and whose output had deteriorated towards the end). The other

74

highlighted scrap he could make out started with the phrase 'that one hit the jackpot'; it was a reference to a well-known song the man had written.

A number of questions to ask Helen Murphy came to Tim's mind - if only he could find a way of doing so that would not reveal how he had been snooping around their place. He looked at his watch, and realized he would need to rush. The funeral party might well have reached the graveyard by now. He brushed the dirt off his hands, and wiped them on the pile of fresh grass cuttings to the side of the compost heap. A crumpled paper hanky from his pocket completed the job. It would have to do.

As it turned out, his timing was impeccable. The last stragglers were walking through the gateway of the graveyard as he parked his battered old Fiesta at the end of the row of cars parked at the side of the road. He joined the mourners gathering around the graveside. It was quite a sizeable turn-out for a 'blow-in' like Murphy, but maybe a lot of them were Helen's friends and relatives. It was hard to say if anyone from America had turned up. Maybe the elegantly-dressed lady, her long hair tied severely into a knot, standing to the left of Helen Murphy, and a good head-and-shoulders over her? No, catching her profile, he could see that she was much too young, no more than a teenage girl, really. She could only be the daughter, Tara.

Further back in the small crowd he noticed Jeannie Staunton, in a black trouser suit and dark glasses. Tim tried to catch her eye, but she gave no sign of recognizing him. She seemed to be the only representative of the band present.

The graveside ceremony was brief and conventional, up to a point. That point was reached after the coffin had been lowered into the grave, and the priest stood back to allow the mourners to cast fistfuls of earth onto it. At the same time, two young people, a boy and a girl, unpacked guitars and began to sing in harmony. It dawned on Tim then what a high proportion of the mourners were young people, probably P.J.'s guitar students. Maybe the priest had not allowed guitars in church, and this was their only chance to say goodbye in their way?

What they sang was an Irish folk song about a sailor boy lost at sea:
   "'Twas early, early in the Spring,
   When my boy Willie went to serve the king,
   The night was dark and the wind blew high,
   It was then I lost my dear sailor boy."
Since the dead man's name wasn't Willie, and neither had he been a sailor boy, it had probably been chosen for its basic topic of loss. Or was there some hidden message? (Had he gone to serve a king? If so, which

one?) Maybe it was just someone's (Helen's?) favourite tune. The tune itself (Tim mused) had been used for a number of songs, all about death and loss: 'The Croppy Boy', about a 1798 rebel captured and sentenced to death, was probably the most familiar one; and there was 'Lord Franklin', about a ship lost in the polar ice on a failed attempt to find the North-West Passage (the present graveside singers' harmonies seemed to have been borrowed from a recent recording of that song.).

Before he knew it, the song was over - they must have reduced it to three or four verses - and the performers had launched into an instrumental coda. For this, the tune had metamorphosed into a variation that it took Tim a good thirty seconds of frustrated brain-racking to finally identify. It was the obscure Bob Dylan song, 'Lay Down Your Weary Tune', probably dating from the master's Greenwich Village days, when he was strongly influenced by the Clancy Brothers. Tim had it on an early bootleg recording, which made him probably the only one besides the performers who could recognize it. He knew it to be on the recently issued 5-LP *Biograph* set, but he hadn't so far been able to afford that, and he doubted if anyone else here would have.

The musical interlude had been strangely moving. Though Tim had connected only very briefly on the human level with the dead man, he knew now, that his death had left a gap in many people's lives. So what if he was just a has-been rock musician who had failed to reach his full potential? There and then, Tim determined that if there was any foul play involved in his death, he was going to find out.

He got in line to express his condolences to Helen and her daughter. The daughter didn't know him from Adam, of course (they might have met, but hadn't, at the hospital), and even Helen had to do a double take before she placed him. His being in plain clothes didn't help.

"Ah, Garda O'Driscoll, isn't it? I didn't know the Gardai sent a delegation to the funerals of accident victims!"

"Not normally. Besides, I'm here on my own account. I hadn't mentioned it before, but I think I met your late husband briefly earlier this year. I'm sorry if I was less than frank with you on our last meeting."

A faint smile came to her lips. Was she admitting to herself that she, too, had been less than frank?

"On what occasion might that have been?"

"It was in the West Cork Hotel in Skibbereen, after an Eascra concert at the end of June." She said nothing, inviting him to go on. "Anyway, as a result of that meeting, there are a number of questions I'd like to ask you

76

that might help us to clarify the circumstances of his unfortunate death." God, he was already retreating into officialese! "Would this afternoon be convenient?"

"Look, I've arranged for sandwiches and drinks for a group of friends at the Westgate Inn after the funeral. It should take about an hour. If you're willing to hang around that long, I'd talk to you after that."

He was. And since he was off duty, he was able to get into the spirit of the occasion and enjoy two more pints before deciding he'd had enough and needed to stay relatively sober for the interview. For the last quarter of an hour he nursed a glass of mineral water.

The crowd began to break up, and soon Helen Murphy came over to the snug where he'd been sitting and chatting with a few kids who (he'd rightly guessed) had been taking guitar lessons from the late P.J. It suited him that the kids took her arrival as an opportunity to break free from his possibly intrusive interrogation and make for the door.

"Now what was it you wanted to know?" she asked as she sat down opposite him, placing her nearly empty brandy glass on the table.

"First of all, on the occasion I met your husband, I had to intervene to prevent an act of violence against him."

"Act of violence?" She seemed genuinely puzzled.

"Yes. He was on the point of being attacked by a member of the band he subsequently worked with. On very little or no provocation, as far as I could make out."

"Attacked? By which of them?" She looked as if she were mentally working through all the possibilities, including Niamh having a go at him with her fingernails, or Jeannie bashing him over the head with her bodhran.

"It was Dónal. He'd borrowed your husband's guitar, and seemed to get insulted when he wanted it back. As I said, little or no provocation. And Dónal *had* been drinking."

She digested this information, and Tim decided to give her more time to think. "Can I get you a fresh drink?" She took a look at her glass and nodded. "Any mixer with the brandy?"

"No, straight's fine. Thanks." He returned with the immediately served brandy, then went back to pick up the fresh pint he'd ordered for himself.

"Do I understand you right, that P.J. never mentioned the little incident at the West Cork Hotel?"

"Not a word."

"Can you explain why he might have wanted to keep it to himself?"

"Well, maybe he didn't want to worry me. He was keen to take on this job. I think he saw a chance of getting back into the mainstream of the music scene. Possibly even a faint chance of the kind of success that had always eluded him."

"And you weren't so keen?"

She frowned. "No. As I told you the last time, I didn't want him to be getting his hopes up, only for them to be dashed again. He'd been doing fine in the secluded rural scene he'd mapped out for himself."

"What about the money? Surely that would be very welcome?"

"Sure, but not necessary. P.J. did suffer a bit from the macho delusion that he should be providing for me. It was always a sore point. Silly really."

Silly, but understandable, Tim thought. "In that context, do you think the news of your relapse - I mean your need for extra radiation treatment - could have affected him adversely?"

"You mean, enough to throw himself off the top of a castle?"

"If you must put it so bluntly, yes."

She took a sip of her brandy. "Well, it wouldn't be very logical, would it, to put an end to all chances of providing financial support."

"No, but in despair people sometimes don't act according to logic. And you had said something like manic depression."

"That was all a long time ago. Of course I can't rule it out, and he probably was somewhat upset - God, so was I! - but that was a whole week before his ... fall. And as I told you, he seemed to have cheered up a lot in the meantime." She paused, and took another sip of brandy. "Do you have some evidence that he may have jumped?"

"We're still waiting to get the reports from Kilbrue, the post mortem results, and the statements of those present at the time. So no. To be honest, I have no evidence of anything at the moment. So let's explore a different avenue. What about Richard Murrough?"

Were her eyes taking on a more guarded look? "What about Richard Murrough indeed?"

"I mean, what exactly was your husband's attitude to him?"

"Did P.J. say something to you about him?"

Here, Tim decided to stick his neck out. "Yes. Before the incident I described, I couldn't help overhearing someone from the band - Jeannie, I think - mentioning his name as a possible producer for their next album. I got the impression that your husband had had some previous dealings with the man."

It worked. Obviously, Helen Murphy was considering whether she could get away with the 'knew his reputation' spiel she'd tried the last time, but had to decide against it. After all, she couldn't know what her husband had or hadn't said in Skibbereen.

"He had some dealings with him back in the early seventies, in San Francisco. It didn't go too well."

"Wasn't it something to do with The Hawks? I didn't quite get what the connection was there."

"P.J. was one of the Hawks, at least at the beginning, when they started performing around the West Coast. Murrough got him thrown out just when they were getting successful."

"After they'd landed their first record contract?"

"Right."

Aha! Bingo! A situation reminiscent of The Beatles and Pete Best! But what did it all mean?

"And what was Murrough's justification for ejecting him from the band?"

"That was before my time, as I told you. But from what I was told, Murrough seemed to regard P.J. as unreliable. And there were genuine health problems."

"Were there any more precise disagreements, for example about the direction the band was taking, or about song-writing ...?" Now Helen looked startled. Tim had been fishing on the basis of a scrap of newsprint found on a compost heap, but she wasn't to know that.

"Did P.J. say something ...?" Tim wasn't going to let her off the hook.
"Well, P.J. always did claim that Murrough had stolen one of his songs, and passed it off as his own. His most successful one, actually."

"'Light and Shade'?"

"Yes. P.J. maintained that Murrough had changed some of the words, but the tune was basically his."

So, no wonder Murrough hadn't wanted him in any band he was working with! "But surely it's not so easy to simply steal someone else's song, I mean, there are ways of establishing one's copyright, aren't there?"

She smiled ruefully. "P.J. was never very organized, never kept records of anything. And besides, we were all a bit spaced out back then. Easy pickings for anyone with a bit of business acumen."

Tim was sceptical . "Didn't he ever try to establish his rights?"

"Oh, sure. He once employed a lawyer who took his money only to tell him he didn't stand a chance in court. In the end, it was I persuaded him to stop hitting his head against a brick wall."

"Do you think that was wise? I mean that song must have been worth millions!"

She shrugged her shoulders. "Have you heard of Noel Redding?"

Now what was all this about? "You mean the Jimi Hendrix bass guitarist?"

"The very one. He lives just down the road from here, near Clonakilty. Came here about the same time as us, a bit earlier even." Tim hadn't known that. Maybe because he had left West Cork around that time, and thus lost contact with the local scene.

"Anyway, everybody who knows anything about rock music knows Noel Redding. Even you know who he is." Did she mean, even a stupid rookie cop? Tim decided to let that pass. "Yet Noel is owed millions of dollars by Hendrix's record company. And he can't prove his entitlement in a court of law." She paused for effect. "Now, what chance do you think a complete unknown like P.J. would have?"

"Point taken."

There didn't seem to be any more information to be extracted from her at the moment. Except maybe for one point. "Now Mrs. Murphy, why did you chose to conceal this possibly relevant piece of background when I questioned you last? As I remember your statement, you said the P.J. merely knew of Murrough's reputation for ruthlessness."

"I didn't think it could be relevant."

"That is always for us to decide."

"Now, if it had been Murrough who had ended up dead on the pavement in front of the castle, there would have been your possible motive for murder!"

Tim agreed that that would have been a neater constellation entirely, but he had to deal with what was, rather than what might have been. "Very true. But you can never know what will prove relevant at the early stages of an investigation. And directly denying knowledge of a fact could be seen as obstructing the course of justice. Please don't walk into that trap again."

She smiled ruefully.

"There's one more thing I wanted to say to you in private and very much off the record."

She looked at him inquiringly.

"On our visit to your cottage I took a look around the back, when there was at first no answer to our knock. Being a keen gardener myself, I couldn't help noticing some rather exotic plants in your conservatory."

Helen grimaced. "OK, it's a fair cop."

"Easy does it. I have no intention of taking this further. I don't really want to get you into trouble over this totally unrelated matter." She took a deep breath.

"But I can't guarantee for my colleague, Garda Brennan, who may be a bit more conscientious about enforcing the letter of the law. There is a real danger that someone may turn up some day with a search warrant."

"So I'd better destroy the plants quick."

"Either that or ... Look, I know of the medical use of cannabis, and wouldn't want to deprive you of its benefits." She waited for his suggestion.

"They're an indoor variety, aren't they?" She nodded.

"And even if they weren't, you wouldn't want to expose them to the kind of weather we've been having. So here's an address where you could stow them away until the coast is clear." He scribbled the address of Dan's farm on a page torn from his notebook, and added a rough sketch of its location. "Hire a van if necessary. There's a greenhouse at the back that I take care of. If the farmer is there, say the plants are for Tim. Old Dan wouldn't know a cannabis plant from ... an artichoke."

Not waiting for any further reaction from Helen Murphy, he placed the directions on the table, got up and left.

Chapter 11

The file with copies of the Limerick PM report and the witnesses' statements arrived on Tim's desk the following day. He had dutifully gone through the proper channels, and for once it had worked. When they hadn't turned up on Monday, he worried for a while that the documents might have landed on Detective Inspector Feeney's desk, or that Sergeant Mike Mulligan might be hogging it just to spite him. But a few discreet inquiries through the secretarial grapevine had put his mind at rest. The Superintendent had seen no reason to put a more senior officer on the job, since as far as he was concerned, there *was* no investigation - and were there to be one, it would be handled by Kilbrue. But he seemed to regard it as appropriate that Garda O'Driscoll should finish the job he had started, tying up any loose ends with regard to the local victim of a fatal incident. As long as it didn't interfere with his other duties.

So, having dealt with the more urgent matter of series of local burglaries and put together a relatively coherent report from Mike's scribbled notes, Tim thought he could reasonably devote an hour or so of his working time to the Kilbrue affair.

The most attention-grabbing element in the file was the folder with five photographs of the scene of the fatal incident, all taken by Sergeant Casey. The sergeant had arrived there at 9.32 p.m., in reaction to Richard Murrough's emergency call to the local Garda station. Two of his photographs were taken while waiting for the ambulance (called by Sean Mills, who had found the seemingly lifeless P.J. lying on the pavement on returning from the local pub). Their usefulness for a police investigation was somewhat limited by the ongoing efforts to revive the victim: rightly or wrongly, both Sean and Sergeant Casey claimed to have discerned some possible signs of life - or at least could not be certain he was dead. If they erred, they erred on the side of caution. The close-up of the upper part of P.J.'s body, with (presumably) Sean's hands applying heart massage made him look very dead indeed.

But photos can be highly misleading in this respect.

The long shot of the scene showed the victim's position relative to the main entrance to the castle: his feet nearly touching the doorstep to the left, and his head extending towards an array of plants and shrubs lined up against the wall. Grotesquely, P.J.'s black peaked cap was perched on top of what looked like a dwarf pine. This photo also caught what appeared to be Niamh Ní Ghráda standing in the doorway, wearing a light-coloured dressing-gown. Her expression of shock could be attributed either to the scene she beheld or merely to the flash of Casey's camera.

The more forensically useful photos (apart from the more gruesome ones included with the PM report) were those Casey had taken after the ambulance men had removed the victim. Casey had taken care to mark the position of P.J.'s body with chalk, so that Tim could now discern that his head had landed beside the edge of a wooden pallet loaded with the plants he had seen in the long shot of the scene. If the fall had not been immediately fatal, the softer wood might be the explanation. But the fourth photograph suggested another: It focussed on the demolished neon sign over the door, the right half of which lay in shards at what had been P.J.'s feet. Though no longer lighting, the remaining lettering was quite legible:

CAISEAL G...

recording ...

This was something else that might have broken P.J.'s fall. But it also opened up a whole can of speculative worms. It certainly made suicide seem a lot less likely.

At that moment Barbara came into the office. "Mike wants that report on the burglaries - pronto!"

"Sure - it's on that pile over there. But what's the rush?"

"Cork is on to him about it, he says. They suspect it's the work of the same gang that's been doing the western suburbs of the city."

"Wouldn't be surprised. But look here - what do you think of this?"

"Huh? What's this all about? Is it that Limerick accident, or whatever?"

"Whatever. Yeah. But look closely at the scene of the fall."

She did, though only after first looking at the more spectacular of Casey's photos. Tim waited patiently until she had finally given her attention to the one with the broken sign. Getting no immediate reaction, he finally pointed out what had seemed so obvious to him: "Anybody who wanted to take their own life would surely have the sense to jump clear of the building, wouldn't they?"

"I suppose so. You mean it doesn't look like suicide?"

"What do *you* think?"

"Well, he might have changed his mind at the last minute, or rather second, when it was too late to save himself, and tried in vain to cling to the wall."

"Hmm. Maybe."

"Well, if he didn't jump, does it look more like he fell or was pushed?"

"You'd want to be a real eedjit to fall off that place." Tim pointed to the fifth of Casey's photos, one taken up on the roof, showing the gap in the battlements overlooking the front entrance. There was a low but intact wall about a foot high, and a red-and white warning tape across the gap at the height of the completely reconstructed battlements. "It's not as if you could mistake it for the staircase. And neither is it a place where you'd bend over to kiss something like the Blarney Stone, as far as I know."

"Maybe he was drunk."

"The PM report will show that. I haven't got around to it yet."

"Can't you check it now?" Barbara was getting interested, he thought. Obligingly, he leafed through the report, skipping the details of the fatal or other injuries, until he found the alcohol level in the blood. It was negligible.

"About the equivalent of having had a beer at lunch time."

"Hmm. Any witnesses?"

"Apparently not, according to the old man. I mean, of course, Superintendent O'Driscoll, Kilbrue District."

"You were talking to your father about it?"

He had been home for Sunday lunch, and of course had tried to get as much as he could out of the old man, but with little success. "He was extremely cagey about it. Said it wouldn't be right to discuss the matter until I'd got access to the file through legitimate channels."

"But he obviously told you something, even if it was negative."

"Yeah. He said not to expect too much from the statements, if and when I did get my hands on the file." He grinned as he pointed to the file on his desk. "None of those questioned at Kilbrue admit to seeing or hearing anything."

"That makes it more like suicide again. Surely, if he fell or was pushed, someone would have heard a scream?"

"Yeah, it does seem a bit odd. But there may be other witnesses that haven't yet come forward."

"What makes you think so?"

"Well, Cathy and I did a detour to drive past the castle on the way to the old folks for Sunday lunch ..."

"Of course."

"Yes, of course. And I couldn't help noticing that someone had spray-painted a slogan over a side wall. You know it's been plastered and painted cream ..."

"Yeah, I read about that in the *Cork Examiner*. But what kind of slogan was it?"

"Oh, something like 'Save Our Heritage - Out with MacMurrough' ..."

"But his name isn't MacMurrough, is it?" Barbara hadn't been present at the interview, but she'd obviously read Helen Murphy's statement with some interest and attention to detail.

"No, that must have been a smart-alecky reference to Dermot MacMurrough, you know, the fellow who is blamed for inviting the Normans to invade Ireland back in 1169."

"Educated vandals, then."

"But not educated enough. Or not so hot on logic. Without same Dermot, there wouldn't *be* any Norman castles to call part of our heritage! Anyway, it appears that the vandalism must have occurred in the same night as the fatal incident. Murrough reported it next morning. So whoever sprayed the castle wall may well have seen something."

"Or have had something to do with it?"

Tim pondered that for a moment. "Possibly. But not likely. What could a bunch of protesters have had against a hack musician? Whatever you think of the style of renovation, poor old P.J. had nothing to do with it."

"But he was part of a bunch of pop musicians desecrating a historical site. Anyway, you said yourself they weren't strong on logic!"

Tim frowned, still sceptical.

"Or it could have been a case of mistaken identity. Maybe they weren't too sure what this Murrough person looked like. They must have been roughly the same age, mustn't they?"

That was true enough. And though Tim had never met Murrough in the flesh, he had to agree (having seen his photo with the *Irish Times* interview) that there were some similarities between the two: greying, of similar build ... But surely nobody could mistake a long-haired ageing hippie with a hang-dog appearance for the dynamic businessman that Richard Murrough so obviously was, oozing success from every pore, and even wearing his handicap to good advantage? "Yeah, I guess so. P.J. was aged 39, and Murrough ..." He leafed through the file until he found the relevant vital statistics. "Murrough was born in 1946, so that makes him at most two years older. Almost exactly two years older in fact, less a month: 25th September 1946, as opposed to 25th August 1948. I suppose those idiots of protesters just might have taken him for Murrough."

"Well, curiouser and curiouser!"

"You can say that again!" But before she might be tempted to, he got back to his main concern, namely to cover as much as he could of this investigation on office time, without trying his superiors' patience.

"Look, I don't know if they'll be able to track down any additional witnesses. But right now I'll have to read this lot," - he pointed again the file on his desk - "to find out where everybody was, or claims to have been, at the time, to find out if someone really should have heard something."

"OK, I'll leave you to it. But keep me posted." It was good to have Barbara in his court.

As well as the vague possibility of additional witnesses, Tim had garnered a few additional items of interest on his weekend visit to his parents. One being that the protest group had not been completely ruled out as suspects, either. Barbara's speculation was not all that way out.

Though his father had played down any suggestion that the Celia Ryan incident back in May had been anything other than an accident, he had to acknowledge that the ESB indeed suspected sabotage. They had been adamant that none of their men had been working on the outside power lines at the time the two women reported seeing someone there, which was exactly the time the electricians inside the building had registered a sudden power failure. And if any anti-renovation protesters were capable of such recklessness, then ...

But the Gardai had found no concrete evidence to support the claim, or even anything to support it in Maggie O'Keeffe's statement. This Tim found somewhat surprising. (Had the woman not been muttering something about a strange dark car when he picked her up at the corner that day?) A cable had indeed been cut through, but by whom? There were no unaccounted-for fingerprints, and the footprints in the muddy soil all seemed to have been caused by the kind of rubber boots worn by the ESB workers. Which did not mean a saboteur had not acquired them, together with whatever tools, insulated cutters, climbing gear and protective gloves would have been required to do the job.

Which elicited the obvious question as to whether any of the known protesters might have had such access. The Superintendent prickled at the imagined implication that his officers had not thought of something so elementary. "Of course we checked that. And one of them does have an uncle in the ESB, but we weren't able to pin anything on him."

"His name?"

"Aidan Flynn." As Tim took a note of the name, it dawned on him he had come across it before.

His mother, as usual, hadn't wanted any discussion of police work over the table. She had participated to an extent in the chit-chat about the obvious vandalism to the castle, expressing a surprising amount of sympathy for the protesters. She had been speaking to Miss O'Brien, the primary schoolteacher after Mass last Sunday, and apparently had come to share her views as to what a Norman castle ought to look like. But enough was enough, she said firmly, as she served the leek and potato soup.

The lunch had gone well. Cathy (who on previous visits had managed to get on the wrong side of his mother with her liberal views, and his father with her barely concealed doubts about police career prospects) was on her best behaviour.

"Absolutely delicious, Mrs. O'Driscoll!" she exclaimed after she'd polished off her helping of apple tart and cream. "And the pastry - it's not just ordinary short-crust, is it?"

So while his mother explained about the addition of a small amount of brown sugar, and invited Cathy into the kitchen to consult her extensive file of pastry recipes, Tim took the opportunity to get back to the Castle Green case with his father, taking care to assure him that he wasn't expecting him to discuss the content of the witnesses' interviews until he got legitimate access to the file. "But I would like to know if you got one from the guitarist as well."

"Guitarist? What guitarist?"

"You know, the fellow I tipped you off about last week. Dónal Ó Gráda is his name."

"Oh, yes, they're trying to track him down."

"Track him down?"

"Yes, he wasn't to be found at any of his usual addresses. Nobody seems to know where he is. But to be honest, I've no idea what reason you had to suspect him of anything."

Tim gave him the bare bones of the Skibbereen incident. "So he's obviously a bit of a hot-head, and could be nursing a grudge. I know there's nothing to put him at the scene of the crime, but you have to admit, it does look a bit suspicious if he can't be found!"

Superintendent O'Driscoll automatically took exception to his son's loose use of the term 'scene of the crime', but Tim had obviously given him some food for thought. After a pause, he somewhat grudgingly said, "I suppose it wouldn't do any harm to put out a general alert to all other Garda stations."

Tim nodded. "Maybe even check the ports."

His father raised his eyebrows. "Well, if the fellow really has something to hide, it could be too late for that now. But don't worry, we'll track him down sooner or later."

In the meantime, Tim had enough in the way of statements to keep him busy for a while. He opened the file, and first skimmed the post mortem report. As expected, it held no surprises. P.J.'s ultimately fatal brain injuries consisted of severe haemorrhaging in the right occipital and parietal lobes, and related clearly to a massive skull fracture extending from the back of the head to the right parietal bone. There was additional heavy bruising at the back of the neck corresponding to internal damage to the brain stem. This bruising was more pronounced on the left, and probably corresponded to the point where his head had hit the edge of the wooden pallet - which may in fact have prevented the fall from being immediately fatal. After a fall from that height, they would otherwise probably have been scraping brain tissue off the stone paving, Tim thought with a grimace. Not that it did him any good in the end.

There were two other fractures - the right humerus and a hip bone; numerous other bruises, plus, on his right arm, an array of scratches and one rather deep cut (from the neon sign?), but no noticeable damage to his hands; no other internal injuries. Stomach contents suggested a last meal of coffee and biscuits taken in the afternoon; his last solid meal (traces of meat) must have been at least two hours before that. Lunch. With a pint of beer, perhaps, as indicated by the barely discernible alcohol content of the blood.

A separate forensic report gave details of the scene (this just put in words what he had seen in the photos), and the victim's clothing. One leg of his jeans and one arm of his threadbare orange-coloured cotton jacket ripped. In one pocket of his jacket, a half-full packet of cigarettes (Marlboro) and a cheap lighter; in the other, an unopened piece of chewing gum (Chiclets), and a plastic bag with a piece of old pottery (now what's that?). Watch on left wrist (mechanical, Omega), glass broken.

Then Tim gave his attention to the accounts of those present in or near the building on the evening in question. Having read through all of them once to get a rough impression, he began to take notes on the computer. Soon he had assembled a spreadsheet with a column for each of those present at any time that evening, giving him a good overview of who was where when. As far as he could make out, all the accounts seemed to tally.

The last generally agreed interaction with the victim had been around 6.15 p.m. The recording session had ended just before 6 p.m. Previous to that, all three Eascra members, plus P.J., plus Murrough, plus his wife and recording engineer Georgie Hayes, had all been present in the studio.

No others had been present in the building at that time. The cleaning lady (Mrs. Maggie O'Keeffe!) usually worked only mornings. The two workers on the roof (not builders, but garden centre employees) had left at 5 p.m. An archaeological survey was going on to the west of the building. Still present there after 6.15 p.m.: Ms. Sheila McCarthy, archaeologist, plus two students.

The security arrangements were lax: The main gate was generally locked, operated by key-pad code, known only to authorized personnel. But the periphery (a natural hedge) would be easily breached. The main door was locked only overnight, usually from 10 p.m., with keys available to late returnees; it was unlocked at the beginning of each working day.

Of the group involved in the recording session, Sean Mills (the piper) and Jeannie Staunton (percussionist) had absented themselves first, and gone for a Chinese meal in Limerick in Sean's car. They therefore *seemed* to be in the clear. Niamh Ní Ghráda had retired to her room shortly after six for a snack and (as she put it) an early night. P.J. had gone to his room a little later, after first re-stringing his guitar in the studio. The latter was observed by Sean, who had hung around there chatting while waiting for Jeannie to get ready.

Sean was therefore the last to report seeing the victim alive. Richard Murrough had remained in the studio even longer ('tidying up', as he put it) but could not strictly speaking be said to have 'seen' either him or Sean. Being in the glassed-in control room, neither could he be expected to have heard their conversation. He said he'd been vaguely aware of their presence, but did not know when they finally left.

Murrough himself reported leaving the castle at around 8.30. p.m. to return to the farmhouse for an evening meal. But not before first annoying Niamh by calling her down by mobile phone to listen to some alternate fiddle takes. His arrival back in the house was confirmed by his wife Georgie, who said she'd left the castle shortly after 7 p.m., having first spent about an hour 'working out' in the basement gym.

Her presence in the gym was confirmed by one of the archaeology students (Tom) who had briefly visited the men's toilet in the basement, though neither could give an exact time. They had a brief exchange, in which Tom mentioned a possibly significant find in their dig. She went to take a look before returning to the house to prepare a meal. Sean had also been alerted to the find (some prehistoric stone structure), and taken a brief look before heading for the Golden Dragon in Limerick with Jeannie.

Because of this possibly significant find, archaeologist Sheila McCarthy had stayed on up to about 6.45 p.m. before retiring to her van 'to write up the day's findings', which by her account took about ten minutes. She had asked the remaining two students (Una O'Riordan and Tom Kinsella - the other student Declan having left earlier that day) to continue excavating as long as there was any daylight. Which they did, after some grumbling, finally heading for Ryan's pub shortly before 8 o'clock.

Before leaving, both Sheila and the students reported hearing Niamh practising her fiddle, probably in her room, since that window was open. The students also said they'd spotted P.J. up on the roof just before they left, which had Tom quipping about Niamh serenading him.

In the pub, they had been joined later by Jeannie and Sean, back from Limerick. Their arrival there at about a quarter to nine was confirmed by both Tom and Una, the latter being just on the point of leaving. Tom was a lodger at Ryan's Guesthouse.

The fact that Sean was the one to discover the victim lying on the pavement in front of the castle (after being the last to admit to seeing him alive) had to do with his decision to 'get a bit of fresh air' by walking back from the pub to the castle, leaving his car and car keys to Jeannie. The walk had taken him about a half an hour, by his account. This tallied with the alarm being raised at about 9.20 by a phone-call from Murrough's house.

So far, no obvious gaps or discrepancies.

Any further deliberation on Tim's part was soon to be cut short by regular police duties. In ten minutes he was due to go on patrol with Barbara outside the local discos (for one hour only, before they both went off duty at 10 p.m.) with a view to detecting (or more likely, deterring) any drug-dealing activity. At that relatively early hour it was just a matter of showing police presence - the colleagues on night duty could expect to see more action in that respect. But it had to be done.

There was one more matter, however, that he just had to check out first. He rang Cathy's number.

On leaving his parents' home that last weekend, he had persuaded Cathy to do one more detour before making their way back to Cork. This time to the pub on the edge of the village known to be frequented by personnel from Castle Green. He wasn't sure what there was to be gained by this, but thought it might be worth trying.

As it was, his cover was blown as soon as he went up to the bar. Just his luck - the daughter and son-in-law who now ran the place wouldn't have known him from Adam. But Celia Ryan was serving, and she greeted him in her usual cheery fashion. "Well, if it isn't Superintendent O'Driscoll's boy! It's Tim, isn't it?" Her high-pitched voice carried across the room.

"That's right, Celia. And how are you keeping? I hear you had a nasty accident earlier this summer."

She nodded, and immediately her hand began to shake as she served him his drink. She assured him that she had made a fair recovery, but still had these recurring headaches. And she thought it had affected her memory "I don't do much work here in the bar any more. My head for figures isn't what it was, I sometimes get a bit addled dealing with the money. So I only help out here once a week on Sunday evenings, so that Bernie and Joe can take a night off. So would you check your change and see if I got it right? I don't want to be making any mistakes."

He did, and assured her it was correct. Then he got back to the main issue. "It was a terrible thing to happen. And I heard that somebody may even have cut those wires deliberately ...?" He looked at her inquiringly. She was shaking her head vehemently, but he pressed on. "Did you see anyone prowling round the area before it happened?"

"No, just the people working on the site."

"No strange cars on the road?"

She shook her head. "And why should anyone do such a thing, anyway?"

"There was talk it may have been someone with a grudge against the renovation of Castle Green."

"No, that's just the ESB trying to cover up their own negligence."

Her phrasing pointed him in the right direction, "So I suppose you're suing the ESB for damages?"

"Of course. Bernie says I'd be a fool not to, and I suppose she's right. My son-in-law Joe has taken the matter in hand, and found me a good solicitor." She had probably also been told she'd be a fool to countenance any suggestion that some anonymous saboteur may have been to blame. But Tim nodded in apparent agreement, and brought the conversation round to the more recent Castle Green incident.

"Another terrible accident! And so bad for business! My good friend Maggie does the cleaning there, and she says the boss is absolutely

91

devastated. They're going to go on as best they can, but you can imagine, a lot of customers are going to be put off by a thing like that."

"The boss, have you met him yourself?"

"He was here once, making arrangements with Maggie. But he left a huge tip, even though they'd only had tea and scones. And Maggie says that's quite typical of him. Generous to a fault. And he has such good manners ... She says you can sometimes forget he's blind, he manages so well."

"But he's not a regular customer here, then.?"

"No, I wouldn't think he's a man for the drink. But the people working in the studio sometimes come here. And a couple of students working on the dig are staying here."

"The dig? You mean the archaeological site?"

"Yes, but they call it the dig. That's them over there. They're both Dubliners, but really nice boys, actually. They've been good guests all the summer. This is their last week before they go back to college."

Tim turned around as soon as he thought he could safely do so without it being too obvious. He saw that Cathy had already sidled away at some point in the conversation, and was now deep in conversation with the two boys in question, one of slight build, dark-haired with Buddy Holly-style glasses, the other fresh-faced with a liberal sprinkling of freckles, and a mop of ginger hair.

But Celia was onto another topic, namely his own career prospects. "Your Dad must be delighted that you've finally joined the Gardai. He often said to me it would be a shame if there were no O'Driscoll from this generation in the force." He kept up a bit of good-natured banter, as was expected of him, until her attention was taken by some other customers.

On the subsequent drive to Cork, he'd asked Cathy what the conversation with the students had been about.

"Archaeology. Fascinating subject."

"I didn't know you were interested in archaeology."

"There's a lot of things you don't know about me, Tim! That was before your time, when I was an undergraduate at UCD." Tim did know she had originally studied History and German with the intention of becoming a secondary school teacher, before turning to the more promising world of computers and joining the same diploma course as Tim. The rest was history. But archaeology? "In my first year, I joined two university clubs in order to broaden my circle of friends: the Student Choir, and the Archaeological Society. It was fun. Even visited a couple of digs."

92

"Digs."

"Yes, digs. Though they wouldn't let me even scratch at the surface in case I messed things up for them. Anyway it gave me enough background to know what the two boys back there were talking about." Tim looked at her inquiringly. "Apparently they've found a row of upright stones that could well be part of some megalithic structure."

"Megalithic?"

"Yes, just means big rocks. And probably from the Neolithic period - Late Stone Age to you. Maybe part of a passage grave."

"You mean, like those things at Knowth or Newgrange?"

"Yes. Or Lough Gur, come to that. There's a megalithic tomb there, too, just a few miles from this Castle Green place. You should know that, you lived in the area, for God's sake!"

"Yeah, but only for a few years. And I suppose I did know it, I just was never interested in Lough Gur except as a place for picnics."

"Anyway, the two students I was talking to are naturally a bit frustrated that they find something interesting just one week before they have to go back to college. And they'd been hacking away at the grounds of the castle all the summer, for four whole months, they said, and finding nothing more than broken bottles and bits of farm machinery! And now the really interesting work will have to be handed over to the professional academics."

"So it was just pure luck - or bad luck, if you will - that they found this structure so late in the game?"

"I suppose so. If they'd conducted their survey clockwise around the grounds instead of anti-clockwise, they might have hit pay-dirt earlier. On the other hand, one of them said it was only within the last month that they'd gone that deep into the mound the castle is built on. That was always the really promising area."

"Hm. So now I suppose they're doing overtime to get as much of the job done as possible."

"That's what they said. And there was some banter between the two about who was or wasn't pulling their weight. Tom, that's the younger, red-haired one, he was complaining about Declan always calling it a day around five o'clock and leaving the hard work to him and Una - that's the third member of the crew, she lives locally."

"And did he admit to the crime?"

"Yes, your Honour, but there were extenuating circumstances. Declan is an early riser, and likes to get work over with as soon as possible. So a few weeks back he'd brought his bike down from his home in Dundalk by train, and took to starting early, usually around six or seven in the morning. You see, with the bike he was independent, and didn't need to wait for Una to drive him to the site."

"Sounds reasonable."

"Yes, but he's doubly frustrated now, because he can't do it that way any more. You see, his bike's gone."

"Gone?"

"Yes, stolen, probably. It happens all the time, even in sleepy little villages like that."

"Who are you telling?"

"I did encourage him to report the loss, saying sometimes the Gardai do get lucky. He was sceptical , he might even have latched on to the fact that I was here with a member of the force - that elderly barmaid you were chatting up practically announced it to the whole pub! He agreed that maybe he should."

"So that was it?"

"Yes."

But maybe there was more to it than that. The thpught came to him two days later. Luckily, Cathy was at home, and answered after the first two rings.

"Hi Cathy, it's Tim. Remember that conversation you had in Ryan's pub with the archaeology students? The one whose bike was stolen - did he say when he missed it?"

There was a pause. She was used to being ambushed with abrupt questions like this, but liked to emphasize that a more civil introduction would have been more appropriate. "Yes, I think he said it was gone on Thursday morning, that he had walked the whole way out that morning, and waited for a lift the next day because it was raining."

Thursday morning. The day after. "Thanks, Cathy. That bike may very well be a clue to something." He wasn't sure himself what he meant by that, so he was glad she didn't ask. Instead, Cathy was starting to make arrangements for next weekend. But Barbara was already at the door waving the keys of the squad car and telling him to hurry up. "Sorry, Love. Gotta go, duty calls."

"Now what was all that about a bike?"

He explained as they took up their posts outside the first of the three local discos.

"Curiouser and curiouser!" So she had managed to say it again.

Chapter 12

He really should have brought Cathy along. Cathy knew all the gossip, and would have saved him from making a minor fool of himself. But it had been his considered decision to go it alone, even though Cathy's suburban apartment was at most a ten-minute drive from the Cork City address given as Jeannie Staunton's residence.

His consideration - only half admitted to himself - was that he had sensed a certain rapport on the occasion of their brief encounter a few months back in the West Cork Hotel. Pure imagination, possibly, and based on nothing more than a faint smile. She might not even remember him. But it was potentially something that could be built on.

Musically, he had always regarded her as the heart and soul of Eascra, her rhythmic innovations giving the band its direction at every point in their development. And she was certainly more of his type than the more overtly glamorous Niamh. A bit like Cathy, really, just with shorter hair. The colour of which was commonly referred to as 'mousy', but could more charitably be described as light brown or (Cathy's favoured term) dark blond.

But who was he to be critically reflecting on degrees of mousiness, when it could just as well apply to his own mane, were it not for the fact that its coarse and unruly nature might call for an even less complimentary animal analogy? Tim began to wonder somewhat uneasily whether his attraction to Cathy (and now Jeannie) could be based on the fact that they were softer, smoother versions of himself. He dismissed the uncomfortable thought, and got back to the matter in hand.

When phoning to make the appointment, Tim had mentioned the Skibbereen incident - without getting much of a reaction. But over and above his legitimate police credentials, it may have tipped the balance towards Jeannie agreeing to speak to him.

Since he was still on the evening shift, it had to be a morning. And Saturday, 11 a.m. had suited her. So this rainy Saturday morning saw him joining the queues of suburban shoppers looking for parking spaces in the city centre. In the vague hope of jogging Jeannie's memory, he had tried to remember what he had been wearing that night in Skibbereen, but to no avail. Jeans certainly, but in June it had hardly been the black leather jacket he was now wearing, as appropriate for the October weather. Cathy would have remembered, but he hadn't wanted to ask anything so silly.

The address given had puzzled him a little. Down by the quays to the east of City Hall, somewhere between the gasworks and the electricity station - it didn't exactly sound like a prime residential area. True, he had seen plans for a new quayside apartment building in the window of a city estate agent, but didn't think anything had gone up there so far.

For a moment Tim thought there must have been some mistake. The building in question looked like an old warehouse. In fact it *was* an old warehouse, as indicated by the faded 19th-century company name on the side: Biggs & Sons, Lumber Merchants. But the door was modern, and it had a doorbell which he could hear ringing in the higher reaches of the building. As he waited, he noted that the lower floor was occupied by some kind of a workshop, though it was hard to make out what kind through the wooden laths of the blinds covering the tall windows. A voice crackled in the intercom, and soon a buzzer afforded him entry, with instructions to go straight up to the top floor.

The voice had not been Jeannie's. Or rather, it hadn't sounded like her, though one couldn't be sure because of the crackling distortion. The person who greeted him at the door of the apartment was a cheerful-looking woman whose round face was framed by a mass of untidy chestnut curls.

"Hi. I'm Anne. Anne O'Halloran. You must be the cop Jeannie's expecting."

Tim confirmed her assumption, and even volunteered to show his Garda badge, but she brushed it aside.

"Jeannie'll be back in a moment. She had to dash over to Crowley's in MacCurtain Street to pick up some sheet music she'd ordered. She said to make yourself comfortable."

He was led in to an airy open space that seemed to extend the full length of the building. On the somewhat creaky (though highly polished) old floorboards, he passed a kitchen-and-dining area to the black leather sofas facing a floor-to-ceiling window. This afforded a spectacular view westwards over the river and the city. The rain had stopped, and the sun breaking through the clouds now made the bridges of both branches of the Lee look positively Venetian. Were it not for the absence of a garden, Tim could imagine living quite comfortably here.

A loft, in fact. Would this remain an idiosyncratic anomaly in its otherwise dreary surroundings? Or was it the beginning of a Little Tribeca on the Lee? Only time would tell. In the meantime, hats off to Jeannie (or Anne) for the initiative and the originality that had gone into it. "Nice place you've got here. It must have taken some doing up."

"Not an awful lot, actually. The building was perfectly sound, and we kept as much as we could. That big window is new of course, and all the plumbing and wiring. But it was well worth the investment, I think you'll agree."

"You mean you own the whole building?"

"Yes."

"Quite a large investment, then?"

"Well, it was Jeannie's money that made it possible. I'm just a struggling artist."

Artist. That might explain the workshop - or studio - on the ground floor. But first Tim needed to sort out how this woman connected with Jeannie. "You're not a relative, are you?"

Anne laughed. "Relative? Oh, no, you could hardly call me that! I'm ... er... her partner. We've been together for three years now."

Partner. Of course. It was probably common knowledge. This was where Cathy might have prevented him from looking rather foolish. It also explained Helen Murphy's mirth at his suggestion that she might have been concerned about her husband's closeness to Jeannie. But never mind ...

"Sorry, Anne, I guess I'm just a bit dumb." She grinned indulgently. "But you said your name was O'Halloran. Would you be any relation to Eamonn O'Halloran? I mean, Eascra's manager?"

"Sure, he's my brother. That's how I met Jeannie."

"Aha! That would make you a Dubliner. So how did Jeannie manage to drag you away from the metropolis?"

"With great difficulty. No, not really, not after we found this building. Places like this are hard to find in Dublin, and renting studio space was getting exorbitant. And space really is what I need: I work in wood or stone, sometimes both combined, and I like to create rather large objects. That also calls for some pretty heavy machinery, especially for stone-cutting, as you can imagine."

"So is that your studio on the ground floor?"

"Yes. I'll be going down there in a second to work on an altar-piece that's been commissioned."

"Altar-piece?"

"Yes. For St. Anthony's in Ballincollig. The Church may not approve of my life-style, but since it hardly rubs off on the sculptures, it's none of their business."

"And the other floors - what are they used for?"

"Well, Jeannie uses the floor under this as a music room, keeps her drums and things there, But one floor is still vacant. We were thinking of doing it up as extra studio space to rent out to other artists. But in the meantime we've got wind of another rather similar project in the vicinity, and there may not be enough demand for both. An old factory building has been bought up by a group of artists just a few blocks away, and I heard they're planning to call it The Sculpture Factory."

"Copycats?"

"Maybe, but if so, fair play to them! Imitation is the sincerest form of flattery."

At that moment they heard footsteps on the stairs, and Anne took the opportunity to break off the conversation. "Here's Jeannie now, so I'll leave you to it." Through the open door, Tim could hear her remark as she passed Jeannie on the stairs. "Your cop's waiting!"

Jeannie did remember her cop. "I'm sorry if I was a bit obtuse on the phone. You're the one who helped P.J. out with the words of 'Skibbereen'." She pulled off her raincoat, hung it on a hanger to dry, and dumped a white plastic bag with a cartoon-style drawing of a dreadlocked and multi-instrumented musician on the glass-topped table.

"The very one. The one with the croaky voice."

She smiled, but didn't contradict. "P.J. told me afterwards that Dónal had turned a bit stroppy, and that it had taken a Garda sergeant to calm him down. That was you?"

"Yes, except he got the sergeant bit wrong. It's still plain Garda O'Driscoll."

"And this is what you might call an extracurricular visit?"

"Correct. I won't be reading you your rights, etc. You can, of course, remain silent, in other words, tell me something I'm asking about is none of my business. But on the other hand, nothing you tell me here can be used in evidence against you or anyone else. It might, however, help to point the investigation in the right direction. So I hope you'll help us out with some background."

"I'll do what I can. Though I'm not sure why you chose me."

"Well, I would like eventually to talk to everyone involved in the business. But since Bandon Garda Station has only a limited role in this investigation, I doubt if they'll be sending me up to Limerick any time soon."

"So it's just that I'm within convenient reach of Bandon?"

"No, it's not just that. I believe you also had quite a close relationship with the victim. By the way, I'm sorry I couldn't make it to any of your south coast gigs this summer."

"You knew about them?"

"Yeah, P.J. invited me and my friend Cathy, but I was on night duty on every occasion. Cathy managed to go to one, though, at the Lobby I think it was."

"Yes, that one went well."

"She was particularly impressed by your version of 'Bean Pháidín'. Very strong and emotional. she said."

"The song of a scorned woman. Jealousy - a wonderful murder motive! Could you be imputing it to me?" She smiled as if to take the sting out of the remark.

Tim decided to be honest. "Well, I've played through all sorts of possibilities in my mind. But I think I can exclude that one now."

"Having familiarized yourself with my household arrangements?"

"Maybe."

"And now you're thinking maybe Anne could've done it."

She was teasing him. But so what? "Could she?"

"She was in Edinburgh all that week, she had some pieces in an exhibition there. I think that rules her out. You will want to check it out, I suppose?"

They would, so he accepted the flier announcing the exhibition that she obligingly dug out of a drawer. He was relieved that there did not seem to be any need to broaden the field of possibilities. The situation was complex enough already.

"And my sexual preferences don't necessarily let me off the hook either, do they? After all, I could have been angrily rejecting *his* advances!"

More teasing. "Having read all the statements so far, it seems to me that you also are the only one with a perfect alibi for the time in question."

"Perfect alibi? Now surely that should be making any self-respecting detective suspicious!"

"It did. But I see no way round it, beyond a huge conspiracy. So can we start being serious?"

"I'm sorry, I assure you, I don't feel quite as flippant about it as I sound."

"No, I didn't think so. You were the only one to turn up at the funeral, I noticed."

"The only band member, you mean? Well, to be fair, Sean just couldn't make it, and Niamh thought she might attract too much publicity if she turned up. Helen Murphy apparently agreed it would be better if she stayed away ... But what are these serious questions you want to ask me?"

Tim thought for a moment. "Let me go through all this in chronological order, and flash back to Skibbereen. The night Dónal created that scene. You seem to have left the bar even before things turned nasty. Were you expecting something like that?"

"No, not at all. But in the state he was, Dónal was obviously trying to get a rise out of me. I mean with that song he chose to sing."

"What about it?"

"Dónal and I don't exactly see eye to eye on political matters. In fact he's pretty close to his brother Séamas, who everyone knows to be actively involved with the Provos, at least on the fund-raising level. But it's OK as long as we keep off the subject."

"And that song was his way of starting a political discussion?"

"It was an in-your-face attack on me, if you really want to know. You see, he knows my family history, which doesn't have the same Republican credentials as his. My grandfather was a sergeant in the RIC - the pre-independence police force that was replaced by the illustrious one you belong to. And he was killed in an IRA raid on Kilmallock police station in 1920."

Tim decided to ignore the touch of sarcasm, though he could have pointed out that two elder brothers of his paternal grandfather had also been pre-independence policemen, and that as a result of numerous late-night family arguments he was therefore perfectly familiar with both views of the Royal Irish Constabulary: as despised upholders of the power of the British Empire, or as a perfectly respectable police force, unfairly demonized by the IRA because they were easy targets. "That song, if I remember it right, was about a similar raid on just that station in the course of the earlier Fenian Rising."

"Right. I have heard him sing it before. I knew he was being deliberately provocative, so I just slipped away."

"Ironic, isn't it, that the scene of the crime - if it was a crime - was just a few miles from Kilmallock?"

"Yes, but hard to read much into it. Are you suggesting Dónal managed to finish the job he had started in Skibbereen?"

"Well, he would have had a real strong motive by then, now that there was talk of permanently replacing him in the band."

"Who told you that?"

"I don't think it would be quite fair to reveal my source. After all, you'll want me to treat anything you tell me confidentially, won't you?" She smiled, but said nothing. "Anyway, is it not true?"

"True enough in respect of recordings, though nothing was definite."

"But of course we have no evidence that Dónal was anywhere near the area."

"He may have been."

"What do you mean?" Was Jeannie trying to hit back at the obstreperous Dónal by casting suspicion on him?

"Well, one of the archaeology students working at the dig near the castle said that she wasn't sure, but she thinks she passed him on the road that night just after she left Ryan's."

"You mean Una O'Riordan, the one who lives in Kilmallock?"

"The very one. She's a real fan of Dónal's, and had been really disappointed to find out he wasn't taking part in the recordings, so when she saw him - or thought she saw him in his green metallic BMW - she stepped on the brakes ..."

"There was nothing about this in her statement."

"I imagine a lot of things are missing from our statements. We all decide what we think is relevant, and if we're not asked about it directly, why volunteer something that may have no bearing on the matter? Besides, as I said, she worships this guy, and wouldn't want to get him into trouble unnecessarily."

"So maybe we should talk to her again."

"It might be wise. Especially now that Dónal has gone missing."

"You know about that?"

"Of course." She explained about their abortive effort to get him back so that they could complete the recordings.

"Have you any idea where he might be?"

"No. But it might be an idea to check up on that IRA brother of his. That's the kind of person who would know places to hide."

The Kilbrue District detectives had probably already thought of this possibility. They were now taking Tim's original tip seriously enough to mount a full scale manhunt. The forensic report (not included in the original file sent to Bandon from Kilbrue, but now belatedly in their possession) had helped. It had revealed distinct signs of a scuffle on the roof of the castle: damaged border plants near the battlements, disturbed gravel, but unfortunately no clearly identifiable footprints, and the only fibre evidence came from the victim's orange anorak. On its own, this evidence would

101

never convict anyone of anything, but at least it was pointing in the direction of foul play rather than suicide or accident.

This evening's TV news would probably include an appeal to anybody who could help to locate the whereabouts of Dónal Ó Gráda, or had seen the green metallic BMW with the recent Dublin registration, to contact their nearest Garda station. Dónal being a fairly well-known personality, it should not take too long to track him down, one might imagine. Though uncomfortable thoughts of the Lord Lucan case (when did *he* disappear? – mid-70s, wasn't it?) destroyed any such certainty.

Just in case the Kilbrue Gardai were not aware of the IRA connection (with associated possibility of the use of its network of safe houses in Britain and elsewhere) he would pass on the tip to his father. Together with the suggestion that they question Una O'Riordan about her possible sighting of the suspect near the scene of the crime. For this is how it was now being referred to.

"You knew Dónal fairly well. Do you think he would have been capable of actually killing P.J.?"

Jeannie thought for a moment. "I really don't know. I can't see him as a cold-blooded murderer, or someone who would plan his revenge on someone. But he was pretty hot-tempered and impulsive. It's an O'Grady trait, to be honest. When either he or his sister are annoyed about something it's best to get out of the way, was always my policy. So I could imagine him lashing out and doing more damage than he intended."

The scenario of a scuffle on the roof gone wrong had already occurred to Tim. That would make it manslaughter. Also a crime, if a lesser one than the murder he had been speculating about, and certainly one that called for its just retribution. He only needed to think back to that windswept graveyard ... But now that the wheels and cogs of the criminal justice system were beginning to creak in the general direction he had nudged them, Tim was beginning to wonder if now was the time to back off and let the County Limerick colleagues get on with the job. After all, nobody was asking him to put in the extra effort. Still, there were a number of annoying loose ends that needed tying up ...

"If we could now move on to the actual recording session. I've been told by his widow that it was you recruited P.J. for the project."

"Yes. After Dónal dug in his heels and refused to 'go into retreat in the middle of nowhere', as he described it. Since I'd been doing gigs with P.J. over the summer, I knew he'd be up to the job."

"Now, it's pretty obvious why P.J. should want the job. But I've been wondering if he confided in you concerning his mixed feelings about it."

"Do you mean, regarding Richard Murrough?"

"Yes."

"Well, he did tell me he had previous dealings with the man back in the States, and was a bit worried about getting on the wrong side of him again. But it had been nearly fifteen years ago, and P.J. let himself be persuaded that Murrough would probably have forgotten all about him. Besides, as you probably know, Richard Murrough is blind." Tim nodded. "So there would be no danger of him being recognized anyway, unless he decided to make himself known."

"Did he?"

"Not that I know of. After a while, they seemed to get on OK, and Richard seemed pleased enough with P.J.'s work."

"And did Richard Murrough give any indication of knowing who he was?"

"Not while I was around. It helped, by the way, that P.J. had been known as Phil back then. The 'P.J.' was apparently part of his effort to create a new existence for himself in Ireland."

"And blend better with the scenery?"

"Yeah, I guess so."

"Did P.J. explain the nature of his quarrel with Murrough?"

"Well, he told me he'd been a member of The Hawks in their early days, and Murrough was instrumental in getting him kicked out - just before their first hit album. In 1972, I think it was. Whatever reasons were behind it, I could understand him being peeved."

"Did he tell you anything of those reasons?"

"No, and I didn't ask."

"He never mentioned claiming writing credits for the tune of 'Light and Shade'?"

"*What?*"

"Yes. I'm told he felt he'd been cheated out of his fair share of the royalties."

Jeannie laughed. "Even a small share of those would have provided a comfortable financial cushion. He certainly wouldn't have needed any odd jobs from us!" She lay back on her leather sofa. "But honestly, I'm sceptical."

"Why?"

"Well, popular music is to a large extent a collaborative art. People in a band are always picking up each other's ideas and developing them. And Richard is no different. As a producer, it's his job to mess around with whatever rough material we come up with and polish it until it shines. He even admits in his charmingly self-deprecating way that his job is essentially parasitic, that he'd be nothing without us working musicians."

"I seem to have read some such comment of his in an interview."

"Yes. And Richard Murrough definitely has an opportunistic streak, always on the lookout for what the next big thing is going to be."

"Like latching on to the trend for re-Americanized Irish folk rock?"

"I guess that's a fair description of what we're doing at the moment, especially with the addition of P.J.'s bluegrass guitar." She paused as if considering what musical implications P.J.'s demise might now have. "But seriously, whatever about a producer's opportunism, when it comes to publishing songs, it's generally clear who contributed what. There's usually plenty of witnesses, even if nothing got written down at the decisive stage. It's not so easy to steal someone's song outright. Or someone's tune, or even a particular arrangement."

"But it has happened, hasn't it?"

"Oh, yes. A lot of black musicians, particularly blues singers, got cheated out of the rights to their songs. I can think of a couple of examples. But that was then, this is ..."

"Hang on. That was the spaced out early seventies in San Francisco!"

"Well, I can't really say how spaced out P.J. was back then. But it seems unlikely that anyone could be so dumb as to let a gold-mine like that slip away from him. Surely he could have gone to court to establish his rights? That is if he had any legal leg to stand on."

"According to Helen Murphy, they tried. But were advised they didn't have a legal leg to stand on."

"My point exactly. I just can't see anyone letting a gold-mine like that slip away from them so easily. Unless ..."

"Unless what?"

"Unless Richard Murrough had some kind of a hold over him."

"Any idea what kind of a hold he might have?"

"No, I'm just speculating. But one thing *is* rather odd ..."

"And what might that be?"

She hesitated. "Well, sometime in the middle of the recordings, I forget what day it was ... Anyway, as part of our cross-cultural emphasis, we were looking for an American standard to give an Irish make-over to, and somebody suggested Murrough's 'Light and Shade' ..."

"Can you remember who made the suggestion?"

"I think it was Sean. Sean Mills, our piper. Anyway, Sean laid down a creditable Irish version of the tune on his pipes. Not half bad, by the way, made it sound as if it had come from Galway ... And the next day we kept experimentally adding other instrumental tracks. It was to be purely instrumental, by the way, no vocals this time."

"Did P.J. get to make his contribution?"

"Oh yes. God, that must have been the Wednesday ..."

"The day he died."

"Yes. Now I wonder if that's why he was so moody!"

"He was moody?"

"Oh yes. Right from the start, actually, but particularly on that day. I had been attributing his mood-swings to his wife's illness - I suppose you know she's got cancer?" Tim nodded. "Well, he'd got some bad news from her over the phone about her tests at the Regional."

"Do you think he was depressed enough to want to kill himself?" The suicide option had not yet been ruled out, so he thought he had better check out her opinion on the matter.

"Well, in the first week it might have been. But his wife's next call was a bit more optimistic. And his mood seemed to have lightened a bit when Richard suggested that we use P.J. for our next album as well."

"It was Murrough suggested that?"

"Oh yes, he was quite impressed with his work - it suited his cross-cultural aims right down to the ground."

From Jeannie's revelation about the use of the disputed tune in the recordings, Tim had been speculating on a scenario involving some kind of confrontation on the roof of the castle between P.J. and Richard Murrough, instead of Dónal. Somehow ending in P.J. being sent flying to his death. But the mind boggled. A blind man would have been at a huge disadvantage in any such skirmish. And if P.J. had fallen as a result of such a scuffle, then all Murrough would need to do would be to report to the Gardai that he had been attacked by this threadbare old hippie, with unfortunate results. That is certainly what a worldly-wise opportunist like Richard Murrough would do.

And the fact that Murrough had just opened up some real professional prospects for P.J. made the whole 'confrontation' scenario seem a lot less likely.

"Jeannie, can you tell me if it was Richard Murrough's habit to go up on the roof? Or P.J.'s?"

"Well, P.J. often went up there, in fact we all did, when the weather was any way pleasant. It was our favourite place for a snack, or to read a magazine, or simply to cool off from a particularly strenuous session. The view from up there was spectacular on a fine day. But I've never seen Richard up there."

"The spectacular view would hold no attraction for him, of course."

"Quite. But he must have gone up there some time. He was very keen on this roof garden they were putting in, and knew all about its lay-out and design. I often heard him arguing with his wife about it - especially about all the delays in getting it finished."

"Surely that hardly mattered any more, since nobody would be able to appreciate it until next spring?"

"Well, it was important to be able to complete the battlements. The situation up there was potentially dangerous. As we all know now."

"Did you not know before?"

"Oh, sure, there were signs warning us off the roof, but nobody took any notice. It was OK if you were careful. And the signs were mainly to avoid any liability in case of an accident."

"Indeed."

"But there was also the big house-warming party - or rather, castle-warming party - that Richard and Georgie were planning. The roof-garden was supposed to be an important element."

"When was the party planned for?"

"October 31st. Halloween."

"How appropriate!"

"Yes, they were deliberately latching on to Castle Green's spooky reputation. I was quite looking forward to it."

"You were invited?"

"Oh, yes, the whole band. We're very important clients for building up the studio's reputation. Plus anybody who is anybody in the Irish music scene, the Dublin press ... But that's off now, of course."

"Of course."

"But they may have it instead on New Year's Eve. Not quite the same as Halloween, though."

"And you'd need to wrap up pretty well to enjoy your champagne on the roof garden!"

"Besides, I doubt if I'll be able to make it. We'll be having our own party here."

"Probably true of a lot of people."

"Anyway, you'll have to talk to Richard if you want to know about that."

Richard Murrough's party plans were unlikely to have any relevance to the case. However, there were several other points Tim would like to be able to question him (and his wife Georgie) on. The problem was, how to engineer such an interview.

"As I told you, I have no official standing in this investigation, so that would have to be arranged privately. Do you think you could put in a word?"

Jeannie looked sceptical . "I can try, but I doubt if it would do much good. I doubt if Richard will want to talk to any more cops than he has to. Now if you were a journalist ..."

"What about the others?"

"The band, you mean? Oh, I imagine they'd be quite willing to talk to you. I'll give them a ring."

"Thanks. Now maybe we can get on to the situation in the week or so before P.J.'s death. What was the atmosphere like?"

"Oh, the recordings were going quite well, everything seemed hunky-dory."

"No strained relations between any of you, or with the staff?"

"No, and as regards staff, they didn't have many. If you discount the Garden Centre workers, and the archaeological crew, there was only Maggie."

"The cleaning lady, Mrs. Margaret O'Keeffe."

"Actually, she was a card ...

"In what way?"

"Oh, the way she took a strong liking to people - or a strong dislike. She absolutely adored Richard - he could do no wrong in her eyes. And Niamh and Sean were also in her good books, she was always offering to make them pots of tea, but never when I was around."

"So she'd taken a dislike to you?"

"I must have rubbed her the wrong way from the start. Maybe when I asked her - politely as I thought - not to use detergent on my bongo drums or my bodhran. Or maybe she just disapproves of lesbians."

"She knows about your private life?"

"Oh, she reads all the tabloids and gossip columns. She's certainly well informed on such matters. Though how she managed to forgive Richard his multiple divorces is anybody's guess!"

"How did she show her dislike of you?"

"Oh, the way she spoke to me, very icy and distant. And the teapot discrimination I mentioned. And the touchy way she reacted to any question of mine. Like when I asked her if she had seen the canvas bag I transported my bongos in, or had maybe tidied it away somewhere. Acted all insulted, as if I'd been accusing her of stealing! I just couldn't get it right with her!"

"Was there anyone else she disliked besides yourself?"

"Well, poor P.J. didn't exactly meet with her approval."

"Why not?"

"No idea, maybe it was just his hang-dog, ageing hippie appearance. But I doubt if that would give her a plausible motive to knock him off the roof with her sweeping brush, in case that's what you're thinking. Besides, she was only there mornings."

"Anyone else?" Tim wasn't quite sure why he was asking all this - just fishing for the telling detail that would provide the key to everything, he supposed.

"No, I can't think of ... Oh, there was Sheila McCarthy, the archaeologist. She got on the wrong side of Maggie by tramping down to the basement toilets in her muddy wellies one day - just after Maggie had cleaned the floor and stairs!"

"And the relationship never recovered?"

"Right. But the funny thing was, she often got it wrong. I certainly never meant her any harm, whereas Sean - one of her pets - was always making fun of her behind her back. He even stole her whiskey!"

"Whiskey?"

"Yes, she's a secret drinker, always has a 'baby Power's' stuffed in her pocket, or a larger bottle stashed away somewhere. On our last day at the castle, Sean mentioned having found one in the broom cupboard, and served us all a round. I must admit, I didn't say no, we were all a bit rattled at the time."

"That was the Friday, wasn't it?"

"Yeah, we broke up for the weekend, and decided there was no point in coming back the following week. The studio would have been vacant, but without a guitarist, there wasn't much we could do."

"If we could get back to the chronology ... We had got as far as the Wednesday, and the work you were doing in the studio. Was there a lunch break?"

"Yes. And for once, the four of us all had a pub lunch together at Ryan's. No particular signs of tension, as I suppose you were going to ask. Except for P.J. being a bit silent, which wasn't all that unusual."

"And the afternoon?"

"Just another day's work. We had been concentrating on P.J.'s guitar accompaniment in the morning, as I already told you. And in the afternoon, Niamh came up with some nice counterpoint melodies for 'Light and Shade'. This made Richard re-think the accompaniment, and he had me and P.J. experimenting with various rhythms, without recording any of them at first. It was just one of those wild improvisations. A lot of fun, really, until P.J. managed to break a couple of strings. But then it was time to call it a day anyway."

"Your statement takes it from there. Was there any particular reason why Niamh and P.J. didn't join you for the Chinese meal?"

"Oh, Niamh is pretty faddy about food, doesn't like Chinese. And P.J. just didn't feel like it, wasn't hungry enough, he said."

"And who was in the pub when you turned up there after your meal?"

"Oh, all three of the archaeology students. We joined them at their table. Plus a couple of locals at the bar. I don't know their names, but they were familiar faces. And Bernie Ryan was serving at the bar."

"Did the students make any reference to the scene back at the castle? I believe they'd stayed on a bit longer than you."

"Oh, yes, they mentioned they'd waved to P.J. up on the roof, where he was probably having his snack. Tom went on for ages about Niamh serenading him, as he called it. Apparently Niamh had been practising some fiddle variations in her room."

"Una O'Riordan left pretty soon, is that right?"

"Yes, about 10 minutes after we arrived."

"And Sean left when?"

"A bit after that. Must have been about ten to nine. It was well before the 9 o'clock news came on the TV in the corner."

"Did he give any particular reason for wanting to leave earlier?"

"No, just said he wanted a breath of fresh air and would appreciate the walk. He's not the most social person at the best of times, and the constant banter may have been getting a bit on his nerves."

"Enough to leave you his car?"

"Oh, that's no big deal, we often do it that way."

"Have you ever walked from the village to the castle or vice versa?"

"Oh, it's a nice walk on a fine day, especially if you take the longer way, directly south from the castle. But I wouldn't do it at night. Sean probably chose the other way, because it has some street lighting along the main road before the side-road turns off."

"How long does it take to walk that way."

"It takes me about half an hour. Sean could probably manage in 25 minutes or so."

"By the way, when Una O'Riordan set off, she would have been heading for Kilmallock, wouldn't she? Yet you said earlier she'd passed Dónal's car on the road. Can you think of any reason Dónal could be coming from that direction, instead of from the Limerick or Dublin side?"

"No idea. Unless ..." She paused for thought.

"Unless what?"

"Well, Dónal's current girlfriend lives in Adare. That's west of Limerick city. I don't know what route you'd take from there, whether you'd go through the city or if there's some other way."

There was. Tim was familiar enough with the topography to know that from Adare, the shortest route to Kilbrue was through Croom, joining the main road at the north end of the village, but south of the point where Ryan's pub was located.

"Can you give me the name and address of this girlfriend?"

"Her name is Christine Allain. She's French, lectures in the language in Limerick." Jeannie wrote out the name on a scrap of paper, and Tim copied it into his notebook. "I don't have an address or telephone number, but Niamh certainly does. Besides, you'll be able to find it in the telephone directory."

"Thanks. Now, as regards the rest of that eventful day ..."

"I didn't turn up at the castle until it was all over."

"I know that. I've read your statement. But I'd like to know something about the situation after P.J. had been taken to the Regional. Who told you what had happened?"

"I saw some of the mess that was left, and there were some local Gardai still hanging around. It was Sean who gave me all the graphic details. He was coming down the spiral stairs after carrying Niamh up to her room. Apparently she'd collapsed with the shock."

"Did you go to see her?"

110

"No. Sean said she'd come to, but had then taken some kind of sedative and was asleep. So I just went to my own room. Found it hard to get to sleep, I can tell you!"

"Were there any further disturbances that night? Any strange noises?" Tim was thinking of the protesters who had sprayed the castle wall. It was still not clear when they'd carried out their art-work, let alone who they were.

"Funny you should ask that. I did hear some footsteps and whispered voices around one o'clock. At first I thought it was just Sean and Niamh, but then I realized the sounds were coming from downstairs. Couldn't figure it out."

"At first you thought it was Sean and Niamh? Why?"

"Oh, God, I seem to have put my foot in it! But what the hell, you're going to find out from somebody sooner or later. Sean and Niamh have been having an on-going but on-and-off affair for years. For the last couple of months it's been off, or so I thought. Mainly because Niamh wanted out, I believe."

Tim thought back to the overheard quarrel in the West Cork Hotel, and wondered.

"Anyway Niamh's been making a great show of her family life recently, both to us and to the public. I'd been taking her word for it that she just wants to be a good wife and mother from now on, but it's hard to know how much is real and how much for show."

"Or whether she's tired of promiscuity or just tired of Sean?"

"Quite. I've been wondering myself."

"So that banter in the pub about Niamh and P.J. could have got on Sean's nerves for another reason?"

"I'm pretty sure it did."

"So why didn't you tell me?"

"I didn't want to be the first to spread the gossip. And besides, it's hardly relevant."

Tim said nothing to that. He was getting tired of telling people it wasn't for them to decide what was or wasn't relevant. In this case he wasn't sure. Sean had been first on the scene, of course - always very suspicious. And now there was a hint of a possible motive. But he could hardly have had the time to commit murder (or manslaughter) and be able to raise the alarm by twenty past nine, as had been the case.

"Very well, Jeannie, you've been a great help. If I've got any other questions I presume I can give you a ring, is that OK?"

111

"Sure, any time."

As he left the building, Tim caught a glimpse of Anne the sculptor systematically indenting a piece of dark wood with what looked like a sledge-hammer. He decided it wouldn't do any harm to have that Edinburgh alibi checked.

Chapter 13

Not for the first time, Garda Tim O'Driscoll bemoaned the absence of a good encyclopaedia of popular music. He did have one covering jazz. but he could find nothing on the market covering the broader field of popular music - or even dealing with rock music in an equally systematic way. It would be nice to be able to look up alphabetically any singer, song-writer, musician, band-leader, or producer, and find listed there all their works and pomps, plus their cross-connections with other artists.

As it was, all he had was a rather impressionistic and opinionated *History of Rock* - and his own collection of LPs, now gradually being augmented by these new-fangled CDs. However handy and indestructible the latter were, Tim hadn't quite taken to them yet. They weren't ... physical enough.

Though his vinyl collection was extensive, a perusal of the record-sleeves of the relevant period had yielded only scant references to Richard Murrough as producer - one on an early Hawks album (1972), and one compilation called *San Francisco Scene*. He could find no references at all to P.J. Murphy - or Phil, or Philip Murphy.

Tim wasn't too surprised at the meagre results of his research. Producers weren't always mentioned on record sleeves. And poor P.J. had never (after being kicked out of the Hawks) advanced beyond session musician. They practically never got mentioned.

The name 'Murrough' turned up a few times, however, in brackets after song titles, usually in combination with some other name. Tim made a list of these titles. Some he knew well, some he didn't. He could find only two giving Murrough as sole author, both of those being on the Hawks album, tracks 2 and 3 on the B side.

He pulled the album out of its sleeve, blew off the dust (it hadn't been played for years, and had obviously been put away dusty), and put it on the turntable. He directed the stylus manually to track 2. It was a standard country-rock number, with quite a catchy tune, but not all that memorable. The second number, however, was the one everyone knew. From the kitchen, where Cathy was making some espresso to round off their meal (she claimed Tim never made any coffee that didn't taste poisonous), he could hear her joining in:

"... And though your dreams begin to fade,
You fear you'll never make the grade,

It matters less once you accept
That life is made ...
Of light and shade."

Rather banal words, actually. But a haunting tune. Tim could just about imagine it played on the pipes, and would be interested to hear what Sean Mills had made of it.

"Isn't that the song written by that Murrough guy, the one you're going to get to interview?" commented Cathy as she re-emerged from the kitchen with two tiny coffee cups on a tray.

"Yeah, but 'interview' is hardly the right word." It had taken some persuasion, but his father had finally agreed to let him tag along when one of his Detective Inspectors was due to interview the Murroughs on the subject of the vandalism to the castle walls. "I may be able to get in one or two questions, but hardly much more."

"As regards that vandalism, did they find out who did it?"

"Well, not exactly. Remember that bike that was stolen?"

"You mean the one that belonged to the archaeology student - Declan was his name, I think."

"That turned out to be a useful tip off, Cathy, thank you very much."

"You're welcome. But in what way was it useful?"

"Well, the bike was found abandoned near the river south of the village. Since I'd suggested rather vaguely that there might be some connection with the goings-on at the castle, they checked it for fingerprints. There was one set that didn't belong to Declan."

"And were they able to match them with anyone? I mean, I suppose they'd fingerprinted all the suspects, that's what they usually do, isn't it?"

"Yeah, for exclusion purposes, as they usually put it. And it did seem to exonerate all the castle occupants and workers as potential bike thieves. At least their prints didn't match the odd set on the bike."

"So whose did? Quit the tension-building!"

"A girl called Róisín Casey. She belongs to group of radical environmentalists that had been kicking up a stink about the reconstruction of Castle Green. They'd all been questioned as vandalism suspects, but denied any responsibility for the spraying."

"And now this Róisín admits to borrowing the bike to get to the castle?"

"No way. She still denies being anywhere near the castle that day. Claims she just went joy-riding and abandoned the bike by the river."

"Does that sound likely?"

"It doesn't convince me. Joy-riding is something little boys indulge in."

"Are you into gender profiling now?"

"Whatever it takes. Anyway, Róisín Casey is an eighteen-year-old Leaving Cert student. Respectable. Apart from her radical tendencies, that is. There's something fishy about the story."

"Hmm. Anyway, what's all this about?" She was pointing to the mess of LPs strewn over the floor.

"I'm trying to get enough background to ask Murrough a few intelligent questions if I get the chance."

"Any success?"

"Not much, beyond refreshing my memory about things I knew already. And I doubt if a trip to the County Library or even UCC would turn up anything worthwhile."

"What about on-line data banks?"

"You still need to know where to look. ... Wouldn't it be nice if I could just switch on the computer, type the name 'Richard Murrough' into a request box, and up comes a list of the relevant data banks on screen ... click on any one, and there's the information ..." A dreamy look had come into Tim's eyes.

"Oh, come on, we may get there yet ... But in the meantime, it's not that bad. My company subscribes to several good data banks, and maybe I could do a search for you in a quieter moment."

"Would you? You're sweet!"

"So when is this interview of yours. I mean, how much time have I got?"

"Saturday, October 31st."

"Hah, great day to visit Castle Green!"

"Why? ... Oh, it's Halloween, I hadn't realized. Anyway Kilbrue didn't have much choice of a day to arrange the interview. The Murroughs are in London at the moment, won't be back till the end of the month. And early in November they're heading off to L.A. for some producing job."

"Sounds like their castle studio isn't exactly doing great business."

"Mmm. The murder, or suicide, or whatever it was may have thrown a spanner in the works. Besides, I imagine for Murrough and his wife it's no more than a hobby. They certainly don't need the money."

"Oh, I don't know. Remember that article you showed me. An interview in the *Irish Times*."

"What about it?"

"Well, hobby or not, I got the impression that this studio project *is* important to him. Some people just can't rest, they need constant reassurance that they are the tops."

"Yeah, that article ... where did I put it?" Tim pulled out the lower desk drawer and began to rummage in the concertina file labelled 'Interesting Articles'. If he was lucky, he'd put it there, and not on the pile on the floor for later sorting; more often than not, that pile sooner or later got shunted into the waste paper.

He was lucky. It was filed under 'M', whether for Murrough or Music, didn't really matter. He skimmed the article, Cathy looking over his shoulder.

"Wouldn't it be an idea to contact the *Irish Times*, or even the journalist who did the interview? They often get a lot more information than is actually printed."

"Yes, there might even be a tape of the complete interview." But then he shook his head. "Nah, journalists are notorious for not wanting to share their information with the police."

"But it's worth a try. It's just harmless background you're looking for, after all."

"Yeah, I guess you're right. And I think I know the best way to go about it." He pulled out his address book. "I'm looking for the phone number of Colin Leahy - remember him?"

She didn't. He was from Tim's undergraduate days, before they met.

"Well, he's now a sports writer with the *Times*. He might be able to help."

He dialled the Dublin number, but only got Colin's answering machine. Rather than leave a cryptic-sounding message, Tim decided to try again later. Then he glanced again at the article, and frowned.

"What time is it in New York?"

"Huh? Why New York?"

"Well, us Driscolls have contacts everywhere. And my Uncle Fred is one of New York's finest." He was quoting a phrase from the Murrough article. "Actually he's my father's cousin, which makes him ... oh, what the hell, we call him Uncle Fred."

He dialled a New York number, having roughly estimated himself that it was a civilized time to phone there, and was luckier than with the Dublin number.

Fred Driscoll didn't exactly pick up the receiver, but he was within shouting distance of whatever extension Tim reached in Manhattan's 32nd Precinct.

"Uncle Fred? Tim here, Bandon, Ireland calling! What's the time over there?"

"Hi, Tim, me boy - it's 4.30 p.m. and I'm just going off duty. But you hardly rang to find out what time it is in New York, now did you? I suppose you want something from me as usual!"

"Well, yeah ..."

"You're lucky to catch me, I was nearly out the door. Wouldn't have been reachable then for at least an hour and a half. That's how long it takes to get from the Upper West Side to the far end of Queens!"

"Jeez - all that commuting must be the devil."

"You get used to it. Anyway, what is it you want?"

"Well, you see, I'm working on a case with some American connections ..."

"I didn't think they'd let a rookie like you loose on a serious *case*."

"They wouldn't. I'm just on the fringe, dealing with a few minor aspects. But one thing leads to another."

"OK, what's the problem?"

"Hard to know where to start. I may have a several questions for you over the coming weeks. But for starters, something close to home. Could you check if there was an officer called Murrough in the NYPD in the fifties - probably from 1956 to some time in the early sixties?"

"Could you spell the name?" Tim did.

"Well, I believe they've got a pretty good archive in the Personnel Records Section. That belongs to the Employee Management Division, and I know someone who works there. Shouldn't take too much persuading."

"Great. How long will it take you to check?"

"Depending on Julie's cooperation - maybe by the middle of next week. But if you have more information to go on, it might speed things up."

"The officer in question is supposed to have died in a car-chase."

"Piece of cake. There's a special Memorial List of officers who died in the line of duty. I can check that myself. Maybe by Monday. So is that it? I gotta rush for the express train."

"That's it for now." He didn't get a chance to elaborate on his thanks, because Fred had already gone to join the West Side throngs making for the 125th Street subway.

It was just as he put down the receiver that Tim and Cathy heard the knock on the door. But somebody could have been knocking there for some time and not be heard over Tim's raised voice. The connection hadn't been that good. There was no bell. Or rather, there had once been a bell downstairs, but it didn't work any more, so the side door of the hardware store over which Tim temporarily lived was usually left unlocked. Any

117

visitors had to climb the narrow stairs and use their knuckles on his door on the second floor. As somebody was doing now.

Tim opened the door. Standing there on the landing was Helen Murphy in a camel duffel-coat. Carrying a small and very scuffed brown suitcase. And looking to all intents and purposes as if she was intending to move in.

She must have suddenly realized how ridiculous she looked, because her mouth opened and closed as if lost for words. Or maybe she'd seen Cathy over Tim's shoulder.

"I'm sorry to bother you at this hour, Garda O'Driscoll. But I tried earlier in the day and you weren't here. I didn't want to go to the Garda station, or phone."

Tim thought he knew what she was nervous about. After his uncle had acknowledged the arrival of some funny-looking plants at the farm, he had phoned Helen Murphy once last week, to check how often they needed to be watered, when she would be wanting to harvest the crop, etc.. But he understood that she would be wary of phoning him even privately. She was now probably wondering what she could or couldn't say in Cathy's presence.

"Won't you come in? By the way, this is my girlfriend, Cathy Cronin."

"Hi, Cathy."

"And this is Helen Murphy, wife of P.J. Murphy, the victim in that case I mentioned."

"Mentioned? It's all he talks about these days, Helen!"

So that there would be no more uncertainty or pussyfooting on either side, Tim tried to sum up the missing information for Cathy as briefly as possible. Cathy might well have mixed feelings about him risking his Garda career with such reckless benevolence (and she showed it in her frown), but she would at least know how to keep her mouth shut.

"It's OK, Helen, Cathy has nothing to do with the Gardai." He grinned. "I mean, on an official level."

Though not seeming fully reassured, Helen began to explain her presence. "There was a raid at our place this morning. Two of your colleagues turned up with a warrant."

"Jeez. Barbara told me she had finally decided *not* to report the cannabis!"

"If you mean the female officer who was with you that day at our place ..."

"Garda Brennan, yes."

"... well, she didn't. Apparently someone else she'd confided in put in the report. Garda Brennan phoned to warn me about an hour before the cops came. I didn't tell her I'd already been tipped off."

Tim raised his eyes to heaven. Thank heavens for small mercies. God only knows who she might pour her heart out to about that. The Super?

"Anyway, your colleagues weren't in the best of humour when they found nothing suspicious in the conservatory. So they strip-searched the whole house. Even insisted on going up into the attic. When they found this, ..." - she pointed to the scuffed case she'd deposited on the floor - "... they picked the lock, since I didn't have a key. No drugs in it, of course, just a lot of old papers."

She clicked open the rusty lock to make her point, and an odour of dust and mould rose from the case. "I thought you might possibly be interested."

Tim took a closer look. He would indeed be interested. There were old music magazines, newspaper clippings, dog-eared sheet music, photocopies, brochures ... all jumbled up in no discernible order. Any dates he saw were from the early seventies.

"It seems to be stuff P.J. held on to from his early career in L.A. and San Francisco. I can't make much of it, and I don't think I could face the job of sorting it all out, but if you want, you can have it."

"Why me?"

"Well, apart from one good turn deserving another ... You were asking about those days, especially about P.J.'s time with The Hawks. And you seemed to be genuinely interested in finding out what really happened to him up in Limerick, which is what I want, too. I doubt if any of this old rubbish is in any way relevant, but you never know."

"Thanks. I mean for trusting me with this. Can we offer you some coffee? Cathy's made some espresso. Or a cognac?"

She took the coffee. "By the way, Cathy and I are driving down to Dan's farm tomorrow. I need to take care of my organic garden down there - including the adopted plants. If you'd like to come along ...?"

She shook her head. "I doubt if you'd want to be seen in my company, after this raid on my place." Tim agreed it might not be wise.

"I'll go down there separately next week. I imagine the crop should be ready for harvesting by then, and you can destroy any evidence of collusion." Helen Murphy thanked them and left.

Cathy looked with distaste at the case on the floor with its burgeoning content. "You're not going to deal with that lot right away, I hope."

"No fear. Sunday night will be soon enough." Cathy would have left on a business trip to Frankfurt by then, and it wouldn't matter what he stank of.

The Indian Summer that had been promised at the beginning of the week had proved short-lived, and by Friday, there was a definite chill in the air. The north-west gale that came in on Saturday definitely called for winter woollies for their trip to the farm, especially if they also wanted to go for a cliff-top walk somewhere out the Mizen Peninsula.

So they weren't too surprised that old Dan had his stove burning. Except that Dan usually couldn't be bothered to do anything more than plug in the electric heater.

"Your sister Brid called in yesterday, and she stoked the fire for me. She's a good girl, Brid. A good girl." Brid was a doctor, and had recently expressed some concern at the state of Dan's health.

Dan had never married. Being the eldest in the family, he had felt obliged to wait until he had inherited the farm before even thinking about marriage. And when that time finally came, it was too late. Like many old bachelors of his generation, Dan wasn't too good at taking care of himself. But since Brid had recently set up her practice as a GP in Schull, only about ten miles further west, at least someone competent was within easy reach.

"I only needed to put a match to the fire this morning. Just look at those flames. A great fire."

That seemed a bit exaggerated. Compared to the magnificent open fire that had graced this very spot when Tim's grandparents were in residence, it was pathetic. Dan himself, to Tim's imagination, was looking more and more like the image of his grandfather. As he puffed on his pipe, he could almost *be* the grandfather Tim faintly remembered sitting there in the glow from some real flames from the open fire, musing on times past.

But Dan was musing on times present. "Your garden is doing fine. Not too many slugs and snails around in this cold weather. But you'll have to harvest what's left of those green things soon - what do you call them? Long stripy green things, they are ..."

"Courgettes," said Tim. "Zucchini," said Cathy. Simultaneously. But it didn't faze the old man, who seemed noticeably relaxed and mellow.

"And those big yellow fellas ..."

"Pumpkins?" said Cathy.

"Yeah, them's the ones. But your one from the veggie shop will be in next week to help herself to some of them." That was Mary Coughlan, with whom Tim had built up a good business relationship over the past year.

120

"Didn't she take a box of courgettes last week?"

"Yes, and she'll be back for more next week. But there'll be plenty more left. Big stripy things. Getting bigger all the time." Dan took another puff of his pipe, and smiled beatifically. A sweetish smell familiar from a totally different context finally reached Tim's consciousness.

"Dan, that pipe of yours. It smells a bit ... different."

"Does it now, me boy?"

"Dan, have you been helping yourself to any of those new plants in the greenhouse?" Tim looked at him sternly, and Cathy's jaw dropped with astonishment.

Dan smiled more beatifically than ever. "A wonderful plant, indeed."

"But Dan ..."

"Now, Tim, I'm not as green as I'm cabbage-looking. The way that hippie woman was hiding them plants behind your tomatoes, I thought there must be something special about them. So I took a closer look at that poster in the guards' barracks, you know, the one where they ask you to be on the look-out for illegal plantations ..."

"But how did you know what to do with it? It's not as if ..."

"Now what else would you do with it? You pick a few leaves, dry them over the fire, then you ..."

"... put it in your pipe and smoke it." All three stated the obvious simultaneously. Dan chuckled gleefully.

The rest of the day - both the working part in the garden and the purely recreational out at Mizen - was dominated by Cathy's recriminations concerning the way Tim was endangering his career.

"You don't think you can stop Dan from talking, now do you?"

"He won't talk."

"But you know the way he goes on when he's had a few drinks!"

"Look, why should you care about my 'career' as you call it. You never wanted me to join the guards anyway!"

And more in the same vein. The subject also kept coming up sporadically over what might have been a relaxing Sunday. So it was with a sense of relief that Tim waved Cathy off on her way to the airport, and retired to his solitary cell. The musty suitcase beckoned.

He began by spreading the mess of papers out on the floor, and sorting them into rough categories.

The music magazines kept catching his eye, with their fascinating glimpses of a glorious era in rock history, so that he had to force himself to be systematic. In the end, he had a rather high pile of such magazines, a smaller pile of clippings (most of them brief references to the Hawks' appearances at various clubs), another small pile of diverse photocopies, some sheet music - not a lot, so that he combined that with the loose leaves of manuscript notation.

The latter seemed to provide the most promising avenue to investigate. Since notes on paper did not immediately convert themselves into imagined sounds in Tim's musically untrained mind, he rummaged for his old tin whistle where he had last seen it (in a kitchen drawer), found it, and began trying to realize some of the melody lines.

The limitations of the tin whistle forced him to try to convert everything into the key of D. This worked well enough with the simpler keys C, G and F, but anything written in a more exotic key was beyond him. Jeannie Staunton would be the one to help him out here. Still he persevered with a few of the more legible manuscripts.

Some of them had two melody lines, in which case he concentrated on the top one. None of these lines were identified as relating to a particular instrument, but some had names scribbled at the beginning: The lower melody line (usually sparsely notated) was often prefixed by 'Pete'. (Was he the groups bass player?) The guitar chords on top were occasionally marked "me". And the rough line of X's below were allocated to Frank (their drummer?).

A few plausible-sounding melodies occasionally emerged from Tim's whistle, but nothing he recognized. Until he tried a piece entitled 'Up and Down'. It was written in C, so that the transposition was relatively unproblematic. Undoubtedly, it bore a strong resemblance to a tune he knew very well indeed - the one practically everyone now knew as 'Light and Shade'. Notwithstanding a few variations, it was basically the same, familiar tune.

There were several corrections scribbled into both melody lines, And whole stretches of what Tim took to be indications for the drummer had been crossed out and replaced in someone else's handwriting (Frank's?).

Though this might not amount to hard evidence of authorship, it gave a strong indication of work in progress. And there had been witnesses to that work. So why had P.J. not called on them to back up his claim? Tim wondered what had become of Pete and Frank, presumably co-members of the Hawks. He knew that two of the group had been killed in a plane crash, putting an end to any chances of a comeback after their acrimonious break-up in 1979. But he could not remember who. Maybe *someone* could be tracked down ...

Now was the time to give in to his natural interest in rock history. He checked the magazines and clippings for references to the Hawks' line-up at different stages of their development. Almost all included a reference to Phil Murphy as the group's lead guitarist. Only one, dated January 1972, mentioned 'the Hawks' new guitarist, Jon Greene'. Together with Pete Cunningham (bass guitar), Ramon Ortiz (keyboard) and Frank Gerwig (drums), that completed the line-up familiar from Tim's record collection.

An interesting side-light was thrown on the band's choice of name. Apparently they had originally called themselves the 'Hawks and Doves'. But in the course of their growing popularity on the club scene it had inevitably been shortened to the first element in the name - giving rise to occasional consternation: How the hell could such a bunch of peaceniks and draft-dodgers be called 'The Hawks', of all things? Tim vaguely remembered hearing of the origin of their name before. What was new to him was that it had been Phil Murphy who had persuaded the others that it would be a wise move to keep the seemingly inappropriate short form, and make it their official name. He was quoted in a 1971 article as defending it for its attention-grabbing potential. He seemed to have been proved right. It certainly hadn't done the group any harm, even if Phil himself hadn't hung around long enough to share in the benefits.

As to the reasons for the change of guitarist, Tim found nothing in the various clippings. Strange.

Tim now turned his attention to the pile of documents, mostly photocopies, but some that might be originals. Practically all of them, he now realized, related in some way to the Vietnam War, and more specifically, to the Draft. There was, for example, what looked like an original application form for the ROTC, or Reserve Officer Training Corps. This, Tim vaguely remembered, had been a popular way of avoiding active service at the time. It was conceivable that P.J. - or rather Phil, as he had called himself at the time - had done just that, as he would probably have just finished college at the time, and no longer be eligible for a student deferment. (The latter term turned up in an information brochure in the pile.) But hadn't Phil avoided the Draft through ill health? Wasn't that what Helen had said? Something about drugs, and a mental breakdown?

Looking closer at the ROTC application form, he realized now that it was only partially filled out. So it may well have been that Phil had never actually sent in such a form. Tim rummaged further in the pile, and finally found a document certifying that Philip James Murphy, born August 25th, 1948 in Baton Rouge, Louisiana, had been judged unfit for military service.

Clipped to this document were two other sheets of paper. The rust from the paper clip had worked its way through all the layers of paper it was holding, so that the corner of one of them partially crumbled as Tim tried to separate it. This gave the results of his physical examination in May 1970: most parameters there seem to have been OK. It was the smaller piece of paper that seemed to have been decisive. This was a photocopy of an older medical report, dated October 1961, from Brooklyn Children's Hospital, New York, and certified that Philip Murphy, born August 25th, 1948 in Baton Rouge, Louisiana, now resident in Benson Avenue, Brooklyn suffered from ... what? Since all the variable details had been entered in handwriting, it was hard to make to what: the first of two words was illegible, but a fair guess was that it ended in '...itis'; the second word seemed to be 'pigmentosa'. Sounded like a skin disease - surely a childhood skin disease couldn't get you off military service? But after the printed heading 'Prognosis", it said 'progressive, incurable', so you never knew, maybe it could. Something to ask Brid about.

Nothing more of interest could be found, so Tim stacked everything together and arranged them in a somewhat more orderly fashion than before back in the case, taking care to place the more intriguing items on top. He closed the case, put it in the hallway where its musty stink was less likely to bother him, and went to scrub his hands and fingernails.

On Monday morning, Tim took the earliest opportunity to ring Colin Leahy at the *Irish Times*. Colin was quite eager to help, but when he rang back it was to report that Dervla Cassidy, the features writer who had done the Murrough interview, was off on a four-week holiday in Katmandu. Or maybe Katmandu was just Colin's metaphor for exotic places way off east. Anyway, Dervla wouldn't be back until November 8th. Her colleagues had checked, but could find no tape or a transcript of the interview in question anywhere in the office. He had left a note for Dervla to contact Tim when she got back, and gave Tim Dervla's extension just in case.

New York came up with a more decisive result. Uncle Fred rang back that evening - actually only late afternoon in New York, but after 10 o'clock Bandon time - to say that no Officer Murrough had died in the line of duty in the fifties or sixties. "And that covers people tripping over the cable of the coffee machine - it all counts as death in the line of duty," he added. Not only that, but Julie had checked the personnel archive and could find no record of any Murrough in the NYPD in the period 1955-65. "Is that any help to you?"

Tim didn't know. But it had him wondering what else Murrough might have invented.

Chapter 14

"But you said no good would come of it - and you were right!"

Maggie O'Keeffe sipped her tea. Celia made it good and strong, but as a result it was always too hot at first. Rather than add more milk, Maggie chose to wait till it cooled down, dunking her gingersnaps in the hot brew in the meantime. She had no ready answer, so Celia went on.

"And this would be your chance to get out. The studio has had no business since the accident - or whatever it was - and it's not sure if it will ever get going again ..."

"Oh, it will. They've got a booking for the first week in November." She pursed her lips to hint at distaste. "Some rock band, I think."

"They got a special cheap rate, I suppose!"

"The Murroughs aren't desperate - either for money or for customers."

"Maybe not. But what's in it for you to be at their beck and call?"

Quite a lot, actually, though Maggie wasn't sure if she wanted Celia to know all the details. "Mr. Murrough has offered me a fixed weekly wage, regardless of whether the studio's working or not. When they haven't got recordings going on, I'll only need to go there once a week to do some dusting."

"So, an offer you can't refuse, as they say?"

"You could put it that way, Celia." The other point in favour of accepting Richard Murrough's offer was his graciousness after he discovered her little secret habit. The problem had started when someone from the band that was there at the time had found her bottle of Tullamore Dew in the broom cupboard, and put it in the fridge.

She suspected that drummer girl, though she couldn't be sure. That one certainly had it in for poor Maggie from the start, always complaining about how delicate her precious drums were, and even practically accusing her of stealing that bag she carried them in. Handmade, my foot! It may have been a sturdy and serviceable container for those precious bongos, as she called them, but it was a crude-looking thing, nothing to create such a fuss about. If Ms. Staunton had not been so rude about it, Maggie might well have told her when she found the damn thing lying around later. As it was, she didn't feel like doing her the favour.

Anyway, after her whiskey had been put on public view in the fridge, she didn't dare help herself to it (though judging by the way the level went down in the bottle, somebody else did!). She tried a different hiding place for the replacement bottle, and that was fine until Mr. Murrough had stumbled on her retrieving it one day. What a sense of smell the man had! But he had been very understanding about it. He even well-meaningly suggested she keep her bottle in the broom-cupboard! After she explained why that wouldn't work, he said he'd think about it, and next day brought her an earthenware jar from the house, one with a nice secure screw-top . It was ideal - nobody would know what was in it! He had seemed to understand that she needed her regular sip just to function normally. Maybe it was because he had an even worse handicap himself.

"But what about your health? Those dizzy spells you've been having ... that's surely from all the stair-climbing you have to do there. That awful spiral staircase would put anyone in a spin!"

It was true. Maggie hadn't been feeling too well, lately, and often had to sit down to recover from a dizzy spell, especially after climbing those stairs. But she was pleased to be able to knock that last objection of Celia's on the head. "That won't be a problem any more. They've finally got the lift put in."

Celia had to return to her only trump card. "But the murder ..."

"They're not sure it was murder. And if it was, it was the fellow who's on the run ..."

"You mean the guitar fellow the guards were looking for on TV?" Her voice took on a knowing tone. "To help in their inquiries, as they say?"

"Yes. Donal O'Grady. They say he had a grudge against the fellow who got killed, because he had taken his place in the band. Except that that means he wasn't there that day. I don't understand it."

"There's talk that he was seen on the road near the castle that day."

Maggie had heard that talk, too, but wasn't sure what credence to give it. She had also heard talk of signs of a fight on the roof of the castle. She'd had a nightmare the other night in which she had plied the two men with whiskey up on the roof of Castle Green, and watched them getting more and more aggressive until one of them ended up dead on the pavement below. She had woken up just as the other fellow was about to push her over, too ...

Not a very probable scenario, she realized. More likely the poor fellow had just fallen, or jumped. But either way, she didn't want people getting ideas. As Mr. Richard had said, "No need to let people think your whiskey had anything to do with it." She felt sure she could trust him to keep her little secret.

***

127

Georgie Hayes was bored. Another day spent shopping in Bond Street and Regent Street, the third in a row. Each shopping orgy followed by a dinner party (twice) or a music awards ceremony (once). And another dinner party (this one in Hampstead) lined up for this evening.

It wasn't as if she didn't enjoy the occasional dinner party. She had even organized the odd one herself, back in Dublin, but that would have been for people she knew - colleagues from the studio, clients from the music scene, struggling musicians. Somehow her parties were always a good bit jollier than any of these stiff London gatherings, with everybody trying to impress everybody else. Business or artistic success, intellectual brilliance, social connections, or charming eccentricity - whatever was one's stock in trade, it was traded over the linguini and crêpes suzettes.

But to be honest, she would have to play that game herself tonight, and many other such nights, if she wanted to make a go of their Irish studio project. It was all about connections. And she certainly did want to make a go of Caiseal Gréine, especially now that Richard seemed to be losing interest. It was all well and good for him, he could do his producing act just about anywhere in the world. As he was doing here in London this week. And would be doing in L.A. late November.

But there wasn't much demand for free-lance sound engineers, since every studio had its own well-oiled team. Which meant that mostly she was reduced to looking on, making the occasional suggestion, and feeling totally superfluous. Those were the moments when she wondered if she had a hope of getting her old Windmill Lane job back. They probably wouldn't take her seriously any more, since everyone knew she didn't need the money.

But she was seriously bored. She already had all the clothes and jewellery she needed, and this afternoon had been particularly unproductive. All she had to show for the three hours after she had abandoned Richard in the St. John's Wood studio was a silk scarf.

So Caiseal Gréine must be kept in business. It was her insurance policy in more ways than one. She knew she could make a decent, satisfying life for herself there, half way between her family in Galway and her old pals in Dublin. In the short time she'd been there, she'd even begun to build up some sort of a social life, especially since joining that theatre group in Limerick. A good balance between work and play.

And all this (a thought she kept banishing) would be true with or without Richard. Though being with Richard was a lot of fun, it would be foolish to imagine it could last forever. Not with Richard's marital history, it wouldn't. It hadn't taken the pre-nuptial agreement to drive that point home. So she had taken care to ensure that the Irish castle would go to her in case of a break-up.

Another thought that kept creeping back in spite of sporadic banishment was that a failure of their joint project would make a break-up that much more likely. After all, where else would he need a recording engineer for a spouse? Others could play the trophy wife role a lot better than she could, or would want to.

So once more unto the breach ... She had to pick up Richard from the St. John's Wood studio, dash in the Peugeot to their Notting Hill apartment for a quick shower and change of clothes, and then back north to Hampstead for the dinner party. There they hoped to meet (among others) the manager of a London-Irish rock band that had expressed some interest in recording at Caiseal Gréine. It was to be hoped that the recent incident there had not put them off, that it may even have added a certain frisson to the project.

"I'm sorry, Mrs. Murrough, but your husband said to tell you it will take about another half-hour. If you would wait here, please."

Mrs. Murrough? She had, admittedly, tried on the moniker for size, before discarding it. Even Georgie Hayes-Murrough made her sound like a Sloane Ranger. She thought she had made it clear to everyone concerned that she was still Georgie Hayes ... Oh dear, all this wasn't putting her in the best of humour for the dreaded social evening to come.

***

When Sean Mills got home after walking his dog, his wife Cora had already put the three younger children to bed. She was probably watching TV with the two oldest, Siobhan and Dermot, so it should be safe enough to join them. No kiddy squeals, quarrels, floor-thumping; no adult recriminations. But first he wanted to get in a half-hour's practice on the pipes, so he pulled off his jacket and gloves, left them at the back door, and slipped up the back stairs to his den in the attic,

He needed to work out a new arrangement of that Murrough tune, one that dispensed with guitar, or at least was less dependent on that instrument. Jeannie would certainly be able to find some replacement guitarist, should they need one, but it would be best to make that part optional. Rhythm to be provided purely by Jeannie's percussion - probably purely bodhran this time, to emphasize the Irish element in a tune not normally thought of as part of the tradition. The main melody on his pipes as a slow air - much slower than the song is usually sung. And a high counter-melody for fiddle, coming in on the third repetition.

The latter element being essential. Niamh must not be given a chance to back out of the remaining recordings. Sean simply could not accept that their relationship was over. Her protestations that she wanted to patch things up with her husband and devote herself to her family were to be taken with a pinch of salt. Especially in the light of her appalling behaviour with the American guitarist.

He could well understand her having occasional pangs of guilt, since he was familiar with such pangs himself. But he knew how easy they were to put aside. Niamh would never belong to that boring husband of hers - accountant, or solicitor, or whatever he was. That she would never belong exclusively to him, either, was the other side of the coin.

If the abortion was meant to make the latter point, it had succeeded. But he could live with it. He didn't need another child. But he needed Niamh. And now he knew how to hold her, for the moment at least.

Niamh had never satisfactorily explained what she'd been doing out of her room late at night on the 30th September, the day P.J. fell to his death. It was only later he'd put two and two together, relating it to the phone-call she'd received in her room after he had carried her up the stairs and deposited her on her bed. Just as she came to from her faint, that mobile phone of hers tinkled some silly tune (was it really 'Yankee Doodle'?). Putting it to her ear, she had gasped, "Dónal ...?" and was then silent, listening for at least a full minute before saying "OK, I'll do it", and putting it down. He could only guess what favour Dónal had asked of her. But in any case, it was something she didn't want mentioned. It certainly wasn't in her statement to the Gardai, or they would have questioned him about it.

He would keep quiet about it, too. As long as Niamh played along. She needn't know that he was being economical with the truth for his own sake as much as hers.

**

Niamh put down the book of fairytales and tucked in her sleeping child.

"Ciara, *a ghrá*, don't let your mammy ever go away again."

Vaguely aware that she was falling into her old habit of making other people responsible for her actions and her well-being, and that this was a bit of an unfair burden to put on a six-year-old child, she added the resolution, "Your mammy is finished with that band. It's brought her nothing but trouble."

That wasn't quite true. It had brought her a beautiful lakeside home, for one thing. It had brought her fame, and a degree of notoriety - which was something she usually perversely enjoyed. But enough was enough. From now on she would go it alone musically, picking and choosing collaborators as she needed them. And they would not include Richard Murrough or Sean Mills. Probably not Jeannie Staunton, either. Though she would, of course, first have to persuade Jeannie to accept a fiddle solo as her contribution to completing Eascra's last album. She would get that recorded in Dublin, had in fact already contacted a studio there.

The only way forward was to put that horrible business at the castle behind her, to pretend it never happened. That this would only be possible as long as her brother Dónal succeeded in evading the Gardai, was a thought that kept creeping into her consciousness. She usually suppressed such unpleasant thoughts by thinking of something more pleasant.

Now it was to consider what fiddle tune she would choose to put on the album. "What about a lullaby, Ciara?" She picked up her fiddle and bow and began softly playing the first few lines of 'Báidín Pheilimí'. Ciara slept on, quite used to such nocturnal serenades.

The phone in the hall was ringing. Niamh abandoned the lullaby and went to answer it. It was her mother.

"They've found Dónal. In England."

Chapter 15

It wasn't quite as bad as Tim feared. The Murroughs at least made a show of not standing on ceremony. Kathleen Smith and himself were soon ensconced in comfortable soft leather armchairs in what had been the parlour of the old farmhouse, with a tray of tea things in front of them. A log fire blazed in the fireplace, the flames reflected in the ornate tiles inset in the antique cast-iron surround.

Though, Tim reflected, he probably wouldn't have got beyond the front door without the authority emanating from the presence of Detective Inspector Smith of Kilbrue District.

Kathleen did most of the initial questioning, which concerned the vandalism to the castle. Their instructions had been to concentrate on this aspect, and avoid any speculation on a possible connection to the recent fatality.

Apparently there had been a series of threatening telephone calls, starting in mid-August, and ending the weekend before the death. The voices had been alternately male and female, plus a number of nuisance calls where nobody spoke at all. The messages had all been in the form of short slogans. The one sprayed on the castle wall had been repeated a few times, but also 'Desecration!', 'Foreigners out!' and 'Death to the Invaders!'. Since both were native Irish born, and one had spent all her life in the country, the Murroughs were particularly incensed by the latter two. Kathleen had to calm Georgie down to get her to concentrate on the main job in hand, which was to try to reconstruct when the calls had been made. They hadn't kept a record, but thought there had been six voiced calls in all, at irregular intervals.

There had also been two anonymous threatening letters constructed out of words cut out of a newspaper, with slogans similar to the spoken ones. Kathleen thought they would want to take these into evidence, for fingerprinting and possible identification of the newspapers used. Georgie Murrough had been holding them fan-like in her left hand to assist her memory as she tried to write out a list of phone-calls and rough dates. The reference to fingerprinting caused her to drop them suddenly on the table. Kathleen consolingly explained that it was not that easy to obliterate fingerprints, but held them carefully by the corners as she slipped them into a folder.

The obvious question was asked, why had they not reported all this to the Gardai?

"We just didn't take them seriously. After all, no real damage was done. I mean, apart from that wire-cutting, and then this ... incident." Richard Murrough was certain he would be able to identify the two voices if he heard them again, and agreed to come to the Garda station to listen to some recordings of the suspects. Time would be a problem, since they would be doing recordings all next week, and were leaving for L.A. in mid-November. Would the week after next be OK?

Not really. The sooner the better. They finally agreed on the coming Wednesday evening.

Tim's opportunity came when Murrough's wife Georgie took Kathleen to the upstairs study to peruse the file she had kept on the subject. This included the two anonymous letters she had mentioned, but also their considerable legitimate correspondence on the subject of their renovation plans with the various authorities. The heritage board *An Taisce* had apparently finally given its blessing to the project. There were also newspaper cuttings that might be of interest, such as letters of protest to various newspapers.

Richard Murrough could not, of course, contribute anything to this, so he helped himself to another cup of tea, put his feet up on the sofa.

"Mr. Murrough, would you mind if I stayed behind and asked you a few questions concerning the fatal incident? My father may have mentioned ..."

"Your father? Do you mean Superintendent O'Driscoll?"

"Yes."

"Ah. Now I know who you are. Your father did mention that his son was stationed in the District where the poor fellow lived. So go ahead. Shoot." Tim registered for the first time consciously that Richard Murrough was not wearing glasses, and had not been since they arrived at the house. They apparently were just for show.

"Mr. Murrough, were you aware that you had had previous dealings with the dead man?"

A brief hesitation. "Not at first. But it dawned on me."

"And when might that have been?"

"It must have been the day before he fell to his death. No, it was the morning of that day."

Tim waited.

"You see, one guitarist sounds much the same as another basically - if you discount the real geniuses, that is. And the name P.J. Murphy is so

133

commonplace that it didn't ring a bell. Besides, if he is who I think he is - or rather was - he used a different form of his name back then."

"Phil."

"Right." Tim was expecting Murrough to ask how he knew, but he didn't. "Also, I don't have the advantage of sighted people in constantly getting visual jogs to the memory. By the way, what did he look like?"

"About your own build, and age."

"I know that."

"A bit bedraggled. Your typical ageing hippie." Murrough smiled. "So what did finally jog your memory?"

"It was the riff he played for a song of mine, It took me back to 1970, '71 ..."

"The early days of The Hawks? And the Janis Joplin sessions?"

Tim was trying hard to make Cathy's dutiful research pay off.

Richard Murrough smiled. "Yes, those were good days."

"And the song in question was ..."

"'Light and Shade'."

"Mr. Murrough, are you aware that P.J. Murphy - or Phil Murphy as he called himself back then - claimed to have written the tune of that song?"

Murrough sat up and put his feet back on the floor. "Good heavens, no! Though to be honest, he could have claimed *some* contribution. The point is, he never did."

"Any idea why?"

Murrough shrugged his shoulders. "Maybe because he was constantly drugged to the eyeballs. That's why he didn't last long in The Hawks."

"He was replaced by Jon Greene, I believe."

"A much steadier character. Technically brilliant, though maybe not quite so creative."

"Anyway how *do* you see Phil's contribution to the songwriting? You said he might have reasonably claimed some contribution to 'Light and Shade'."

"That riff of his. It sparked something off, it may well have been the starting point for the melody. Songwriting is a mysterious process. It's often hard to pin down where ideas come from. But in this case, I do think Phil could have claimed some credit."

"Did you ever feel guilty about taking advantage of a hopeless junkie?"

"Oh, he wasn't a junkie. Just pot. And LSD. The usual for the time and place." Murrough took a deep breath. "But yes, at first I did feel a bit guilty, particularly since he missed out on The Hawks' big time. But the feeling passed. Besides, it was his own fault."

"Do I understand you right, there never was any court case about the songwriting credits?"

"Oh, no. I'd remember that!"

"And on the day it dawned on you who he was, did you speak to him about it?"

"No, I left it to him. After all, he must have known who I was."

"He did. So did he make himself known to you?"

"No."

"Earlier in this conversation, Mr. Murrough ..."

"Call me Richard."

"OK, ... Richard, you referred to the incident as him 'falling to his death'. Is that the way you really see it? Or was it just a manner of speaking?"

"I really don't know. Considering his background, and the fact that the past was beginning to come up again, with all its failures and frustrations ..." He tailed off.

"Well, what?"

"I think he probably jumped."

"In spite of the fact that we now have a prime suspect for murder? The other guitarist, the one who's been tracked down in England?"

"Yes. Admittedly, I don't know anything about him. But I still think suicide is more likely."

"But everybody says he was increasingly cheerful. Hadn't you offered him some more permanent role with Eascra?"

"True enough. But that was before what's-his-name, the piper ..."

"Sean Mills."

"Yeah, before Sean Mills suggested that blasted song of mine. Phil's guitar track was sounding more and more aggressive with every take."

"Did you keep those takes?"

"Sure."

"Could I hear them?"

"Sure. If you wish, I can take you over to the studio after your colleague is finished with collecting evidence."

"Thanks." They could hear the two women closing the study door and making for the stairs. "One more thing ..."

"Yes?"

"I read that interview you gave to the *Irish Times*, last June it was. Very interesting."

"Thanks. It was a good one."

"One detail worries me. You referred to your father as joining the NYPD, one of New York's finest, as you put it."

"Sure."

"And you said he died in a car-chase, in the line of duty as it were."

"True. Though actually it was a heart attack he had in the course of the car-chase."

"But nobody called Murrough is listed in their Memorial List for that period. In fact, there was no Murrough in the NYPD in all of the 50s and sixties. So did you just make it up for effect?"

Murrough laughed out loud. "I like a man who does his homework. But this one is easily explained. You see, my old man didn't call himself Murrough - he was plain Jack Murphy!"

Tim was feeling a bit deflated, but soldiered on regardless. "So you changed your name."

"Right. Murphys are two-a-penny. And awfully Irish, at a time when being Irish wasn't as fashionable as it is now."

"A bit like Ronald Reagan, you mean? He didn't like the usual form 'Regan', so he ..."

"... accidentally brought his name closer to the original Gaelic form 'Ó Réagáin'. The difference is, I knew what I was doing. The old Irish names 'Ó Murchú' and 'Mac Murchú' have been variously anglicized over the ages as 'Morchoe', 'Morrow', 'Murray', 'Murphy' and 'Murrough' - with or without an appended 'O' or 'Mac'. Remember the infamous Diarmaid Mac Murchú - or Dermot MacMurrough - that the protesters have compared me with?" He guffawed again. "I think it's as good a form as any."

Tim was spared the need to reply by the return of the two women. As they concluded their business, he began to re-gather his wits about him. Sure, Murphys are two-a-penny, both in this country and America. But surely it was too much of a coincidence that the two men whose paths had crossed so contentiously - and ultimately fatally - should share a name?

The studio was cold, as the heating there had been set to minimum. No recording had been done there since the Eascra sessions, Murrough said apologetically. But they wouldn't have to stay there long. Kathleen Smith had departed in the squad car on Tim's assurance that he wouldn't mind walking back to the village. Now, Murrough was fumbling with some tapes at the control desk. Tim wondered if he had them marked in Braille for his convenience, but never got to ask, because a jangle of guitar strings assailed his ears. No wonder P.J. had broken his strings.

"I seem to have started with Phil's last version," came Murrough's comment over the microphone. "I think you get the message. For comparison, I'll play an earlier take."

The riff was vigorously played, but steadier than the other, later take. "Yeah, I see what you mean." Murrough had now emerged from the control room. "By the way, it's not quite the riff used on the Hawks' recording of 'Light and Shade', is it?"

"No, we changed to a smoother line for the recording. But this was the way it started, which is why my ears pricked up when I heard him play it that ... day." There was an awkward silence. "Anything else you'd like to hear?"

"What about those fiddle takes you were working on that same evening? You and Niamh, I mean."

Obligingly, Murrough returned to the control desk and flipped a few switches. Then he groped on a shelf behind him and pulled out two spools. They did indeed seem to have Braille markings on them.

"This is the one we decided to use." A melancholy wail came through the speakers. Tim tried to imagine how it would blend with P.J.'s riff.

"Now here are two of the rejects." What followed was a more ornate version of the same, and an equally melancholy passage that contained a few recognizable notes of the basic tune. When he was done, Murrough shut off the machinery and rejoined Tim, who was seated all the while in the carpeted 'dead area'.

"How about something more cheerful and positive to finish the day?" Murrough groped for what he must have known was standing there. It was an old-fashioned microphone, such as was used in the fifties. "My most treasured possession. It was used for some great recordings by Patsy Cline and Willie Nelson, in Nashville, and may even have graced Sun Studios in Memphis." Tim was impressed.

"Though there's no proof of the latter, so I can't call it the Elvis Mike. Instead, I call it the Maggie Mike, in honour of my present cleaning lady - have you met her?".

Tim told him she had done some work for his family during his schooldays. There was nothing to be gained from mentioning their more recent encounter.

"Go on, take it in your hand, everybody does!" Tim did, and put on a little Elvis act to go with it.

"Now you also said you wanted to inspect the scene of the ... whatever. Luckily, we can now take the newly-installed lift. Makes a huge difference, I can tell you! If you wish, you can walk down, and inspect the other floors." They had climbed the spiral staircase to the studio on the first floor, but did the remainder - the equivalent of three floors - in more comfort, and in silence. Somehow the atmosphere of the place was getting through to both men, in spite of the shiny new high-tech equipment.

As it hummed to a halt, Tim broke the spell by querying how Murrough had managed to get planning permission for such an anachronistic feature. As expected, the question didn't faze the man. He even managed an impish grin. "I did get a few people to put in a good word for me. But as it turned out, the authorities didn't take much persuading. After all, the place was just a pile of old stones. You must remember that, if you once lived locally, as I'm told." Tim nodded. "Anyway, from the second floor up it's been pure reconstruction. It was this or nothing."

They emerged on the roof, to view a clear, starry sky. A crescent moon was visible low in the sky, reflected in the waters of Lough Gur on the northern horizon. This was the way it would have been roughly a month ago, on the day P.J. must have stood at this very spot, overlooking the entrance to the castle. The roof garden now seemed to be complete, however, with two neat rows of potted conifers down the middle. The heavy machinery, the winch and cement mixer Tim remembered from the photographs, had long been cleared away. The battlements were also complete, with no danger of stumbling to one's death on the pavement below. Tim held on to the cold stone and looked over.

He wasn't normally superstitious, but the sudden chill he felt seemed out of proportion with the actual night temperature. Together with the night that was in it, it had him wondering if might have come from the older ghosts said to haunt the castle, or from a more recent one.

"You probably heard we had planned a Halloween party here. Would have been fun."

Yes. Would have been.

Chapter 16

"Would you mind if we continued our talk outside of the house? You see, my wife will be back from her mother's in about half an hour, and I'd rather ..." Sean Mills tailed off, and just raised his burly hands in supplication. Tim had often marvelled that such solid flesh was capable of producing such filigree sounds on the pipes.

"Sure. You mean go to a pub?"

"Well, what about a walk?"

"OK."

But first he wanted Tim to drive his car down to the pub first. Something about not giving rise to awkward questions. Tim decided he needed to humour him. After all, his original appointment had been for tomorrow, Monday, and Sean had graciously agreed to the change after Niamh phoned with a headache, asking to put off their meeting till Tuesday.

Tim had taken two days off after the weekend to meet as many as he could of the witnesses, using his family home as a base. Tuesday had originally been earmarked for Maggie O'Keeffe and the spraying suspects, since Maggie spent Sunday with her sister in Limerick. Now it had to be tomorrow for all of them. Luckily it was a school holiday.

Which left only today for a chance to call on Sean at his home in Kilkenny. A good three-hour drive there and back. He hoped he would make it back in time for his meeting with Una O'Riordan, now arranged for 8 p.m.

Since the afternoon was pleasantly warm by early November standards, a walk would be no hardship. As they left the house in this visibly affluent suburb of Kilkenny, Tim was rather surprised to see Sean pull on a pair of sheepskin gloves. Noticing his stare, Sean explained. "Gotta keep my fingers nimble for my solo gig in Clonmel tonight. They're very sensitive, and I've got a reputation to keep up!"

"Yeah, sorry about that. I realize you don't like to be distracted before a concert. But it had to be today or not at all." Sean's expression suggested that 'not at all' was an option he could have lived with. "So thanks for agreeing to talk to me."

"Jeannie persuaded me. She assured me you were OK. Said you were the same fellow who managed to subdue Dónal that night in Skibbereen."

"With your help."

As they drove away from the house, Sean asked if Tim had been able to interview the same Dónal. Like everybody else, he'd heard in the news that the fugitive had been apprehended in England.

"No way, he's still in custody in Birmingham. He'll be extradited eventually, but it'll take a while. I did, however, talk to his girl friend yesterday."

"Christine?"

"Yes. She just confirmed what she'd already told the Kilbrue Gardai ... I'm afraid I'm not free to give you the details." These were that Dónal had driven down from Dublin early that fatal evening and had a meal at her place. Driven away again, and returned briefly about an hour later, only to ransack her supply of ferry timetables and drive off again.

This information had not been gladly divulged, nor had the facts emerged all at once. According to Tim's father, it had taken some gentle pressure to convince Christine that cooperation was the best policy. In the end, a combination of none-too-subtle hints about consequences for her resident status (whatever about the European Community ...), repeated use of the term 'accessory after the fact', and the continental European's inbred wariness of the police, had done the trick.

Combined with Jeannie's tip about Dónal's brother's IRA contacts, the crucial hint about the ferry timetables had put the Gardai - and subsequently the British police - on the right track. It turned out that the IRA 'safe house' where Dónal had been allowed to take refuge (and hide the all-too-recognizable BMW, probably allowing for its use, when equipped with new number plates, for other purposes) had been under surveillance for some time.

"Anyway, what I can tell you is that Dónal is still denying any involvement in P.J.'s death."

"So why did he run?"

Tim let that question hang in the air. Having parked the car at a nearby pub, the two men set off on their walk.

"You like to walk, it seems."

"Sure."

"Just like the evening P.J. was killed?"

Before suggesting the walk, Sean had already recounted most of the events of that day, and there were no glaring discrepancies with what was on the record, or with what Jeannie had told Tim. The only mildly interesting addition being that P.J. had seemed 'a bit distracted' when he left him in the studio re-stringing his guitars.

"Sure. Plus I'd had enough of the drink. One pint is more than enough for me after having drunk the better part of a bottle of Beaujolais with the Chinese food. Very middling Beaujolais at that."

"No other reason?"

"No. Do I need one?"

"Just asking. I believe the students in the pub that evening were joking about some apparent flirtation between Niamh and P.J. earlier in the evening."

"So?"

"You might have wanted to check up on the goings-on back at the castle."

"Hah!"

Tim waited for him to elaborate. He did.

"Look, I see there's no point in denying that we've had a bit of an affair. Jeannie told me she'd mentioned it, since it was bound to come out any way. But it's over."

"Even that evening?"

He hesitated briefly. "Yes." Tim decided not to probe that area any further for the moment.

"On your walk back to the castle that night, did you meet any traffic going in either direction?"

Sean relaxed visibly, possible relieved at the change of subject. He was silent for a moment. When he spoke, the tension was back. "One car came against me. At some speed, if I remember rightly. In any case, I had to retreat onto the grass verge. I was walking on the right, of course."

"What kind of car was it?"

"A biggish one. Pale-coloured, I think. It was a dark night, Not much of a moon."

"Make?"

"Dunno. I was dazzled by the headlights.

"Could it have been a BMW?"

"I suppose it could have. Or a Merc. But I suppose you mean, could it have been Dónal's, and the answer is yes, it could have been. I heard someone else claims to have seen him in the area. But I didn't see the driver, and only noticed the pale colour after the car passed me. I certainly didn't get the registration number."

"Could you pin down the exact time and place? According to what you told the KIlbrue Gardai, you left the pub around 8.50 p.m. ..."

"It m ust have been pretty soon after that, about five minutes into the walk."

"And where did you meet the car?"

Sean looked as if he was thinking hard. "It must have been just where the road begins to rise, on a curve to the right. It came over the top of the hill at me suddenly, so that I had to jump to get out of the way."

"Do you think the driver saw you?"

A pause. "Don't know. Not necessarily, because of the curve. A bit like the one we're on now." He demonstrated the evasive action by ducking into the shade of a hawthorn bush.

"And you reached the castle when?"

"About a quarter past nine. God, do I have to go over all that again? I've told everything to the Kilbrue cops!"

"Well, there are a few details I've been wondering about. What did you notice first about the scene?"

"The broken glass on the path. Some of it had scattered pretty widely. Then P.J's legs sprawled across the doorway. His head almost hidden by those plants stacked to the right of the entrance."

"Did you immediately realize who was lying there?"

"I'd have recognized that ghastly jacket of his anywhere. But I immediately turned him over to see his face."

"He was lying on his face?"

"No, on his side facing the wall. Anyway, as I touched him, I got the impression he might be still alive, so I attempted a bit of heart massage, yelling for someone to call an ambulance."

"Who did you expect to hear you?"

"Niamh should have been in her room. And there might have been someone in the studio."

"But nobody came?"

"The walls are pretty thick. So after no more than a minute or two I went in and rang 999 myself."

"From what phone?"

"The ground-floor office. Then I ran down and banged on Murrough's door. You must know the rest."

"OK, let's skip the arrival of the ambulance and Gardai, and even Niamh's melodramatic scene. What about afterwards, when everything had quieted down: Did you just all go to bed, or were there some further discussions among you?"

"Well, I stayed in the ground-floor sitting room for a while talking to Georgie ..."

"Murrough's wife."

"Yeah, and our recording engineer. We were just rambling on about how awful it all was, and whether he was going to survive ..."

"What was the assumption about what had actually happened?"

"Oh, an accident. At least we weren't admitting at the time that there were other possibilities. Then Jeannie turned up, and we had to go over the whole story again."

"How did she react?"

"Shocked, of course. But she had enough presence of mind to ring the Regional to try to find out how he was. Not that they told us anything. Insisted that they had first to notify his next-of-kin ..."

"Meaning his wife, or rather widow. But she didn't get to be officially notified until the next morning - through us at Bandon Garda Station!"

"Maybe in the confusion nobody realized that Jeannie was the one who could have given them the correct name, address and telephone number. Anyway, this talk of notifying his next-of-kin suggested the worst."

"So what did you do then?"

"Nothing, We all retired to our respective rooms."

"Did you call in on Niamh again?"

Was Sean tensing up again? "Yeah, I looked in her door. She doesn't lock it. She was sound asleep, had taken some sleeping tablets earlier, after she had recovered from her faint."

"And you didn't speak to Niamh any more that night."

"No."

"Jeannie thought she heard your voices whispering about one o'clock that night."

Sean looked sullen. "OK, I did look in on her once more. I couldn't sleep, and though she might need some ... comforting."

"And did she?"

"No, she woke up as I opened the door, and said she was OK."

"You didn't stay?"

"No. She didn't want me to."

"Actually, Jeannie says she heard the voices from downstairs, that is, not from the room next door to hers."

Sean's eyes had taken on a guarded look. "She must be mistaken. Or if she did hear something, it wasn't us."

"You heard nothing strange that night."

"No, nothing. But I got to sleep shortly after, and once I'm asleep, it takes a lot to wake me."

Tim suggested turning back, since he didn't have much more to ask. He took the opportunity to pull out his notebook and look at his notes.

"You got along well with the cleaning lady, I believe?"

Sean seemed a bit taken aback by the sudden change of topic, but immediately relaxed. It was, after all, a less fraught subject. "Maggie? Sure, we got on well. Why do you ask?"

"Well, I'm told you helped yourself to some of the whiskey she'd hidden away in the broom cupboard."

"Oh, I replaced that for her before we left. No harm intended. When I found it, I was a bit in need of a sip myself, and then it ended up in the fridge."

"When *did* you find it? I mean, what were you doing in the broom cupboard, of all places?"

"Oh, that was the same evening, as P.J.'s fall, I mean. After Niamh came to after her faint, she felt nauseous, and then vomited on the floor. We cleared it up, but she thought it left a bit of a stain, and asked if I could find some strong detergent. I went to the obvious place for it."

"And then put it back again.?"

"No, I left it with Niamh, she said she'd replace it when she was finished with it."

"I see. Well, that's all I need from you at the moment. If any further questions occur to me, I'm sure you won't mind if I give you a ring?"

"No, that'd be OK. Though I can't imagine what else might be of interest." After a question about detergent, just about anything was possible, he may well have been thinking.

Tim was a good ten minutes late for his appointment with Una O'Riordan, who was down for the long holiday weekend from Dublin. Her parents' home proved to be one of the solidly-built detached houses up the Railway Road, which, in spite of its proletarian-sounding name, was Kilmallock's best residential area, where the doctors, lawyers and teachers tended to live. Tim had often passed this way in his student days, catching the train to Cork at Kilmallock Railway Station (now closed down, of course). The sitting-room Una showed him into was comfortable, decorated in restrained good taste, and heated by a roaring log fire.

Since Una insisted she was going out with her friends at half-past eight, Tim got straight to the point. "There are just two things I want to check up on. One is if you're certain it was Dónal Ó Gráda you saw driving toward Castle Green on the night of P.J.'s death?"

"Oh, absolutely. I'd know him anywhere. I'm a real fan of his, I've been to several Eascra concerts ..."

"But wasn't it already dark when you were leaving Ryan's? Twenty to nine, I believe it was."

"Yes, but as I turned onto the main road, I caught him in my own headlights. It was him all right."

"Was he speeding?"

"No, he couldn't have been at the point I saw him, just about to turn right into the side road." She considered for a moment. "He may have speeded up after that, though. The engine sounded quite loud as he drove off." She hesitated again. "Look, I'm not happy about this at all. I like the fellow. But If he had anything to do with this other guy's death then he ought to answer for it."

"How well did you know this other guy?"

"Not well at all. I think I spoke to him only twice, once when he took a look at what we were doing at the archaeological site, and once in the pub. He wasn't all that sociable, but pleasant enough."

"But you knew him well enough to recognize him when you saw him up on the roof earlier that evening?"

"Oh, yes. Though to be honest, it was already getting dark at the time, just before eight o'clock, it was. We were already packing away our tools for the day. But I'm pretty sure it was him." She closed her eyes as if trying to conjure up the scene. "There had been a bit of a sunset, and that orange jacket of his reflected the remaining rays of light."

"I believe there were some joking comments made about him in the pub afterwards."

"Mainly by Tom - one of the other students on the dig. It had to do with Niamh's fiddle music we could hear at the same time. Tom made out she was serenading him!"

"Playing something romantic?"

"No, actually it was fast dance music. But Tom thought it was funny enough to stretch a point."

"Could there have been something to it? I mean, do you know anything about the relationship between the two of them?"

"No, I wouldn't know anything about what went on inside the castle. As I said, the fellow who died hardly ever came to the pub, and Niamh never did."

The Caseys lived in the new council estate that straggled along the river to the east of Kilbrue village, spoiling (to Tim's eye) what had once been a pleasant, grassy riverbank, suitable for occasional picnics and other adolescent rendezvous. Though, to be honest, he had not much appreciated the landscape at the time, still rankling under his enforced transplantation from his earlier home in West Cork. The chorus of a Joni Mitchell song ran through his mind, the one about not knowing what you've got till it's gone: "They paved paradise, and put up a ..." ... council estate with a miserable concrete walkway where the rushes used to be. Tim checked the thought. He was still much too young for nostalgia to be setting in.

The Casey's house was an end-of-terrace with a passably well-kept garden. He rang the doorbell. The woman who opened the door was expecting him. It had helped that the children's father was a brother of Sergeant Casey. There were a lot of Caseys in Kilbrue. Even Maggie O'Keeffe, whom he hoped to interview later, was one of the clan.

He hoped he wasn't up against a conspiracy of silence. He would have preferred to interview the three kids separately, but didn't want to push his luck. They had already been interrogated by the Kilbrue Gardai (Róisín, the eldest, having been questioned by his father personally). Besides, they would by now have had ample time to coordinate their stories. He would just have to prick up his ears for any uncertainties in their answers and try to interpret their demeanour as best he could.

Their mother showed him into the slightly musty-smelling front room, one that was probably only used for special visitors. At least it was already heated by a gas fire, whose mock flames made some gesture toward the concept of cosiness.

The two 14-year old boys were ushered in. Identical twins, to all appearances. From what Tim had heard of identical twins, interviewing them separately probably wouldn't have made much difference - they probably would have been capable of telepathy over a distance.

The mother retreated into the narrow hall, and could be heard yelling up the stairs, "Ro-o-o-sheen!". The eldest girl was probably in her bedroom listening to her favourite boy group over headphones, or swotting for her Leaving Cert. (she had a certain reputation for studiousness), or both. Eventually she joined them in the sitting room, pale, slender girl dressed in black jeans and a close-fitting horizontally striped turtle-neck, her reddish wavy hair tied back in a ponytail. She took the other chintz armchair facing Tim across the fireplace. The twins were already sprawled at either ends of the sofa, a defiant look on their faces.

"Now which one of you is Liam?"

The one on the left, in the yellow sweatshirt, raised his hand. The other boy, Cormac, was wearing red. They were probably colour-coded for the family's convenience.

"Well, Liam, Cormac, I'm told you've admitted to spraying that slogan on the wall of Castle Green. And damaging the plaster." The boys nodded in unison.

"It wasn't much damage. Dad's paying for it," said Cormac.

"And it's being taken out of our pocket money," added Liam, looking sullen.

"Look, I'm not all that interested in the rights and wrongs of your little caper. I'm just interested that you were there, on a day when something far worse happened."

"We had nothing to do with that!" said Liam, a touch of fear penetrating his defiance.

"I'm not saying you had. I just want to know what you saw and heard."

He faced Róisín. "You still say you weren't there."

She shook her head. "I wasn't. As you probably know, I went for a cycle that evening ..." Róisín was adopting the same defiant expression as her twin brothers.

"On somebody else's bike!"

"I just borrowed it."

"Why?"

"It was a nice bike. I saw it when I passed Ryan's pub on my way back from my friend Jodey's. There was no one there, so I just tried it out. I meant to bring it back"

"And why didn't you?"

"I was going to do a round and cycle back via the back road ..."

"You mean past Castle Green?" He checked his copy of her previous statement, taken by the Kibrue Gardai. "At eight thirty in the evening?"

"Yeah, why not? But I never got there. When I turned off the main road at the river, I saw my mother standing with her back to me talking to a neighbour under a street lamp, so I just hid the bike in the bushes. Then she saw me, and I had to pretend I'd been walking home."

"Do you often do things like that?"

"No, never."

"So why this time?"

"It just came over me. It was stupid."

Tim looked at her sceptically. She looked away. He decided to leave it at that, and turned to the twins. "What's the name of the new owner of Castle Green?"

"Mr. Murrough." they answered simultaneously.

"How do you spell that?

"M-U-R-R-" they started simultaneously.

"-O-W, " continued Liam.

"-A....," said Cormac, and petered out.

"Look, it's obvious they got the idea from me," put in Róisín. "I can show you the kind of thing they must have copied." She got up and retrieved a few papers from the top of the upright piano. They were leaflets from the protest group announcing a public meeting, including (in large print) one of the slogans that had got spray-painted in the castle walls: 'SAVE OUR HERITAGE'. Also, in the body of the text, the smart-alecky reference to 'MacMurrough'.

Róisín must have known she would have to give some explanation for her kid brothers' surprising literacy. If she was covering up for her own presence at the scene, the question was why. An eighteen-year-old might well have to face severer penalties for such vandalism. Or was it because she had seen or heard something she didn't want to talk about?

The leaflets were already familiar to Tim from the file he had been allowed to peruse at Kilbrue Garda Station. "I'm told you were involved in the making of these leaflets."

"Well, I wrote the text. Nobody else wanted to do it, and my friend Jodey told everyone I was good at composition, so..." She shrugged. "But Aidan did the design on his computer, and got them printed in Limerick."

"Aidan?"

"Aidan Flynn." Yes, of course. The one with ESB connections.

"Her boyfriend," added Cormac, with a broad grin.

Róisín glared at him. "Aidan is studying environmental science at Limerick NIHE. I know him from school, he was a few years ahead of me." Tim was momentarily puzzled, until he remembered that the local convent school was now co-educational. "Anyway, it was he and Miss O'Brien ... I mean Mary O'Brien ... it was they that started the protest group.

"Mary O'Brien being your teacher?"

She was my teacher at primary school. But in the group we're supposed to call her Mary. It was her idea to call the Yank 'MacMurrough'".

Tim already had a list of the members of the protest group, so he didn't need to follow up that line. Róisín's reference to Aidan and Mary sounded a

148

bit like an effort to spread the potential blame a bit wider. "Anyway, can you honestly say that none of you - Mary or Aidan or whoever - were involved in the spraying?"

"We weren't. I've already told the guards that."

He knew that. The others all had cast-iron alibis for the evening of P.J.'s death. (According to his mother, Miss O'Brien had been highly incensed at having to provide one!) Of the two organizers, Tim would have liked to question the enigmatic Aidan, in spite of his proven participation in a local hurling match that evening. But at most, he might have nailed him for the earlier sabotage of the power lines. It was more important to interview those with shaky alibis or none.

Tim turned to the boys again. "And did any of them put you up to it?"

"No. We did it for fun," said Liam

"Found one of those stupid leaflets lying around and sprayed some bits of it on the wall," said Cormac.

Maybe now he would get to the interesting bit. "OK, tell me how you went about it. When did you go out there that evening?"

"Just after our tea." That would make it about 6.30.

"Did you cycle?"

"Yeah, but only half way up the back road," said Cormac.

"We didn't want our bikes to be seen when we were doing the job," said Liam.

"There are several spots where you can climb the ditch and get through the bushes."

"The easiest one is from the field to the east of the castle," added Cormac. "That's where we got in."

This was more or less what Tim had expected. "That evening there were people working around the castle, coming and going. How *did* you manage not to be seen?"

"We hid in the bushes behind the castle," said Liam.

"Just down the slope from the car park." said Cormac.

"What was going on in the grounds at the time?" asked Tim.

"We could see those people digging in that hole on the other side."

"How many people?"

"Three," said Liam.

"Two," said Cormac, simultaneously. They glared at each other.

"It was only two," said Cormac. "A man and a woman, I don't know their names. The boss woman was walking away from them when we hid in the bushes."

149

"Yeah," Liam conceded. "She went to her van in the car park."

"And she stayed there how long?"

"Not long at all," said Liam. "After a few minutes, she got out and went into the castle."

Tim sat up. This was something new. He took out his note-book. "Are you sure?"

"Sure we're sure!" they answered simultaneously.

"And when did she come out?"

"Don't know. Could have been any time," said Cormac.

"You see, we weren't watching the entrance all the time," added Liam. "But her van was still there when we looked last ..."

"... at about twenty to eight," completed Cormac. "I wanted to start spraying, thought we couldn't wait any longer, it was beginning to get dark."

"And even if she went back to her van she wouldn't have seen us from that side."

"But what about the other people at the archaeological site?" asked Tim. "The people digging in the hole, I mean. They would surely have seen you?"

"Oh, we waited for them to move away. You see we wanted to borrow their ladder."

"And anyway, while we were spraying we heard two cars drive away. We knew we were safe enough after that."

"I see. But had ye seen or heard anybody else around? On the roof, for example?"

"The roof? Oh, yeah, ..." Cormac looked at his brother, as if wondering whether he should have kept his mouth shut on this point.

Liam took over. "Just as we were getting the ladder, we saw a grey-haired fellow standing with his back to us up on the roof. So we ducked into the hole until he went away."

"Who did you think it was?"

"Oh, we were sure it must be yer man, Murrough," said Cormac.

"But it could have been the fella who fell off the roof that night ..." added Liam.

"Or was knocked off!" said Cormac, with a barely suppressed grin. He seemed to relish the ghoulish thought.

"But we had nothing to do with that!" Liam glared at his brother.

"OK, the fellow you saw had grey hair. Anything else you noticed?"

"No, he had his back to us. And it was only for a few seconds that we saw him."

"And you heard nothing from up there?"

"No," said Liam.

"But we heard someone inside the castle all right," said Cormac. "Someone playing the fiddle."

"How do you know it was live music?"

"Oh, it kept stopping and starting, the same sort of thing over and over again, sometimes a bit different ..." Cormac tailed off helplessly.

"And whoever was playing seemed to be moving about ..." added Liam.

"You'd hear it more from the left side, and then from the right."

Tim did a mental flashback to the Skibbereen concert, with Niamh promenading backwards and forwards on the stage. "What sort of thing was the person playing?"

"Oh, jigs and reels and things ... diddley-eye, diddley-eye, you know." Tim knew.

"And you weren't worried that person might have seen you?"

"Not really. It sounded high up in the castle, and nobody could stick their heads out of those narrow little windows."

That sounded like a reasonable bit of risk-taking, assuming a certain determination to carry out this crazy little caper. "And how long did it take ye to paint the slogans?"

"Dunno. Maybe ten minutes."

"No, a quarter of an hour, about." corrected Liam. "I had to shift the ladder a couple of times to paint the higher-up slogan."

"The 'save our heritage' one?"

"Yeah, whatever. Cormac did the 'out with yer man' one."

"And then?"

"And then we ran off," they said together.

"Which way?"

"Across the fields back to our bikes, and then back home along the back road, said Liam.

"Do you know what time it was when ye ran off?"

"It was a quarter past eight when we got to our bikes," said Cormac, proudly displaying his digital watch with its large fluorescent dial.

"And ye didn't see or hear anything strange at the castle before ye ran off, did ye? A bang? A crash? A shout?"

"No, nothin' like that, said Liam

"Just that fiddle music," added Cormac.

151

Since Maggie O'Keeffe hadn't (by all accounts) been anywhere near the castle on that fatal evening, any corroborative detail that could be expected from her would be about the relationships, the atmosphere that prevailed in the castle before and after the event. But that could well be of prime importance. There were also some open questions about Celia Ryan's accident.

In any case, Tim was rather looking forward to the chat. The Maggie he remembered from his schooldays could be extremely loquacious, which might now be a very useful trait. She lived in one of the older terrace houses just over the bridge, just a five-minute walk from the Caseys.

When he couldn't hear the bell ring inside the house, he tried the knocker. Well-polished brass, as one might expect. When his second knock failed to elicit a response, he tiptoed over a pruned rose-bed and peeked in the sitting-room window. Nothing. At his third, and louder knock, the next-door neighbour's door opened, and a head covered in curlers stuck out. A dejected-looking Irish setter was whimpering at her feet. She caught it by its collar before it could slip out the door.

"If it's Maggie O'Keeffe you're wanting, you won't find her here. She was taken to hospital yesterday."

"Hospital?"

"Yes, the Regional."

"What's wrong with her?"

"I don't know. She'd collapsed. A good thing her sister rang me yesterday to find out why she hadn't taken the bus to Limerick, as she always does after mass on Sunday. She wasn't answering her phone. I have a key, so I checked. Found her lying there, and called an ambulance."

"She hadn't been attacked, had she?"

"Oh, no, I don't think so. It was probably just the dr..."

"The drink?"

"Me and my big mouth. It's none of my business."

The neighbour clammed up, until Tim reassured her by showing his Garda badge. "Anyway, she did fancy the odd drop. And there was a half-empty whiskey bottle lying on the floor beside her, with Trudy lapping up what had spilled."

"Trudy?"

"Yes. Her dog." She bent to pat the reddish-coloured setter, who had looked up at the sound of his name. "The poor thing hasn't stopped whining ever since."

Chapter 17

There was no point whatsoever in calling to the hospital. When even his second phone-call on Tuesday morning yielded the information that Mrs. Margaret O'Keeffe was still in a coma, Tim saw that he would have to stick to Plan A - no, it was already Plan B - and drive out to Scarriff to interview Niamh Ní Ghráda. And then on to meet Sheila McCarthy. A lucky fluke had placed her on an archaeological site in County Clare, the site being within easy reach of Niamh's lakeside home near Scarriff.

Niamh had insisted on him coming in the morning, while her husband was still at work in Ennis, and her daughter Ciara still at school. Tim had hoped this was so that she would be able to speak freely. In this, it looked for a while as if he was going to be disappointed.

It wasn't that Niamh was in any way obstructive, or reluctant to speak. She had graciously seated him in a wicker chair in the airy conservatory overlooking Lough Derg, and gone to fetch a thermos of coffee and a plate of biscuits from the kitchen.

She was looking good - not quite as relaxed and glowing as when Tim had last seen her on stage at last Eascra concert, but composed. Somehow, both Jeannie and Sean had led him to expect her to be pale and haggard. OK, pale she was, but not haggard. She wore Calvin Klein jeans, loafers, and a green silk blouse. Her auburn hair hung loose, and she kept brushing it back from her face - possibly a nervous gesture, possibly a habitual mannerism. She sat with her back to the magnificent view and smiled as she promised to answer his questions as fully as possible.

But nothing Niamh said added anything to - or cast serious doubt on - what he had already heard from Sean or Jeannie or Richard Murrough, or from those who had heard her playing the fiddle on the evening in question. She added a few details - the names of the tunes she'd been practising ('The Kid on the Mountain' and 'Miss McCleod's Reel'), the kind of tablets she'd taken (just Valium, not proper sleeping pills).

Of course she also admitted to the affair with Sean. How could she get away with denying it? Tim didn't bother, however, to confront her with the rumours of an abortion. If there had been one, she would most certainly not confide in an officer of the law. Abortion was not just illegal in the Republic, but, since 1983, the ban was enshrined in the constitution.

Besides, he couldn't see any relevance, and concentrated instead on the situation at the time in question.

But she stated quite calmly that the affair was over, and had been at the time of P.J.'s death. She conceded that at that point, Sean had not yet quite got around to accepting the fact. Her account of their various meetings tallied exactly with what Tim had heard from Sean.

The possibility of collusion occurred to him. It would only have taken a brief phone-call for Sean to tip her off on the points he had already been forced to concede. But no amount of oblique questioning brought about any deviation from her story. And only on one point did she betray any inner turbulence.

"Can I trust you that none of this will be made public? It would ruin my family ... My husband knows nothing of all this ... and he doesn't need to know, now that it's all over."

Tim had to be honest here. "I hope I won't need to make use of this information in any way. But I can't give you any absolute assurance, if it proves to have some relevance for the investigation ..."

"Oh, I can assure you it hasn't!"

"Then nothing more will need to be said about it. But what about the jealousy aspect? You probably know of the gossip that's been going round, about you flirting with P.J. ..."

"Oh, that's a lot of ... nonsense. Flirting, my foot!" Spots of colour rose to her face.

"You mean it was more than that?"

She seemed to realize that Tim was trying to provoke her into some kind of admission, but did not rise to the bait. Instead she became calmer again.

"No, that is not what I mean. I know I have a reputation for being ... flirtatious, as you say. But all it means is that I like men, and I like being admired." She smiled her little helpless smile at Tim, and he had to acknowledge its potential effect. No man could be quite immune, he thought ... except perhaps for Richard Murrough. He wondered if that was a train of thought worth following up, and decided against it.

"And if you're implying that Sean might have got upset about it, enough to ..." Niamh struggled for words, probably failed to find any appropriate euphemisms, then ploughed on. "Enough to knock poor P.J. off the roof ... Well, I think Sean knows me better than that."

She would say that, wouldn't she?

"Besides, he wasn't there at the time, was he? He came back from the pub and found him lying there."

154

Tim acknowledged that that seemed to be correct. "But what about yourself? You were there."

"I'm not sure if I know what you're getting at."

"Sean may know you well enough not to take your little flirtations seriously, but maybe P.J. didn't. Could he have imagined you were seriously interested in him ...?" Tim was ad-libbing. A scenario had just developed in his mind in which Niamh joins P.J. on the roof, and a series of misunderstood intentions leads to her pushing him over the edge. The mind boggled, but it was just about possible. At least as possible as the scenario involving a scuffle with Murrough. And a shade more plausible that Niamh might then panic instead of declaring it an accident ...

"Are you suggesting that I ...?" She stared at him blankly. He stared back, smiling quizzically, daring her to go on.

"Look, I know it's your job to examine all possibilities ..." She tailed off. Tim wondered if she really believed that. Surely she must realize that it most certainly wasn't the job of a junior cop from a different district to get so involved in this investigation? It was probably just tact, or flattery.

"But I couldn't have done it! I went nowhere near the roof that day, or evening." She paused, as if trying to remember. "I was in the studio, and then in my room, practising. You said yourself that some people heard me."

Tim conceded that this was true, and that she was not exactly a prime suspect. "After all, that honour falls to your brother."

Niamh took a deep breath. "I was wondering when you were going to mention the obvious fact. Your questions so far seem to suggest that you're not quite as convinced of his guilt as the rest of your colleagues!"

"It doesn't matter what I think. As things are looking now, Dónal will be charged with the crime of manslaughter as soon as he is extradited from the UK."

"Manslaughter?"

"Most probably. There's plenty of circumstantial evidence pointing to his presence at the scene of the crime, and also as to motive. But it would be difficult to prove premeditation."

"So he won't be charged with murder?"

"Not unless new evidence turns up pointing in that direction. I suppose there's no point in asking what you think?"

"I know Dónal is not capable of premeditated murder. As regards the possibility of him losing his head turning violent ... well, I honestly don't know."

"Have you had any contact with him since he absconded?"

155

"No."

"What about the evening of the death?"

Was Niamh suddenly looking a bit disconcerted? She had turned away and busied herself with the coffee flask. "If he did come to the castle, he certainly didn't call to see me."

"Any phone-calls? Did he perhaps ring you to say he was coming, or anything about what was worrying him?"

"No." Niamh got up and walked to the window and stared over the lake. Then she turned back to face Tim. "All right, there was one phone-call. It was after ... it had all happened, about 11 o'clock that night. Dónal rang from somewhere on the road, using his car-phone. He said he'd turned up at the castle meaning to challenge Richard Murrough about the suggestion of replacing him in the band. He saw the body on the pavement ... he called it 'the body', he thought P.J. was dead ..." Niamh was beginning to look a bit green in the face. Tim remembered how she was supposed to have reacted to that same sight. "Anyway, he swore that he'd had nothing to do with it. But he thought it better to disappear for a while."

"He didn't say where he was going?"

"No, that would have been foolish. I might have told the cops."

"You said nothing whatsoever of all this to the Kilbrue Gardai!"

She looked away. "True. I couldn't bring myself to. After all, he's my brother. But now that there are witnesses who saw him near the castle, I suppose it can't do him any more harm."

"You realize that withholding such information could be construed as obstruction of justice?"

"I know. That's why I couldn't find a way to come clean about it, after having concealed it so long."

"Well, we may not need to make use of this new information. But there's one thing I still don't understand, namely *why* Dónal phoned you. Wouldn't it have been better from his point of view to keep completely quiet about being anywhere near the castle? After all, he didn't know then that he'd been seen."

Niamh walked to the window again. Without turning around, she said, "He asked me to do something for him."

"Do what?"

"He said that when he saw the ... body, he had first thought of alerting whoever was in the castle. He touched the doorknob. After driving off, he realized too late that he must have left fingerprints on it. So he asked me to wipe it."

"And you did?"

"Yes, I used a bit of detergent to be sure."

Most probably, the same detergent Sean had brought up to remove the stain on the bedroom floor. But that was a minor point. "When did you do this cleaning job?"

"Later that night. Some time after 1 o'clock, I think."

So that was the noise Jeannie had heard. But hadn't she said something about whispered voices? About thinking it had been Niamh *and Sean* ? "Did you meet anyone while you were out of your room?"

"Oh, no!"

Wasn't she being a bit too emphatic here? So what if she'd woken someone, and they'd come to investigate? Could it be that she was still trying hard to play down the relevance of her relationship with Sean? But there didn't seem to be much point in pressing her on that subject. So he changed it.

"By the way, is there any chance of Eascra coming together again? I was quite a fan of you guys!"

"I'm afraid that vessel is smashed for good," she said with a faint smile, playing on the meaning of the band's name. "Nothing but shards left."

Yes, shards. That was the next item on Tim's agenda. Time to break off the interview - which had proved enlightening enough after all - and head for his lunch date with Sheila McCarthy.

The archaeological survey that McCarthy & Co. were now carrying out was on the proposed site of an 'interpretive centre' for a newly-discovered cave complex just north of Ennis, on the edge of the Burren. The Burren being that famously weird County Clare moonscape noted for all sorts of exotic flora and fauna. This eastern edge was less spectacular, but each community wanted its own slice of the tourist pie, and interpretive centres were the order of the day. The environmentalists were up in arms against it, of course, and their hope was that if the environmental impact study didn't put a stop to the project, maybe the archaeological survey would.

All this Tim had gleaned from the press and the other media, not from Sheila McCarthy herself, who - seated in the passenger seat of his car on the way to a highly recommended pizzeria on the outskirts of Ennis - was being studiously impartial on the subject. Declining to express any opinion at all on the rights and wrongs of interpretive centres, she obviously preferred to chat on the impact of Ireland's erratic weather on her line of work.

She had been surprisingly amenable on the phone, in spite of it being a cold call, without the benefit of any introduction or recommendation. As arranged, he had picked her up from the site, where she was immediately recognizable as the only woman there. Otherwise she hardly lived up to any stereotypes Tim may have been holding, whether of 'archaeologist' or 'businesswoman'. A short, somewhat stocky figure in a Barbour jacket and wellingtons, the latter being exchanged for a pair of Hush Puppies before stepping into his car. A few strands of greying fair hair escaped from under a kind of floppy sou'wester. On removing said headgear in the car, she apologized profusely for spattering Tim with raindrops. Her jovial manner probably stood her in good stead at work in the field. She insisted on first-name terms.

Tim ordered a bottle of Chianti to wash down the pizzas. After all he was officially off duty, and feeling generous. As it turned out, Sheila only sipped at one small glass, leaving the greater portion for Tim to finish off. Which he did, with the result that by the end of the meal he was feeling distinctly mellow, and wondering if he would be in a fit state to drive back to Bandon that evening.

While consuming their pizzas (*funghi* and *quattro stagioni*) Tim went over the sequence of events covered by Sheila's original interview with the Kilbrue Gardai. She filled out some detail, like explaining why she hadn't after all followed on to join Jeannie and Sean at the Chinese restaurant that evening.

Apparently there had been too much to write up about the day's findings. After months of finding next to nothing, they had finally come across something that looked like a Neolithic structure - possibly a passage grave, though with the roof stones missing. On the same level they had also found a few rough shards that might possibly also be Neolithic, but would need careful examination to determine.

Word had spread among the inhabitants of the castle, and a few of them had come to take a look, Sean Mills and Georgie Hayes, for example. No, P.J. had not been among them, as far as she knew, though she had not been present all the time.

It had taken her about an hour to write up the findings as she sat in the van. She had finally driven away at about ten to eight. This tallied with what the Casey twins had said. She also agreed with the twins that the fiddle-player (presumably Niamh) had seemed to be moving about in the castle. No, she hadn't seen anyone on the roof: she wouldn't have been able to from the perspective of the car-park.

Now to the first of two sore points. "By the way, did you enter the castle at any stage that evening?"

"Oh, no, I had no reason to."

"Then how do you explain that two witnesses that happened to be in the area saw you walk from the van to the entrance?" He chose not to reveal that these 'witnesses' were the rather untrustworthy Casey twins.

Sheila McCarthy's mouth opened, then shut again. Then she smiled. "Oh, yes, I'd quite forgotten. I did go to the toilet. That's in the basement of the castle."

"I see. Which reminds me - better do the same myself before setting off. That's been well over a half-liter of wine, and roughly the same amount of water!" This was true enough, but it was also a cover for a different plan of action. "If the waiter comes, would you order me an espresso, please."

As expected, there was a pay-phone near the toilets.

He returned to find two tiny cups of coffee already on the table. "I've asked for the bill. We're going Dutch on this, of course."

"No, this is my call." Sheila gave in gracefully.

"Now, I'm sorry, Sheila, but I had to check that story of yours. Georgie Hayes was working out in the gym in the basement at the time in question. I've just spoken to her on the phone. While she was in the gym, only one person passed her on the way to the toilets and that was the student, Tom Kinsella."

Sheila's features stiffened. "Yes, I saw her there. She must have forgotten."

Tim decided to change tack. "There's one more thing I've been puzzling about. That pottery shard that was found in P.J.'s pocket. That obviously came from the site, didn't it?"

"The Kilbrue Gardai have already asked me about that."

"I know. You told them you had no idea how he got it. You were not aware that he had visited the site that day, you said?"

"No, but he might have when I wasn't there."

"It was in a plastic bag, obviously already neatly filed away."

"We always file things away neatly as soon as we find them."

"But this '21/5' - isn't that obviously a date? Long before you say anything interesting was found."

"No, it has to do with stratification ... Look, you wouldn't understand ..."

"Try me."

She said nothing for a while. "I don't need to give you any more details. You told me yourself, you have no official standing in this investigation. And the Kilbrue Gardai were perfectly satisfied with what I told them."

"OK. But I have to tell you that I've already figured this one out. And what it comes to is fraud. Maybe even murder." Tim was chancing his arm, but by the shocked look on Sheila's face, it seemed to have worked. Her previously ruddy complexion had paled dramatically, and now provided little contrast to her wispy, ash-blond hair. "Even if it has nothing whatsoever to do with P.J.'s death, it will not reflect well on McCarthy & Co."

Sheila still said nothing.

"I don't necessarily have to take this little matter of fraud any further if you cooperate in figuring out what happened to P.J. Murphy. It's up to you."

Sheila's stony face finally crumpled, and she was obviously near to tears. "All right, I did go into the castle to look for P.J. You see, I'd found that shard earlier, and stored it in the glove compartment of the van."

"You hadn't reported that find because it wasn't ... convenient?"

"Right. It was found ... I found it when we were excavating the area intended for the car park. Richard Murrough had made it quite clear that that should not be held up by anything."

"Was there some form of bribery involved?"

Sheila's 'no' was barely audible. Tim decided not to labour the point. "OK, go on with your story.

"As it happens, nobody saw me find the shard, the students had just finished work. I didn't want to risk the company being kicked off the job ..."

"Surely he couldn't do that?"

"He'd have found a way. Anyway, I thought it better not to risk any unpleasantness, and stored it away, intending to 'find' it in a more convenient spot."

"And how did you know P.J. had it?"

"He was the only one besides myself who'd been in the van since I'd last seen it there. When he turned up early on the first day of their recordings, it was lashing rain, and he was worried about his guitars. I let him take shelter in the van. No one else could have taken it."

"So you went to his room on the night of his death?"

"Yes, I knew his room was on the top floor, Georgie had once shown me around the castle. I was hoping to simply ask the fellow if he had the shard, and get it back unobtrusively. He had hardly meant to steal it, and I doubt if he was looking to cause trouble."

"But you obviously didn't get it back."

"No, he wasn't in his room. But ..." Though Sheila hesitated, it coincided with a discernible brightening of her face. She was obviously beginning to regain her composure.

"But what?"

"I was really surprised when nobody answered my knock, because I thought he had to be in there. You see, I'd just seen Niamh come out of his room, carrying her violin case."

"Niamh?"

"Yes, I assumed they'd been doing something musical ... though I hadn't heard anything at that point."

"Are you sure it wasn't the studio you saw her coming from?"

"Of course I am. I know which is the door to the studio. We'd been warned often enough not to go near the place when the red light was on ... and as a matter of fact it *was* on as I passed it on my way up that evening."

"Yes, it would be. Mr. Murrough says he was working there at the time. You must have been there just after 7 o'clock."

"A quarter past. A clock chimed in the hallway as I went up the spiral stairs ... just as I reached the top floor and saw Niamh, as a matter of fact."

"Did Niamh see you?"

"I don't think so. I ducked back into the stairwell, the part leading up to the roof ..."

"And went up on the roof?"

"NO!" Word had obviously got around that that was where the unfortunate P.J. had probably been at that moment. "As I told you, I knocked at his door assuming he must be there ..."

"And then?"

"I opened the door - it wasn't locked - and looked inside. There was nobody there. So ... I took a quick look around, anywhere he might have put the plastic bag. Opened a few drawers ..."

"How long did you spend there, about?"

"Not long, I was too nervous, thought he might walk in on me any minute. I must have given up after about five minutes. Maybe ten at most."

"By the way, where did Niamh go after you'd seen her leave P.J.'s room?"

"I don't know. But since I was on the stairs going up, she can only have gone down." Logical enough.

"So then what did you do?"

"I gave up and left the castle. I could hear Niamh fiddling in her room as I passed. Then I drove back to my Limerick hotel."

"When did you hear about P.J.'s death?"

"Next morning, when I turned up at the site."

Having finished their coffees, Tim settled the bill. Then he drove Sheila back to her job, and headed south again. Passing through Ennis, he looked for a public phone, found one, and dialled Niamh's number.

No, no way could she give him a second interview that day. Ciara had just arrived back from school ...

OK, he would just have to ask her over the phone.

"Niamh, I've just spoken to a witness who saw you coming out of P.J.'s room on the evening of his death. You never mentioned that to me."

There was a long silence. He would have given anything to see her face. Finally she answered. "Yes, I ... We were working on a new tune at the time, and I wanted to suggest a counterpoint to a guitar riff of his, so I went up to his room with my fiddle. But he wasn't there."

"So why hadn't you mentioned it before?"

"I'd forgotten all about it."

Funny what people manage to forget.

Though Tim now felt sufficiently sober for the trip to Cork, he prayed he wouldn't run into any of his colleagues on the way.

Chapter 18

As Tim re-entered his shared office at Bandon Garda Station after his extended weekend break, a somewhat shocking sight assailed his eyes. Sergeant Mike Mulligan was bending over Barbara Brennan as she sat at her desk, his brawny right hand resting on her shoulder. He appeared to be absorbed in some report Barbara had been writing, though Tim doubted that that was the object of the exercise. As Mike began to move away, he appeared to give Barbara a playful slap on her tightly-uniformed left hip with his previously unused hand. Though if Tim had been called as a witness, he couldn't have sworn to the latter, so unlikely did the scenario seem.

"What was that all about?" demanded Tim, as soon as Mike was out of earshot.

"Oh, we made a couple of arrests last Saturday night at the Stardust Disco. Ecstasy dealers. The paperwork it brings on is a pain in the ass!"

"I don't mean the paperwork."

"So what do you mean?"

"Jeez, Babs, you ..."

"Don't call me Babs!"

"Don't call you Babs? What's a little nickname by comparison with ...?"

"OK ... Timmy. Maybe I am a bit too touchy about the 'Babs'. It was what my Auntie May used to call me, and I never could stand it!" She seemed determined to avoid the subject.

"But you can stand being pawed all over by that ... jackass?"

"Oh, that jackass, as you call him, really doesn't mean any harm. It's just his manner. They're all like that where he comes from."

"I'll bet. I'd call it full-scale sexual harassment!"

"It's not har*ass*ment, it's *har*assment."

"It's that all right. And it makes it worse that he's a rank above you. I've half a mind to report him."

"Oh, don't do that!" She seemed genuinely worried.

"Why should you care if he gets into a bit of trouble? He's never done either of us any favours, always pulling his little bit of rank ..."

"Look, I just don't want any trouble. Can't you just leave it at that?"

Tim shrugged. If women don't want to stand up for their rights ...

"Have a good weekend? I don't suppose you wasted it on all those interviews you'd been planning!"

"Huh? Why shouldn't I? And what makes you think it would be a waste?"

"Well, they've found your man, haven't they? The fellow who was on the run, I mean. The sexy guitar player. Whatsisname ..."

"Dónal. Yeah, they found him all right. In an IRA safe house in Birmingham."

"So that's it, isn't it? Your dad must be proud of you!" Her smile was so unctuous it was obvious she was teasing him . "Wasn't it you put them on to him? You said all the time he must have done it."

"I never exactly said that. I just pointed out that he was a hot-head with a strong motive, and it needed looking into. And as it turned out, Dónal *was* seen near the scene of the crime."

"If it was a crime."

"Quite. And even if it was, the evidence against said Dónal is still rather flimsy. Purely circumstantial. Needs backing up."

"And you think the Kilbrue crowd can't manage the backing up?"

"Oh, I'm sure they can, Only too well, if I know them at all."

"Spoken like a man with a strong police background."

"Oh, I'm not suggesting they'd manipulate the evidence, it's just ..."

"Just what?"

"Well, now that they've started to build up a half-way respectable case, I wouldn't put it past them to put on their blinkers and not see anything that points in an inconvenient direction."

"And what direction might that be? Are you suggesting that someone else may have done it? Or that maybe it was suicide after all?"

"I really don't know. What I do know is that if Dónal *is* innocent - and I'm not saying he is - I couldn't rest easy knowing I contributed to putting him behind bars!"

"Hmm. Maybe your dad won't be so pleased with you after all."

"You can say that again. He let me tag along when one of his Detective Inspectors was interviewing the Murroughs over that vandalism I told you about. But that was arranged before Dónal was tracked down. Now I'm the loose cannon that might wreck their case. I can't expect any more favours."

"But you're going to plough ahead regardless?"

"I suppose I'll have to."

"So what did you come up with over the weekend that's causing all this soul-searching?"

"Nothing decisive. But lots of questions. I'm getting the impression that everybody involved has got something to hide."

"Everybody?"

"Well, almost everybody. As regards the band, the only one who seems completely on the level is Jeannie Staunton. And even she was a bit cagey for a while, careful not to spread any damaging gossip about the others."

"Hah! That's often the best way of spreading it. Are you sure she's in the clear? No hidden motives for wanting your man dead?"

"None that I could find. I may have already filed it away under 'Cases Pending'".

"What?" It took Barbara about two seconds to twig that Mike Mulligan had just stridden into the room, heading purposefully for the large metal filing cabinet in the corner. "Oh, yes, here it is, thanks." Tim busied himself with the pile of papers on his own desk until Mike retreated.

He then went over the details of Jeannie's cast-iron alibi. "Besides, she's the only one who seemed to care a whit for the fellow. At least she went to his funeral."

"That could have been for show."

"Sure. For a while I harboured a few suspicions about her ... girl friend, or partner, or whatever you say."

"The one with the sledge-hammer?"

"Oh. I told you about her, did I? Sorry, I'm losing track." He now remembered Barbara's prim reaction ("I'm not well up on celebrity gossip!") to the revelation about Jeannie's sexual orientation. He'd been somewhat relieved to hear he wasn't the only one out of the loop in that respect.

"Anyway, Kilbrue have checked Anne O'Halloran's alibi, and it really is rock-solid. She was at an exhibition in Edinburgh all that week, and besides, no one has come up to say they saw her anywhere near the scene of the crime. It really looks like both of them are in the clear."

"If I remember rightly, the bit of juicy gossip that Ms Staunton let slip out concerned the affair between two other band members - right?"

"Yes. Niamh Ní Ghráda and Sean Mills. The fiddler and the piper."

"So did you manage to confront them on the matter, like you said you would?"

"Oh, they both admitted to it. They had to, since they knew Jeannie'd been talking. But both claimed it had been all over, even on the day in question."

"And how convincing did that sound?"

"Not very, especially on Sean's side. There could be a strong motive there. The trouble is, Sean seems to have a fairly good alibi. He was with Jeannie in the pub up to about ten to nine, then he left to walk back to the castle, where he found P.J. on the pavement, and raised the alarm at 9.20."

"And does it really take a half an hour to walk that distance?"

"About that. I tested it, and did it in 25 minutes. Actually, Sean must have done the same, since he says he attempted a bit of heart massage before raising the alarm."

"Maybe he jogged back in time to climb up to the castle roof and do the deed ..."

"Having found Niamh and P.J. in a compromising situation? Just about possible, I suppose, even though Sean doesn't strike me as being all that athletic. He certainly isn't in the clear yet."

"And hey, wasn't there something about a stolen bike?"

"Yes, and it was taken from outside the pub. Very suspicious. But they've now pinned that on someone else."

"Hmm. So what about Niamh?"

"Ah, yes, Niamh. She may seem an unlikely killer, but she does *not* have an alibi for the time - beyond having been heard practising her fiddle practically non-stop."

"Couldn't that have been a recording?"

"Apparently not. Anybody who reported hearing it is adamant that it was live - stopping and starting, moving about in her typical style, etc."

"They could still be mistaken."

"Sure. But besides, there were no recorders found anywhere in the castle - apart from the studio, of course, where they had full professional equipment. Nobody needed to carry around anything as primitive as a tape-recorder. No, the real problem with her faulty alibi is that we still don't have a precise time for P.J.'s fall from the roof. She could have been fiddling her heart out for hours, then joined P.J. on the roof after all the potential listeners had left, and for whatever reason, knocked him over the edge."

"Maybe he'd interpreted her flirting as something more serious and got brushed off in a more brutal than usual fashion."

"I thought of that, yes."

"But as regards the time frame, surely they've narrowed it down a bit by now?"

"Not much. It could have been any time between the last of the archaeology crowd departing, which was about ten to eight, and Sean raising the alarm."

"That makes it about an hour and a half."

"Right. Maybe we can chop a quarter of an hour off the beginning, since Kilbrue have come up with another pair of witnesses who were on the scene up to just after eight o'clock. They would surely have heard something if it had happened while they were there."

"Maybe they did, and aren't admitting to it. Who might those witnesses be, anyway?"

"The boys who have admitted to spraying slogans on the castle walls."

"You spoke to them, too?"

"Yes."

"And how believable did they seem?"

Tim shrugged. "As believable as any 14-year old kids after they've been caught doing some mischief. Which is not very, I suppose. But the one I'm most suspicious of is the elder sister, Róisín."

"You think she put them up to it?"

"At the very least. She's a member of the local protest group who objected to Murrough's radical reconstruction. But I also have a strong hunch she must have been on the scene as well. Her story for the evening makes no sense at all."

Tim brought his colleague up to speed on the finding of the bike with Róisín's fingerprints all over it. He then recounted the joy-riding story, which was sounding more unlikely at each telling.

"Could she have done it? Killed your man, I mean. Maybe she mistook him for Murrough!"

"Well, strange as it may seem, that's who the kids thought they'd seen on the roof! Unlike the other witnesses who saw P.J. up there, they'd never met either of them, had only seen pictures of Murrough in the local newspaper."

"So could she have done it? Physically, I mean, and time-wise."

"Well, I suppose she could have got into the castle, the main door wasn't locked. But she's only a wisp of a girl, would hardly have dared to tackle a grown man single-handed!"

"Maybe she had help?"

"Well, there's a boyfriend, and he's active in the same protest group. What's more, he's strongly suspected of a nasty bit of sabotage earlier this year. An old lady was injured ..."

"That's it, then."

"No, I'm told he has an alibi for the evening of September 30. He was playing in a hurling match in Limerick. Though I didn't get to interview him."

"Hmm. But maybe Róisín *could* have managed it on her own. Thinking she was dealing with a blind man might have given her the courage to tackle him."

Tim was impressed. This was an avenue of speculation he had not yet ventured down. "True enough." He considered the scenario for a moment. "But if Róisín *had* entered the building, she would have left some traces of her presence. Fingerprints, for example, since she was so careless with the bike. She would definitely have left some on the ... "Jeez, Babs, I've just thought of something!"

Barbara grimaced at the hated nick-name, but swallowed any protest.

"The doorknob. It had been wiped clean."

"You mean by the cleaning lady?"

"No, she was given the following day off, told to hold her fire until the forensic squad had done their thing. It was Niamh."

"Niamh?"

He recounted the explanation he had finally got for the noises Jeannie had heard in the night.

"So she could also have unwittingly been doing Róisín a favour as well as her brother."

"Yes."

For a moment, both Barbara and Tim gave some of their attention to the paperwork on their respective desks. In Tim's case it was definitely just for show. Mike Mulligan had made another foray into their office. After his retreat, it was Barbara who resumed the conversation.

"Does all this mean you've dropped your idea that Murrough himself may have done it?"

Tim pulled at his wiry hair to indicate frustration. "I may have to. I just can't make the pieces of the story fit together in any convincing way. But I'm not there yet. I just can't bring myself to think that their past connections are nothing but a coincidence."

"Connections?"

Tim briefly summed up what he had learned about the two men's shared San Francisco past: P.J. being kicked out of The Hawks, the song-writing grudge, plus the intriguing titbit that the band had been working on an instrumental version of that same song in the studio the day P.J. died. But also Murrough's disarming frankness on the matter.

Barbara suggested that this may have been mere bluster, to cover up a real murder motive. "He wouldn't have wanted P.J. finally putting in a claim for his share of the royalties."

"I don't see how he could have, at this late stage. Not very convincingly anyway. All Murrough would need to do would be to play down P.J.'s contribution. He probably wouldn't deny it completely, since he's admitted it to me, and there may be other witnesses from the past ... If it came to a court case, Murrough would probably offer to pay a derisive sum in settlement, and that's off his back. It certainly wouldn't be worth risking murder for."

Barbara shrugged. One more nice theory knocked on the head.

"But there's one more really weird connection."

"And what might that be?"

"His name. He's really a Murphy. Murrough's just a fancy version!"

"Oh. ... So are you thinking he might be related to the victim?"

"The thought crossed my mind."

Barbara laughed it loud. "Then maybe he's related to the makers of Murphy's stout. Or to me."

"You?"

"Yes, why not? My mother's maiden name was Murphy. There's a lot of Murphys around."

"That's what the man said. He wanted something more distinguished."

"I can understand that, especially if he's as vain and self-centred as you described. You know what my Auntie May once told me ...?

"The same Auntie May who used to call you 'Babs'?"

"The very one." Barbara scowled. "But she's also an amateur genealogist. What she doesn't know about the Murphy clan isn't worth knowing ... Anyway, she's fond of pointing out that 'Murphy' is the most numerous Irish name of all."

This didn't sound encouraging. But maybe the aunt could be useful ... Tim had dutifully passed on the hint about the identity of name to Kilbrue, suggesting that they check for any family connection. But he wasn't confident they would try very hard, now that they were sure they'd got their man. "Do you think your aunt could be asked to do us a favour?"

"A favour? You mean track down a family connection?" Tim's grin told her she'd got it in one. "It'd be a tall order. But she likes doing that sort of thing. So write out all the details you've got: dates of birth, who emigrated from where when, etc. etc., and I'll pass it on to her." A tall order indeed. He would need to consult Helen Murphy to find out what she knew of her late husband's family. And of course Uncle Fred of the NYPD. "Actually, I think she'd be tickled pink to help nail a murderer!"

"I'm not saying Murrough's a murderer..."

169

"But he hasn't got an alibi." Barbara had once carefully studied Tim's chart, which he now pulled out of a drawer.

"No, he hasn't got an alibi. He was in the castle up to 8.30 by his own account, working in the studio."

"Alone?"

"Apart from one visit from Niamh, to discuss something about a fiddle track."

"And she backs up his story?"

"Yes. And what's more, the phone-call he made to ask her down is on the phone company's records. Apparently it's easy to check mobile phone calls."

"Good to know. I've just got myself one. Must remember not to use it to plan a murder."

"Yeah, better not. But the phone-call, and Niamh's half-hour visit, still don't put Murrough in the clear. There was plenty of time otherwise. If only I could work out the logistics of a blind man managing to knock a sighted, able-bodied man off the roof!"

"What about his wife? She's able-bodied and athletic, isn't she? She could have helped him out."

"Hard to see how. She was at home in the cottage from 7.15, preparing a meal and watching TV. The Kilbrue Gardai checked her story. She was able to give a fairly detailed account to them of the obscure Channel 4 program she'd been watching, as well as the RTE News after she'd switched over to it at nine. She'd made two phone-calls in the commercial breaks, both from her mobile phone. Apparently they haven't got a regular phone in the house yet."

Barbara shrugged. The slowness of the phone company was legendary. "Both calls checked, of course?"

"Of course. One was to her mother in Galway, and the other to the secretary of a theatre group she's involved in in Limerick. The third call didn't need to be checked. It was to the Kilbrue Gardai at 9.26 precisely."

"So she's in the clear."

"Looks like it."

"Thank heaven for small mercies. You're still left with ..." She started counting on the fingers of her left hand: "Murrough himself, Sean, Niamh, Dónal, and the girl protester ...what's her name..."

"Róisín Casey."

"That makes five suspects."

"You can add one more: Sheila McCarthy."

"And who she when she's at home?"

"It's who she is when she's *not* at home that counts here, She's an archaeologist, and the co-owner of a commercial operation doing archaeological surveys."

"Oh, the one in charge of the dig. Yeah, but what makes her a suspect?"

"The fact that P.J. had pinched an archaeological artefact from the glove-compartment of her van."

"And why should he do that?"

"No idea. Curiosity maybe." He went over Sheila McCarthy's story of the missing Neolithic shard, and its potential for embarrassment at the very least, and serious damage to her professional reputation at worst.

"I see. So you're suggesting she went after P.J. to get the evidence back ..."

"Or to silence him. Though she's only admitted to the former. And that only because she'd been seen entering the castle."

"Seen by whom?"

"The Casey twins. The boys who sprayed the castle walls."

"Oh. But in any case, she obviously didn't manage to get the thing back."

"No. Her story is that she searched P.J.'s room, failed to find it, and then went away. But the interesting thing is that before going into his room, she'd seen Niamh leaving it."

"What? So that brings us full circle. Back to Niamh and Sean. My head's spinning!"

Tim admitted to a similar state of confusion.

For once, a silent interlude devoted to paperwork was not attributable to Mike Mulligan's baneful presence. It was finally broken by a remark from Barbara. "What about all the background dirt you were hoping to get from the cleaning lady?"

"Jeez, Barbara, thanks for reminding me. I've got to make a phone-call. The cleaning lady's in hospital, I wasn't able to speak to her."

"So you're ringing the hospital?"

"No, Kilbrue Station. I was warned off contacting the hospital directly."

"I thought you said you weren't going to get any more help from Kilbrue either!"

"Not from the old man. But one of his Detective Inspectors promised to give me the low-down."

"And what are you expecting him to tell you? Is it something suspicious, something connected with the case?"

"I don't think so. Maggie O'Keeffe is known to be an alcoholic. She was taken to hospital on Sunday in an alcoholic stupor. Kilbrue are checking the circumstances just in case." He didn't bother to point out that his prospective informant was a she, not a he. That might have brought on some banter on the sexual politics of police-work, which seemed to be a sensitive topic at the moment.

"So maybe something to do with the case drove her to over-indulge?"

"Maybe. Listen, Babs, I'm not supposed to be spending so much time on this, so would you do me a favour? I want you to go out and chat up Sergeant Mike to keep him off the phone. Did you know he often listens in on other people's phone-calls?"

Barbara seemed a bit startled, but obligingly selected a suitable page from those strewn on her desk, and made for the door. "Yes, I know. He does that."

Since he was starting the week on the late day shift, it was already half past two, and DI Kathleen Smith may well have gone off duty. Luckily, she was still in the office, and had two items of information for him.

Maggie O'Keeffe had come out of her coma, but was being kept under observation, and was not yet available for interview. There was a preliminary bulletin on her physical state, which, however, contained so much medical jargon that Tim asked for it to be faxed to him. (He would have to stand guard over the fax machine.)

The other concerned the Murroughs' attempt to identify the voices that had made the nuisance calls, some of which had been quite virulent ('Death to the Invaders!' etc.) The couple had kept their appointment at the Garda station that morning, and from a selection of ten recorded voices (five male, five female), had separately and effortlessly picked out two as sounding very close to what they remembered hearing. They were the voices of Róisín Casey and her boyfriend, Aidan Flynn.

Chapter 19

The waiting room was only about half full. But for every patient summoned to the doctor's presence, another one would arrive. It was impossible to know how many of them had appointments, but Tim feared it was probably the majority. When he turned up at the reception desk at 10.30, - without an appointment, of course - and expressed a preference for Dr. Brid rather than her colleague (it was a joint practice), he was told he would have to be prepared for a long wait.

It was now approaching noon, the official end of morning office hours. At least there wouldn't be any more new arrivals. Knowing he wouldn't be satisfied with the usual spread of magazines, he had come armed with the *Irish Times,* which also served as additional protection for the large brown envelope he was carrying. By now he had exhausted the national and international news, the sports pages and the Letters to the Editor, and was well into the cryptic crossword.

He just had to be out of here by one o'clock, or he wouldn't make it back to Bandon in time for the start of his afternoon shift. He had asked Barbara Brennan to cover for him in case of any delay, but didn't want to push his luck.

Tim was finding it hard to concentrate on the crossword. The possibility of a family connection between the two Murphys had been exercising his mind ever since he had activated Barbara's Aunt May on the subject. That had been only yesterday, and it had already caused one near-sleepless night trying to figure out what such a connection might mean - if it existed. Two phone calls had come up with the basic data to work on: Jack Murphy (Murrough's father) had emigrated to New York from Nenagh, County Tipperary in 1956; P.J. had known of an ancestor called Cornelius Murphy (from Dungarvan, County Waterford) who had entered the USA through Ellis Island in 1893. It didn't sound promising ...

Tim's fellow-patients had now dwindled to three - or rather, two, to be optimistic, since the rather addled young mother with the pasty-looking toddler probably counted as one. 'Patient' - what an appropriate word, Tim thought. And wasn't there something in the Down clues about putting up with delays? Yes, there it is, 17. down: *Irishman that is not, in short, calmly enduring delay in treatment.* Of course - PAT+IE+NT! And it fits! So 17. across starts with a P - *Where the preacher may make a mess of it*:

PULP+IT. Which leaves only 28. across, now with E as third letter: *The artist's forte is to score with this technique.* Of course, an anagram - F+SCORE = FRESCO - why didn't he see that one before?

"Mr. O'Driscoll, please." The mother with the cranky toddler glared at him, though it was hard to see why. Tim had definitely been waiting longer. Maybe she had an appointment with Dr. John for 11.30 or so, and thought Tim was being unjustly favoured. Tim smiled back at her, and was ushered down the corridor to Dr. Brid O'Driscoll's consulting room.

"Tim!" she nearly shrieked. "What the hell are you doing here? Don't you have any doctors back east?"

"Sorry Brid, but this seems to be the only way I can catch you this week. I'm on late shift until Friday. and I may need some medical advice before the weekend."

"So what's wrong with you?"

"My mind's distracted and confused." (Why the hell was he quoting an old Simon and Garfunkel song?) "No, seriously, it's not me, it's ... someone that may have some connection to a case I'm working on." He pulled out a page from the brown envelope. It was, in effect, a photocopy of a fax of a fax, so its legibility left something to be desired. "What do you make of this?"

Brid squinted at it. "I see you've covered over the name in question before photocopying this." It was his somewhat half-hearted gesture towards confidentiality. "But knowing you, you'll probably let slip sooner or later who this is all about." She looked at her brother quizzically, but he just shrugged his shoulders. She scanned the document.

"For starters, this is from Limerick Regional Hospital, so would it be correct to assume that this has something to do with that Castle Green case? Dad mentioned on the phone yesterday that you were nosing in on the investigation."

"Is that what he said? OK. I admit it. But please don't let him know I got my hands on this." He pointed to the photocopy. "It wasn't supposed to go beyond Kilbrue Garda Station, but I persuaded someone there to fax it to us in Bandon."

"And why were you so interested?"

"It's someone I wanted to interview last weekend, but who was taken to hospital before I turned up."

"A suspect in the case?"

"No, just someone who worked at the castle ... who might have some background information, I thought."

174

"And you think her hospitalization might be suspicious in some way? Foul play, as you say."

"Well, there's an off-chance. Even Kilbrue thought it worth checking out. By the way, I never said it was a she!"

"Well, there's a reference to a previous pregnancy further down the page - in the summarized case history. I imagine that clinches it."

Tim looked sheepish. "OK, you'll have her name out soon. Anyway, what do you think?"

"Well, they certainly haven't found any indication of foul play. It looks like a clear case of alcohol-induced coma."

"Yeah. I saw that they'd checked for barbiturates and what I think are tranquillizers." Tim pointed to the reference, and Brid nodded. "And the tests came out negative."

"They were probably speculating on a suicide attempt. Barbiturates and alcohol are a popular combination for such purposes."

"But couldn't the coma have been caused by some other toxic agent?"

"Possibly. But they'd need to know what to look for, to test for it. And if there are no symptoms pointing in another direction ... By the way, do you know anything of the circumstances in which she was found?"

"Lying on the floor with a spilled bottle of whiskey beside her."

"Need I say more?"

"But there *are* some references to other symptoms. Now I think I know what 'advanced cirrhosis of the liver' means ..."

"A scarring of the liver tissue probably due to years of alcohol abuse."

"But what the hell is 'haemochromatosis'?"

"It also affects the liver. But it's basically a metabolic disturbance, usually genetic, that causes an excessive uptake of iron from food and other sources, and resulting deposits in the liver and elsewhere. Alcohol makes it much worse, by the way."

"Now how did they hit on this haemo-whatever business?"

"You've made a fair point there. In a case like this, the differential diagnosis is very difficult ..."

"Huh?"

"Telling apart the effects of alcohol from the abnormal iron metabolism. It can be a chicken-and-egg situation. And there is such a thing as iron poisoning which can, in extreme cases, cause coma. But as regards hitting on the idea in the first place, some observant person must have noted some abnormal pigmentation of the skin."

"What kind of pigmentation?"

175

"Usually greyish patches, especially on the face and neck. Anyway, they've obviously done some tests to check the suspicion." Brid pointed at a reference to 'serum ferritin levels'. "Though to be perfectly honest, alcohol can also mess up the results of those tests."

"So they're still not sure?"

"No, but the case history does seem to clinch it. Look, there had been a previous incidence of hospitalization some twenty-five years back."

"That's the reference to her pregnancy?"

"Yes. Apparently she'd taken iron supplements, as she must have thought all pregnant women are suppose to do ..."

"To stave off anaemia?"

"Correct. Only in her case, she not only didn't need it, but couldn't take any more. She must have collapsed, if she needed to be taken to hospital on that occasion. You don't happen to know if she was already drinking that far back?"

"No idea."

"Is the lady still in a coma, by the way?"

"No, she's just come out of it. But they're not allowing police visitors just yet. I'm told there'll be a chance at the weekend ..."

"I doubt it. But if you do get to speak to her ..."

"What then?"

Brid hesitated. "Let me ask first, does she have any relatives?"

"I'm told she's got a son in England, and a sister in Limerick."

"Well, it's usually no good telling habitual drinkers they should lay off the booze. But if that sister in Limerick were to keep an eye on her, maybe get her into Alcoholics Anonymous, she might have a chance. Otherwise ... well, she may not last long."

"I'll see what I can do."

"It really is quite disgraceful the way people in this country turn a blind eye to the problem of alcoholism." Brid was really getting into her stride on what seemed to be one of her pet topics. "The people around this lady have probably been just shaking their heads and smiling indulgently at her secret tippling. Just imagine the fuss if she'd taken to smoking pot, a relatively harmless drug!"

How very true. Tim began to pack away the photocopied bulletin, and in doing so, was reminded of his second reason for making the trip out to his sister's office. "Brid, there's one more thing I've been waiting for a chance to ask you about." He fumbled in the envelope and pulled out the plastic folder that was keeping the other scrap of paper from falling apart.

"What do you make of this? It was found in the victim's papers, and is apparently the main reason he got out of serving in Vietnam."

She took the transparent folder and scrutinized it.

"Maybe you can decipher it better than I can. Sounds like a skin disease to me. Could it really be something that might have disabled him from military service?"

Brid looked at her brother sceptically. "It sure would!" she finally answered. "It means he was going blind."

Now this was the last thing Tim had expected. "Blind?" was all he could manage to say.

"Yes, blind. *Retinitis pigmentosa*, it says here. It's a degenerative disease of the retina, of genetic origin. As it says here, it's progressive and incurable. So if the victim was diagnosed with it in ..." - she checked the date - "...1961, his field of vision would already have been considerably narrowed down by ... When was Vietnam?"

"He got out of the draft in 1970."

"They sure wouldn't have wanted him with a gun in his hand or piloting a helicopter by then!"

"But ... But P.J. Murphy wasn't blind."

"No?"

There was a long pause.

"Richard Murrough is."

Chapter 20

Cathy Cronin was seriously peeved. Not only had her previously attentive boyfriend absented himself over the course of the long weekend, forcing her to invent excuses for him at Gráinne's Halloween party, but he was now trying to back out of next Saturday's planned trip to Dublin for the Van Morrison concert. She had slammed down the receiver in disgust when he rang with the news at the beginning of work that morning. Something about visiting someone in hospital. Of course it had to do with that Kilbrue case he'd got himself involved in. With regard to which Tim seemed to have lost all sense of proportion.

Sure, he had turned up Tuesday night on a flying visit, as he called it. Obviously thinking she ought to be grateful for whatever couple of hours he could manage to spare from the investigation. As if she didn't know damn well that what he was now doing amounted to free-lancing, way above the call of duty now that the case was officially solved.

It had never had much to do with Bandon Garda Station in the first place. Far from furthering his career (something she might have approved of even if she had little understanding for his weird career choices), he was now probably hindering it. Why Tim couldn't just bask in the glory of having given the decisive tips leading to the arrest of Dónal Ó Gráda was beyond her.

On Tuesday night he had been full of excitement about some new revelations concerning a whole host of suspects. But it hadn't become clear to her what all these new facts added up to, and she doubted if Tim was making any more sense of them himself.

He had at least graciously acknowledged that her internet research had enabled him to hold his own in conversation with the record producer Richard Murrough last Saturday night – when he should have been at Gráinne's with her, of course. But the Murroughs weren't the only possible suspects, apparently; he had also been rabbiting on about this dodgy archaeologist whom he had caught out in some little deception. Also about those kiddy vandals, and his conviction that their elder sister may have been on the scene, up to no good. Apparently it was her unconvincing story about pinching the student's bike that made him smell a rat, though the rat in question still remained to be caught.

Here Cathy had to remind Tim that it was *her* conversation with the archaeology students in Ryan's pub that had brought the matter of the stolen bike to light. So if anything significant were to emerge from that tangle of loose ends – which she doubted - she expected to get some credit for it. "Oh, yeah, sure" was all he had said to that mild protest.

And now this. No way was she going to miss out on the Van Morrison concert. Of course it would be no problem to get rid of the tickets, if she wanted to. The concert had been sold out for weeks. Peter in Accounts, for one, had even put a small ad in the *Cork Examiner* in the hope of getting some on the black market. And there had been several other such ads. But at most, she only intended to get rid of one.

Not only was Cathy a serious fan of the singer in question, but this concert fitted in very neatly with two other Dublin dates - her kid sister's 21st birthday party on Sunday night, and a business meeting on Monday morning. As regards the latter, she had tried in vain to interest Tim in how important it was for her own career development. Peter might conceivably show more interest. He was a bit shy and (to be honest) boring, but if he was also a fan of Van the Man there must be some hidden depths there. Maybe he would be glad to get just the one ticket. He wasn't married, and as far as she knew, didn't have a regular girlfriend.

She rang Peter's extension. As expected, he jumped at the chance. You could even say he was over the moon, so effusive were his thanks. He had long ago given up hope of getting a ticket, and now … "Gee, thanks, Cathy, I don't know how to thank you!" By shutting up she thought.

Before she could get back to the job in hand - de-bugging a new piece of custom-made software for an important client – her phone rang again. It was Tim. Saying he'd changed his mind, and could make the concert after all. Explaining he'd even managed to swap shifts with someone and take Monday morning off, so that they could travel back together. And asking – after her silence indicated something was wrong – why she wasn't delighted, now that everything was hunky-dory after all.

Hunky-dory! What a word to use!

"Well, there's just the little matter that I've promised your ticket to a friend of mine."

A brief silence, then, "OK, let her have it."

"Him."

"OK, let him have it. I'll come along anyway and do something else for the time. It can still be a good weekend, with your sister's party and all."

Something fishy there. "Look, Tim, you're putting me in an impossible situation! It wouldn't work like that. ... OK, I'll try to explain to Peter that it was all a misunderstanding. But you've got to promise me you're not going to back out again!"

"I promise."

"You're sure?"

"Sure I'm sure."

She sighed, hung up, and rang Peter's extension for the second time in ten minutes.

Tim realized he had seriously put his foot in it, and would need to tread very carefully over the weekend. He could not possibly now explain that his change of heart was mainly due to the diminishing prospects of being allowed access to Maggie O'Keeffe, still under observation at the Regional Hospital. The other factor being his diary entry for November 8, indicating the prospective return from Katmandu (or wherever) of a certain *Irish Times* reporter.

Of course that matter could have been dealt with over the phone. As he had just now - the second time in two days - checked a detail of P.J.'s past with Helen Murphy. With an indecisive result. (No, as far as she was aware, her husband had never lived in New York, though he did have an aunt in Brooklyn.) But given the choice, Tim always favoured the face-to-face confrontation.

The fact that November 8 was a Sunday was only mildly puzzling. It was common knowledge that daily newspapers worked Sundays, the only remaining question being whether a features writer like Dervla Cassidy would be at her desk on that day. Colin Leahy had given him his colleague's home number as well as her office extension. Either he would be able to arrange a meeting for Sunday evening (and somehow manage to slip away from the party), or for Monday morning (to coincide with Cathy's business meeting). The latter being by far the easier option under the circumstances.

Cathy had been somewhat surprised at Tim's professed interest in attending her sister Deirdre's twenty-first. She herself was attending only out of a sense of family duty, since both of her parents had opted out, saying they didn't feel up to travelling from Tralee. There had been a bit of family friction involved, the parents saying they would have been quite willing to finance a big do at Benner's Hotel, and Deirdre replying "Thanks, but no thanks!" Her new Dublin friends were obviously more important to her than anybody back home in Tralee. Those old school friends that mattered were also studying or working in Dublin anyway.

As a result, the party was a low-budget affair in Deirdre's shared flat in Rathmines. That their parents would not have blended well with this scene was putting it mildly. Looking around, Cathy estimated that she and Tim were probably the oldest of the guests.

The people from the upstairs flat had been apparently been invited, and their space annexed for the purpose of depositing coats, etc. Probably for some other purposes, too, which would emerge in the course of the evening. With the maturity of her twenty-eight years Cathy was beginning to look indulgently at the wild-oats-sowing of the younger generation.

The first hour or so of the party was pretty grim. First of all, Tim seemed totally distracted, and was making absolutely no effort to circulate and be sociable. The first thing he did on arrival was to ask to use the phone. Apparently he was trying to contact Colin Leahy, an old college friend of his. He said it wasn't all that important, but if so, why did he keep trying?

She herself did put in an effort, but not to much avail. For one thing, talking about last night's Van Morrison concert didn't cut much ice with these kiddies – OK, teens and young twens. "I wouldn't cross the road to see that old codger!" was one comment. "Isn't he the one who looks like a bank clerk?" was another, from a girl who she knew to be one of Deirdre's flatmates. Though the latter remark would honestly have had to be answered in the affirmative, it totally missed the point. Cathy changed tack and asked the flatmate about the journalism course that she and Deirdre were doing, but the girl was already eyeing a rather attractive dark-haired boy at the other side of the room and didn't seem to understand her question. Conversation was difficult anyway against the over-amplified music, so Cathy gave up and went to get her glass re-filled.

Through the doorway to the hall she noticed Tim standing with his back turned to her. So he had found someone to talk to at last, someone of their own generation, it seemed. No, on closer inspection Cathy had to revise her opinion that she and Tim were the grey eminences of the party. The person Tim was deep in conversation with was at least in her mid-thirties. This needed checking out.

Tim had been highly frustrated at his failure to contact Dervla Cassidy. At her home number he kept getting her answering machine, and at the office he had been told that Dervla had been in earlier in the day, but was now off work and wouldn't be in again until Monday morning.

His last attempt had been from the pay-phone in the downstairs hallway of this rather run-down Georgian house now converted to student flats. At least it was relatively quiet down here. The ground floor apparently consisted of bedsits, the occupants of which had either joined the party in the larger flat on the first floor, or gone elsewhere to avoid the din. He left a message this time on the answering machine, requesting Dervla to contact him at his city centre hotel. At least Cathy's business meeting ensured that they had decent accommodation.

The party was now in full swing, but it wasn't really his scene. Cathy, however, seemed to be enjoying herself, so it was probably a bit premature to suggest that they leave. Glumly cradling his rum-and-coke, he retreated into the hall of the flat, where the decibel level was somewhat more tolerable than in the living room (currently Madonna, 'Who's That Girl?' - not a favourite at any level of volume). It was also a degree less crowded. There was a phone there, too, and he thought it might be worth trying once more. He picked up the receiver.

"It's not working. You'll have to use the pay-phone downstairs."

The speaker was a tall woman, probably in her late thirties. That in itself made her stand out from the rest of the company, but she was also quite strikingly dressed, in a black silk blouse and pants with lots of clunky silver jewellery, and her frizzy hair had (had been given?) a reddish tinge.

"Oh, thanks. But it's not important. The person I'm trying to reach probably isn't home yet. Are you a … er … relative, by the way?"

"You mean because you don't think I belong in this rather youthful social scene?" She didn't wait for him to come up with an answer. "No, it's just that I was Deirdre's mentor when she was doing her first spell of practical work experience at the newspaper I work for."

"And what newspaper would that be?"

"The *Irish Times*."

"Oh."

"And what about yourself?"

Fair question. "Oh, I'm with Deirdre's elder sister. By the way, if you work for *the Irish Times*, maybe you know Colin Leahy?"

"You mean, in the Sports department? Yeah, I know Colin. What's the connection?"

"We were at college together."

"And what line of work are you in?"

"I'm a cop." Tim was still trying out varying ways of answering that question.

"I didn't know Colin went to - cop school." Her smile went some way towards taking the sting out of that one.

"He didn't. We both did science at UCC, and we were on the college cycling team together. It was only later I went to cop school, as you call it." Tim supposed it was as good a term as any for the Garda College at Templemore.

"And have you kept it up, the cycling I mean?"

"Nothing competitive. I did a bit at Templemore, but now it's just recreational. I do still own a pretty good racing bike, though." He was already running out of small talk.

The frizzy-haired lady spun it out by referring to Stephen Roche's marvellous win in the Tour de France that year. Tim countered by relating how he had watched the exciting finish behind the locked doors of O'Sullivan's pub in Crookhaven during the so-called 'holy hour' Sunday afternoon closing time. A risky manoeuvre for a Garda on probation, but having cycled out from Bandon towards Mizen Head, it had been the only way to avoid missing the finish. They both recalled the RTE commentator's immortal words as Stephen hurtled down the Champs Elysées: *Nothing can stop him now! Nothing can stop him now! ... Oh, anything could stop him now ...* , and frizzy-hair had to control a fit of giggles. "I don't think I got your name, by the way."

"Tim."

"Dervla." Dervla? Not exactly a common name ...

"Not - Dervla Cassidy, by any chance?" He was about to add, "late of Katmandu", but thought better of it.

"Oh, have you read some of my stuff?" She seemed genuinely pleased.

"Oh sure." He thought fast. Apart from the Murrough interview, what else did he remember reading under that by-line? "Mostly travel, isn't it?"

"Travel and Lifestyle, yes. And occasionally I'm let loose on celebrity interviews."

There was his opening. "Wasn't it you did that interview with Richard Murrough?"

"Murrough?" She crinkled her brow, as if trying to place the name. Apparently Murrough wasn't that much of a celebrity. "Oh, the record producer, yeah, sure. That was some time last spring, or early summer I think."

"Published in June."

"Right. Did it impress you so much, or have you some special interest in the guy?"

"Both, really. Look, I don't know how to put this … When you get home you're going to find a rather odd message on your answering machine. You're the person I've been trying to reach on the phone all day."

She looked at him suspiciously, as if this were some new pick-up line.

"Seriously. If you've been away for the last five weeks you may not have been paying attention to much local news recently."

"Well yes, I have been in India. Just got back yesterday."

"Katmandu, I was told."

"There as well. But what earth-shaking event am I supposed to have missed?"

"You may not have registered the suspicious incident at that castle of Murrough's down in Limerick, and certainly not the subsequent investigation."

"Well, I do remember a report about an accident at a castle used as a recording studio. That and the reference to the group Eascra did make me think it might be Murrough's place. That was just before I left for points east, so I haven't given it any thought since."

"Well, in the meantime, somebody's been arrested in connection with the incident."

"Not Murrough, though?" She smiled at the unlikely thought.

"No, Dónal Ó Gráda."

"What? You mean the Eascra guitarist? God, I really am out of touch! Tell me more." He did.

She listened in silence. Finally she asked, "So you think I can help you in some way?"

"It's a long shot, but I've been wondering if there was more to that interview you did than actually got published."

"Well, there was a bit more, but I have no idea how significant it might be. Richard Murrough had made it a condition of giving the interview that he would have the right to go over the transcript and cut anything he didn't want printed."

"And that's what happened?"

"Yes."

"What sort of things got cut?"

"Well, I got the impression that Murrough was very careful of the image he was putting across. The whole interview for him was probably in the nature of a P.R. exercise for that new studio he was setting up. But I remember thinking that some of the bits he wanted cut couldn't possibly have done him any harm."

184

"Like what?"

"The break-up of his last marriage, for example. And his new relationship. But all that was already in the public realm. It had been chewed over in several gossip columns, even on the social pages of our own newspaper. But though he answered my questions on that topic quite openly, as I thought, he subsequently insisted on cutting that section from the published version. Any readers not already in the know might be left with the impression that the sound engineer was a he! ... What's her name again?"

"Georgie Hayes."

"Right. And I couldn't see any great significance in the other cuts, either. But as I said, it was a condition he made, so that's the way we did it."

"Some colleagues of yours in the Features department said they couldn't find the original tape recording of the interview. Do you happen to have it?"

"Oh, no. That was another of Murrough's conditions, that he could take it away with him."

"Isn't that unusual?"

She smiled ruefully. "A bit irregular, yes. But my boss thought it would be worth stretching a point here."

"So you only have your memory of what was actually said?"

"Oh, I kept a copy of the transcript. I took it home with me as a precaution, just in case Murrough started harassing us to confiscate any printed copies as well. He did seem a bit paranoid."

"A copy of the whole uncut interview?"

"Yes. As far as I remember, the sections to be cut are marked, but in any case, it should be possible to compare it with the published version."

"Do you think you could let me take a look at it?"

"I don't see why not. Can you prove to me you are with the Gardai?"

"Well I don't have my badge with me right now. But if I were to call to your office tomorrow, I would be carrying the necessary identification."

"OK, I'll bring the transcript in with me. Could you call around 10 o'clock?" Cathy's business meeting started at nine. Things were working out very nicely indeed. He wouldn't even need to make any special effort to cover up his ulterior motives in joining her on the Dublin trip.

That was the point where Cathy joined them. "I see you've found some kids your own age to play with, Tim!"

"You're flattering me," said Dervla. Introductions followed.

"Would you believe, Cathy, Dervla is the person who did that interview with Richard Murrough earlier this year."

"Really?"

"Yes, she's going to let me have a look at the original transcript tomorrow morning. It should suit you, you'll be at your meeting."

"No objection. But why are you bothering? I know you're quite obsessed about that Castle Green case, but I thought you'd lost interest in Murrough as a possible suspect!"

"Not really. His previous dealings with the victim just have to mean something. And it can hardly be just a coincidence that ..."

"Can't be a coincidence? So what do you call running into his interviewer at my kid sister's birthday party?"

Cathy had a point there. Unfortunately, this was not the appropriate moment to explain what had revived Tim's interest in Murrough as a possible suspect. Namely, the fact that he had in the meantime discovered something that had the appearance of a real motive. And that the 'coincidence' of the same surname - with or without an actual family connection - may have provided the key.

The *Irish Times* offices were only a short walk from their hotel. As he strolled along the quays, the November sun glistened on the waters of the Liffey, turning mud to silver. Tim had the strong intuition that he was about to learn something that would have a similar effect on the murky circumstances surrounding P.J. Murphy's death.

His hopes were, however, not immediately fulfilled. Dervla was expecting him, and he easily followed the directions he got at the information desk to her office on the third floor. As promised, she had the transcript with her. But on examining it, he had to admit that the cuts in the interview did seem as harmless as Dervla had said. Tim could find no great revelations in any of them.

"As you see, I had to mess around a bit with the phrasing of the remaining questions to give the impression that nothing had been cut. Murrough insisted on that, too. It's a bit borderline, but I decided it was just within the bounds of acceptable practice."

Questions of journalistic ethics were of no immediate concern to Tim, so he just shrugged his shoulders and went back to perusing the document. He noted the cut that kept any uninformed readers in the dark as to the sex of the top technician lured away from Dublin's Windmill Lane Studios. The remaining reference to Georgie Hayes as 'one of the best' carefully skirted the issue.

Apart from the question about rumoured plans for re-marriage, two items referring to Murrough's early years had been cut. With a smile, he noted that one was about his change of name. The answer given was more or less what he had said to Tim when challenged on the subject at Halloween.

"How on earth did you find out that his father's name was plain Jack Murphy?"

"Basic journalistic research." She did not elaborate further. "But at least it's clear why he wanted that passage cut. However he managed to justify it, adopting a new, fancier-sounding name gives off a strong whiff of vanity!"

Tim had to agree with that assessment.

The second such item was more puzzling. Tim read it again:

But isn't it true that you had originally aimed at a totally different career?
You mean medicine? Yes, as a kid, I'd always had the idea that I'd like to be a doctor. And when it was finally diagnosed that I had indeed inherited the genetic defect that leads to blindness, it made me all the more determined. Oh, I had no illusions that I could ever be a surgeon, for example. But I thought I might go into medical research, and maybe even find a way of preventing genetic diseases breaking out in other people. So I did do a year of medical school. But as the damn handicap took hold, any kind of study just became too difficult. I decided to play to my strengths instead. So I dropped out of college and made a career of my hobby. I think it was the right decision.

Dervla saw over his shoulder what he was looking at. "That one made him seem almost human, could have got him oodles of sympathy!"

"So why on earth did he want it cut?"

"I don't know. He didn't explain. But I could hazard a guess."

"Which would be …?"

"That it suggests failure, weakness, improvisation, making the best of a bad lot. I think he wants to give the impression that he has always done exactly what he wanted, with no deviation from his chosen course. The one thing he can't stand, I imagine, is to be pitied."

Tim thought about that. It did indeed tally with the attitudes Murrough had expressed elsewhere in the interview, and with the impression he had got of him face to face. But this realization had the perverse effect of making Tim feel something like, yes, pity.

He was becoming more and more convinced that Richard Murrough had had *something* to do with P.J.'s death. What, remained to be discovered, and – if he had indeed actually killed him - the even greater question of how.

187

But what did he want to do about it? After all, P.J. was dead, and pinning the blame on somebody wasn't going to bring him back. Then the scene at the funeral came back to him. The small crowd ... Helen ... Tara ... the guitar students ... He shook himself free of his momentary weakness, reminding himself that justice and retribution were as valid human impulses as pity. Besides, he had to *know*.

Tim leafed through the transcript again as if he might have missed something.

"Was there nothing more said about his songwriting, or about his work with The Hawks?"

"If it isn't there, it wasn't said."

"And he didn't elaborate any further on the Vietnam War?" Tim scanned the interview and found the brief reference, in Murrough's answer to a question about the meaning of the 'Light and Shade' lyrics: "... not the whole story. There are references in there to the Vietnam War, which I wasn't involved in ..."

"As I said, if it isn't there ..."

Tim finally gave up on that count. No point in antagonizing a useful contact, one who had proved most obliging. He asked if you could make a copy of the complete transcript, and she had no problem with that.

"You know, I've been thinking. Your interest in the interview has brought something back to me. It was just before I left for India." She paused as if trying to reconstruct the details. "I remember getting a phone-call that week from someone asking if the newspaper would be interested in background information on Richard Murrough's past.

"Did the caller say what kind of information?"

"I don't think so, but the implication seemed to be that it would not be flattering."

"And did you say you would be interested?"

"I was non-committal. Of course I had to say it would depend on the nature of the information. We would listen, and judge it on its merits. He said he'd ring me back later that week."

"So it was a he. Did he give a name?"

"No, no telephone number either."

"And did he ring back?"

"No, not while I was around, anyway."

"Can you remember the exact day you got that call?"

"It must have been in the middle of the week." She opened her desk diary and leafed back to the week in question. She found the brief cryptic

188

reference, which Tim was able to read upside down: INFO on R.M.?? "Yes, it was the Wednesday. Wednesday morning to be precise."

Wednesday, September 30th.

Chapter 21

Barbara was off sick, so Tim was made painfully aware of how useful she had been to him as a sounding-board for his various hunches and theories. No, that wasn't quite right - 'sounding board' was far too passive for her occasionally very insightful comments and questions, some of which would cause him to see a familiar fact in a new light, or set off a whole new train of thought. Just chewing over the ramifications of the latest set of revelations in his own mind wasn't the same. He had the strong feeling he was missing something important.

The feeling was similar to that of being stumped with a crossword puzzle. Very often, the stalemate would only be broken when he did a logical side-step, as it were, and suddenly began to read a clue in a wholly different way. The words would take on new meanings, and the relationships between them would add up to something totally different to the kind of solution he had been vainly straining after.

If Babs had been here, they would have been sharing the early day shift again, and he would have used morning tea-breaks like this one to occasionally pick her brains on the subject. Liam Dwyer, a fresh-faced rookie recently arrived from Templemore, was totally uninitiated in the matter, though he may well have read about Dónal's court appearance in today's *Cork Examiner*, before passing the news section that contained it to Tim. He was now perusing the racing pages of the sports section. Mike Mulligan had taken his mug of tea back to his desk. He was the last person Tim would have considered discussing the case with.

Cathy, though initially helpful, had become increasingly allergic to the topic, and seemed to regard any further efforts to solve the Castle Green conundrum as a waste of time, and counterproductive to what she called his career prospects. So he had avoided the topic both on the trip back from Dublin, and on the following shared weekend.

The latter, which according to the duty roster was to be Tim's last free weekend until Christmas, had been spent down on Dan's farm. Cathy had, for once, graciously put up with the rather primitive living conditions, and even mucked in to help with the very necessary work of tidying up the vegetable garden for the winter. She had been somewhat disconcerted to see one huge cannabis plant still there, now nearly touching the glass roof of the greenhouse, and looking more conspicuous than ever now that the tomatoes were gone. He had tried to reassure her that Helen Murphy would be harvesting the remainder and clearing away the evidence within a week or so, which she had reluctantly accepted. So it had seemed diplomatic to avoid what had become a sore topic.

Not having had either Barbara or Cathy as a sparring partner, Tim had been sorely tempted to confront Richard Murrough directly on what he had learned from his sister Brid and from Dervla Cassidy. Just to get some kind of a reaction. The Murroughs were due to leave for L.A. on the Sunday, so this would be his last chance until their planned return four weeks later.

It would have meant spending another weekend in the Limerick area, which (on the plus side) would allow him to call to see Maggie O'Keeffe. The lady, he had been informed by his present Kilbrue contact DI Kathleen Smith, was now out of hospital and resting at home.

All this would undoubtedly have put a further strain on his relationship with Cathy. But what finally decided him against another trip to Kilbrue was a rough cost-benefit analysis, which came out decidedly negative. After all, what Murrough might have to say on the matter could run the gamut between total denial and disarming frankness, without really getting him anywhere.

That the medical report found in P.J.'s suitcase had been manipulated was now evident. On a closer examination than he had originally given it, Tim could make out that the heavily written 'Philip' may well have obliterated an original 'Richard'. There would have been no need, of course, to mess with the surname. And it would have been a simple matter to change Murrough's date of birth - 9/25/46 - to P.J.'s - 8/25/48. The place of birth - Baton Rouge, Louisiana - showed no signs of manipulation, so it had probably been inserted on a space that had been left blank in the original.

A few nights ago, when Tim was again having a bit of trouble falling asleep, he had (as an alternative to counting sheep) run through some possible reactions on Murrough's part:
- *Could you describe it to me please? ... Good heavens, it does sound as if it might have come from my medical records, but I have no idea how Phil could have got his hands on it.*
- *Oh, that! Yes, I remember Phil asking if I could oblige with something like that. But I had no idea that he'd actually used it.*
- *Sure, I helped him get out of the draft by letting him manipulate an old medical report of mine. We needed him in the band, for God's sake! It was 1970, I think, some time before he took to the drugs and had to be replaced. At the time, he seemed grateful.*

A remark of Jeannie Staunton's had also exercised his mind that sleepless night: "...unless Richard Murrough had some kind of hold over him." Could this have provided it? It was, after all, a criminal act to forge a document, and one that Richard Murrough could credibly deny any complicity in. Neither would it have been covered by President Jimmy Carter's subsequent amnesty for draft dodgers, (When was that? 1976 or so?) So it could well have been the reason P.J. never dared to challenge Murrough in court on the song-writing issue. At least while resident in the USA. And after that he had clearly been discouraged from taking any such action by his wife.

So had something snapped at some time during the Caiseal Gréine recording sessions? Had P.J. been finally goaded into turning the tables on Richard Murrough? If he had, in fact, been blackmailed all those years into letting Murrough claim sole credit for that hit song, was he now trying to blackmail him in return? Or merely taking revenge for all those lost years and the success that had since eluded him?

On the issue of the phone call to the *Irish Times*, Tim had also run through some possible responses:

- *What? He didn't say a word to me about dishing any dirt to the* Irish Times.

- *Yes, he told me he was thinking giving the whole story to the* Times, *but would reconsider if I made a fair settlement to acknowledge his contribution. I agreed of course.*

- *Yes, he told me he was going to give the whole story to the* Times, *and I said, 'OK, do your worst, my lawyers can deal with this - and don't expect any more work with me!'*

- *Sure, he threatened to reveal all, which could certainly have hurt my image. You bet I wished him dead! But what could I do about it?*

The latter question posed a real problem. Tim could not picture any scenario that might have involved Murrough in P.J.'s death. And lacking any concrete evidence of such an act, alerting Murrough to the fact that he was still a suspect (in Tim's eyes, if in nobody else's) might well be a fatal mistake. Especially now that he was on the point of leaving the jurisdiction. Should he really have something to hide, he might then be in no hurry to return to Ireland. And without first building up a case against him, there would be no chance whatsoever of extradition.

Extradition. Yes, in Dónal's case, that had been accomplished very efficiently. The file of evidence submitted by the Kilbrue Gardai to the Director of Public Prosecutions in late October had been accepted as sufficient to bring charges. Of course it would, Tim thought ruefully. It included his own contribution, didn't it? The British authorities, on their part, had raised no bureaucratic obstacles - probably mindful of their interest in getting similar cooperation from the Irish authorities when they needed to extradite the occasional IRA suspect. Less than four weeks, it had taken. Must be a record!

Glumly, Tim re-read the item in the *Cork Examiner* that now served to emphasize his feeling of helplessness and stalemate:

Eascra star charged with manslaughter

Mr. Dónal Ó Gráda (26) appeared in Limerick District Court yesterday charged in connection with the death at Caiseal Gréine Recording Studio, Kilbrue, County Limerick, on September 30th of Philip James Murphy (38). Dónal Ó Gráda is the well-known lead guitarist and vocalist with the successful folk-rock group Eascra. Mr. Murphy was a session musician temporarily employed by the band.

The search for Mr. Ó Gráda, initially to help the Gardai with their inquiries, and his subsequent arrest in Britain, attracted considerable publicity (see our previous reports). He was extradited from Britain this week. Superintendent Patrick O'Driscoll of Kilbrue District Garda Station expressed full satisfaction with the cooperation of the British authorities.

Mr. Ó Gráda was charged with manslaughter, and remanded in custody in Limerick Prison. An application for bail was refused. The trial on the charge of manslaughter was set to open in the Central Criminal Court on January 4th.

Questioned by our reporter after the hearing, Mr. Gerard Prendergast, Counsel for Mr. Ó Gráda, said his client intended to plead Not Guilty to all charges ...

Yeah, yeah ... purely circumstantial evidence ...

Maybe he should call to see Barbara. The flu, she was supposed to have, and contact was discouraged. But she'd been off work for over a week now, so must be over the worst of it. Besides, Tim had never had the flu in his whole life, so he felt he must gave some natural immunity. In any case, he was prepared to risk it.

She commuted daily from one of Cork City's western suburbs, Bishopstown, he thought it was. As far as he remembered from previous conversations, she lived in her old family home with her mother, an invalid

193

in need of considerable care, and (sometimes) her delinquent kid brother. Her father was dead. All in all, it sounded like a pretty dreary set-up for someone recovering from the flu, so maybe his visit didn't have to be purely self-serving, Maybe she could do with a bit of cheering up.

He went out to the main office to get Barbara's address and telephone number from the relevant filing cabinet. As he jotted it into his notebook he sensed Sergeant Mike attempting to look over his shoulder. Turning in a sudden movement, Tim pretended to accidentally bump into him. "Oh, Sorry, Mike, want to get at the cabinet? Let me get out of your way first." He resolved to wait until he got back to his flat in the afternoon to make the telephone call.

What did one take on a visit to a recovering flu victim nowadays? Feeling a bit foolish with the bag of seedless grapes he'd bought at the small greengrocer's shop adjoining the hardware store over which he lived, Tim nipped back up the stairs to his flat to augment his offering with something stronger. He rooted in the dark cupboard that passed for his wine-cellar, and pulled out a dusty bottle of Chianti. That should do. On second thoughts, why not give her a choice? From his living-room cabinet he took an already opened and somewhat depleted bottle of Hennessy cognac, and put the two bottles, a corkscrew and the bag of grapes into a plastic bag, and headed down the stairs and around the corner to where his car was parked.

With his offerings propped up between the diverse rubbish clogging up the boot of his old Ford Fiesta, he chugged along the N71 towards Cork. At the Bishopstown roundabout he headed north, had to stop twice to consult the city map, but finally found the correct address, a semi-detached house surrounded by a rather scruffy, overrun garden. Yeah, who was there to take care of it? Hardly the surly-looking boy who at this very moment was emerging from the front door dressed in motor-bike leathers. Probably around nineteen, he must be the delinquent kid brother that Barbara often half-jokingly referred to.

Meeting him at the gate, Tim first got a hostile glare in reaction to his question if this was the Brennans' place, then a mumbled "Sure!", before the boy noisily took off on his motor-bike. Barbara was more welcoming.

"You'll have to keep your voice down, 'cause Mother is resting upstairs." Tim noted the wheelchair parked in the hallway, and the chair-lift the old lady obviously used for negotiating the stairs. Tim asked the obvious questions. "She's not well at all. Muscular dystrophy and an associated heart problem. She may eventually have to go into a nursing home, but we're

194

doing the best we can with home care at the moment. She gets meals-on-wheels, and a nurse looks in on her once every day."

Barbara herself was a bit pale, but obviously over the worst of the flu. She felt perfectly OK, she said, and even admitted that she could easily have gone back to work at the beginning of that week. "But I'd been given a doctor's certificate for two weeks, and I'd be crazy not to use it under the circumstances." She gestured in the direction of upstairs. Tim grunted sympathetically.

"Look. Tim, I'll be back at work on Monday, but I don't know how long more I'm going to stay on the job. I'm thinking of giving notice."

"No!"

"Yes, I'm serious. I've missed the chance to give notice to the end of the year, so I'll have to keep going another few months ..."

"But you love the job!"

"Maybe," she acknowledged with a real look of sadness in her eyes. "But it's all getting a bit too much. What I need is a part-time job, and you can't work part-time with the Gardai Siochana!"

"Can't that delinquent brother of yours help out a bit?"

She laughed. "Oh, I've been maligning him over the years, I know. But Kevin's OK, he's been off the drugs for years, and hasn't been in trouble for ages. I should really stop calling him a delinquent. It's just got to be a habit, and he practically encourages it by putting on his surly, tough guy act."

"I got treated to a bit of that on the way in."

"Everybody does. But he doesn't mean any harm. And to be fair to him, he does his bit in looking after Mother, as best he can."

"So where's the problem?"

Barbara looked into the middle distance. "It's just that his best isn't enough. And my best isn't enough either, trying to keep down a full-time job at the same time. Mother is getting to be more and more of a burden."

"So maybe full-time care in a nursing home would be the best option after all?"

"I don't think we can afford it."

"You'd be less able to afford it with only a part-time job! ... Or with no job at all, which is what all this might lead to!""

Barbara looked away, and didn't answer.

"You can't do this to yourself, Babs." He could have kicked himself for falling back into the habit of using a nickname he knew she hated, but she made no protest this time. "Barbara, you love being a cop, you said so. You're not cut out to be one of those self-sacrificing full-time carers who usually end up totally embittered ... You've got a life to lead, for God's sake!"

Barbara finally turned around to face him. "Look, I know you mean well, Tim. But I'd rather not talk about this any more. I'll have to make my own decisions." Tim shrugged. "Now what have you got in that bag? You said you wanted to cheer me up, not make me brood!"

Tim extracted the bunch of grapes, and Barbara laughed out loud at their hospital-visit implications. So they did, at least, seem to have a cheering-up effect, even more so when their rather battered and soggy condition became evident, having shared a car ride in a plastic bag with two heavy bottles and a corkscrew. She got a plate to put them on, and some kitchen paper to help deal with the squishier ones. Tim cut off her automatic move to put on the kettle for a cup of tea. "You can have the tea later, I've brought a choice of booze. Which do you prefer?" She went for the Chianti, and he set to work on it with the corkscrew.

"Now what was it about the Kilbrue case that you wanted to chew over?"

"Oh, it doesn't seem so important any more."

"Out with it!"

"Well, OK. First of all, there's your Aunt May's contribution."

"Has she come up with something already?"

"No. She phoned this morning to say that the Murphys of Tipperary and Waterford were two largely separate branches of the clan, so there would be no obvious connection between the two men in question."

"And didn't one of them emigrate some time in the 19th century?"

"Yes, in 1893. Anyway, your aunt couldn't exclude some individual connection, possibly through the female line, but that would involve considerable research. I thanked her, and told her to wait a while before investing any further effort in the matter."

"Why that? She enjoys this stuff. And however unlikely, she might still have come up with something!"

"Because we may not need to establish a family connection. I've found something else that ... might possibly explain the significance of the shared surname."

He produced the manipulated medical report from the same bag he had transported his offerings in, noting that while its plastic folder was now smeared with grape-juice, the document itself didn't seem to have suffered. He used some of the kitchen paper Barbara had so thoughtfully provided to wipe away the smears, and let her examine it. He explained where it had been found, and what it had probably been used for.

"Now that you point it out, even I can see it's been manipulated. There are even slight differences in the handwriting," she noted. "Could this Philip Murphy really have got away with it as proof of his own disability?"

"It does sound strange, but I must admit, I hadn't noticed the manipulation at first glance. It took my sister's explanation as to what *retinitis pigmentosa* actually is, to make me take a closer look. And I can well imagine, back in the early 70s, when thousands of young men were being called up to the recruiting stations daily, those given the job of processing the medical reports were probably seriously overworked. P.J. was probably chancing his arm in his desperation to avoid the draft - and just got lucky." Then he explained its possible significance for the Castle Green case.

Barbara listened to his rambling account, carefully wiping her fingers after each grape to take a sip of Chianti. "So what you're saying is, this record producer first allowed him to use - or rather, misuse - this medical report of his to get off the draft, and then threatened him with exposure of his crime should he claim his share of the royalties for that hit song?"

Put that way, it sounded unlikely. "Yeah. But it needn't have been planned like that from the start. Maybe Murrough really did want to help him get off the draft. And only got tempted to use his knowledge to pressurize P.J into silence later, when a lot of money was at stake."

"It's possible."

"It might not have been even necessary to make an explicit threat. Just a hint, maybe. Or even the bare fact of Murrough being in the know might have been enough to keep him silent. Can you imagine the situation ...?"

"Yes, I can imagine it very well indeed," Barbara said stiffly.

"You know, everything I've heard of Richard Murrough, and even my own brief experience of speaking to the guy, tells me he's an absolute genius at flying by the seat of his pants."

"You mean improvising, living by his wits?"

"Yeah, turning every circumstance to his advantage."

"But aren't you forgetting a couple of awkward facts?

"I suppose you mean the one circumstance that it would be very hard to turn to anyone's advantage?"

"Yes. The fact of being blind. His *retinitis pigmentosa* , or whatever you call it."

"No, I'm not forgetting it, I'm painfully aware that the crime in question simply could not have been carried out by a blind man - except perhaps by a freak accident ..."

"In which case it wouldn't be a crime ..."

"... and wouldn't have needed to be concealed."

"But what about the other awkward fact? Namely that Kilbrue are satisfied they've got the right man - with your help, of course."

Tim grimaced.

"Why are you now so sure he didn't do it?"

"I'm not. It's certainly looking bad for Dónal. And my own evidence isn't going to help him any ..."

"You're going to be called as a witness?"

"You bet! The old man isn't going to let me off the hook in that respect!"

"So why can't you just go with the flow, and see what comes out in court?"

Tim's stubborn silence made it adequately clear to Barbara that 'going with the flow' was not an option. "OK, let's postulate that Murrough wanted P.J. dead - whether to save his money or his image is beside the point. He himself is not in a position to carry out any such act. But he knows of somebody else with a grudge against P.J. Would it be beyond the bounds of possibility for him to ..."

"To provoke Dónal into doing his dirty work? Babs, you're a genius!"

"This is wild speculation, Tim, don't get carried away!"

"I know, but it would be completely in character for Murrough to try to stage-manage things to his advantage." Tim thought back to what Jeannie and the others had told him about the progress of the recording sessions. "And you know what probably enraged Dónal enough to drive down from Dublin that day?"

Barbara looked at him inquiringly. "Murrough had been promising P.J. a permanent role recording with the band. Somehow, Dónal must have got wind of it."

"Or maybe Murrough phoned him directly with the news?"

Tim wasn't sure if Jeannie had said as much. If so, it should be in his notes. "There would be no guarantee of success, of course ... "

"But he might just have got lucky ..."

"And in the end he'd have someone else to take all the blame."

They sat in silence for a while, sipping Chianti and finishing off the last of the sticky grapes.

"God, I wish I could talk to Dónal."

"Can't you?"

"No way. Kilbrue are not going to let me anywhere near him. And I can understand them. They'd be crazy to let me rock the boat at this stage!" But that wasn't the only obstacle, he realized. "And to Dónal's lawyers I'm the enemy!"

As Tim was closing the garden gate behind him (having taken his leave of his colleague with a friendly 'See you on Monday!') he could hear the noise of a motor-bike approaching. He looked down the road. It was already dark, but the street lighting was quite good in this suburb. Sure enough, its rider was the same leather-clad figure he had briefly encountered on his arrival. The bike screeched to a halt just as Tim was fumbling with his car keys, slightly encumbered with the now depleted plastic bag in one hand, and the precious folder in the other.

For a moment it looked as if the boy was going to ignore him. Just a short glare, and he turned away to begin manoeuvring his impressive machine through the garden gate.

But no. "Hey, you!" After parking his bike, the boy had turned around to face him.

"You mean me?" Tim affected a friendly expression.

"Yes, you. You're from the Bandon Gardai, aren't you?"

"That's right, I'm a colleague of your sister's."

"I'd know a cop anywhere."

"Do you have a problem with that? After all, your sister's a cop!"

The boy didn't have an answer to that, so he changed tack. "Look, I know all about you. You're the one who's bothering my sister."

"I have no idea what you're talking about!"

"You're the one who's forcing my sister to give up her job!"

"Kevin, please ...!"

The use of his name seemed to have enraged him further. "It's 'Mr. Brennan' to you!"

"Please calm down, Kev... Mr. Brennan! What the hell are you ...?

"I've got some friends out in Bandon," Kevin managed to give the word 'friends' a sinister ring. "Now that I know what you look like, they can cause a lot of trouble for you. That is, if you don't lay off my sister!"

Kevin may not have been in trouble 'for ages', as Barbara had put it, but if it was his style to go around threatening police officers like this, the truce wasn't going to last much longer. Tim banged his car door closed again, and approached the boy in what he hoped was a conciliatory manner. But the net result was to receive a nasty thump in his chest which sent Tim reeling backwards towards the car, dropping the plastic bag in his effort to keep his balance. A nasty crack told him the Hennessy bottle had suffered in its

199

unplanned contact with the pavement. A good thing there hadn't been much left in it …

When he'd picked himself up, the boy had already retreated into the house, banging the front door. Tim waited for a moment to see if Barbara had registered anything of this peculiar scene. But apparently not. The TV was on in the living room, he could see its pale glow through the window. And the overgrown buddleia in the front garden would have obscured the view, had she chanced to look out. He considered knocking at the door to try to clear this matter up, but then decided it would be easier without Kevin hovering around. He would talk to her about it on Monday.

On his way home, Tim stopped off at the Garda station to pick up his uniform jacket. It had been too awkward to wear under his raincoat in the afternoon downpour that had coincided with the end of his shift earlier that day, and he would need it first thing tomorrow.

He was due to be picked up by Liam Dwyer in the squad car at six o'clock sharp on Sunday morning to head down to Kinsale as potential reinforcements in a drugs raid. Neither of the two rookies had been fully initiated in the background of the case. But putting two and two together, it was plain that the authorities had grounds to expect an incoming shipment of *something* (cocaine? - heroin? - or just cannabis?) on a private yacht. As many times before, it would probably come to nothing. Or they might make a few arrests. Either way, he and Liam would have to be there. In uniform.

As he retrieved his jacket from the hook, his eye was drawn to a rather large note on his desk, weighted down by a stapler and written with a green felt-tip pen in what looked like the Superintendent's hand. It said:

Phone call for Garda T. O'Driscoll Sat. 3.15 p.m. from Mr. Gerard Prendergast (of Prendergast and Partners, Solicitors, Dublin)

Please return call Monday morning!

The Dublin telephone number was underlined twice. Whoever had made the call must have made it sound urgent.

Chapter 22

In summer, the early shift had its redeeming features, allowing as it did for long afternoons on the beach, or the odd bit of gardening. In late November it had none. Even night duty was preferable to having to drag oneself out of bed at 5.30 in the morning. Yes, Tim could just about manage to shower, dress, have a cup of tea, and sprint the 200 meters of dark, empty street in the allocated half an hour, but it was never pleasant.

This morning he did have the added motivation of the intriguing phone call from Dublin. But in his experience, lawyers were seldom to be found at their desks at 6 a.m., so it would be a few hours before he could satisfy his curiosity in that respect. Ahead lay, instead, at least three hours of paperwork, most of it ensuing from yesterday's raid.

From the official point of view it had not been a complete waste of time. Five kilos of cannabis resin had been found on board the *Marianne II*, a two-masted sailing boat taking advantage - the crew had originally claimed - of the fresh winds and unseasonably good sailing conditions for their final pleasure trip of the year. Four men had been taken in for questioning: two Frenchmen, and two locals. They would be formally charged later in the day. At least Tim would not need to appear in court, since he and Liam had been there merely as reinforcements. Considering his own recent involvement in cannabis production, he was grateful to be let off the hook.

As he approached the side door of the Garda station, suddenly Barbara was by his side. In the darkness of the November morning he hadn't noticed her lurking in the car park. Apparently she'd been waiting in her car to ambush him on his arrival.

"Tim, I've been waiting for you to turn up." She signalled to him to retreat back around the corner of the building. "Kevin told me how he treated you outside our house on Saturday. God, I was mortified!"

"Never mind, no great harm done, except to the dregs of that bottle of brandy I was carrying. But what the hell was he going on about?"

"It seems he mistook you for someone else." She looked really embarrassed.

"And who might that be?"

"Mike."

Tim had to ask her to continue with her explanations.

"Well, I had mentioned at home that Mike had been getting on my nerves a bit, getting awfully familiar ..."

"It didn't seem to bother you when *I* raised the subject."

"Well, there isn't much I can do except keep out of his way ..."

"Which isn't easy since he's nearly always on the same shift."

"Right. Somehow he manages to arrange it like that. That's why I wanted to clear this up out here. He'll be all over the place, won't give me a moment's peace."

Tim began to recall Kevin's actual words. "To the extent that he's practically forcing you to give up your job?"

"Oh, not exactly. Mother's illness is the real problem, But ..." she tailed off.

"But you'd have found some other way of dealing with it if it weren't for Mike, is that it?"

"Maybe."

"But for God's sake, there's surely a less drastic way of getting him off your back. I mean a less self-punishing one. You could report the bastard!"

She shook her head. "Remember that drugs raid on Helen Murphy's place last month?" He did. "Well ..." She took a deep breath. "I was the one who tipped her off, and Mike knows it. He was listening in on the call I made."

"What?" Tim wasn't referring to Barbara's phone call, which he'd heard about from Helen Murphy, but that was how she took him up.

"Yes. You know I'd been worrying about whether I should report the cannabis find. But I didn't. I decided that you were right, that we should make an exception in her case. But I mentioned the matter to Daisy one lunch-break." Daisy did the secretarial work for the lower ranks. "I thought she'd understand my dilemma, since her father had just died of cancer."

"But she spilled the beans to Mike."

"Or to somebody. In any case, as soon as I heard a raid was imminent, I phoned Helen Murphy."

"From the office."

"Yeah, I didn't have a chance to go out to a phone box. The boys were already on their way!"

"And since then, Mike had been practically blackmailing you?"

"Oh, not in so many words. But he does refer to it occasionally."

"In what way?"

"Oh, when we're on our own, he'd make little jokes about it. And in company he once went on and on about how the hell the Murphy woman had been able to get rid of the evidence ..."

"And speculating about whether she'd been tipped off? With a knowing wink? "

"Exactly. Apparently there wasn't a trace of anything in the house when the boys turned up. Murphy must have nearly killed herself lugging those huge plants out of sight in the half hour or so she had to do it!"

"She had a good bit more than half an hour."

"What?"

"It wasn't you tipped her off. I warned her earlier that she'd be safer stowing them away somewhere else." He decided not to tell her yet that he knew exactly where.

Barbara's mouth fell open. "You ...?"

"Yes, me. And I'm going to make it quite clear to smarmy Mike."

"But you can't ..."

"Well, he'd be a lot less likely to harass me on the job!"

"He'd get you thrown directly out of the force, more likely!"

This was indeed a strong possibility. Maybe it would be possible to make a *cause celebre* of it, in the interests of drug law reform? In his radical student days, he had been briefly involved (together with Colin Leahy) in such a campaign ... Then he thought of the old man. In the long run, even more desperate remedies might be called for. "We'll figure something out. In the meantime, don't even *think* of giving notice." He looked at his watch. "By the way we're nearly five minutes late. Let's not blot our copybooks any more than we have to."

Barbara followed him meekly into the office.

Nine o'clock seemed a reasonable time to return the call. Answered by a secretary, kept on hold for at least a minute and a half. (Was Prendergast indulging in a power game?) Finally ...

"Ah, Garda O'Driscoll! Thank you for returning my call. Gerard Prendergast here. I am contacting you in connection with the manslaughter case brought against my client, Mr. Dónal Ó Gráda."

"I guessed as much. But you must realize that Bandon Garda Station is only very peripherally involved in the matter. Are you sure it isn't my father you need to contact - Superintendent Paddy O'Driscoll of Kilbrue District? They're the ones responsible for the investigation."

"No, no, I quite realize that. As a matter of fact, I have already been in contact with your father in matters connected with the official investigation.. No, it's you personally I wish to speak to."

"I'm not sure if I can help you in any way."

"My client thinks you can."

Tim stifled his surprise and tried to maintain his neutral tone. "Before we go any further, Mr. Prendergast, I'd better make one thing clear. Though I am not part of the investigating team, I may very well be called as a witness - for the prosecution!"

"I am aware of that possibility. But is my understanding correct, that you haven't yet been called to give evidence against my client? In other words, that it is only, as you said, a possibility."

"I have not yet been officially notified, that is correct."

"Then there should be no impediment - yet - to a meeting with my client."

"A meeting with your client?"

"Yes, if you would agree to it. You are under no obligation, since it would not be part of your regular police work. We would of course, refund your travel expenses ..."

"But why?" There had to be a catch somewhere. "I don't think I can be much use to the defence in this case!"

"Maybe not in court. And the purpose of the meeting would not be to influence your testimony in any way. It would, in any case, be in circumstances that could not be described as confidential ..."

"In Limerick Prison, I presume?"

"Yes. In my presence. You will understand that I have to insist on that."

Tim understood that only too well. What he didn't understand was why Dónal's counsel would even countenance such contact with the other side. But the explanation was impending.

"It will come as no surprise to you, I am sure, that it is not on my advice that my client is seeking a meeting with you. In fact I expressly advised against it. But my client can be rather headstrong."

"Yes."

There was a short silence. Prendergast was probably wondering if Tim was being mildly sarcastic. "Do I understand that you have no objection in principle to such a meeting?"

Tim pretended to hesitate. "Very well. I have a day off tomorrow. Could it be arranged for Tuesday afternoon?"

It could: 4 p.m.

Tim had only once before been inside Limerick Prison, though he was very familiar with its forbidding walls, having passed them almost every day for two years on the bus into the city, on his way to and from Sexton Street school. His one visit inside, in the course of his training at Templemore Garda College, had made quite an impression on him. He even remembered the visiting room where he now sat. The air of gloom was the same, and the seasick-green paintwork of the walls didn't seem to have been changed.

He sat on one side of a broad laminated table, Dónal Ó Gráda and his counsel on the other. A prison guard stood impassively by the door. Since Tim had his back to him, he could more or less ignore the official presence. This was not the case for Dónal Ó Gráda, who would not be allowed for one second to forget the situation he was in.

Introductions had been cut off by an almost simultaneous 'We've met before!' on both sides. In both cases it had been accompanied by a degree of embarrassment at the memory. Dónal covered up his by trying to reconstruct the actual date of their meeting. "In June, wasn't it? The night of our last concert ..."

Tim examined the man's features. Gone was the fiery belligerence of that night in Skibbereen, and the sneer with which he had greeted the intervention of an officer of the law. Instead what Tim imagined he saw in his undoubtedly handsome features was a kind of deflated resignation, and possibly bewilderment. He probably wouldn't like his many fans to see him like this.

"Look. I'm sorry about that stupid little incident, and the trouble it caused you ..."

The trouble it caused had been mainly to himself. Without it, the attention of the Gardai might never have been drawn to the matter of missing guitarist; witnesses to his presence at the scene of the death might never have come forward. After his initial panicky flight, Dónal might have returned with some trumped up explanation for his brief absence, professing total ignorance of the matter. And he might have got away with it.

On the other hand, maybe he wouldn't have. Accepting responsibility for the man's present situation could even be a kind of self-aggrandizement. Even without Tim's intervention, Dónal's suspicious behaviour on the day of P.J.'s death and afterwards might have put him in the situation he now found himself. Rightly or wrongly? Tim did not know.

"Why did you want to see me?"

"I was told you'd got yourself involved in the case, above the call of duty, as it were."

"By your sister, I suppose?"

"Well, yeah. But it was Jeannie Staunton who thought it might be an idea to talk to you. Niamh agrees with Mr. Prendergast here that it would be better to leave the cops to do their own job." The said Mr. Prendergast smiled weakly in agreement with the sentiment if not with the wording.

"I thought you and Jeannie didn't get on all that well?"

"I don't get on well with a lot of people, to be honest. And with Jeannie there's the political thing. She sees me as a rabid republican, and all that ... But she's straight. She thought her own evidence might have helped to put me behind bars, and was worried in case justice might not be done. She says you're the only one with an open mind on the matter."

"But I have no official standing in the investigation. That's all in Kilbrue's hands."

"All the better, she said. At least you're independent of the party line."

"In spirit, maybe. But I'm still a member of the force. You couldn't possibly employ me as a private eye, for example, if that's what you had in mind."

Dónal shook his head, and Prendergast looked shocked at the thought. "I'm just glad that somebody out there wants to get at the truth, whatever it is."

"What do *you* think it is?"

"I don't know, except that I didn't do it." He looked imploringly at Tim, as if willing him to believe it, against all appearances. Tim had to remind himself that the man was a professional performer.

"So how do you think you can help me get at 'the truth', as you call it?"

"I can only quote Jeannie: 'If you really didn't do it, just tell him what you know, and see what he can make of it'." Jeannie was a wise girl. "So if you're interested, I will."

"Shoot." Dónal launched into an account of his relations with the band, and his mixed feelings about getting a session musician to fill in for him on the Caiseal Gréine recordings. Tim had heard all that before, from various sources. It got interesting when he reached the point where he got the news that his temporary replacement was being considered for a permanent role with the band.

"And who was it told you that?"

"Well, Niamh had mentioned in the course of the first week of recordings that things were going quite well, and made a couple of sisterly sarcastic remarks about doing fine without me. Then the producer fellow - Murrough - rang up, on the Friday or Saturday, I think, saying that if it was OK by me, they might use this P.J. Murphy for the follow-up album as well. I told him fuck off."

Prendergast raised his eyes to heaven, but since he'd already reminded Dónal that he did not need to reveal anything to anybody about his state of mind in the days leading up to the incident, there was nothing more he could do. Nothing from this meeting could be taken down to use directly in evidence against his client, but even so, Dónal should be more careful not to damage his own case.

"Then there was another phone-call from Murrough ..."

"When?"

"Wednesday lunch-time." The day of the incident. "This time saying he was about to do a deal with Murphy for the next album, and if I had any objections, I or my manager should come down and discuss it."

"When was the deal to be done?"

"Before the end of the week, he said. I said I'd be down to meet him the following day. We made an appointment for 2.30 p.m., and he gave me the code for the gate. Then I changed my mind and headed down that afternoon. Stopped off at Christine's place first."

"Christine being your girlfriend?"

"Yes, she lives in Adare, just outside Limerick. She had a meal ready, then I made for the castle, meaning to tackle Murrough on the matter of the recording contract."

"You reached the castle when?"

"About twenty to nine, it must have been. As I was stopped at the gate, I thought I saw Murrough walking down the path leading to the house down to the left. Apparently that's where he lives."

"That's right. You didn't call out to him?"

"No, I thought I'd park the car first, then knock on his door in a civilized way. Wouldn't want to be scaring a man who I knew couldn't see me, no matter what our business relationship was!"

"Of course."

"Then I drove up towards the parking area. The first sign something was wrong was the broken glass on the drive. I stopped half way up so as not to damage my tires. Then I saw ... the body."

That meant that Richard Murrough had just walked right past it. But of course the man was blind ...

"What did you do then?"

"I went and took a closer look. I had to practically climb over him to get a look at his face. When I saw who it was ..." He broke off.

"You recognized him?"

"Yeah, from that night in Skibbereen. I may have been a bit sozzled at the time, but it doesn't affect my memory."

"I'm told he'd had a haircut in the meantime."

"Yeah, but he was still wearing that same threadbare old jacket." He paused.

"Go on."

"Then I thought of Niamh, who must have been in her room at the time. She hardly ever goes out in the evening. I went to the main door, found it wasn't locked - and then thought better of it."

"Why?"

"Well, I'd first thought it must be some kind of an accident. Then I realized what it might look like to someone else ... It was as if I'd been set up to arrive just then."

There was Barbara's latest theory. "You mean by Murrough?"

He shrugged. "Anyway, I didn't want to be anybody's fall guy, so I got back in my car and sped off as fast as I could."

"Didn't you have to open the gate first?"

"No, I'd propped it open on the way in. Didn't think my stay would be very long."

"And it wasn't."

"No, even shorter than I expected." He grinned faintly.

"And that was it?"

"Yes. You know the rest, I think. Stopped off at Christine's first to get her ferry timetables ..."

"OK, you needn't go into that. You also phoned your sister from Wales late that night, I believe."

"Yeah, she told me you'd got that out of her."

"One more thing: Did you see Sean on the road on your way back to the main road?"

"Sean Mills? Oh sure, nearly knocked him off his bike, but I didn't feel like stopping to apologize!"

Bike? Coming from anybody else, in any other circumstances, this piece of information would have put Sean back on the list of suspects. It would have given him the decisive ten minutes needed to commit the crime and then 'discover' the body. But now it appeared to put him in the clear. According to Dónal, the deed - if it was a deed - had already been done.

"Can you put a time on that, and say where exactly you passed him?"

"Must have been around nine. It can't have been much more than a quarter of an hour since I arrived at the castle. And I passed him just as I drove out the gates. I remember thinking, OK, he can close the gates for me ... as if that mattered!"

In its total irrelevance, that little item had the ring of truth to it. Tim wondered whether it would be fair to apply this impression to everything else Dónal had said.

"Well, Mr. Ó Gráda," he said with a deliberate air of formality. "You've given me a lot to think about. I hope I can make good use of your information."

The fifteen minutes allocated to the meeting had not yet been used up, and Dónal was in no hurry to be ushered back to his prison cell. "Well, I hope you can come up with something before my trial. I'm absolutely desperate, I can tell you, at the thought that I might be stuck in here for years, if not decades!" Before Prendergast could butt in, he went on, "Though my legal counsel here says I shouldn't worry too much, the cops haven't got enough evidence to get a conviction ..."

"That is correct," Prendergast finally managed to say. "The evidence for the prosecution is purely circumstantial, and rather flimsy at that. My position is that we do not need to prove what actually happened, just to cast doubt on the prosecution's case."

"He doesn't even want me to take the stand and give evidence on my own behalf." Dónal seemed to want to get Tim involved what was apparently a dispute over legal strategy.

"I'm sure you're getting the best legal advice from Mr. Prendergast."

"But you never know what the jury is going to make of it. Without some facts to prove my innocence, I mean." Prendergast was probably more worried about what a jury would make of the accused ranting on about the unfairness of being ousted from the band he had helped to create. Tim repeated his recommendation to follow the advice of his legal counsel.

"By the way, did you hear they're planning a big party and press conference to mark the release of the new album?" Tim hadn't. But then he had not spoken to any other members of the band for over three weeks.

"When is it planned for?"

"New Year's Eve, at the castle."

"At Caiseal Gréine?"

"Yeah. And that's going to be the title of the new album: *Eascra at Caiseal Gréine.* Trust Murrough to go for maximum impact! And apparently he's trying to link it up with that archaeological find, that passage grave or whatever they've dug up on the grounds. You know, Eascra, Beaker Folk, all that Neolithic stuff."

"Sounds like a good idea. For the publicity, I mean. Even you must welcome that."

"Oh, sure, publicity is what the man understands! But it's got nothing to do with me. I probably wouldn't be invited even if I were out of here!" Dónal seemed to be totally incapable of concealing his resentment. Prendergast was right to keep him off the witness stand.

Chapter 23

"So Sean told you to go to hell!"

Sean's actual phrase had been the one used by Dónal Ó Gráda to tell Richard Murrough what he thought of his planned replacement. But for some reason, Tim had toned it down for Barbara's consumption. Though why a wish to consign someone to eternal damnation should be considered milder would not bear logical examination. Besides, Barbara was probably used to a lot worse from that kid brother of hers.

"Yeah. Well, not at first. He readily admitted to having borrowing Declan's bike ..."

"I suppose he had no choice but to admit it."

"Quite. He had at first pointed out his fingerprints weren't on it, but luckily I remembered seeing him putting on gloves on a relatively mild day. He made a point back then of how careful he has to be with his hands, etc. So he hadn't a leg to stand on. Anyway, as regards having lied about it at first, he made a fair point: What did we expect in the circumstances?"

"Meaning how would it have looked if he'd admitted to rushing back to the castle?"

"Yes. Even *you* were speculating that he might have jogged back in time to do the deed!"

"Hmm. But now that you know he would have had sufficient time, it doesn't help you pin it on him."

"Yes, ironic, isn't it?"

"Could this Dónal fellow be lying?"

"Sure he could. But how would it help him? On the contrary, it rules out another possible suspect."

Barbara had to brake suddenly as she steered the squad car round a curve, only to come up against the hind ends of a herd of cattle, completely blocking the road on their way back to the meadows after the morning milking. The two Gardai were on their way to the scene of a reported burglary about five miles outside Bandon. Seeing the Garda insignia on the car, the farmer made more of an effort to herd the cattle to one side than he might otherwise have done. They inched past. "Sorry, what were you saying?"

"I forget. Anyway, as regards nicking the bike, Sean said he thought it wouldn't be missed, that he originally intended to bring it back early next morning in time for Declan to use it. Claimed he was looking forward to the bit of exercise."

"Sounds as if he was real chatty and cooperative, not at all like you said!"

"At first, yeah. And without being asked, he even cleared up the mystery of the noises in the night. Apparently he'd parked the bike around the north side of the castle out of sight, as soon as he saw something was wrong. And since he realized the bike might cast suspicion on himself, he resolved to cycle it back to its rightful position during the night, as soon as things had quieted down. That's when he bumped into Niamh."

"So she wasn't the only one trying to cover something up!"

"So it seems. But whereas Niamh succeeded, Sean wasn't able to carry out his plan. The bike was already gone, he said."

"Oh?"

"Yeah, he went on about not knowing what had happened to it ... I tried to get back to the main issue, which he'd skipped. Namely how he had spent the extra ten minutes or so gained by cycling back from the pub. That's where he got all bolshie and said he had no time to say any more, was rushing to a gig, was under no obligation to talk to me anyway, and if I didn't like it I could ..."

"Go to hell."

"Yes." He'd missed his chance for linguistic accuracy, and besides, other things were more important. "Now, knowing Sean had rushed back to the castle, what do *you* think he would have done on arrival at the scene?"

"Well, if the reason for his rushing had been to check up on Niamh, I suppose that's what he would have done."

"I agree. Especially if the person lying on the pavement was the other half of the suspected couple."

They had arrived at the isolated farmhouse, the scene of the burglary. Duty called. Apart from taking down the details of the stolen goods, and examining the point of forced entry, they had to deal with the distraught farmer's wife, who went on and on about how only a few years ago they never even bothered to lock their doors in this area ... Barbara made a valiant effort to console her by saying how much worse things were in the Cork suburb where she lived. That didn't help much. It had the poor lady foreseeing the day when drug-crazed urban gangs would be roaming the previously peaceful countryside ...

On the way back, they tried to pick up the conversation where they had left off.

Though Barbara in no way shared Tim's personal obsession, she seemed to find the Castle Green affair an intriguing mystery - possibly providing a foretaste of the detective work she hoped to get into if (and this was now a big 'if') she stayed in the force. "But what I don't understand is what happened to the bike. Isn't it the same one you say some schoolgirl had admitted to taking?"

"Exactly."

"But if Dónal and Sean are now telling the truth ..."

"And why should they be lying?"

"... the girl can't have stolen the bike!"

"Not as early as half-past eight, anyway, like she said."

Barbara was beginning to read the hidden signals. "Do I understand that you've found out how she got her hands on it?"

"That's right. And I think I've figured out a couple of other things, too,"

Tim had managed to challenge Sean on the discrepancy in his story soon after his meeting with Dónal. He had driven to Kilkenny on spec, and been lucky enough to catch Sean before he left home for a gig in Waterford. He would dearly love to have challenged Róisín Casey in turn first thing next morning. It was his second day off duty. But it being mid-week, this would have meant dragging the poor girl out of school. Which would not do at all, even if he managed to get the authority of Kilbrue Garda Station behind him. He decided to wait until after school, and call on Maggie O'Keeffe instead.

She greeted him with some apparent enthusiasm, saying her friend Celia had talking about him recently. "She said you were working on that awful murder case out at Castle Green, asking her questions about the people there." Tim wondered whether Celia Ryan was trying to play up her own importance by turning a harmless bit of small talk at the bar into an interrogation. Or whether she'd been percipient enough to realize that he really had been fishing for information at the time. "But that's all cleared up, now isn't it?"

"A man has been charged with manslaughter, yes. But we're still looking for additional evidence, and you weren't well the last time I tried to call here." She looked at him warily, as if wanting to avoid the awkward subject. "May I come in and ask you a few questions?"

"Oh, certainly, I'll make you a cup of tea." He followed her into the sitting room, and then waited while she busied herself in the kitchen with the tea-making process. Though rather cluttered with ornaments and mementos, the room was spotlessly clean, the mirror over the fireplace freshly polished. A coal fire blazed in the grate. All in all, no sign of an incapacitating illness. Maggie seemed to be coping well enough - whether with or without the booze remained to be seen.

She returned with a loaded tray.

"You know, I don't think I'll have anything of interest to tell you, Tim. Sorry, I mean Garda O'Driscoll."

"That's all right, Maggie, you can go on calling me Tim." She probably saw him as the sixteen-year-old he had been way back then, and nothing else would come naturally. And besides, he'd been calling her Maggie.

He decided to deal with the least important matter first, and asked her to go over again what she remembered of Celia Ryan's accident. She was a bit taken aback, as if this was the last thing she'd expected.

"You weren't making much sense when I picked you up on the Limerick road that day. I suppose you were too upset. It must have been a terrible moment, with Celia unconscious, and you not knowing what to do!"

Grateful for the sympathy on a matter she had nearly forgotten, she exclaimed, "You don't know the half of it, Tim! There I was, and not a soul in sight! I thought, Where are all the cars when you need them? One had just splashed me, and another ..."

There it was. He hadn't imagined that element in her story. "Wait a minute, Maggie. What was that about cars? Celia said there weren't any."

Maggie shifted in her chair. "Well, there was the one we'd seen at the site. Pale blue, it was. It belonged to one of the students, I found out later. It came from behind, and splashed me badly, but that hardly matters now."

"No, but what about the other car? There was another car, wasn't there?"

Maggie was obviously feeling very uncomfortable indeed. In the end she sighed heavily. "Yes, it was a bit odd. A small dark car had passed us earlier, as I was standing at the entrance to the site. It should have been long gone when we turned the corner after setting off from the castle, but we saw it start up and head off towards the main road."

"Start up from where?" Maggie said nothing. "Was it from the place where Celia came in contact with the live wire?"

She shrugged. "Yes, it could have been roughly there, near the gate."

"A small dark car, you say? Could you make out the colour, or the make?"

"No, but it could have been black or brown."

"Did you see the driver?"

"No!"

Wasn't that a bit too emphatic? But Tim obviously wasn't going to get any more out of her, and let her off the hook by changing back to the main topic of P.J.'s death.

She smiled gratefully. "I wasn't even there that evening, and I never even saw the fellow they say killed poor Mr. Murphy."

"But you knew the people there. And you cleaned up the day after, didn't you?"

"Oh, no, I was told to stay away, the guards were all over the place. It was two days later before I was allowed to do any cleaning. And it certainly needed it by then - all sorts of things thrown around, and white dust all over the place ..."

"Fingerprint dust."

"That's what I was told."

"Did you notice anything strange?"

"Strange? Everything was strange! As I said, the place was a mess, and everybody was a bit shook."

Not knowing what to ask for specifically, Tim had to leave it at that. Instead, he asked about her relations with the people involved, and came up with a neat confirmation of what he'd already heard. She had nothing bad to say about any of the men: Mr. Murrough - "a darling man"; Sean Mills - "a great sense of humour "; even P.J. Murphy - "a bit shabby looking, but very serious and quiet". Nor about Niamh: "a gorgeous girl". Georgie Hayes also met with her grudging approval: "a very gracious lady, if a bit cool". But her face clouded over completely at the mention of Jeannie: "a nasty piece of work, no manners" - and Sheila: "loud, inconsiderate".

Having grown to like Jeannie, Tim would have liked to get behind this strange antipathy. But all he got was examples of trivial frictions and disputes. "She was always accusing me of messing things up for her. Once she practically implied I'd stolen something of hers. Something that it turned out later she'd just left lying around!" Nothing about objecting to her lifestyle or sexual orientation. But then it was already growing unfashionable - even in rural Ireland - to admit to such prejudices.

Now to what was really irking him about Maggie's possible role in the whole affair.

"I believe you've had a nasty spell of bad health. As I said, I tried to call on you some time back - and you'd just been taken to hospital in a coma."

Maggie looked uncomfortable. She busied herself with pouring him a second cup of tea. "Yes, but I'm all right now."

Tim decided to take the bull by the horns. "You know we had to check the possible causes, in case there might be a connection with this other business." Maggie nodded. The 'we' he had used was pushing it a bit, but he had decided to take advantage of Maggie's implicit assumption that he was part of the official investigative team. "According to the medical report, there was no suggestion of foul play. The coma was brought on by over-indulgence in alcohol. Is that how you see it?"

"I suppose so," she said humbly. "That's what the doctors say. But ..."

"But what?

"But my little sup of whiskey had never caused me any trouble before ... I thought I'd got used to it."

She looked confused, as if she wanted to say something more, but couldn't find the words. Tim helped out. "That's what being addicted means - getting too used to the stuff. I hope you're taking your doctors' advice and keeping off it from now on."

"Yes, my sister has got me into this group ..."

"Alcoholics Anonymous?"

"That's right. Gertie drove me in to their meeting place last Tuesday. They seem to be nice people."

"So you'll keep on going?" Maggie nodded rather glumly. It was clear she would need all the support she could get to stay sober. "But I think you were going to say something else about your illness?"

"Yes. But that nasty spell I had ... the coma, as they call it ... OK, I believe what the doctors say, that the whiskey must have brought it on. But something like that had happened to me before, long before I took such a liking to the whiskey."

"You mean twenty-five years ago?"

She looked at him in surprise. "You know about that?"

"Your medical history was all there, in the report. It was during your pregnancy, wasn't it?"

"Yes, when I had Brendan. He's in England now," she added irrelevantly. Tim nodded, wanting her to go on. "It was those iron tablets I'd taken. Gertie gave them to me, told they'd be good for my blood."

"But they didn't agree with you."

She nodded. "But the funny thing is, the dizzy spells I had then, in the days before I collapsed and had to be taken to hospital ... Well, it was very like that this time, too. For several weeks I'd been feeling a bit weak, and occasionally dizzy."

"But you surely haven't been taking iron supplements recently?"

"No, of course not. But maybe there was something else in my food. You just don't know what you're getting in the shops these days."

She may have been right there. But even so, it was important that she should not play down the role of the alcohol in causing her collapse and ruining her liver. Before leaving, Tim repeated the dire warning that his sister Brid had asked him to pass on.

He waited on the bridge over the river that Róisín Casey would have to cross on her way home from school. From that vantage point, he could see the entrance to the convent school. Luckily, she was in the first group to emerge. She reached the bridge in the company of a bunch of other girls, all in their dark green uniforms.

Róisín may have been embarrassed to be picked up by a Garda in uniform, but Tim figured that she would like it even less to be questioned at home. He gave her the choice of going to the Garda station to answer a few questions that had turned up, going to her home, or sitting in Tim's car. She chose the latter. Her nervousness was palpable.

Tim took out his notebook to ensure that the official nature of the proceedings was emphasized in spite of the informal surroundings. He got straight to the point.

"Miss Casey, we have reason to believe that the account you gave us of your actions on the evening of September 30th was not quite accurate." That 'we' wasn't quite accurate either, but what the hell!

She stared at him, saying nothing.

"To be precise, we now know that you did not take Mr. Declan Sheehan's bicycle from outside Ryan's pub, as you claimed."

She still said nothing, just staring stubbornly ahead to the street corner where three of her friends were nudging each other, and occasionally looking back over their shoulders.

"As late as a quarter to nine it was still there. And shortly after, it was parked at Castle Green. Now would you please take up the story from there." He looked at her sternly. She had gone distinctly pale, and now a flush was creeping up her neck to her cheeks. It looked as if she was going to cry, but Tim decided to give no mercy. "You have the right to remain silent, of course. But if you do, or if you continue to tell that cock-and-bull story about joy-riding, you may end up being suspected of a crime worse than bike-stealing!"

217

This rough paraphrase of the usual police warning might well have had her refusing to say another word without the presence of a solicitor. She was a smart girl. Luckily, however, she decided to talk.

"OK, I made up that story because I didn't want anyone to know I'd been on the castle grounds that evening."

"With your brothers?"

"Yes."

"And with anyone else?"

She looked a bit disconcerted, but finally answered with a firm "No."

"How did you get there? Did you walk?"

She hesitated. "No, I got a lift. Aidan dropped me off there, before driving to Limerick for a hurling match. We'd been at Jodey's before that. He was helping us with our maths homework." She was getting a bit voluble, which was often a sign of trying to distract from the main issue.

"Aidan Flynn, I presume you mean?"

"Yes."

"What kind of a car does Aidan have?"

"Huh? It's ... a brown Opel." Interesting, Tim thought.

"And Aidan is the same person who, with you, made those threatening calls to the Murroughs?"

Her face had by now turned crimson. "We didn't mean them any harm. Just wanted to give them a fright, to get them to think about how they were messing up our countryside."

"All right, get on with the story. Where and when did you meet up with your brothers?"

"About half seven, behind the bushes on the north side. I made sure they did nothing until it was safe, and they wouldn't be seen."

Did you take part in the slogan painting?"

"No, I just told Liam and Cormac what to write where."

"And otherwise the account they gave is correct?"

She nodded. "I sent them off some time after eight, and stayed back to tidy up."

"Tidy up?"

"To put back the ladder. We'd borrowed it from where the archaeology crowd were digging. I lugged it back there." Now if Kilbrue had bothered to fingerprint that ladder, this matter might have been sorted out a lot earlier.

"And then?"

There was a long pause, as if she was wondering how much she should tell. "I went around to the entrance, walking close to the wall."

"Why?"

"Why go to the entrance? Or why close to the wall?"

She was stalling. "Both."

"Well, we'd seen this man up on the roof. We thought it was Mr. Murrough. I saw him again when I was putting away the ladder, from the archaeological site."

"So?"

"So I got the idea I could give him a real fright. I knew the door wasn't locked - I'd seen people going in and out - so I thought I might go inside and try to find my way up."

"Wasn't that a bit risky?"

"Maybe. But since the man is blind, he wouldn't know who was yelling at him." So another of Barbara's theories had proved correct.

"Like your threatening phone calls?"

"She looked sullen. "Yes," she practically barked.

"But what about the person you'd heard playing music? Weren't you worried that that person might see you?"

"That was the reason I stayed close to the wall. ... It was Niamh Ní Ghráda playing, wasn't it?" Tim nodded. "Well I thought I saw her at one of the windows once. But I knew she wouldn't see me if I kept close to the wall."

"But weren't you afraid of being seen once you got inside?"

"Oh, sure, I knew that was a risk, but thought I'd find somewhere to hide." Róisín turned around to face him, as if she'd suddenly decided to be completely frank. "All I could think of then was how marvellous it would be if I managed to pull it off. I could tell ..." She tailed off.

"... Aidan and all your radical friends?" She said nothing. "Was it Aidan gave you that idea, of taking advantage of the man's blindness to give him a scare?"

She frowned again. "I don't remember."

"So you climbed the spiral stairs, and then ...?

"No, I never got as far as that. I never even got inside! I was crouching behind those big pot plants that were stacked on a board near the door, just to make sure the coast was clear ..." She paused again.

"And then?"

"Then I heard a crash, and the sound of breaking glass. Something seemed to have fallen from the roof. I looked around, and saw ..." She broke off.

At last - a witness! "A crash, you said ... A scream?"

219

"No scream. Just a crash. Looked like he hit the neon sign, and then the board with the plants. He was just lying there, his head stuck behind those plants, near where I'd been hiding!"

"What time was that?"

"I'm not sure. Well, it was ten past when I put away the ladder - I looked at my watch as I was making up my mind to try to go inside. So it must have been about a quarter past eight, or maybe twenty past."

"So what did you do?"

"I saw ... the man lying there, the man who'd been on the roof. With broken glass all around. I didn't know what to do ..."

"You didn't think of calling the Gardai? Or any emergency number?"

"I couldn't! I wasn't supposed to be there! And besides, I thought ..."

"What?"

"Oh, nothing. Just how it might look. The Gardai might think I had pushed him over the edge, or ..." She tailed off again.

"Or that one of your friends had got there before you?" She didn't answer. "Did you think maybe Aidan hadn't gone to his hurling match after all?" Aidan's alibi had been checked, and was solid. But Róisín wasn't to know that.

"I don't know what I thought!"

"You knew it was Aidan cut the wires back in May, didn't you? And nearly killed Celia Ryan!" Suddenly it dawned on him why Maggie O'Keeffe - Róisín's aunt - had been so cagey about the car she'd seen. "Maybe you were even there yourself!"

She said nothing. He pressed ahead. "So you knew what he was capable of. How reckless he could be. That's why you've been lying to us up to now. You thought he'd done it."

"I just knew I had to get away from there!"

She can't have left just then. But first things first: there was another underlined item in Tim's notebook that needed clearing up. "By the way, Róisín, had the music stopped by then? Niamh practising on the fiddle, I mean:"

"Oh, no, that was still going on, practically non-stop. She only stopped around half past eight." So Róisín was still hanging round then.

"Jigs and reels and things?"

"Yes. Well no, she also played a slow tune. It's one I know, because we learned it as a song in school. 'The Coolin'." Yes, *An Cúlfhionn*, 'the fair-haired one'. Very popular as a slow air for fiddlers and pipers, because of the scope it gave for elaborate ornamentation. "When was that?"

220

"Oh, just as Liam and Cormac were finishing up their spraying."

"Your brothers didn't mention a change in musical style."

"Oh, they've both got tin ears, they would hardly notice the difference, even if they'd been listening."

"This was shortly after everyone else had left the grounds? When the cars had driven away, I mean?"

"Yes, about then. It was nice. I like that tune. But she suddenly broke it off and played another reel. Then she got back to 'The Coolin' again."

"And she stopped playing around half past eight, you said?"

"Yes."

"And you left then?" Tim knew she couldn't have, but was testing her.

"Not directly. I first had to pick up the bag of spray-cans and things that I'd had with me. It had a notebook of mine in it."

"With your name on it, I suppose?"

"Yeah. I thought I'd left it near the ladder at the site, so I went back there first. But it couldn't find it there. Then I remembered I'd carried it with me as far as the door, and stuffed it behind the pot plants."

"So you went back to retrieve it."

"Not yet. I wanted to, but just as I was climbing up the slope to the car park, I saw Mr. Murrough coming out the door. That was a shock, I can tell you!"

"You mean, you'd thought he was dead!"

"Yes, it was only then that I realized that the dead man must be somebody else. There was no doubt that this was Murrough coming out, with his white stick and all."

"By the way, the man lying on the ground was not dead at the time. If you'd called an emergency number at the time, his life might have been saved."

"I'm sorry. I didn't realize ... I didn't think ..."

"As it was, it took nearly another hour before the alarm was raised. By which time it was too late."

She looked at him sharply. "But what about the other people who turned up there shortly after?"

So she knew about them. "Tell me what you saw."

"Well, I was stuck where I was, behind the bushes. It was dark, and I didn't want to go out the back way, through the fields. So I waited until Mr. Murrough had walked down the path. I grabbed my bag, and thought I might then manage to get back onto the road. But then I heard a car approaching, and ducked back again. I could see the headlights as it stopped at the gate. Then the car came about half-way up the drive. The driver got out ..."

"Can you describe the driver?"

"No, I couldn't see him clearly against the lights. But it was a man, that's all I can say."

"So what did he do?"

"I think he first bent down to see what was lying there, then he went to the door. But I don't think he went in. Anyway, he soon got back in his car, did a three-point turn and drove off."

"Go on."

"I saw that the gates had been left open, which would make it easier for me to get out. I was on my way to the gates when another man turned up - on a bike. I had to hide behind a different shrub."

"And what did that man do?"

"He pushed the bike up the slope, and dropped it when he saw the mess on the pavement. I think he shouted 'Jesus Christ' or something. He bent down and I think he turned the man on the ground over, probably to see who it was. Then he looked around. I thought he might have seen me - it was a very small shrub - but apparently not. He picked up the bike and wheeled it round the corner to the north side of the castle, then went inside."

"Into the castle?"

"Yes."

"And stayed how long?"

"I've no idea. That was my chance. I went round the corner, grabbed the bike where he had left it. Luckily he hadn't bothered to lock it, and the gate was still open. I put my bag on the carrier, cycled down the slope, and took the back road into the village."

"And that's when you dumped it near the river."

"Yes."

"Now Róisín, do you realize that one of the two men you saw arriving at Castle Green is currently charged with manslaughter? That is, of having caused the death of P.J. Murphy, the man you saw lying on the pavement."

She said nothing for a while, so that Tim was sorely tempted to shake her to force a response. But finally: "Afterwards, I thought the man in the car might have been Dónal Ó Gráda, but I wasn't sure. I didn't see him clearly."

"You would still be an important witness. Your testimony could make a huge difference!" She stared stubbornly ahead. "Did you want to be responsible for an innocent man being convicted of something he didn't do, and put behind bars for ten years or so?"

At last she showed a touch of conscience. "Yeah, I thought about all that. But all in all, I didn't think what I would say would make that much difference. After all, who would believe me, after I'd made up that other story?"

She had a point there. One more unreliable witness certainly would not have the prosecution rushing to drop the charges. But for Róisín, it was obviously a case of believing what she wanted to believe. He drove her to the corner of the street where she lived, dropping her off at the point near the river bank where she had dumped Declan's bike.

A short visit to his mother (the old man was in Limerick on business), and then he needed to get on the road back to Bandon. But as he reached Ryan's pub, he stopped on an impulse.

As luck would have it, Celia was serving. "Garda O'Driscoll! How nice to see you again! ....What are you having?"

"Just a glass of Guinness, please. Can't risk any more, I'm driving back to Bandon tonight."

"I suppose you've been visiting the old folks at home."

"That's right, Celia." And he embarked on the usual round of small talk. This time he didn't need to make any special effort to bring the conversation round to what interested him. Celia did it for him.

"I believe you've also been visiting my good friend Maggie O'Keeffe." News travels fast in this village. "She had a nasty turn recently, but I suppose you know about that."

"Yes, it was the weekend I wanted to talk to her about her work at Castle Green. She'd just been taken to hospital. But she seems to have made a good recovery."

"A marvellous recovery." Celia lowered her voice. "It helps that she's keeping off the booze. You know, we'd all been turning a blind eye to her little habit, pretending we didn't know ..."

"Yes, that happens a lot in this country. My sister Brid is always going on about that."

"She's a doctor, now, isn't she? Down the country somewhere."

"That's right, she has a country practice down in West Cork."

"Isn't that where ye all grew up, before coming here?"

"That's right, Celia." The conversation was de-railing. Better get it back on track. "But as regards Maggie, is her sister keeping an eye on her regularly?"

"As regular as she can manage, coming out from Limerick a couple of times a week. The rest of the time it's up to me. Some of her Casey cousins call in on her, too, but I've got a bit more time. I call once a day - usually in the evening if I'm not working here - to see that she's OK. And ..." She lowered her voice again, "... to check that there are no bottles of whiskey stashed away anywhere."

"And so far she's managed to stay off the stuff?"

"So it seems. But I'm worried about her going back to work at Castle Green."

"She's going back to work? She didn't mention that to me."

"Probably because she knows everybody is trying to talk her out of it. You know, I never quite understood why she was so keen to continue working there after that awful affair, the man getting killed, and all that." She paused, and Tim made sympathetic noises. "Oh, she talked about the regular pay, and how friendly the Murroughs were, and so on. But it turns out it wasn't just that."

"No?"

"No, it all came out at a wedding we were at together some time back. Now Maggie practically never drinks in public, pretends she doesn't like it much. But this time she drank some sherry to be sociable, and got a bit tipsy. She even joined in a sing-song, you know the one, 'Whiskey in the Jar'." Who didn't? It was the bane of Irish pub life, the one song guaranteed to get the noisier elements going. With the eloquent chorus:

Wisha ring dum-a-doo dum-a-da,
Whack fol-de-daddio,
Whack fol-de-daddio,
There's whiskey in the jar.

"Well," Celia elaborated, "After joining in a couple of choruses, Maggie went rambling on about there being whiskey in the jar out at Castle Green - 'and a very fine jar it is, too' - those were her very words."

"Did you find out what she meant by that?"

"Apparently Mr. Murrough, the owner of the castle, was being a bit too accommodating. When some musicians there helped themselves to her 'little bottle', as she called it, he arranged for a better hiding place for it. And I think he even provided a special container. That must have been the jar she was giggling about, though she was sounding a bit confused."

"Did you ask her about this afterwards, I mean when she was sober?"

"Oh, I tried, but she pretended not to know what I was talking about. Maybe she really didn't remember what she'd been saying."

"That's possible."

"But my point is, there's no way I can keep an eye on her out there. If Mr. Murrough is so indulgent, she could easily slip back into her old ways."

"We've got a problem there, I can see that. Maybe someone could talk to Murrough."

"Could you? I mean explain to him that she's an alcoholic and just has to stay dry?"

Tim doubted very much that Murrough needed any such explanations, but didn't want to go into that with Celia. "Not me, I won't be around here much. But maybe my father could, or someone from Kilbrue Garda Station ..."

Celia thanked him profusely, and he was on his way.

As he drove through the night, he went over in his mind the new elements that had been added to the puzzle, and the old ones that had to be re-arranged, or seen in a new light. He had the distinct feeling that some new patterns were emerging, but so far they were failing to coalesce into a satisfying whole.

As he often did when stumped by a crossword puzzle, he tried to temporarily switch off his logical faculty, and instead, toss around the various elements in the style of a brainstorm:

ROOF - RIFF - RIFT - LIFT - LEFT ...

OPPORTUNITY - OPPORTUNE - OPPORTUNIST - OPPORTUNISTIC ... ...

It dawned on Tim that for the first time, he now felt he knew with a fair degree of certainty who had brought about P.J. Murphy's death. The WHO implied the WHY. He thought he could make a fair stab at WHERE and WHEN. What remained to figure out was the HOW.

But the latter point was decisive. Without it, there could be no concrete proof of his theory. Nor even an alternative scenario to cast doubt on the prosecution's case. In other words, nothing to save Dónal Ó Gráda from an unjust conviction.

Chapter 24

"Dublin? But you never wanted to live in Dublin!"

Cathy's phone-call could not have come at a more inopportune time, but Tim did not want to say why. So he was doing his best to feign interest in her tale of woe. She didn't have much choice, she patiently explained, Celtic Technologies having been taken over by a German outfit called Tech-Soft, who were consequently reducing the number of Irish offices to one.

Tim vaguely remembered that Cathy's convenient business meeting following the Van Morrison concert had had something to do with meeting their new German 'partners'. She had been proud then to be one of the chosen few to be kept on, 'mainly because of her German degree'. Now she was arguing that the whole thing might be a blessing in disguise. Being heavily into computer translation, her new bosses were putting her in for a computer linguistics course at DIT. Everything might work out fine, if only...

"If only what?"

"Well, I've been thinking. Your probation is nearly up, and you could easily put in for a transfer to Dublin. Maybe even to Harcourt Street headquarters."

"Hah!"

But she was undeterred, and continued to rabbit on about Tim being more than adequately qualified for the computer crime division.

"OK, I'll think about it."

The squeaking door seemed to have registered on Cathy's ears. "Is there somebody there with you?"

"No that was just the cat." The black-and-white cat was a recent acquisition, as yet nameless. Rescued only that weekend - by Cathy - from the roof of the extension just below Tim's bathroom window, its owner had still not been found. In spite of the notice pinned up in the window of the hardware store downstairs. It wasn't so much that Tim had adopted it, as that it seemed to have adopted Tim. Two attempts to get it to find its own way home had failed. Each time Tim had placed it in the back yard it must have climbed up from, the cat (though it was really little more than a kitten) had cowered in a corner, and then followed him back through the alley to his front door.

"Maybe it needs to be fed." Cathy, bless her, had a soft heart. "OK, see you Friday. And do think about what I said."

The cat was actually snoozing on Tim's one comfortable armchair. The squeaking door had been caused by Barbara, returning from the kitchen with a jug of fresh milk for the mugs of tea already making rings on the scratched surface of what passed for a coffee table. Surrounding the mugs was a confusion of photographs and papers extracted from the official file Tim had brought home from the office.

"You didn't need to lie to her. After all, we've got nothing to hide! It's not as if ..."

He cut her off. "Sure, she'd know that." He wasn't all that sure that Barbara's steady boyfriend in Cork would put their relationship beyond suspicion, but what the hell ... "No, it's just that spending more of my free time on this business wouldn't go down all that well with her either." He indicated the mess on the table.

She took her place at the other end of the lumpy sofa, and resumed her perusal of the spreadsheet Tim had created for the events of the evening of September 30th. A print-out of the latest version, the one incorporating Róisín Casey's most recent admissions.

The phone call had come at a point when Barbara had drawn his attention to some still unexplained discrepancies in the post mortem report. Now he had it. Somehow, through Cathy's distracting rigmarole, his unconscious mind had gone on processing the information.

No scratches to P.J.'s hands ... his silent fall ... the bruise on the left side of P.J.'s skull, though the fatal fracture had been on the right ...

"You know Barbara, we have to start thinking in terms of a two-part deed." He explained what he meant.

Barbara thought for a moment. "I can see that opens a whole new can of worms. So he was knocked out before being pushed over the edge."

"Exactly."

"So now all you need to do is find the weapon used to knock him out."

"Not an easy task at this stage."

"What's that?" Barbara was pointing to the photo taken on the roof, indicating to the left of the cement mixer.

"That's the winch they used to lift heavy objects onto the roof."

"No, not that. The thing propped against it. It could be a spade or something."

It certainly could. And there may have been more of the same lying around the roof. After all, they were setting up a roof garden at the time.

"Sure, but if so, it probably belonged to the garden centre. I doubt if they could trace the tools they actually used there."

"Though maybe the winch itself has some potential - the hook itself looks hefty enough! Give it a good swing, and ..."

Tim was sceptical . "Yes, they might just about be able to trace that piece of machinery. But I doubt if there'd be any traces left of its use as a weapon."

"But at least we can show it wouldn't have been hard to find a potential weapon up there. Surely the more important point is *who* did!"

"Of course."

As Barbara began to consult Tim's table of events to check who was on the spot at the time, Tim made an additional point. "It must be said that the first part of the deed needn't have been up on the roof at all."

"What? But the victim was seen walking around up there only shortly before!" She consulted the table again, and pointed out that the archaeology students had noticed him around a quarter to eight, and the Casey boys several times up to about eight o'clock. "And this Róisín person saw him as late as ten past!"

"I've been thinking about that. Remember, Róisín and her brothers thought it was Murrough up there."

"But they weren't familiar with either of the men. And they were sort of fixated on Murrough as the object of their protests."

"Yes, but what if they were right? What if it really *was* Richard Murrough up there?"

"Oh." There was a long silence before she went on. "But what about the other witnesses? They knew both men."

"Yes, but it was dusk, and the only details anyone mentioned were his clothing. In particular P.J.'s ugly rust-coloured anorak."

"You mean ..."

"Murrough could have worn that jacket and cap to give the impression that P.J. was still alive at the time."

"But wait a minute! All this points in two different directions. First of all, it involves Murrough in some way. .... But it also means P.J. could have been knocked unconscious long before that."

"And anywhere in the castle."

"Mmm." She consulted the table again. "Any time from 6.15, if it comes to that. And that brings a lot of suspects back into the equation."

"That's exactly what was bothering me. I've come to the conclusion anyway that at least two people must have been involved. However unlikely it may sound."

"One being Murrough?"

"Yes, almost certainly. But it may have been unpremeditated and, well, opportunistic."

"I seem to have heard you use that term to describe him before."

He agreed that it would certainly be in character for Murrough to come across some situation and take advantage of it. To get someone else to do his dirty work, as it were.

"But who? And how?"

"Let's take the 'who' question first. I think it's the easier one."

The next hour was spent going through the list of suspects one by one - namely all those present in the castle after 6.15.

They decided they could eliminate the archaeology students, only one of whom had briefly entered the castle (to go to the toilet), and none of whom had a motive. Sean was briefly back in the picture, except that his motive - the one that had him rushing back to the castle on a 'borrowed' bike - had only emerged later.

Barbara finally zoomed in on Sheila McCarthy. "After all, she was around in the castle a bit longer, and she only admitted it when forced to."

"You mean she may have been lying about finding P.J.'s room empty?"

"Yes, maybe he was snoozing on his bed, or something ... You'd need to check are there any handy cast-iron candlesticks or heavy ornaments there!"

"Maybe we should. Still, that scenario sounds a bit unlikely if she could have just quietly retrieved the incriminating shard and slipped away."

"What about P.J. blackmailing her, or directly threatening exposure of her professional misconduct?"

"Now that I can just about imagine. She might well have had enough physical strength to knock him out, especially if he was taken by surprise."

Barbara's eyes were attracted to another point listed on the spreadsheet. "In either case, Sheila's talk of seeing Niamh entering P.J.'s room would have been an attempt to cast suspicion elsewhere, just in case any traces of violence were found in the room."

"Right. But now let's complete that scenario. What might have happened then?"

Barbara thought for a moment. "Then Murrough appeared on the scene, possibly attracted by the noise ... and, well, offered his assistance in covering up the crime."

"Yes, that's exactly the sort of thing I've been considering. Between them, they could have lugged the unconscious P.J. up onto the roof. Since his room is on the top floor, it would only have been one flight of stairs from there."

"Then Murrough would have waited until Sheila and everybody else had left the grounds to push him over the edge."

"Plausible enough," said Tim, though with a frown. "I see just one little snag."

"And what might that be?"

"If Murrough was alerted by the sound, why not Niamh? Her room was directly under P.J.'s, and at the time she was either there, or in the studio with Murrough."

Barbara shrugged. "Maybe she was wearing earplugs. Or headphones. But OK, let's consider the remaining suspects." She checked her list. "What about Georgie? Could you say she had a motive?"

"You know, Babs, she's the one person I haven't been able to figure out. Maybe because I never managed to speak to her on her own. I do not know what makes her tick."

"Why she married Richard Murrough, for example? For love or money?"

"Yeah, things like that. She seems to be a fairly down-to earth person, and respected in her profession. Why a person like that should choose to be another one of Murrough's trophy wives is beyond me." Tim shrugged his shoulders, "But as regards motive, she might well have wanted to help her new husband out of a tight spot."

"She was working out in the gym from shortly after six. She could easily have gone back up into the studio while her husband and P.J were there. After all, it was her place of work."

"And then?"

"Maybe she was witness to a quarrel. That could have been the point where P.J. made it known to Murrough who he was, and threatened revenge for his ruined life, for whatever wrongs - real or imagined - he had done him. That disputed hit song, for example. Though P.J. never seemed to be to be the kind of person to suddenly snap..."

Barbara began to leaf through Tim's notes. "Did you say there was some reason why things should have come to a head on that particular day?"

Tim summed up what he had learned from various sources about the band working on a new instrumental version of 'Light and Shade'. "And there was that phone-call to Dervla Cassidy of the *Irish Times*. You know, the one who did the Murrough interview."

"It was that day?"

"That morning, to be precise. We don't know for certain that it was P.J. who was offering to dish the dirt on Richard's Murrough's past, but it seems very likely."

"That's it then. There was a quarrel, P.J. said he'd contacted the national press, and they were interested in hearing more. Then he either demanded silence money or some kind of compensation, or said he was going ahead with the exposure anyway."

"That fits very well with the evidence I've collected. P.J. was hoarding documents that would have proved that for over ten years, Murrough had been effectively blackmailing P.J. into silence, and collecting 100% of the royalties for a hit song that should at least have been shared with him. May have said he no longer gave a damn, now that he was living in a foreign jurisdiction."

"Or maybe the statute of limitations for document forgery has run out?"

Tim nodded. "It probably has. We can check it. So under the circumstances it's very plausible that a quarrel may have ensued as soon as Murrough and P.J. were alone in the studio together. Especially with P.J. being goaded by the re-use of the very tune that he claimed to have composed. The last straw may have been Murrough pretending to be unconcerned, possibly saying 'Go ahead, do your worst!' or similar. They could well have come to blows ..."

"And nothing would be heard outside due to the soundproofing."

"Right. And remember, Sheila McCarthy reported the red light was on when she passed the studio door on the way up to P.J.'s room. I'd been wondering about that. Strictly speaking, it shouldn't have been necessary for the kind of post-production that Murrough was doing at the time. It wasn't actual recording."

"So P.J. may have switched it on to ensure privacy?"

"Possibly."

Barbara thought for a moment. "But even if the men came to blows, I can't see a blind man getting the better of a fist fight!"

"Me neither. But weren't you speculating on someone bursting in on them? Someone who would have known the red light was anomalous?"

"Oh yes, Georgie!"

"That was your idea. She could certainly have entered the studio for whatever professional reason, seen her husband under attack, possibly even thought he was being murdered ..."

"No cast-iron candlesticks there, though, are there?"

"No, of course not. I've been wondering about that, since it had already occurred to me that the studio was a lot more likely a location for the original attack than any bedroom. And as it happens, I have been shown around the studio, by Richard Murrough himself."

"So is there anything there that might have been used as a weapon?"

He thought himself back to the scene, visualizing the high ceiling of the studio, the wooden panelling, the isolation booths, the control room, the parquet floor with suspended microphones, and the grey-carpeted 'dead area'. Suddenly another element in the puzzle slipped into place. "There is. Very suitable, I should imagine."

"Come on, stop building up the tension!"

"Sorry. They've got a beautiful old microphone - you know, the heavy 1950s kind. Purely decorative. But it's certainly what I'd grab if I saw someone being attacked in the studio. I imagine you could crack someone's skull with it, or at least make a nasty bump on the back of an attacker's head!"

Barbara considered this information. "Has it been checked for fingerprints?"

"I think they only dusted the main door, the hall, the immediate roof area, and possibly the stairway. They had no reason to suspect any foul play elsewhere in the castle."

"So why not get it done now?"

"Probably too late. Maggie's probably polished it many times since. You know, Murrough had jokingly started calling it the 'Maggie Mike' after the name she's known by locally. And any person who used it as a weapon would also have had the chance to make sure it was clean." Tim thought back again to his tour of the castle. "Besides, any surviving prints would prove nothing."

"Why not?"

"I imagine everybody who visits the castle gets to handle it, Murrough is so proud of its illustrious history. He even had me doing an Elvis Presley act with it!"

Barbara grimaced with assumed distaste. "OK, I get your point. But those things have deep ridges on top, haven't they? I've seen pictures ... you know, where Elvis or whoever sings into it." Tim nodded, "Well, if it was used as a weapon, some of the victim's skin cells or bits of hair or blood would probably have got knocked inside. That wouldn't be so easy to clean."

"Babs, you're brilliant!" He noted she was no longer objecting to the nickname. "Especially if they find blood or bits of hair. If we're lucky, microscopic analysis might show them to match P.J.'s."

"But I thought Kilbrue weren't interested in looking for new evidence that might cast doubt on their existing case?"

"They needn't see it that way. I could suggest to DI Smith that Dónal may have possibly used it as a weapon. I'm sure she'd get the forensic squad to work on it if she thought it might bolster their case. I'll suggest it tomorrow."

Barbara was beginning to look doubtful. "It can't do any harm, I suppose. But if they only found skin cells, it would just be unidentifiable grunge, wouldn't it? Could be anybody's ..."

"Well, at least they'd be able to recognize how fresh ... No, wait, what am I saying?" Tim got up and began rummaging in the concertina file he kept on his desk. Having failed to find what he was looking for under 'D', he found it under 'G'. For 'Genetic fingerprinting'.

"Ever heard of Alec Jeffreys?" Barbara looked blank. "Well, he's been working at Leicester University trying to find a reliable way to identify a person's DNA for forensic purposes. And only a few years ago ..." He consulted on of the articles he'd retrieved. "... 1985, to be precise, he managed to use the polymerase chain reaction technique, usually known as PCR, to make an identification in some immigration case."

Barbara was looking even blanker. "I'll explain the science later. Anyway, everybody's DNA is different, except for identical twins, and it's found in all the cells of the body. And only last year, Jeffreys' DNA evidence was used to identify the murderer of two girls in the Midlands."

"Oh, yes, I think I know the case you mean. It was how Colin Pitchfork was convicted, wasn't it?"

"Good girl, you're on the ball! But the main point is that it was the first time DNA was used to solve a crime and get a conviction. It's definitely the thing of the future ... the only problem being that there aren't many laboratories equipped for the technique. Certainly none in Ireland yet."

"Maybe you could persuade Kilbrue to get the necessary tests done in England. In Leicester, if necessary, or wherever you said this man Jeffreys is working."

"I'll try. But even if they play along, the tests take at last six weeks. It may be too late for Dónal's trial."

"But getting the tests done might be a way of putting pressure on whoever is really guilty of the crime."

233

He grinned conspiratorially. "That's just what I was thinking."

"And it now looks like a cooperative effort between Murrough and his wife."

Tim was silent for a while. "I'm not sure. I can still see a few snags there."

"Such as?"

"Well, for one thing, whoever burst in on the scene must have come to the rescue from behind, to have a fair chance of overwhelming the attacker. Now just imagine I'm the assailant, and you've just grabbed this weapon." He handed Barbara a rolled-up newspaper, which he could safely assume lacked the destructive force of a 1950s microphone. Then he grabbed the snoozing cat from the depths of the armchair, causing squawks of protest from the unfortunate animal. Also two nasty scratches to his left hand, and finally a hefty blow from the rolled-up *Cork Examiner* on the back of his neck, just under his right ear.

He dropped the cat, who glared at him in uncomprehending hostility. Was this the end of a beautiful friendship? Maybe she would finally depart in a huff, and find her way back to her original owners? Though Tim had been trying to achieve such an end over the last week, he now relented. He couldn't let it end like this. He stroked the animal's soft fur, and after a few seconds of stiff resistance, she rubbed against his arm. "OK, Murphy, no harm intended!" At last she now had a name, however provisional. A logical enough choice, considering she had been playing the part of Richard Murrough, the original form of whose name had seemed more suitable for a feline.

Dabbing his scratches with the tissue proffered by his colleague, Tim proceeded to make his point. "See? You hit me under the right ear, just as any right-handed person would in the circumstances. But the mysterious bruise on P.J.'s head was on the left."

"So what? Maybe Georgie is left-handed!"

"She isn't."

"How the hell do you know that?"

"Elementary, my dear Brennan. When I latched onto DI Smith's interview of the Murroughs last Halloween, I observed her writing out a list of the threatening phone-calls she remembered. She wrote with her right hand."

"OK, but that's not decisive. Depending on her relative position, she might have been only able to get at him from the left."

"True, it isn't decisive. But there's also the matter of logistics. Even if we assume she's strong enough to lug P.J.'s inert body up onto the roof, either alone or with her husband's help, it'd be quite a job. From the studio door that would be four flights of spiral stairs, remember!"

"She'd been working out in the gym, hadn't she?"

"Oh, she's pretty athletic, I know. But ..."

"And maybe there *is* some other way. Didn't you say something about a lift?"

"Oh, that wasn't in operation yet. It was just an empty lift-shaft at the time."

"Sure, but ... maybe with a rope ...?"

A rope. A sudden vision of the scene on the roof flashed on his inner eye. He fumbled among the crime-scene photos again, until he found the one they'd been looking at earlier. Silently he pointed to the winch with the iron hook, the one Barbara had been considering as a potential weapon. "You're right. It may have been possible. Now we need to find out if those lift-shaft doors can be opened."

"You should be able to get your friends in Kilbrue to check them, if you suggest it's a method Dónal might have used, not someone they regard as totally innocent like Georgie."

Tim frowned. "Let's not get too fixated on Georgie. There are a couple of other snags to that scenario. Like the time-scale."

Barbara obligingly unfolded the spreadsheet again to let him elaborate. Georgie, he pointed out, would have needed to get the unconscious P.J. up on the roof - by whatever method - either between 6.35 and five past seven, between her chat with Tom Kinsella in the gym, and her visit to the dig. Or between 7.10 and 7,30. Having (by her own account) gone back to the house to prepare a meal around 7.10 - and even if she'd hung around longer, she would have to have finished the job and retreated to their home by 7.30 at the latest, since Róisín Casey was keeping a keen eye on the place from then on." He pointed to the appropriate column. "She would have noticed her leaving the castle after that. She noticed everything else."

"OK, that still gives her two periods to do it in - one of twenty minutes, and one of thirty. I think we'll have to discount the first option, as that would be largely taken up by the actual attack, but the second would surely be sufficient?"

"Maybe, except some other people were wandering around the castle at that time. Sheila McCarthy and Niamh Ní Ghráda. Neither mentioned running into Georgie, or hearing any funny noises. And if they had seen or

235

heard any such thing, they would have had no reason to keep quiet about it. It would have been in their interest to shift the suspicion elsewhere."

"So they didn't run into Georgie. That doesn't mean she didn't do it."

"No, but there's something else that bothers me even more, and that applies to the Sheila McCarthy scenario as well."

"And what might that be?"

"Both scenarios would have the guilty lady leaving the scene of the crime at either 7.30 or ten to eight, leaving Murrough up on roof waiting for an opportunity to complete the job."

"So?"

"Since Murrough would only have his sense of hearing to go by, this would imply a willingness to take a reckless risk."

"You mean, he couldn't be sure he was not being observed?"

"Exactly. And one thing I know for sure is that Richard Murrough is no fool. He may be willing to take a risk, but it would have to be a calculated one."

"Wait, couldn't Georgie have kept an eye out from the house and phoned him on his mobile phone when the coast was clear?"

"The house is down a slope to the south-west of the castle. The view is completely obscured by bushes and trees. No way could she have been able to help from there."

"Hmm. "

"This may not be the sort of thing Sherlock Holmes is supposed to have meant in saying that when you have eliminated the impossible, ... how does that quote go on?"

"Whatever remains, however improbable, must be the truth."

"Thanks. But Murrough being a reckless fool is as near to impossible as makes no difference."

Barbara shrugged. She knew nothing of the man, had never met him, so could express no opinion on the matter. "So what does remain?"

"Niamh."

"Niamh?

"Yes. I'm now convinced that the scenario you've just built up is correct, except for one little detail."

Barbara looked at him quizzically.

"I mean the scuffle in the studio. I'm pretty sure something like that must have happened. But I don't think it was Georgie who came to Murrough's aid."

"You think it was Niamh?"

236

"It must have been. At least none of my quibbles apply to her."

"Left-handed?"

"Sure, have you never seen her play the fiddle?" But of course she hadn't. Barbara had little interest in music of any kind.

"But I've seen pictures of her, and she looks very slightly built. Surely she would be a lot less able to help get an unconscious man onto the roof?"

"All she would need to do would be to fix the hook onto ... well, I don't know ... maybe P.J.'s belt."

"If he was wearing one."

"We can check that. Anyway, Murrough would have easily been able to work the winch to get him up on the roof through the lift shaft."

"Objection, Your Honour. Why the hell should Niamh want to finish the poor fellow off? She had absolutely no motive to kill him, for God's sake!"

"No, but she may have thought he was already dead. Thought she'd killed him. And got in a panic."

"She could have felt his pulse..."

"Maybe she didn't think of that ... or left it to Murrough. And this is where Murrough may have grabbed a unique opportunity to rid himself of a troublesome ghost from the past. A blackmailer with the means to ruin his wonderful career, or at least cast a blight over it just when his new project was taking off ..."

"Pure speculation."

"Of course, but no more so than before. And this time everything fits."

"OK, go on."

"So he offers to help cover up Niamh's supposed homicide by faking an accidental fall from the roof. Of course she'd comply."

"But what if she realized he was still alive, or P.J. came to in the meantime?"

"Well, if he had come to, it would have been easy enough to call the whole 'cover-up' effort off as an unfortunate mistake. But he didn't. Maybe for some of the time, Murrough was in a position to ensure he didn't. We may never know."

Barbara was silent for a while as she consulted the spreadsheet. "I can see the time-scale is less of a problem in Niamh's case. She was in the castle all the time. Some of it, by her own account, working in the studio with Murrough."

"I'd take her account with a grain of salt as regards the actual timing. My guess is, she went down to the studio a bit earlier than she said in her statement, probably on her own initiative. The traceable phone-call at 7.05

237

was probably part of their cover-up, suggesting it was only then that she was invited down to hear some tapes."

"Yes. Mobile phones are, well, mobile. She may have been sitting right beside Murrough when she took the call!"

"Quite. And we know she lied about spending about a half an hour from then on working in the studio. It was only when forced to that she admitted going up to P.J.'s room ..."

"Because she'd been seen by Sheila McCarthy. And so she was probably also lying about having seen P.J. going upstairs to his room at 6.40."

"That most certainly."

"But wait a minute! What could Niamh have been doing in P.J.'s room, if she knew she'd just knocked him out - thought she'd killed him, even?"

"Probably fetching his jacket and cap, so that Murrough could impersonate him on the roof."

"Oh! Now I see what you mean by things fitting in!"

"But what clinches it for me is that this scenario doesn't involve Murrough being a reckless fool."

"What do you mean?"

"He was able to use Niamh's eyes to make sure the coast was clear."

"Niamh's eyes?" She again consulted the table of events. "But Niamh retreated to her room after that to practice, at least by her own account ... and, yes, that's been confirmed by several witnesses."

"Precisely. But was she really practising?"

"Well, all the witnesses got the impression that it was live music, her moving around, etc. And no tape-recorders anywhere except in the soundproofed studio."

"That's not what I mean. She was most definitely playing Irish tunes on the fiddle. But was *practice* the object of the exercise?"

Barbara looked confused. "What do you think it was?"

"I think she was signalling."

"Signalling?"

"Yes. What Róisín Casey described opened my eyes. Up to that I'd only heard references to her playing a string of reels and jigs, fast dance music anyway. But Róisín was struck by the way she changed her tune sometime before eight o'clock and began playing a slow air, one the girl was proud to be able to identify as 'An Cúlfhionn'-"

"Even I'd probably know that one! But so what? Why shouldn't she play a slow air?"

238

"No reason whatsoever, except she didn't stick with it. After a few bars she broke into a fast jig again. Now that I'd call an unnatural act! No musician would spoil the flow of 'An Cúlfhionn' with a scrap of a jig!"

"I'll have to take your word for that."

"It can only have been an agreed signal: dance music - people still around, hold your fire; slow air - the coast is clear, go ahead."

"I get your point."

"Anyway, she soon reverted to the slow air, and shortly afterwards, P.J. came crashing down, right beside Róisín, as it happens, who was cowering near the door!"

"So Niamh's eyes proved not all that reliable, after all!"

"Not as regards detecting the presence of someone who was making a determined effort to keep out of sight, no. That was a possibility they didn't seem to have considered. But my guess is, she *had* seen Róisín's two brothers running away across the fields."

"You mean, that would account for her suddenly breaking off the slow air?"

"Yes, the intention would have been to warn Murrough to hold back a moment."

Barbara considered all this for a moment. "You know, you've got me almost convinced."

"There's one more piece of the puzzle I can make fit in. Namely what Sean was up to in the ten minutes he gained by cycling back to the castle." Barbara looked at him inquiringly. "My guess is that as soon as he saw P.J. lying there, he checked up on Niamh. He may have found her in a nervous state. Whether she actually confessed her involvement we may never know, but at least he must have suspected something."

Barbara said nothing, so he went on. "This scenario would also make sense of Niamh fainting when she arrived on the scene in her nightgown."

"What? But surely she would have been only pretending this was the first she knew of the incident? I mean, if this scenario is correct."

"True. But it would have been a genuine shock to realize that P.J. was not dead even then. That she, in fact, had only knocked him out with the original blow ..."

"Jesus Christ!" This was the mildest of a string of expletives. Tim had never known Barbara to use such gross language before. "She would have realized there had been nothing to cover up, and that she had been manipulated into cooperating in a deliberate murder!"

"Yes, she had been used, but could do nothing about it."

Another long silence,

"But we have no proof."

"No. With a bit of luck, we may be able to prove that the original attack did take place in the studio. But it will be hard to pin it beyond reasonable doubt on any particular person or persons."

Another even longer silence. Tim finally broke it. "You know, I've been wondering whether Maggie O'Keeffe may know something useful."

"The cleaning lady?"

"Yes. I was finally able to call on her last week, and I spoke to her closest friend, Celia Ryan, the one-time owner of Ryan's pub." He recounted her revelations about the way Murrough had been pandering to Maggie's alcohol habit prior to her collapse.

"So you think Murrough was at least trying to encourage her own self-destruction?"

"You could put it that way, I suppose. It certainly would be a very inefficient murder method, extremely uncertain in its outcome. But considering Murrough's handicap, he may not have had anything better at his disposal, and at least this attempt had the advantage of being totally unprovable."

"But even if it was his intention to speed her departure from this world, at least it didn't work."

"Not this time. But Maggie is totally loyal to the Murroughs, and is determined to go back to work as soon as they get back from L.A. in two weeks time."

"We've got a problem. Can't she be talked out of going back to work?"

"Her friend is trying, but isn't very confident."

"Well, in that case, your best option would be to find out what she knows that might possibly incriminate Richard Murrough. That is, if she really knows something."

"If my theory is correct, Murrough at least thinks she does. But she may not realize it herself. It may be something totally trivial that she does not see the significance of. But that's what makes it so difficult to ask about it directly!"

"Well, if it's something that trivial, she may already have mentioned it. Maybe even you didn't recognize its significance! You should check all your notes again. Or try to remember what she said that you didn't even bother to write down."

What Barbara said made perfect sense. But her advice would be rather difficult to act on. Trying to find the one bit of significant information would not just be like trying to find a needle in a haystack. More like looking for a particular piece of hay in a haystack. Still, he would try.

"In the meantime, we can at least get Kilbrue to work on the additional bit of forensic evidence."

Barbara agreed, and added, "And I think it might be an idea to judiciously leak the information to all the possible suspects that you're following up this particular trail."

"Yeah. As the Yanks say: Let's run it up the flagpole and see who salutes!"

Chapter 25

Except that it couldn't have happened like that.

As soon as Barbara had left, Tim developed a sneaking feeling that there was a problem with the beautiful scenario they had worked out between them.

As he lay in bed trying to get to sleep, it came to him. A small problem, but with serious consequences. Since there was no question of sleep until he had sorted this out, he jumped out of bed and re-opened the file that he had so carefully tidied up.

He searched the documents for evidence that P.J. Murphy had been wearing a belt on the day of his death, but could find no such reference. Every detail of his clothing was listed, down to the contents of his pockets, but no belt. What was even more decisive: On the crime scene photo showing the victim prostrate on the pavement, his jacket had ridden up, revealing the top of his beltless jeans.

So either Sean had removed it on his arrival at the scene - which would bring Sean back into the equation as a suspect again. Or the unconscious P.J had *not* been hoisted up on the roof through the empty lift shaft. Even if some other part of his clothing had been found strong enough to bear his weight - the top of his trousers, maybe - the hook of the winch would have cut a recognizable hole at that point. There was no such mark.

Either way, he would need to rethink the scenario. It took another two hours before he finally dropped off to sleep.

Though somewhat discouraged by the discovery of a fault in his favoured theory, the next day saw him proceed with the more practical elements of his plan. DI Kathleen Smith proved quite amenable to the idea of getting preliminary forensic tests done on the antique mike, and also on any other suitable weapons that might be found in the bedroom that had been occupied by P.J. It was certainly possible that Dónal had accosted his rival in either of those two places, and the identification of the weapon used might well help to bolster the prosecution's case against him.

A warrant would be issued that very day, and she herself and Sergeant Casey would carry out the search. She promised to be particularly careful with the mike. In the Murroughs' absence, they would gain access through the caretaker.

In the two months since the incident, security at the castle had apparently been beefed up, and a full-time live-in caretaker/gardener was now in residence in a newly-built cottage at the corner of the grounds. The fact that he would pass on the receipt for any confiscated items dispensed with the need for a special phone-call on their return. Two other calls, however, needed to be made.

He reached Sheila McCarthy at the company's Dublin office.

"I'm sorry to bother you again in this unfortunate matter, Ms. McCarthy, but for purposes of elimination we need to establish certain facts. Could you please inform us whether you are left or right-handed?"

An understandable pause as she grappled with such an odd question. "I'm right-handed."

"And you would be able to establish that by a handwriting demonstration?"

Another hesitation, as if trying to figure out what consequences her answer might have. "Yes."

"Thank you."

He could only get Niamh's answering machine, and, for once overcoming his aversion to such things, left a recorded message. In her case, it did not need to be a question. Without identifying himself, he requested that she contact DI Smith at Kilbrue Garda Station to confirm that her brother Dónal is not left-handed. He had failed, he said, to get the information from Dónal's counsel. She might or might not recognize his voice. In either case, it didn't matter.

Then there was the problem of finding a way to attend the New Year's Eve press conference. He could not go in an official capacity, that was clear. Police officers would not be welcome, and bursting in on the festive scene with the authority of the law behind him was not what he had in mind.

He had a fair idea of some of those likely to have received invitations. He started with Helen Murphy.

Yes, she had been invited to represent her late husband for his contribution to the Eascra album being released. But no, she did not intend to go. She sounded incensed at the very idea. Her daughter Tara had expressed an interest in attending in her stead, but it was clear she was not being encouraged. She would have to decide for herself. And if she went, it would be with her own boyfriend.

Jeannie Staunton proved more amenable. Of course she'd been invited, and their agent Eamonn O'Halloran had been adamant that they would all have to attend for purposes of publicity. But when Tim expressed an interest

243

in getting in, and asked if her invitation was 'with partner', her slight hesitation spoke volumes. "Oh, yeah, sure. Well, Anne does want to attend, but she can get in as Eamonn O'Halloran's sister. That won't be a problem ..."

Belatedly it struck him that such subterfuge might be interpreted by the press as an attempt on Jeannie's part to get back in the closet. He promised to try to find an alternative way.

"By the way, Jeannie, I've been going through my notes of my original interview with you, and there's some reference there to your bad relations with Maggie."

"You mean the cleaning lady?"

"Yes, but all I've scribbled down is 'damage to instruments - missing items - stealing?'. Could you fill me in on what it was you were accusing her of stealing?"

"Oh, I hadn't accused her of any such thing! She got the wrong end of the stick. I just wondered if she'd tidied it away somewhere. It was a large bag, specially made to fit my two bongo drums."

Tim had seen Jeannie play them on stage. The exotic instruments were about waist high, one fairly broad, one slim. "The bag was made of what?"

"Canvas."

"Strong canvas?"

"Oh yes. The drums are very sensitive, and I wouldn't want the goatskin getting scratched or - God forbid - perforated."

"And when did you miss the bag?"

"That must have been pretty late, when we were thinking of packing up to leave. There had been plenty of little incidents before that when I'd had to ask Maggie to be more gentle with my instruments, so I suppose all that may have led her to think I had it in for her."

"So it was after P.J.'s death?"

"Yes, it must have been Friday morning. Maggie only works mornings. And before that, I'd thought we might find a way of completing the recordings in that session."

"Did the bag ever turn up?"

"No, I've had to get another one specially made. Not too expensive, but it was a nuisance."

Tim was thoughtful as he replaced the receiver. The next chance to visit to Maggie would be the following weekend. He had not intended another trip north before the inevitable family Christmas. But it would have to be. A phone call would not be the same.

"The fuss she made, that one!" Maggie was getting quite red in the face as she remembered her altercation with 'the drummer girl', as she called her. "Sure that old bag was a rough-looking thing, nothing to get so excited about!"

"I know that, Maggie. But Ms Staunton had had it specially made to fit her drums, and only wanted to know if you'd seen it anywhere."

"Hah! She practically implied I'd thrown the old thing away on her! Even though I'd had nothing to do with it."

"And you never saw it after that?"

"Well ... Down, Trudy! Down!" Her dog, a handsome red setter, had been rubbing his nose against her knees, and was now extending a silky paw onto her lap. "Let me get him his dinner, I think he's hungry." She departed to the kitchen with Trudy in tow.

Was this a ploy to gain some time to think? When she returned, her inquisitor insisted, "You were saying, Maggie ... something about finding Jeannie Staunton's bag later?"

"I did come across it later, but only after they'd all left."

"The band, you mean?"

"Yes. They left on ... the Friday afternoon, I think it was. Now, I normally work only mornings, but I was given the Thursday off so that the guards could examine the place. And they left it in a right mess, I can tell you! I was only allowed to start cleaning up at one o'clock on the Friday, and it took me all the rest of the day to sort the place out."

"But as regards the bag?"

"Oh, the drummer girl had already driven away when I came across it. Now, if she'd been a bit more civil about it, I might have got her telephone number and let her know her precious bag had turned up. But as it was, with her practically accusing me of taking it, why should I bother?"

She raised her chin in a self-righteous gesture, and Tim grunted sympathetically. "But where exactly did you find it?"

A small hesitation. "It was at the bottom of the lift shaft, down in the basement."

Highly interesting. "But Maggie, what were you doing in an empty lift shaft?"

Maggie was looking very uncomfortable indeed, and a blush spread upwards over her cheeks. "Well, Garda O'Driscoll, you know that I used to like my wee drop ..."

"Yes, Maggie, and I hope you've been managing to keep off it since that nasty turn you took. It wasn't doing you any good." Maggie nodded. "But back then, you used to keep some at the castle, is that right?"

"Yes, for the occasional wee drop. Especially to give me a bit of strength for all that stair-climbing, you know, before they got the lift put in." Tim did not comment on this bit of gratuitous rationalization, but nodded for her to go on. "Well, someone found my half-bottle of Tullamore Dew in the broom cupboard where I'd been keeping it. It must have been that drummer girl did it, just to spite me! Later I found where she'd put it, in the fridge in the kitchen."

Tim did not correct her. "When did you notice it was gone?"

"Well, I reported for duty as usual at eight o'clock on the Thursday. But they sent me away. That was when I got the news of the poor fellow's death the night before. I could have done with a wee drop when I heard that, I can tell you, but it was gone!"

"So, Maggie, what did you do about the problem?"

"Well, when I turned up for work on Friday afternoon, I had a fresh bottle with me, I just didn't want to leave it in the broom cupboard where it was so easy to find. So I looked around the basement for a better place, and thought the lift shaft might do."

"Could those doors be opened so easily?"

"Oh, yes. You could prise them open, and sometimes they would even spring open without your doing anything. Mr. Murrough warned me about the danger right at the beginning, said to keep away from them doors, or you might risk a nasty fall." She shivered again at the thought. "But there was nowhere to fall to from the basement, was there?"

No indeed. "And it was then you found Jeannie Staunton's bag?"

"That's right. But she had just left by then. And anyway, it wasn't there when I looked for it the next day. I worked the Saturday morning that week, too."

"I see. But did you tell anybody else about the bag, or did anybody else see it?"

"Well, Mr. Murrough may have seen .... Oh, what am I saying? Of course he wouldn't have seen it! But he came down the stairs just at that moment to work out in the gym, as he says. And ... he has a great sense of hearing and sense of smell ... You see, I had just taken a sip from the bottle, and so he immediately copped on what I was doing. But he wasn't at all angry, he seemed to understand ..."

"And he offered to find you a better place for your bottle?"

Maggie stared at him in astonishment, opened her mouth and shut it again, looking down at the floor. It was as if she'd been about to ask him how the hell he knew that, and then thought better of it. Maybe she had a vague memory of her tipsy confidences to Celia, but didn't want to open an unpredictable can of worms.

"Or was it a special jar he offered you?"

Maggie must have decided then that honesty was the best policy from then on, since there was no knowing what this possibly clairvoyant cop already knew. "That's right. A nice earthenware jar with a screw top. I could keep it on the top shelf of the broom cupboard, and no one would be any the wiser."

"And you'd been helping yourself to it ever since from that jar - that is, until your collapse brought you to your senses!"

Maggie looked suitably sheepish. "Well, not exactly. I did at first. But when I got to the end of the jar, I found it had been dirty."

"Dirty?"

"Yes, there was a bit of brown dust at the bottom. It had probably never been properly cleaned. I know how hard it is to clean those jars on the inside. Mr. Murrough had meant well, but after that I preferred to stick with a nice transparent bottle."

Whether Mr. Murrough had meant all that well was highly questionable, but there was no point in saying so to Maggie, whose adulation of her boss was total. "Maggie, have you ever told either of the Murroughs of your earlier health problems, the collapse during your pregnancy?"

Maggie looked puzzled. "Sure why shouldn't I? Mr. Murrough had told me all about his eye problems. So I told him about my sensitive liver. Anyway, as regards my occasional sips of whiskey, I won't be taking any more," she added hurriedly. "Even when I go back to work at the castle. After all, they now have the lift put in, so I don't need it so much."

This was another awkward point. Tim had not been able to arrange any kind of guardian angel from Kilbrue Garda Station, in spite of his vague promises to Celia. But something obviously needed to be done. He inquired when she was planning to go back to work.

"Oh, the Murrough's are still in America. And there won't be any more recordings done there before Christmas. But they want me in the week before Christmas to help get the castle in shape for New Year's Eve. Did you know they're putting on a big party?"

He said he had heard.

"It'll be afternoons this time, which suits me better. And they even want me to help with the serving on the night," she added with undisguised pride.

Since he knew the party in question was to be professionally catered, Maggie's assistance would be of marginal importance, probably meant as a sop to her ego.

His next stop was at the home of Maggie's distant relatives, the Caseys. He asked for the twins, and was told they were at the hurling field outside the village. He accosted them just as they were about to jump on their bikes to head back home.

They looked at him suspiciously, remembering their previous interrogation.

"You're smart boys," Tim said. "I've got a job for you. "

They still looked suspicious. "What kind of job?" asked Liam. At least Tim thought it must be Liam, if the yellow anorak meant anything.

"You're related to Maggie O'Keeffe, aren't you?"

"Yeah, the ould one is a cousin of our father's, or something," said Cormac. What about her?"

"In the week before Christmas she'll be helping out at Castle Green. Her friend Celia Ryan has been looking after her at home, but she can't do that while she's working at the castle."

"You mean, keeping her off the booze?"

Kids nowadays tended to be very well informed of the failings of the older generation. In this case it helped to cut a long story short. "Right. It'll be afternoons, so you should be able to take turns after school to accompany her there. I'll pay you two pounds per afternoon." Maybe he could get her closer relatives to subsidize their payment, but if not, it wouldn't break the bank, even on his meager Garda salary.

The boys looked at each other. Then Liam said, "OK, but what if she doesn't want us there?"

"You can pretend to be Maggie's little helpers. I'll get Sergeant Casey to persuade her that she could do with a bit of assistance, and to explain to the owners of the castle. And there are two more things."

They looked at him quizzically.

"I want you to check whether she's got any bottle of whiskey hidden away there. Probably in the broom cupboard in the basement, but keep your eyes open for other hiding places, too. If you do find one, or maybe a jar with whiskey in it, you're to put it in a plastic bag and give it to Sergeant Casey."

"OK. But you said two things." That was Cormac.

"Yes. The other one is a bit of detective work." The boys' eyes lit up. "You see, I need to find a big canvas bag." He demonstrated its estimated size with his hands. "It was last seen in the basement, but could have been hidden away anywhere, or even destroyed. So if you find this bag, or even any scraps of heavy canvas that might have come from it, do the same with that: Put it in a plastic bag and give it to your uncle, Sergeant Casey. But don't say a word about it to anyone else."

The boys grinned widely. This sounded interesting.

Barbara found Tim's account of the measures he was taking to protect Maggie's life highly amusing, but was less than convinced of their urgency.

"Why are you now so sure it was a deliberate attempt on Maggie's life?"

He told her what he had found out about the seemingly harmless knowledge that might have proved dangerous to the killer. "And neither do I think the attempt on her life was as amateurish as it had first seemed."

"Why not?"

"Iron oxide. It's the coating used on magnetic recording tape. The one thing that would be readily available to a recording engineer, or a producer. And with all that tape at his disposal, even a blind man could manage to scrape off enough powder to lace Maggie's whiskey with. I'd say she had a narrow escape."

"So how *did* she escape?"

"Iron oxide, or ferric oxide, is insoluble in water, and only slightly soluble in alcohol. It would have left a deposit at the bottom of whatever container was used. Maggie thought it was old dirt encrusted in the jar Murrough had provided, and reverted to using her usual bottle. By then the iron had already done some damage - together with her high alcohol consumption - but not enough to finish her off."

"But wait a minute - iron isn't toxic, surely? People take iron supplements all the time, it's supposed to be good for you!"

"It's toxic to Maggie. She has a condition which means she can't tolerate it."

"But how could Murrough have known about that?"

He explained how Maggie had poured her heart out about her various medical problems, including the previous coma she'd suffered as a result of taking iron supplements. "It was all in her medical record. The condition is called haemochromatosis, and my sister explained it to me. She's a doctor."

"But that's just the point. It would take a doctor to understand things like that."

"Or a medical student."

"Huh?"

"Murrough had studied medicine for a while, before being forced to give up by failing eyesight. I only found that out when I got to see the full transcript of that *Irish Times* interview. That was one of the passages that were cut, for whatever reason. The interviewer speculated that he didn't like being associated with failure, with being forced to compromise, or improvise."

Barbara thought for a moment. "Well, if you're right, he's had to improvise in lots of ways."

"Yes, both to get where he is, and to maintain his position."

Another silence.

"But surely he wouldn't try the same trick again, especially since it didn't work first time around?"

"No, and neither do I think he would want a sudden death to spoil his big press conference planned for New Year's Eve. But he might try something even more subtle, as long as it was also more certain in the long run. The best I can do is to try and locate that bag, or find what happened to it, in the next few weeks." He added that this was another job he'd given the Casey twins.

Barbara smiled at the thought of the kids being employed as detectives. Then the smile disappeared as she apparently remembered something more serious. "By the way, that big party could well be spoiled by another development. Did you read yesterday's *Tribune*?" Tim had to admit he hadn't had the time.

She pulled a folded section from yesterday's Sunday paper from her bag. She spread it out, and pointed to a brief item at the bottom of page 5. The headline had a familiar ring to it :

Eascra star hospitalized

Niamh Ní Ghráda, glamorous lead singer of the folk-rock group Eascra, was admitted to St. Joseph's Hospital, Ennis, yesterday in an unconscious state. The cause was said to be an overdose of barbiturates. According to hospital sources, her condition is now stable, and she is expected to make a complete recovery. Both her husband, solicitor John Bolton, and the group's agent Eamonn O'Halloran insisted that the

overdose had been accidental, a miscalculation brought
on by recent pressures of work.

"I'm wondering if it could have something to do with those phone-calls
you made last Wednesday."

Yes. What had he said? Run this up the flagpole and see who salutes? He
hadn't quite meant it like this. Or had he?

Chapter 26

"How did you get over the Christmas?"

This traditional Irish greeting assailed Tim at every turn. Some of those who asked should have known better, namely the colleagues familiar with the duty roster. Tim had volunteered for the unpopular Christmas Day shift, in return for getting both New Year's Eve and New Year's Day off. He would answer with a shrug, sometimes adding the comment that he had 'got over' it by not celebrating it this year.

This was strictly speaking not completely accurate. Cathy had made the brilliant suggestion of doing it German-style, and making Christmas Eve the main event. She had picked up this snippet of cultural information during her undergraduate German studies, and later discovered that this had once been the custom in Ireland, within the living memory of her grandmother.

In any case, this provided sufficient justification for a Christmas Eve dinner in her Cork city apartment: duck *à l'orange,* followed by one of the small plum puddings she always made for such intimate seasonal occasions. Then Midnight Mass in their favourite small chapel. Tim normally saw the inside of a church only on his occasional weekend visits to his parents. However, Christmas was different. He was a Christmas carol junkie, and gladly joined in a final spirited chorus of 'Hark, the Herald Angels Sing'. The cross-cultural occasion was then topped off by two steaming glasses of *glühwein* back at her apartment.

In the resulting mellow mood Cathy had finally seen fit to forgive Tim's previous little deceptions concerning what she called his freelance detective work. She was now fully informed of his intention to gate-crash the New Year's Eve celebration at Castle Green. With good grace, she accepted that she would not be able to go along, since it would only be possible for him to attend as partner of one of the invited guests.

That had worked out all right. He was glad he would not have to impose on Jeannie, nor cadge a press pass from Colin Leahy, an option he had already considered and rejected. He had arranged it so that he would be able to arrive early and take a look around before the official program began. According to intelligence gleaned from Jeannie, everybody of importance would be there - apart from Helen Murphy, and of course Dónal.

Even Niamh was supposed to be turning up. She had apparently made a good enough recovery to put in an appearance in a Christmas Day special on

RTE. Since Irish criminals seemed to take that one day off (and the pubs were closed), Tim had relieved the tedium with the help of the ancient black-and-white portable set stored in DI Feeney's office. The program wasn't live, but judging by some topical references, the pre-recording had been done only days before.

The planned visit to Castle Green had acquired some importance in the meantime.

Preliminary forensic tests on the antique microphone had been carried out. The only fingerprints identified had been Maggie's. The fact that Tim's had not been found on it indicated that the surface had been thoroughly cleaned at least once since Halloween. Tests had indeed revealed the presence of some skin cells imbedded deep in the ridges - a lot more than one would expect from normal handling. No hair, however, so no immediate microscopic identification would be possible. Kathleen Smith had been quite willing to send the organic material to an English laboratory for this new-fangled DNA process. As feared, no results could be expected from that until late January at the earliest.

The Casey twins had not managed to turn up very much. No canvas bag anywhere, though they had snooped in all the cupboards, nooks and crannies they could get near in the course of their employment as Maggie's little helpers. No suspicious earthenware jars, with or without whiskey in them. Liam had found one abandoned Tullamore Dew bottle in the space under the kitchen sink. It had a trace of what seemed to be its original contents in it.

As instructed, the boy had conspiratorially wrapped it in a plastic bag and handed it over to his uncle, Sergeant Casey, who obligingly sent it in for testing. The liquid was indeed unadulterated Tullamore Dew whiskey.

And that was it, apart from an intriguing reference to a bonfire site the boys had noticed in the hollow below the old apple tree that stood between the castle and the renovated farmhouse.

***

Don't get mad, get even. Now who was it had said that? Some American politician, she thought. One of the Kennedys, wasn't it?

"What was that you said, darling?"

Niamh wasn't aware of have spoken aloud, but she must have mumbled something.

"Oh, nothing." No point in involving John in this. She didn't want him inquiring what she was getting at, or - more likely - pedantically consulting a dictionary of quotations.

"You're going to be all right. There was nothing mad about it." So he had heard that word. "It's perfectly understandable, the strain of this whole nasty business ... But please don't make another mistake like that again,"

Yes, the tablets had been a mistake, though not the way everybody meant. Why punish only herself and her family for something that wasn't really her fault? She'd been dragged into it. Fooled.

"And we really don't need to attend Murrough's big publicity do tomorrow, if you don't want to. Whatever Eamonn says."

"I do want to. Whatever about the band breaking up, it is important to promote this last album. And we don't need to stay long. It'll do if we turn up at nine and leave at ten. We can be back here in good time to ring in the New Year with our own friends." She paused, and grimaced. "I nearly used the word 'celebration', but that's not quite the right word this year. Who knows what the New Year will bring?"

"Don't worry too much about Dónal. I was talking to Prendergast yesterday. He's pretty sure he can get him off. Apparently some new evidence has turned up that may even cast some suspicion on Murrough, of all people!" As a solicitor himself - though not specializing in criminal law - John was making good use of his connections.

Since Niamh didn't react, he went on. "The defence is certainly going to apply for an adjournment, to get the new evidence evaluated. It may not be enough to bring charges against Murrough, but it should be enough to sow some doubt in the minds of the jury."

"So he's pretty confident, is he?"

"Yes, within reason."

Niamh sipped at the glass of cognac with which she had been washing down a piece of left-over Christmas cake, then put it down. "I shouldn't have taken a drink. It's brought on that headache again. It keeps coming back, ever since ..." She didn't need to finish that sentence. "Would you mind if I went for a walk down by the lake? A bit of fresh air might do me good."

"Do you want me to come along?"

"No, dear. Would you drive over to the O'Laughlins and pick up Ciara? I promised them I'd pick her up by five, but I don't feel up to driving now."

"Sure. Get your fresh air."

She pulled on her most comfortable woollen jacket, did without gloves since she could stick her hands in its deep pockets, and without a hat so that she could let her long auburn hair blow in the light breeze. She first negotiated the steep steps down to the new pier that had been inaugurated

254

just that summer. The boats were now stowed away in the smart stone boathouse beside the pier. She stood there for a few minutes taking in the view over the lake, the small ripples on the surface given a silver glint by the fading wintry sunlight.

Then she turned left along the path past the old boathouse, a rickety wooden structure now due for demolition. The path beyond that point was rather mucky, so that she regretted not having put on more solid shoes than the elegant slip-ons that had been so conveniently to hand. But that wasn't so important now.

After about five minutes she turned back, and this time stopped at the old boathouse. There was a padlock on the door, but she knew where the key was to be found: in one of the two empty flower-pots under the step. This was for the convenience of her elder brother Séamas, who had assured her that the box he had stored there would be removed by the end of January at the latest. She had allowed it under that condition, mainly because he was her brother, not out of any great enthusiasm for 'the cause', about which her feelings were somewhat ambivalent. She had also made him promise to pick it up either late at night, or (if it had to be during the day) while John was at work.

The reason for the temporary storage had been the betrayal (as Séamas expressed it) of a central IRA dump somewhere in Tipperary. As soon as a new location was decided on, the now scattered material would be brought there, and this minor worry would be off her shoulders. Should the authorities have found it on their land, it would have been easy enough to deny any knowledge of it; but it would have been a huge embarrassment, especially to John.

Though she had only reluctantly complied with Séamas's request, it now fitted in well with her own purposes. She removed the padlock, and pulled out the door, which creaked on its rusty hinges. As soon as her eyes grew accustomed to the gloom, she looked to the left of the entrance for the trap-door which had once been used to stow away boating equipment. She undid the latch and pulled. It was stuck. For a moment she thought she might have to give up. Then it suddenly gave, throwing her back against the side of the hut.

From there on it was easy. The cover of the box lifted easily. She made her selection, and stuffed it into her left pocket. Luckily there was only one kind, so she had no problem deciding what went with what. Lid back, trap-door closed, door padlocked, key in flower-pot, the latter replaced under step. Then she made her way back up towards the house.

The contents of the box had sent her mind back to the exciting stories of fighting men told by her grandfather when she was about ten, and Dónal a few years younger. She remembered her mother's shock when she caught the old man actually fondling an ancient revolver that he had managed to hide away somewhere, and demonstrating how it worked for the children's benefit. Funny how it had been the more sceptical Séamas that had actually followed in the old man's footsteps.

Luckily John wasn't back yet with Ciara. That gave her time to transfer the contents of her left pocket to her favourite Gucci bag. It was, admittedly, a bit large for evening wear, but it would do.

Chapter 27

Once more unto the breach ... This was becoming Georgie Hayes's favourite phrase when facing up to unavoidable social ordeals. And the upcoming one was more serious than most. She had tried to talk her husband out of the album-release press conference at this particular place and time. But he had replied that there would be no better place or time. And that there was no such thing as bad publicity.

Nothing ventured, nothing gained. That seemed to be Richard's favourite motto.

She had put in an appearance with Richard at eight o'clock to greet the more punctual of the invited guests in the festively decorated main hall of the castle. Then she had excused herself, saying she need to check that everything was prepared for the main event at nine o'clock. She left Richard to entertain the guests (he was good at it!), and the professional caterers to ply them with drinks and party snacks. Maggie O'Keeffe was also pottering around, positively glowing at being able to play a part at such an illustrious occasion.

Both the studio and the roof garden had been set up for the press conference, the latter to be favoured if the weather allowed. It was looking good at the moment. Some clouds in the west, but otherwise a clear, starry sky. The four guest rooms below had been converted to press rooms (for interviews) and cloakrooms. Having checked that everything was OK, Georgie slipped out of the castle, she hoped without being noticed. She would turn up in good time for the official part of the evening.

The early guests were creating quite a considerable volume of chatter, she noted as she passed the main hall. In spite of their small number. Of those who had contributed to the recording, there was only Jeannie Staunton, the percussionist, with her partner, Anne O'Halloran - the sister of the band's agent, who was also there with his wife. The McCarthys had also turned up early. She had to be reminded who they were. The couple who ran the archaeological survey company that had unearthed the passage grave would, of course, be honoured guests, since its official opening as a tourist attraction was to be linked with the album release. Not a bad idea of Richard's, she had to admit.

A more awkward moment came when she was introduced to a tall, elegant young woman and her boyfriend. The girl was called Tara Murphy, and she was officially representing the one missing musician: P.J. Murphy. The victim. If Georgie was somewhat stuck for words, Tara covered over quite successfully by speaking with great dignity of the contribution he had made to the recording.

She was also introduced to someone she had previously only known by name. In view of the importance of her interview in publicizing the Caiseal Gréine project, Dervla Cassidy had been one of the specially invited guests, in addition to the regular *Irish Times* music journalists and their photographer. Her partner was a tall, somewhat gawky man who looked as if he would be more comfortable in jeans than in evening attire. She didn't catch his name - Timothy something - though she had thought for a moment that she had seen him somewhere before.

Having escaped from the noise and bustle, if only for half an hour, she put her feet up on the sofa in their farmhouse living-room, from which point she had a somewhat obstructed view of more cars driving up to the car park. Suddenly, a figure appeared only a few feet from her window. He had his back to her, but it seemed to be the young man who had come with Dervla Cassidy. He was now bending down, poking at something on the ground, just below the old apple tree. The one all the locals had warned them should not on any account be disturbed.

With a sinking of her heart, she realized what he was examining. It was the ashes of the rubbish she had burned there, immediately after their return from the States. She was not sure of the significance of the canvas bag, but she knew her husband had deliberately concealed it in the house some time after the death of the guitarist. Being informed that the Gardai had confiscated some items from the studio for forensic examination, she had taken it into her hands to destroy it.

Richard was not an evil man. Whatever Richard had done, she knew she could not bear to see him humiliated and destroyed. Anything but prison. He would not survive it.

The man outside the window now seemed to have found something that interested him. He was retrieving some scrap out of the ashes, and putting it in a plastic bag that he had taken from his pocket. After slipping the bag back in the pocket of his jacket, he was now wiping his hands on the wet grass.

Just then she remembered where and when she had met him before. He had been in uniform.

***

258

It was a good-natured crowd that shuffled its way up to the roof garden. Inspired by the exotic location (and fuelled by the drinks that some still carried in their hands) a substantial proportion of the guests had elected to use the spiral staircase. Even a number of press photographers, who had been expressly advised to take the lift to avoid clogging up the passages with their bulky equipment.

Emerging on the roof, some of those foolish souls who had neglected to pick up their coats from the cloakroom suddenly regretted their decision, causing a bit of a jam. But finally everyone was in place.

The audience sat on white plastic seats arranged in the central area between the two rows of conifers in their antique terracotta pots. A raised platform had been erected against the western battlements, on the opposite side from the lift and staircase door. There, the three surviving active musicians sat at Murrough's right as he stood up to speak, his wife (and sound engineer) at his left. He introduced the new *Eascra* album, especially emphasizing its revolutionary concept.

A bit exaggerated, Tim thought. There had been plenty of recordings that demonstrated the Irish contribution to American music and vice versa. He wondered what Jeannie thought of Murrough's hyperbole, but her expression was nearly as impassive as Sean's. Niamh's smile seemed a bit forced. The carefully chosen snippets from the album played over the excellent sound system sounded intriguing, however.

To Tim's surprise, Murrough then introduced Tara Murphy, saying she wished to say a few words.

It really was only a few words, in which she expressed her gratification at the late recognition of P.J. Murphy's skill as a guitarist. But it was impressive. Where did she get such poise and confidence?

The questions that followed showed that not only the music press was present. Several referred to P.J.'s death and the upcoming trial. Most of these were parried by Richard Murrough, one by Niamh. She insisted on her brother's innocence, expressed confidence that he would be acquitted of all charges, and added, "I expect that any subsequent inquest will bring in a verdict of accidental death."

Her phrasing suggested to Tim's ears that she had been schooled by her solicitor husband, and he wondered idly how all this would play in Saturday's newspapers. The painful topic was cut off by Murrough introducing a talk on the sensational archaeological discoveries, to be given not by Sheila McCarthy, as Tim had expected, but by some academic from UCD. The musicians took their places in the audience.

Though the professor lent an air of gravitas to the proceedings, his delivery was somewhat monotonous. Tim was not surprised that a number of those present took this opportunity to go to the toilet. Particularly understandable in view of the amount of drink that had previously been consumed.

Most were back in their seats by the time Murrough stood up to thank the professor. A number of stragglers, however, had to grope their way in the sudden gloom: on Murrough's signal, Georgie had flipped a switch to dim the lights. As his eyes grew accustomed to the gloom, Tim could just about make out that the seat beside Niamh's husband was still vacant.

Faint music began to emerge from the loudspeakers. As it grew in volume, Tim recognized the tune. It was the Irish traditional-style version of 'Light and Shade' that Jeannie had told him about. The melody was carried by Sean Mills' pipes, a fiddle descant and bodhran accompaniment coming in at various points, and the whole thing underlaid with a distinctly untraditional rock guitar riff.

As the music crescendoed further, floodlights suddenly came on at the west side of the castle, behind the platform where the Murroughs were still standing. The Neolithic passage grave that the professor had droned on about was finally being inaugurated.

Most of the audience left their seats to get good vantage points at the battlements on either side of the platform. Tim and Dervla were some of the few who decided to wait, to avoid the crush. Neither did Murrough turn to look. But of course he wouldn't, stupid thought! He had told him that he could still register some light (and shade) to an extent, but what he was seeing now would be in his mind's eye.

Stranger, however, was that Georgie had not turned to admire the spectacle. As she stared over Tim's head to some point on the other side, she stepped further to the left, away from her husband.

Tim turned to follow her gaze.

Maggie O'Keeffe, standing to the side with a tray of glasses, must have done the same, because her scream and the crash of breaking glass coincided with Tim's reaction.

Niamh was standing in front of the lift, her crocodile-leather handbag dropped to her feet. She was taking careful, double-handed aim with what looked like a Webley revolver.

Tim lunged over three rows of vacated plastic chairs, stumbling over the last one. It was too late. By the time he had grabbed her by the arms, two shots had already rung out. She dropped the gun unresistingly.

People were screaming. Richard Murrough lay slumped backwards over the wall.

Pocketing the revolver, and leaving Dervla to watch over the unresisting Niamh, he rushed to assess the damage. He nearly collided with both Sean Mills and Niamh's husband as they rushed in the opposite direction.

One shot had merely grazed Murrough's shoulder, but the other had knocked off a substantial chunk of his skull, scattering brain tissue over the grey limestone battlements. Georgie just stood there staring, a blank look on her face.

"You've got a mobile phone, haven't you?"

She pulled one out of her bag, and he put in a call to Kilbrue Garda Station.

Epilogue

Barbara had extended her Christmas break to accompany her invalid mother on a visit to an aunt up the country. (Her Aunt May, actually: the sudden flurry of interest in genealogy had reactivated some previously dormant familial feelings.) On returning to the office, the first thing she noticed in her letterbox was a white envelope addressed to her in a familiar hand. She ripped it open.

Dear Barbara,

I handed in my resignation yesterday, so you won't be seeing me back on the job.

With Helen Murphy's consent, I admitted to the Super that it was I who had tipped her off about the raid. So you needn't worry any more about Mike's attempt at petty blackmail. Luckily I didn't need to go into details about where... (This intriguingly unfinished sentence was crossed out.) *Helen is willing to pay the fine, which shouldn't be too painful, and make use of the publicity in the campaign for legalization that she's now got involved in.*

I'd been thinking of getting involved myself, but decided it would be better for all concerned if I kept a low profile for the time being. Not least for the old man's sake. He's just been promoted to Chief Superintendent, and it was his friendship with our own Super that saved me from a dishonourable discharge. My employment has been merely 'terminated' as from the end of January, and I'm even being allowed to take the three weeks holidays that are due to me.

The sensational events at Castle Green over the New Year may have hastened my decision, though in a way I haven't quite figured out yet. In case you've been out of touch with the news, I've left a copy of the Irish Times *on your desk. What the report doesn't include (it wasn't known at the time) was that Niamh had left a full confession - spoken on tape in the studio. So that's where she'd been during the professor's boring speech!*

It was just as you imagined it when you sketched out a scenario involving Georgie. Except that it was indeed Niamh who had come to Murrough's aid, only to be used in turn for his own ends. And that poor P.J. wasn't hoisted by his (non-existent) belt: They had both stuffed his recumbent form into the canvas bag that Jeannie used for her drums. (She had later mentioned its

disappearance - that was the decisive clue that I missed for some time.)
Then Murrough had gone up on the roof, temporarily donning the jacket
and cap that Niamh had retrieved from P.J.'s room. She hid them hid in her
violin case, as it happens, so Sheila McCarthy's account was spot on in that
regard. When Murrough let down the rope through the lift-shaft, Niamh
attached the bag to the hook, and the rest you can imagine. All that
remained was for Murrough to wait for Niamh's musical signal that the
coast was clear.

One interesting little detail: What prompted P.J. to attack Murrough in
the first place was not, as we speculated, the latter's show of unconcern at
P.J.'s threats of going public. Or at least not only that. What Niamh heard
as she entered the studio was P.J. yelling, "You leave Tara out of this!"
Tara is Helen Murphy's daughter, adopted by P.J. when they married. I
have never heard any reference to her natural father, but I think we can now
make an educated guess. It is not a subject I intend to bring up with Helen
Murphy.

This isn't exactly the way I wanted the case to end. But at least the truth
has come out. And I do feel a kind of rough justice has been done.

The one point where I am not sure concerns Georgie. She saw Niamh
taking aim. She could have saved her husband, but didn't. It probably
doesn't amount to murder or manslaughter in any strict legal sense. But
morally? At least a 'sin of omission', as I remember from the catechism we
learned at school. And as regards motive: Well, I suppose she inherits the
castle and may wish to keep the studio going as a business. But there may be
more to it than that.

And as regards Niamh's motives, there may have been some method in
her madness. She probably foresaw the unlikelihood of anything being
pinned on Murrough - even if Dónal got acquitted, which wasn't at all
certain. If she's lucky, and has good lawyers (remember, her husband is a
solicitor!) she may get off lightly. A plea of insanity might have a fair
chance of success, and even if found guilty, her sentence could well be
comparatively light. And think of all the records this is going to sell! I've
already purchased my own copy of 'Eascra at Caiseal Gréine.'

Work-wise, I'll be spending most of the spring down on the farm. I
promise to drop in on you any time I'm passing through Bandon or Cork.

All the best,
Tim.